T0274795

THE SISTER QUEENS

THE SISTER QUEENS

Justin Scott

SEVERN HOUSE

First world edition published in Great Britain and the USA in 2024
by Severn House, an imprint of Canongate Books Ltd,
14 High Street, Edinburgh EH1 1TE.

severnhouse.com

British Library Cataloguing-in-Publication Data
A CIP catalogue record for this title is available from the British Library.

ISBN-13: 978-1-4483-1274-0 (cased)
ISBN-13: 978-1-4483-1275-7 (e-book)

All Severn House titles are printed on acid-free paper.

MIX
Paper from
responsible sources
FSC
www.fsc.org   FSC® C013056

Typeset by Palimpsest Book Production Ltd.,
Falkirk, Stirlingshire, Scotland.
Printed and bound in Great Britain by
TJ Books, Padstow, Cornwall.

Praise for Justin Scott

"Justin Scott's *The Sister Queens* is costume drama, murder mystery, and history book all wrapped up in delicious twenty-first century prose that manages to evoke the rich, sensuous language of the Elizabethans. Reading it, I feel at once in the company not just of Shakespeare but also of a master storyteller from our own time"
Leonard Barkan, author of
Reading Shakespeare Reading Me

"Will leave you as absorbed as the groundlings at the Globe, watching *Hamlet* for the first time"
Kevin Baker, author of *Paradise Alley*

"Continually exciting . . . The climactic sequence is sensational"
Publishers Weekly on *A Pride of Kings*

"Wry, witty, and garnished with sharply observed local color: Scott at his best"
Kirkus Reviews Starred Review of *Mausoleum*

"Historical action-adventure fiction at its rip-roaring best!"
Library Journal Starred Review of *The Bootlegger*

"Combines a vivid historical environment with a top-notch story and enjoyable, realistic characters"
Booklist on *The Gangster*

"Suspenseful reading, full of atmospheric detail"
Booklist on *Normandie Triangle*

About the author

Justin Scott has been writing historical suspense novels, thrillers, and sea stories for fifty years. He is the author of the Benjamin Abbott New England detective series and collaborated with Clive Cussler on the Isaac Bell historical detective series. Born in Manhattan, he grew up on Long Island's Great South Bay in a family of professional writers. Justin holds BA and MA degrees in history, and before becoming a writer, drove boats and trucks, helped build Fire Island beach houses, edited an electronic engineering journal, and tended bar in a Hell's Kitchen saloon. *The Sister Queens* is his 37th novel. He lives in Connecticut with his wife, filmmaker Amber Edwards.

https://justinscott-paulgarrison.com

Lightning struck from thin air twice twenty-eight years ago.

One moment I thought of The Sister Queens, the next I met
AMBER EDWARDS.

We are so lucky to be such stuff as dreams are made on.

CAST OF CHARACTERS

THE LORD CHAMBERLAIN'S MEN,
a Company of Players in London's Globe Theatre

WILLIAM SHAKESPEARE – Popular playmaker of royal histories and comedies, poet, stage-player, and shareholder of the company.

RICHARD BURBAGE – London's most loved actor and double shareholder in the Lord Chamberlain's Men. 'A tragedian of great name.'

JIM MAPES – Former coxswain to Sir Walter Raleigh and the company's new stage-keeper,

STEFANO FOGLIAVERDE – Italian fencing master, engaged by Dick Burbage to teach the players to stage fight with the modern rapier.

WILL KEMPE – Famous clown and jig dancer, contentious shareholder, player of Shakespeare's characters Bottom, Dogberry, and Sir John Falstaff.

HARRY CONDELL and JOHN HEMINGES – Player-shareholders.

EDMUND – The book-holder.

MARC HANDLER – Will Shakespeare's player apprentice, an orphan.

ROBBIE BURBAGE – Player apprentice to his father, Richard Burbage.

SOVEREIGNS

QUEEN ELIZABETH – Elderly 'Virgin Queen,' who refuses to name her successor, iron-willed ruler for forty-two years, defender of Protestant England against Europe's Catholic empires and the Roman Pope, bulwark at home against Protestant–Catholic civil war.

MARY QUEEN OF SCOTS – Beheaded in the Tower of London thirteen years ago. Queen of Scotland since an infant, Queen of France by marriage, cousin of Queen Elizabeth through her grandmother Margaret Tudor. Cherished in memory by England's ostracized Catholics.

JAMES VI – King of Scotland, Queen Mary's son, who converted to Protestantism and who Catholics hope and Protestants fear will convert back if he inherits or captures Elizabeth's throne.

NOBLES

LORD ESSEX – Famous young hero, Robert Devereux, 2nd Earl of Essex, groomed by the Queen to serve England, Master of the Horse, Privy Counsellor, victor at Cadiz, general of an English Army that failed to subdue Irish rebels. Returns to London out of Her Majesty's favor, but still loved by the people.

LORD SOUTHAMPTON – Henry Wriothesley, 3rd Earl of Southampton, Essex acolyte, Will Shakespeare's patron.

THE COUNTESS OF SOUTHAMPTON – Mary Wriothesley, mother of the earl. Newly entitled, upon his marriage, the Dowager Countess.

SERVANTS OF HER MAJESTY

SIR ROBERT CECIL – Secretary of State (traditionally titled Queen's Clerk), Elizabeth's advisor, confidant, and master of her spies. and enemy of Lord Essex. Cecil's father was Lord High Treasurer William Cecil, the Queen's principal secretary for much of her reign, founder of Her Majesty's spy service.

FRANCIS BACON – Queen's Counsel Extraordinary, lawyer, scientist, scholar, and brother of Essex's spy master, Anthony Bacon.

SIR RICHARD TOPCLIFFE – Priest hunter, Tower of London interrogator, known to 'scrape' the Catholic conscience on the torture rack.

SIR WALTER RALEIGH – Spanish Armada hero, sea explorer, courtier, projector of New World expeditions, and a poet, once an Essex rival for the Queen's goodwill, now in the earl's retinue.

SIR FERDINANDO GORGES – The Queen's commander of Plymouth, Raleigh's cousin, powerful courtier, dubbed a knight by Essex.

WALT GRINNER – Warder at the Clink prison; former headsman.

THE HANGMAN – Executioner at the Tyburn Tree.

ANTHONIE KINGSTON and CYRUS CAREW – Armed gentlemen, Sir Robert Cecil's personal guard.

LADY ANN BACON – Lively translator from the Latin of the *Apology in Defense of the Church of England*, commissioned to persuade Catholics to conform to Queen Elizabeth's new English Church. Anthony and Francis Bacon's mother.

SPIES

ANTHONY BACON – The Earl of Essex's master of a vast net of English and European spies, intelligencers, conspirators, and beagles.

ARTHUR GREGORY – Skilled seal-cracker.

NILES ROPER – Landlord of the Queen's Hart Tavern, veteran, reluctant interceptor of conspirators' letters.

LYLE LEET – Secret messenger.

PETER and JOHN – Thames wherry men.

CONSPIRATORS, FORGERS, MURDERERS, and COUNTLESS INFORMERS.

SOUTHAMPTON'S HOUSEHOLD

FRANCES MOWERY – The dowager countess's lady-in-waiting and gatekeeper.

NED – Buttery door halberd man.

STEVEN – Butler, lover of Will's plays.

NELL and SUSAN – Girls at the back door.

COOK, HOUSE GROOMS, SERVANTS, PAGES, and OSTLERS.

RETAINERS – Tutors, painters, clergymen, music teachers, and poets.

WILL SHAKESPEARE'S FAMILY in WARWICKSHIRE

MARY ARDEN SHAKESPEARE – Will's mother, beloved youngest daughter of an illiterate farmer who persuaded a distant cousin of gentle birth to teach her to read and write.

JOHN SHAKESPEARE – Will's father, glover, public servant, 'new man' of business.

ANNE HATHAWAY – Will's wife who manages the family and the household during his long absences.

HAMNET – Will and Anne's only son, who died four years ago, age eleven.

JUDITH and SUSANNA – Their daughters.

WILL SHAKESPEARE'S FRIENDS

BEN JONSON – Player for hire, bellicose army veteran, playmaker and poet, jailed for duels, brawls, and seditious writing.

FATHER VALENTE – Outlawed Jesuit priest.

MRS BROAD – Landlady of Ben's writing garret, stalwart in a pinch.

ISOBEL – Child laundry maid befriended and converted to the Catholic faith fifteen years ago by imprisoned Mary Queen of Scots.

GILES the Swabber and JAKE, BOATSWAIN, GUNNER, GUNNER'S MATE, and the MASTER – Mariners in the ship *Eliza*.

ONE

London, 1600
The Winter Coming On

Will Shakespeare plunged into the hangman's crowd and headed for the gallows. No show drew Londoners like a hanging from the Tyburn Tree. Spectators were wedged thicker than bones in a churchyard. Will wove himself through them, nimble as a boy from a player's ceaseless capers on the stage. Two scarred veterans were matching his pace. He let them overtake. The warriors would clear a path.

Sudden as hawks, they swooped. They pinned his arms, ignored his startled 'Have hold!' and bewildered 'Where go you?', and marched him like their noonday shadow toward the nobles' coaches clustered on a rise that offered the best view.

He spied a drunken blacksmith and imagined an escape, rehearsing in his mind's eye the twists and swerves. He stopped struggling to cozen his ambushers to ease their grip. When one let go to knock the blacksmith out of the way, Will tore loose from the other and ran full tilt, dodging an orange-wife, vaulting an apple-barrow, and cleaving through a knot of carousing apprentices. Too late, he saw the one-legged beggar slide a crutch between his ankles. Trampled ground flew at his face. He was inches from sprawling in the mud when a burly footman righted him with an iron hand.

'Thanks, my good fellow.'

The footman tossed a coin to the beggar and helped the veterans drag Will to the nearest coach – a long, dark, four-horse car with no coat of arms to mark its owner. The coach driver jumped down, brandishing his whip.

'*Help, ho!*' Will roared in a voice trained to thunder to the highest galleries. '*Murder!*' But the swarm of mechanicals, apprentices, laborers, uprooted countrymen, and mercenaries, which ordinarily respected neither person nor authority, gave a wide berth to the dark coach and the hard-bitten crew shoving him through the curtains.

Their master, a cripple bundled in a courtier's embroidered cloak, smothered Will's protest with an imperious gesture of a jeweled hand. Mustachioed and bearded, he lounged on his bench with a shrunken leg in loose silk hose and slipper propped at an ungainly angle on a brass-banded leather chest. The cripple stared, silent as stone, until Will doffed his hat. A man of winter, thought the mystified playmaker, dead coals for eyes, cold visage, and icy tongue.

'Master Shakespeare, many say the Queen grows old.'

'Not I!' How had this courtier – whoever he was, whatever he wanted – known to waylay him at Tyburn? He had told only Dick Burbage where he was going. Who else had been near enough to hear? The Italian swordsman Dick had hired to teach the players the rapier? Their new stage-keeper trimming ropes overhead? An apprentice eager for a tip? London was riddled with spies both foreign and domestic who bribed servants and apprentices to inform. Had spies followed him across London Bridge? But why?

The cripple banged his cane. The whip whistled. The coach jerked into motion, rolling heavily. The cripple winced; there was gout in that foot.

'Others say that if Elizabeth Tudor produced no heir, it is Her Majesty's holy duty to name her successor.'

'Never I, sir.'

The cripple mocked Will's fear. 'Then who is heir to our Virgin Queen? . . . *Name the bastard!*'

'Virtue can't issue a bastard.'

The coach stopped. The cripple parted the curtains. They were beside the scaffold under the three-legged gallows. A Jesuit priest, a vigorous older man of sixty years, knelt on the puddled folds of his robe, head bowed, his prayers white puff clouds in the cold.

His name was Valente – 'Brave Pious Father Val' to Catholic recusants who refused to accept the Protestant Church and hid him from the priest hunters. 'Papist Antichrist' to Protestants who hated Catholics and feared their ambitious Pope. Will had walked to Tyburn on the chance that Valente might find peace ever so brief in the glimpse of a long-ago friend.

'Do you know that Catholic's crime?'

Valente's crimes were no secret. Pamphlets, broadsides, and ballads had blazed abroad news of his execution for scorning every act, article, and injunction that outlawed the Catholic Church. All London knew that the Jesuit had pledged his life to 'return,' as Val put it, every last Protestant to the bosom of the Pope.

'He preaches for Rome.'

'He preaches lies!'

Will covered his mouth before a knowing smile betrayed their friendship. Father Valente had vowed that if the government's priest hunters ever captured him, he would preach his faith from the Tower of London torture-rack. He would preach while they dragged him on the long road to Tyburn. He would preach from the gallows. Saint or madman – portions of both – reckless, foolhardy, steel-hearted, Val never pretended that his disciples' fate on earth would be kinder than his. And he never preached a word he didn't believe.

They were close enough to mingle gazes. Would the cripple notice if Will stared hard to make Father Val look inside the coach? A priest hunted every day and night he spent in England would feel his gaze. Will tried to find his courage as the hangman dragged him to his feet. Too late. The hangman forced Val up the ladder. His lips moved faster. Butterfly wings.

'Some say the Queen is weak,' the cripple droned in Will's ear. 'Too destitute of spirit to guard her throne from Catholics when the Spanish fleet attacks again.'

Will raised his chin to play the patriot and put ice in his own voice. 'Our Queen will sink Spain's next Armada as she sank the last.'

'Twelve years ago, long years in the life of a woman.'

Elizabeth's defiant call to English arms, hurled from astride a warhorse, honed Will's retort: '"Let tyrants fear a woman with the heart and stomach of a king."'

The hangman was fitting the noose over Val's head and snugging it around his throat. The crowd fell silent. Will heard a single crow, its cries falling faint, make wing to a distant wood. The hangman turned Val slowly off the ladder. One foot slipped from the rung and fluttered to find it. Then the other flapped the air. The people cheered. Father Val was hanging by his neck.

'Lord Essex's followers say Essex possesses the domestical greatness of a princely successor.'

Will barely heard him. Val's legs were beating the air in frantic measure.

'Some would make Essex king.'

'*Not I*,' shouted Will, before such talk gained a share of air beside his madly kicking friend.

'Quite,' the cripple agreed mildly. 'It is Her Majesty's prerogative to make a proper king.'

And yet, when his cloak slipped from his shoulder, Will saw a ruff dyed the tawny shade of a bitter orange. The Earl of Essex's colors. Sure as day, *the cripple was an Essex man.* Who could inspire such rebellious boasts of princely succession but the war hero Essex, a handsome young nobleman loved for his dazzling gestures and elegant bearing. Commoners admired his boldness, and even gentles who thought him cocksure could not deny his bravery.

Essex had been the Queen's favorite. Some wondered, none knew, whether Elizabeth had made him her lover despite the wide difference 'twixt their ages. She had appointed him her Master of the Horse, and a privy counsellor, granted him riches with the monopoly on sweet wine import taxes, and given him command of an enormous army to subdue Ireland's rebels.

But an ugly glimpse twelve paces from the stage when the Chamberlain's Men played at court had Will asking whether the greatness Essex looked for would overwhelm him. The Queen, intent on *Much Ado*, denied the earl's whispered request with a dismissive shake of her head. His cajoling smile fell from his lips as if lopped by a sword, his red-faced fury revealing an impetuous schemer who lost all reason in defeat. Soon after, Essex blundered in Ireland – bested both in battle and treaty at the cost of English honor and Her Majesty's treasure. He had stormed back to England, defying the Queen. She banned him from court, angering his friends who boldly affected orange hats or ruffs to pledge loyalty to their hero.

'*Let down the priest*,' shrieked a woman. Scores took up the cry, but not with mercy in their hearts. '*Let him down!*'

Val fell like a sack of millet. Still alive, he watched with saucer eyes the hangman's apprentice, age of sixteen, desperate to please, bring the knife and place the handle in his master's hand.

'Some say Scotland's King James should stay in Scotland.' The trap yawned like a bear pit: Scots King James shared royal blood with Queen Elizabeth. But savage Scots loved France, not England. 'What say you?'

Will's left hand crept unbidden to his mouth. He had broken the habit of unfirm nerves his first months on the stage. But here he was plucking his lips like a lute, thumb and forefinger worrying his mustache above and the tuft below. He forced the hand back down to his knee and commanded his mobile player's face to conceal his fear.

'What say you?' the cripple demanded. '*Should the Scots King stay in Scotland?*'

'So long as our English Queen commands.'

His tormentor leaned close. 'And when Her Majesty has lost her earthly warrant to command . . . Have you no more answers?'

The coach was so close to the scaffold that Will could see Father Valente's lips move. Trembling? No. Forming words. *Ego te absolvo.* Lifting his tethered hands to make the sign of the cross, Val forgave the hangman's apprentice for bringing the knife.

Now his eyes glinted at Will. *Ego te absolvo.* You too, my friend.

'God's Will be done,' said William Shakespeare.

Dark fire flared in the cripple's eyes. 'Would you play words with me?'

Val screamed. Will turned from the butchery.

'*Watch!*'

Will forced a strong voice past his gorge. 'What would you have of me?'

'I would have you make a play.'

'A *play*?'

'A true play. *Watch!*'

But he was already watching the hangman draw Val's heart from his chest, hold it for the man to see and, in the seconds before he died, smear it on his face.

The contempt that Will Shakespeare saw in the cripple's face mirrored the hangman's for the Jesuit.

'You are asking me to write a play?'

'I *command* you to write a play.'

'Upon what subject?'

'A history of an era so recent it is not yet fully chronicled by Holinshed.'

'Why ask me? Holinshed's *Chronicles* is my pillar. I don't write of the present. I trade in the past.'

'You trade most prosperously in what a university wit might dub "political upheaval, betrayal, and assassination."'

'Only in the past. Prison, torture, and death await the writer of political upheaval in the present. Holinshed is always my source. His chronicles of the past are my wellspring.'

'Dead papers!' The cripple pounded the bench with his fist. 'I offer *vigor*! *Living* Holinsheds with breath in their lungs and blood in their veins who partook of events firsthand!'

'*Living* Holinsheds won't have breath in their lungs for long. Neither will the poet who listens to them. Besides, the Revels will never allow it. Actors are not allowed to play living rulers on the stage.'

'We will deal with the Master of the Revels.'

Will stared miserably at the cushions. They were embellished with cloth of gold. He could not deny that the possessor of such a car had the wealth to pay the Revels' bribes. But once performed, such a play would cost the playmaker a death as long and bitter as Father Val's.

'Why do you hesitate to write a play that portrays the Queen as our good and glorious sovereign?'

Will said, 'Recent events are best served by pamphleters.'

'No. These events stir the heart as much as the intellect.'

'Who better to stir hearts than ballad-mongers?'

The cripple stared.

Will met his eye. He was done ducking his head and doffing his cap. The cripple had admitted that he needed what only a playmaker could deliver – three thousand spectators to listen for hours and tell all London what they had heard – a theater show to fire people's hearts and steer their minds.

'What events?'

'*Cuius regio eius religio*. The defense of the faith.'

Will said, 'I know the dead Latin beaten into schoolboys. And you know that those you would sway are only swayed by lively English – what events, sir? What cause do you demand I project?'

He waited uneasily, nursing an empty hope that despite the

cripple's disloyal talk of royal birthright, the play he commanded would not be deemed treasonous.

'The guarantee of a worthy heir,' said the cripple. 'To lead England's triumph over perfidious France, bloody Spain, and the Pope. Do you see where I drift?'

'Succession,' said Will. 'Where you'll drift on reefs and shoals.'

Like any ambitious London man, he feasted on news of palace machinations as hungrily as privateers devoured reports of Spain's treasure fleet. The old Queen's court – the pivot upon which England's power turned and a great dispenser of opportunity – was riven by factions. Courtiers, like this one, were already maneuvering to seize Elizabeth's crown. But when nobles stormed, common people could only look to steeples for which wind blew the weathercocks.

Will's fellows in the Chamberlain's Men were afraid even to revive his *History of Richard II* – the tale of a weak ruler. With succession in doubt, Will had already cut the abdication scene. Now they were wondering aloud whether he might prune a line here and new-write there, to make King Richard steadfast as Elizabeth.

The cripple's command was deadlier than Will had feared, deadlier than sedition or blasphemy. 'You will write a play about the triumph of Elizabeth our Sovereign Queen over the traitress Mary Queen of Scots.'

'*The Sister Queens*!' Will blurted before he could stop himself.

TWO

'You've taken it up! You will be my poet.'

Will Shakespeare cursed his slippery tongue, even as his mind raced.

The death-struggle between the Queen of England and the Queen of Scotland was the greatest story of the age. Royal cousins warred like bitter sisters for nearly twenty years before the headsman's ax put an end to it. But the fear and hatred ran too deep to end. Even after the Scots Queen was thirteen years in her grave, their battle still raged in Protestant and Catholic hearts. Woe to any who stepped between their loyal followers – too many sides to risk taking sides. All faiths: Protestant, Catholic, Puritan. All patriots: English who loved Queen Elizabeth, and Scots who loved their king – Mary's son James.

All were eager to shed blood by the dagger, or the rack, or the hangman. A distant relation of Will's own mother had been implicated in a Catholic conspiracy to murder the Queen and put King James on her throne. No one believed it of him, but reports came to Stratford of Edward Arden's head spiked on London Bridge for the crows.

'I know nothing of it. I was an unbaked youth when Her Majesty—'

'You are thirty-six years old. Thirteen years ago you were twenty-three and already father to a son when Mary was brought to justice for conspiring with foreign enemies to assassinate Queen Elizabeth.'

'But far from London town.'

'Two days' ride – back and forth to Warwickshire like clockwork.'

'Only for gentlemen with coaches such as yours. Thirteen years ago I was a traveling player – north by foot and cart to York, down to Plymouth, and all Wiltshire, Oxfordshire, Leicestershire, and Lincolnshire between. I thought myself blessed to visit my wife and children and my father and mother twice in a year. But more to your point, sir, there are writers who specialize in news.'

'None so popular. The great Greene's slander only elevated you.'

Will still savored the envious slurs poor drunken Robert Greene had cast at an 'upstart' lowly young player turned play-maker. Will's histories of warring nobles and royal usurpers had struck powerful chords in a London haunted even then by uncertain succession, and had drawn bigger houses than gentlemen writers who had scholarized their wit at university. Ten years' work had earned triumphs. The Chamberlain's Men played often at court. His poems sold as fast as his printer could marry ink to paper. He'd bought farms, stables, gardens, and the finest house in the Warwickshire town where he was born with his profits.

He said, 'Greene slandered Christopher Marlowe, too.'

'Marlowe is dead. Stabbed steps ahead of the hangman.'

A venomous reminder that only fools took sides when lords warred. The government had acquitted Kit Marlowe's murderers in a trice, and Will had seen them strutting up Gracious Street in bright new velvet doublets. Of fools, to be sure the majestic Marlowe had known no equals. He had encouraged rumors he was a spy – serving the Queen, no less – had written that religion was a 'childish' thing, and even claimed that he had lectured Sir Walter Raleigh on the finer points of atheism; although from what Will had read of the old naval hero's free-ranging poetry, Raleigh would listen to anyone.

'But court writers, university scholars' – he inclined his head, elevating the cripple to that select fraternity – 'better understand majestical events. *Magnalia regni.*'

'You speak to the groundlings.' The cripple nodded contemptuously at the servants, the mechanicals, the cooks' boys, scullery maids, harlots, carters, and the masterless men and vagabonds pressing closer to see the hangman quarter the priest's body.

Will imagined them as the cripple saw them: grains of gunpowder – a hollow flash of stage lightning if ignited loosely, but rammed hard into cannon, the charge of hot and bloody civil war.

'I cannot write your play.'

The cripple said, 'The authorities again express concern that the large gatherings for plays like yours threaten the peace and breed plague. They would close the plays for the safety of the city, as would the preachers who inveigh against them.'

Will refused to rise to that bait and dismissed it boldly. 'The authorities are *always* threatening to stop the plays, and Puritans rage because our players' trumpet draws thousands more than the sermon bell.'

The cripple's smile hardened. Will imagined a slithery viper's tongue parting his lips. 'Her Majesty might overrule the authorities, being the play-lover she is. But in these parlous days, she might not. Unless I persuade the Privy Council to influence her.'

The cripple's threats cast Will back to the confusion of his boyhood when the newly throned Queen Elizabeth reestablished the English church – supreme again, as her father had founded it – freed of the Pope and ruled by the English monarch. Protestant zealots were emboldened to reform 'gorgeous papist rituals.' Ancient Catholic rites and cherished customs were banned. People were forbidden to pray for indulgences to speed the souls of their dead beloveds through purgatory, forbidden the nuptial blessing, forbidden funeral mass. Even common worldly joys – the long-loved Maypole, the Corpus Christi pageants – were turned topsy-turvy down.

Angered, he shot back, 'You would close *all* the playhouses to force *me*—'

'No need to if the Master of Revels bans *your* next play.'

The trap snapped shut. But there rose in Will Shakespeare a resistance to this extortion. It was proper to doff his cap in respect of station, but disorderly to accept abuse of station.

'Look!' The cripple directed Will's attention to a white-bearded old man pushing to the scaffold with a gleeful smile. 'Do you know who that is?'

'No,' said Will, though the old man could only be the vicious priest hunter Richard Topcliffe who famously haunted the gallows when Catholics were executed.

'Sir Richard himself,' said the cripple. 'Fiercest of the priest hunters. A master of the rack. Proud to "scrape" the papist conscience.' He drew the curtain before Topcliffe could see inside the coach.

Will said, 'Who knows what of my next play? Methinks my poems consume my efforts now.'

'Would you defend your poems in the Tower?'

Will felt his resistance shrivel like a salt-sprinkled slug. Hard-won fame was no armor against savagery. Thomas Kyd – Will's first guide to play-making – had transformed the theater as a storm churned a glass-flat sea into white horses, and his *Spanish Tragedy* remained year after year the most popular drama in London. But Kyd had been racked in the Tower. Will remembered seeing him drag his body up Fleet Street like a cart broken to pieces.

The cripple laid a small calf-gloved hand on his arm. His manner was gentler, almost kindly, now that they both knew he had prevailed. 'Go to the Bel Savage Inn. Ask the Moor about Queen Mary's letter.'

'Your "living" Holinshed?' Will asked, unable to disguise his disgust. He pushed open the curtains with a hand trembling as much from fear as anger. Marlowe, dead. Kyd, dead.

The cripple lowered his lame foot to the floor of the coach and placed the brass-banded leather chest beside him on the cushions. 'Stay a moment longer, if you would.'

Will was struck by a new, tentative note in his voice. Doubt shadowed the man's face. Until this moment, their dealings had been unequal-matched – he like a plowman craning his neck to answer a mounted knight. Now, as if unhorsed, the cripple opened the chest and heaved from within a thick pile of folded paper crammed into a sheepskin binding.

'I have a brother,' he said. 'Who has my deepest love. Love such as yours for your daughter. A learned, yet worldly man. A famous hand at lawyering, a Member of Parliament, and often the Queen's favorite. He has already turned his hand to this play you name *The Sister Queens*.'

A reprieve? If some learned, worldly lawyer had already drafted a version of *The Sister Queens*, might Will not new-write it quickly and give the brother the credit? Let the worldly lawyer defend himself against suspicions of sedition. 'What has your brother named his play?'

'*The Tragical History of the Anointed-Sovereign Queen Elizabeth and the Traitorous Catholic Mary of France and Scotland . . .* Methinks *Sister Queens* is more felicitous.'

Methinks too, thought Will. Two words that promised an

irresistible play. How long before sisters and queens were at each other's throats? By the start of the second scene? Before the first scene ended? But he'd be discovered. There were few secrets at court. None in the theater. The sister queens' warring sides would uncloak which poet to blame sooner than any first scene Will Shakespeare could imagine.

The cripple thrust the many papers at him. Will turned open the sheepskin and his breath stopped short. The front sheet read, *'The Tragical History of the Anointed-Sovereign Queen Elizabeth and the Traitorous Catholic Mary of France and Scotland* as written by Francis Bacon.'

Much was explained and all made much worse.

Francis Bacon was the Queen's Counsel Extraordinary and a staunch friend of Essex, whose many powers included investigating traitors. That made this cripple his brother Anthony, a creature of the shadows who Marlowe had sworn was a master spy whose network of intelligencers served the Earl of Essex in both England and Europe. No wonder they could pluck him from the crowd. Anthony Bacon had countless informers to report his intentions, and countless spies to stalk him.

'My brother and I will be forever grateful.'

A triple-edged sword. The Bacons could be valuable friends. Or terrible enemies. Or – if they miscalculated and were blamed for writing a seditious play and ended up on the wrong side of courtly conflict – deadly millstones hanged about their poet's neck to drown him in the depth of the sea.

'It is but an early version. In private, between us, I fear it lacks the common touch. But it needs only a professional poet to lend flesh to its bones.'

Will hushed a groan. Until his successes freed him from clearing other men's thickets, he had repaired, embellished, new-writ, and lent flesh to the bones of numberless bad and half-finished plays that 'lacked the common touch.' He hefted the heap, six fat sections stitched with strips of vellum. 'It has weight already.'

'It embraces many complicated events, which obliged him to explain with care.'

In other words, the worldly attorney had done the lawyerly thing and dealt with the complications by embracing them all. Will

Shakespeare said the only thing he could until he reckoned a way out of this trap. 'I will read it.'

'Speed is all.'

'The Chamberlain's Men await my tragedy of Hamlet.'

'They and your Danish prince will wait upon *The Sister Queens*.'

But the Chamberlain's Men were in desperate straits, with a lease and lease-fine coming due. The company needed his new play. And he was just beginning to believe that emerging from his new *Hamlet* was a play different than any London had heard. That hope gave him courage to fight. He drew Bacon's foul papers to his chest and conjured a conspiratorial smile: 'As a playmaker, your brother knows that the muse turns the glass in her own time.'

Anthony Bacon nodded, as Will had guessed he would. University wits clung like catamites to the conceit that 'the muse' was elusive. 'How long, do you reckon, for *The Sister Queens*?'

'Foul copy in half a year, I would think. Writ-new another month or two.'

'No! I can't allow you more than three months to performance.'

In truth, a playmaker who couldn't deliver his play in five *weeks* should turn his hand to ballads. 'You allow the impossible,' Will countered firmly, hoping he had at least bought time to work on *Hamlet*. Gripping Bacon's bulge, he stepped from the coach. Anthony Bacon called down, 'Do not burden your young patron with our conversation.'

It was not at all astonishing that this ice-eyed provoker knew that the Earl of Southampton was his patron. So he would know too that Southampton worshiped Essex. But that did not paint him a traitor.

'My Lord Southampton is out of all suspicion!'

'How would *you* know? *Tell no one of our meeting*.'

Will said nothing to acknowledge the command. He had to warn Southampton. No bosom friend of Essex was 'out of all suspicion.'

'Never disappoint me,' said the cripple, with a significant glance at Val's limbs strewn about the scaffold. 'If you do, you will end your days like your priest.'

Will's breath stopped short again, and a thousand fears stormed his heart. How could Anthony Bacon know he knew Val? Not a soul in London knew about Val. *Tell him the truth,* whispered the quiet voice that occasionally spoke deep in Will's brain – a voice that he had learned to trust as a mariner steered by the lodestar.

'You are misinformed, sir. Father Valente was my *friend*. He was never my priest.'

Bacon laughed. 'I'd expect only the bravest acolyte to admit it.'

'You are misinformed,' Will repeated. *Speak truth! Ram it home!* He raised his voice. 'I was never Father Val's acolyte. How could I vow to embrace the single life of a Catholic priest? Die without children? A single, issueless man remembered not to be? Never! My priests marry in England's Church. My priests preach in English. And my priests sire English heirs.'

Bacon laughed again, a grating sound scratching with contempt.

Will said, 'How dare you mock England? I am not a subject of the Pope. I love England. I love my Queen. *I am an Englishman.*'

'But you weren't always, were you, Master Shakespeare?'

'What do you mean?'

'I mean that you were born to a recusant.'

'Nonsense! My father was born Protestant, long before the Queen established the Church of England.'

'Your father was converted to the Roman Church by an *ardent* Catholic.' The serpent tongue slid into another superior smile for the word ardent. 'You would play words with me, Master Playmaker?'

Will Shakespeare felt death in his heart for what he would hear next.

'*Ardent* she was, and *ardent* she still is – your mother – Mary *Arden* Shakespeare, who never renounced her family's Catholic faith – her illegal, foul, recusant Church of Rome faith that foments rebellion against our Queen.'

'That is insane. That is lunacy.'

'Fortunately for your mother, the priest hunters never caught on. And haven't, yet. It only recently came to me through intelligencers investigating another matter . . . I've told no one, even in my most intimate circle. Only I can tell Sir Richard Topcliffe the truth about your mother. And I will, the very instant you disappoint me. Now go and write my play.'

'She is an innocent, an honest woman in her middle age.'

'She is yours to save.'

Anthony Bacon pounded his cane. His driver lashed the horses, and the long, dark car thundered from the gallows.

THREE

'Lord! Bless our Queen with long and happy life . . .'

A shrill ballad-monger sang the news of Val's execution. Remnants of the hangman's crowd stopping to listen and buy broadsides of the verses pinned to his doublet choked the road to Southampton House.

> 'And bring true peace to end this awful strife;
> And give all her subjects wisdom to foresee
> That Pope and England never will agree.'

Not for centuries, thought Will Shakespeare. He shouldered past the ballad-monger and pressed on, shifting the weight of Bacon's manuscript from arm to arm and glancing back to see if he was followed until he realized it didn't matter. They knew where he lived. They'd known to find him at the hanging.

Guilt or innocence had no bearing on Anthony Bacon's threat. Edward Arden, almost certainly not a conspirator, had confessed on the Tower rack that he was. Will's mother faced the same fate. He had no choice but to write *The Sister Queens*.

His admission that he had no choice kindled a glimmer of hope – faint as a candle in a cave. Bacon could not betray Mary Arden Shakespeare to Topcliffe before Will wrote *The Sister Queens*. The spy master clearly believed that only he could write a play that would inflame the groundlings. But could Bacon believe that any poet alive could write even one word while fearing for his mother in the Tower? Or pen a single syllable while mourning her death? Will rated it less a hope than a fragile expectation of less despair. But he picked up his pace.

The Earl of Southampton's London residence was a formidable mansion that loomed like a fortress just outside the city wall. Its guard towers and great hall were built of pale-yellow Caen-stone stripped from the nearby ruin of the ancient Templar Temple. The towers flanked the hall and joined stone ramparts that protected galleries, stables, kitchens, buttery, and lodgings for a hundred servants.

Will slipped around back to the stout, iron-studded buttery door. 'Good morrow, Ned.'

The groom standing watch with an iron-tipped staff and an axe-head halberd close at hand returned a warm, 'Good morrow, Master Shakespeare.' The short hallway behind Ned led to the armory and the rooms where the watch grooms lodged.

Safe inside, Will hurried up the servants' stairs.

The dinner hour was long over, the Great Hall nearly deserted, and the few retainers lounging by the fire took no notice of a pale and shaken poet. When the butler rushed in with more wine, Will caught his eye. More than once he had glimpsed the fellow's moon face shining from the groundlings in the pit.

'Is his lordship about, Steven?'

'Closeted in his chambers, Master Shakespeare.'

'Please carry word that I await his pleasure should he wish to advise me on a thorny matter.'

Thorny it would be. Essex and Southampton were closer than hammer and anvil, but Will had to pry them apart before Essex dragged Southampton down with him. For gratitude, for friendship, for honesty, Will had no choice but to warn him. He would risk 'disappointing' Anthony Bacon. He could only hope for his noble patron's protection.

The butler promised he would pass on the word. Doubt in his voice expressed what both men knew. A nobleman 'closeted in his chambers' would stay closeted for as long as he pleased.

The wintry afternoon was already too dark to read by the small window in Will's room, and Francis Bacon had written far too many pages to squint at in the smoky light of stinking tallow candles. Will lugged the bundle to Southampton's library, which housed an ever-growing collection that the earl and his mother had granted Will allowance to add to from the St Paul's booksellers. Here he was welcome to burn bright candles of sweet-smelling beeswax.

Such luxury was wasted on *The Tragical History of the Anointed-Sovereign Queen Elizabeth and the Traitorous Catholic Mary of France and Scotland.* Will plowed through speeches that knew no

end and scenes as slow as elephants. He plumbed verbal abysses
for some hint of wit. He sought action, found oceans of incidents,
and sought in vain information unknown to alehouse gossips. Flesh
to bones? It had no vigor of bone, only flesh – a gross, quivering,
unfinished creature entirely lacking its skeleton. It would drive
spectators straight from the theater to a bear baiting.

Kit Marlowe – never one to dodge a spear, much less turn his
other cheek – would have been the man to write *The Sister Queens*.
Marlowe would have relished the danger. Envy for his dead rival
struck Will like a thunderbolt. Were Christopher Marlowe alive
today, might not Anthony Bacon have pressed *him* to write an
intricate tragedy of royal personages instead of Will Shakespeare?
Bacon had only to look to Kit's first words of *Edward II*, when
the derelict king wrote to his minion:

> 'My father is deceased; Come Gaveston,
> And share the kingdom with thy dearest friend.'

Could any poet alive promise so much in only two lines?

A story as great as *The Sister Queens* deserved such a
champion.

The butler appeared with a supper tray of bread and cheese.
Consolation. 'I am sorry, Master Shakespeare. I am told the earl
will see no one tonight.'

He lay awake in the dark, praying for sleep to end the dreadful
day. Even steel-hearted Val had screamed. Even after what they
had done to him in the Tower, the priest had been shocked by the
pain of the knife. Will imagined his mother in the Tower, gathering
her courage at her first sight of the rack. He shut his mind to that,
and what did he remember? Thomas Kyd stumbling along Fleet
Street in the rain, months after his session on the rack.

'Hold, Master Kyd!' Will had bellowed, his player's voice surely
heard in the suburbs beyond the city wall and Bankside across the
Thames, but Kyd had scuttled away. He flinched when Will overtook him, eyes darting to see who was watching. His cloak was
mud-spattered, and so thin that his stooped shoulders were
drenched. Only thirty-four, then, barely five years Will's senior,
he was old-faced and frightened.

'It's Will, Master Kyd. Will Shakespeare.'

Kyd's voice was thin as reed song. 'Will. They say it goes well with you.'

Will had murmured flap-mouthed courtesies. 'By God's pleasure. And with you, sir?'

'I am cursed among men, but God's to be worshiped.'

'God's a good man,' flew from Will's mouth. To this very night he hated himself for the empty proverb.

Thomas Kyd had returned a cutting look, a flash of the pride he had once possessed: Will, after all, had modeled *his* revenge play *Titus Andronicus* after Kyd's; and Kit Marlowe could never have conceived his *Tamberlaine* before *The Spanish Tragedy.* Yet Kyd's still out-drew both of theirs.

'I thought, at first, I could bear the rack,' he had droned, like an old man reciting his ailments. 'I was still the most part whole when the rack's master eased pulling. And hadn't told them much, either. Not very much. But he had stopped only to ram a great rock under my back, which bent me like a bow. And then they tore me until I was this dismal wreck . . . You're right, Will. God is a good man. We've few racks in all England and only one rack master. Spain's got scores.'

Will had to speak, had to say something. 'Was it Topcliffe?'

Kyd had surprised him. 'Topcliffe wanted Marlowe.'

'*Marlowe?* Kit made no secret of his foolery. Told all London that Christ was St John's bedfellow. What could you possibly tell Topcliffe about Marlowe?'

'Anything to make him stop. But my trouble was that Topcliffe didn't give a fig's end for Marlowe's monstrous opinions. Topcliffe would not stop until I recalled that Kit told me he was going to Scotland to meet with King James.'

'King James? But why not, King James? Kit was ambitious for a patron. And the King writes sonnets that aren't half bad. What a match they'd have made – majestic poet and poetic royal patron!'

Thomas Kyd shouted, *'Are you artless, Will?* King James wants what they all want – Queen Elizabeth's throne. English courtiers scheming for it are terrified the Scots King will snatch it out from under them. So, when they caught wind that your majestic poet – a fool who bragged he happened also to be a "majestic" spy – made overtures to James, they paid the cruelest interrogator in

England to tear "evidence" from me to "prove" that Kit Marlowe was plotting with King James to overthrow the Queen.'

'But why you?'

'They knew we'd shared rooms They found some atheist writing Kit had there and that was all they needed to drag me in. Here's the jest: scheming whoreson Marlowe was too cocksure to see they were using him against James and when they were done would stab him dead.'

Nothing, thought Will, had changed in the eight years since Topcliffe had tortured Thomas Kyd to confess what his pay masters wanted to hear.

In the morning, he fetched Raphael Holinshed's *Chronicles of England, Scotland and Ireland* from the library and opened it on his table before the window. It had been new printed shortly after the trial, with recent events added by John Hooker after Holinshed's passing. But all Hooker lent to the story were speeches recorded in the Lords and Commons urging Queen Elizabeth to execute Mary Queen of Scots.

Their arguments were compelling: Mary's role in Catholic Anthony Babington's plot to free her and murder Elizabeth; the Queen's safety and the peace of the realm could not be assured with Mary alive; neither strict imprisonment, nor banishment, nor seizing hostages, not even conversion to Protestantism, would deter Mary's followers from conspiring anew 'to make her a head to be set up against Her Majesty.' Proof that Mary had ordered Babington to free her and murder Elizabeth, the *Chronicles* recorded, had been 'collected from her own letters and the confession of Babington, her instrument and conspirator.' Will shook his head. All this was known, had been known since the trial.

Shouts of *Hail* and *Holla* and laughter drifting up the stairs, and the slant of light, heralded the mid-day dinner hour when hunger might stir Southampton from his chambers. Will went down to the Great Hall. Serving grooms were laying places at the head table, which stood at one end on a raised platform, and at the many trestles stationed on the main level. The warm smell of white wheat bread wafted from the kitchens below, and the belly-sharpening pungency of roasting joints of beef.

The earl's retainers, guests, and armed gentlemen lounged about.

At the oyster table at the lower end of the hall, laughing gallants dressed in costumes worth half a city drew swords and scuffled in friendly combat. But all who caroused and gossiped and postured had one eye ever flashing toward the door to Southampton's private chambers.

A groom armed with a birch rod directed a gang of boys who were strewing fresh rushes on the floor and bearing logs into the hall for the deepening cold. Will hailed him.

'Tom. Is my lord coming down for dinner?'

'No, Master Shakespeare. His lordship is not about.'

Will thought that odd. Every man waiting for dinner seemed to have one ear cocked for a summons from his benefactor. The tension in the air was typical when the earl was expected, and his knights and gallants were alert as saddled chargers.

Will left the hall by a back door and made his way downstairs to the buttery, where he took his place at one of the plank tables. Other members of the household were already seated: a young poet whose courtly, if not fastidious, verses had lately caught Southampton's fancy; his music teacher, a taciturn German; a Hampshire clergyman who thought himself purer than his table mates; and a flock of Italian painters, smelling of linseed oil and turpentine, brought over from Verona to decorate the new music room ceiling.

He caught the eye of the harried butler who emerged from the cellar driving wine-laden serving-men before him like a flock of ducks.

'Steven. Has his lordship responded to my message begging audience?'

'I'm certain he will respond in due course, Master Shakespeare. Pray excuse me, sir, I'm wanted in the hall.'

They ate mutton, salt fish, cheese. Their bread was rough rye, their drink thin beer. The nearby kitchen dinned like a battlefield, with clatter and banging, bellowed commands, shouts of alarm – 'Look to the plate!' and 'Have done, have done!'

Will heard Cook revile a serving-groom in rhyme. He opened one of the palm-sized table-books he carried to record phrases and thoughts, slid a silver pin from the binding, and wrote on a page coated with a soft mix of glue and gesso, 'Have hold, Cuckold!'

The butler, driving more wine bearers from the cellar, slowed in passing to whisper, 'His lordship will not see you.'

Will was astounded. 'A thorny matter' conveyed urgency, and it was unlike his patron to ignore an urgent plea. Utterly mazed, he returned to his room and took up paper and quill, ink pot, and blotting sand to transcribe from his table-book the Italian painters' mangled English phrases, and the rhyme Cook had shouted at the serving-groom he was cuckolding. His thoughts were whirling like swifts. He had to warn Southampton. He hoped that the play plot was Anthony and Francis Bacon's own private conspiracy – not countenanced by the Earl of Essex, not even known to him. Were that the case, Will stood a good chance of gaining Southampton's protection. But how likely was it the case?

He was staring with unseeing eyes at the Holinshed and Hooker account of Queen Mary of Scots' trial when he heard the clatter of many horses on the cobblestones below and a rush of servants on the stairs. He peered from his narrow window. The courtyard was a swirl of milling riders and crimson capes. Mary Wriothesley, Dowager Countess of Southampton, had arrived from the country with her company of armed gentlemen and waiting gentlewomen.

Will raced downstairs to join the servants and retainers lining up to greet her. Of all the household, who better to persuade Southampton to grant him an audience than the earl's mother?

High-colored, flushed from her ride, her dark, stone-blue eyes swept the anxious assemblage of porters and maids, cooks, painters, musicians, and poets. Will stood slightly apart – still as a statue – to catch her eye without appearing to presume.

It was she who had transported him into the earl's sphere. It was she who had welcomed him – a penniless commoner – into a noble house, where vast rooms of painting and sculpture, a library of books on a hundred subjects, and halls ringing with music and spiced by the ever-present scent of power were his to explore.

The old stage trick worked.

'Have you a new poem for me, Will?' she called down from her horse.

'If you please, my lady.'

She dismounted and disappeared indoors. Will rushed to his room to cobble one quickly. Then he washed his face and hands in a bowl of purple glass left behind by an alchemist installed by

Southampton's father, shaved cheeks, chin, and throat, and carefully trimmed the hollow dividing his mustache.

The countess's waiting gentlewoman, Frances Mowery, a plain-
faced country lady, met Will at the top of the stairs, where the
floors were strewn with lavender instead of rushes and every
footstep released sweet perfume. 'God give you good morrow,
Master Shakespeare.' Frances's husband, it was said, never came
to London, preferring to sleep in his hall with his hounds, and
Will had wondered, at first, why a noblewoman famous at court
for her wit, her education, and the fashion of her garments kept
such a rustic attendant. But he had come to see that a wise woman
would value a stouthearted, clear-eyed ally in a large household
teeming with retainers. Frances led him to an open door that looked
upon her mistress's chambers.

She was seated at a writing table with pen in hand and a shaggy
white Iceland dog on her lap. One of the bound fair copies of Kit
Marlowe's poems ever floating around London lay open to 'The
Passionate Shepherd.'

She continued to write, and Will took the opportunity to regard
closely the woman whose patronage he likened to a drawbridge
lowered from a wondrous castle. Age had clothed her in angel-like
perfection. She was twelve years his senior and recently named
'dowager countess' when her son married, but her lively spirit
would make Father Time smile, for any implication of aged widow-
hood was a jest no observer could believe. Her skin was smooth,
her hair, laced lightly with strands of silver, still lush and glossy,
and – miraculously – her teeth plentiful and white. The single clue
to her years, Will thought every precious moment he saw her, was
the certainty in her deliberate gaze.

It had been eight years since he fell under her spell. She had
sent for him when his comedy *Love's Labor's Lost* played for the
Queen at Tichfield Park and spoke frankly. She was having difficulties with her son. The boy, then eighteen, had been only eight
when she was widowed, she explained. The Queen's Lord Treasurer
Burghley had made him his ward, conducted his education, sent
him to Cambridge. Now the boy refused to honor his debt by
marrying Burghley's granddaughter, Lady Elizabeth De Vere.

'We are new, they are old.' The countess had explained the

worth of the ancient De Vere lineage. 'Nor can a widow ignore the value of Burghley's friendship.'

Baron Burghley – Lord High Treasurer William Cecil, patriarch of the Cecils – was at the height of his powers then: the Queen's closest advisor, master of Her Majesty's government, and founder of her spy service.

'I've assured Lord Burghley that their marriage would honor my family and complete my happiness. But I find my son not yet disposed to be tied.'

She had smiled her lovely smile at a dazzled Will, who heard Kit Marlowe's true-born words, 'Who ever loved that loved not at first sight?'

'I believe,' said the countess, 'that the poet of *Love's Labor's Lost* can change my son's mind by writing him love poetry in praise of marriage.'

She was, in effect, granting a commoner extraordinary license to advise a noble in matters far more intimate and consequential than his sword instructor and Latin tutor. A poet was expected to praise his patron – in flatterer's coin were nobles paid – just as a tutor was expected to teach, a clergyman to inspire, a counsellor to advise. The Countess of Southampton required Will Shakespeare to perform all four duties at once. He had seized eagerly upon her commission:

> 'From fairest creatures we desire increase
> That thereby beauty's rose might never die.'

But the power of words had limits – or at least the power of *his* words. After three years, two epic poems, and scores of sonnets, Southampton turned twenty-one and promptly forfeited a heavy portion of his inheritance to Burghley rather than marry Lady Elizabeth. Will could only wonder whether the countess blamed him for her son's obstinacy, or – worse – for her need to surrender her independence and re-marry for protection. But he surely blamed himself for letting her down.

With the Lord Treasurer no longer her friend, she had chosen her new husband cleverly – Sir Thomas Heneage, a confidential intelligencer to the Queen with his ear to the heartbeat of every plot. But the old man had died five months later. Will had worried for her with Heneage gone. For a woman born of Catholics and mother to a headstrong son with a reckless penchant for defying the royal will, Heneage had been a wise, even necessary, choice. She must have worried, too, for suddenly she re-married to a soldier – Will's own age – who had distinguished himself at Essex's great victory at Cadiz. The bridegroom was currently fighting in Ireland.

Frances Mowery plodded away, farthingale rustling, heavy shoes crushing lavender like millstones. The countess looked up from her writing.

Will made a long leg, his head bowed low.

'Good day and happiness, my lady.'

'Good day to you, Will.' She regarded him coolly. 'You've not brought me a poem in some time.'

> 'Oh never say that I was false of heart.
> Though absence seemed my flame to qualify—'

'Your muse rises briskly on short notice,' she interrupted with a smile.

She held the key to so much of his happiness that he was forever cautious in her company, expressing his desire at careful remove. It was only in his third sonnet for her son that he had dared:

> 'Thou art thy mother's glass, and she in thee,
> Calls back the lovely April of her prime.'

But today, the plague of Bacons made him brave; caution seemed a waste of precious time when threats loomed deadly.

'The muse,' he answered, 'stands when inspired, my lady.'

Her eyes widened and Will feared she would call for her armed gentlemen. But she favored his boldness with an almost saucy smile. 'What zeal hath inspired thee now, absent so long?'

'Beauty, your ladyship, is never absent. It sweetens our dreams.'

'Sometimes, Will, you have the manner of a gentleman – or at least a courtier.'

'You are very kind, my lady.'

'It must be the poet in you.'

'My mother Mary is of gentle birth,' he ventured. She shared a thin line of cousinage with the Ardens of Park Hall. (There was no shame in Edward Arden's head spiked to London Bridge; nobility, aristocracy, and gentry all knew executions.) 'And though the College of Heralds granted my father gentle, no coat of arms can elevate me higher than the station I hold as your admirer.'

'Is there more to your poem, Will?' A blithe reminder that nobles cared little for the gentry.

> 'As easy might I from myself depart
> As from my soul, which in thy breast doth lie . . .'

Her gaze strayed toward the room where Frances plied her needle. For the couplet, he curbed his voice as he would to prompt a player who had forgotten his line.

> 'For nothing this wide universe I call,
> save thou, my rose; in it thou art my all.'

'Have you read it to my son?'

'His lordship has not yet afforded me the opportunity, my lady.'

'It is moving. Perhaps it will move him too.'

He said, 'I hope so, my lady,' and seized the chance to gain an audience. 'If his lordship is not preoccupied with affairs of business.'

Suddenly she was grave. 'Busy with affairs beyond him.'

Grave and uncertain, Will realized, her gaze bleak. 'Countess Southampton, do you mean his promotion to General of the Horse?'

'Certainly not. It's *Essex* that's captured his heart.'

Will crafted a sympathetic reply. 'Boys admire soldiers.'

'He's no boy!' she snapped. 'He's not been one for years. Surely not since sneaking behind the Queen's back to marry her lady-in-waiting. Besides, it's more than enraging Her Majesty that frights me. Far more, far worse. It's Essex and his stately schemes.'

'Stately schemes' resounded of treason, plots to usurp the throne. Will scoured his brain for the words to ask a noblewoman wise in the ways of the court how far under way were these crimes? *Even further along than extorting me to write a play to inspire the treasonous scheme?* But he needn't ask, for she vented her fear plain and bluntly.

'Noble Essex would be burnished regal. The peer would make himself peerless. While my son, unable to secure Her Majesty's favor, grows discontent and in his despair might follow such company as Essex offers.' She fell silent, then mused, 'His father, too, had a penchant for pretenders – sent to the Tower for the Scots Queen and lucky he wasn't beheaded.'

Will considered his reply. Her new husband was an Essex man, a comrade knighted by him at Cadiz, and had fought beside the earl in Ireland. Thank God he had stayed there when Essex angered the Queen by returning to England against her orders. Possibly, Will wondered, because his wise new wife persuaded him to stay at his post while Essex conjured his plots?

'May I ask, your ladyship, could his lordship turn to some protector at court? An ally? Before things are too far under way?'

'I don't know who. Essex taints all he touches. Her Majesty will never listen to any appeal that reeks of him.'

'May I suggest, my lady, that you persuade his lordship to let me wait on him so that I might make him aware of the danger?'

'No.' The countess shook her head. 'There is nothing you can do. My son is still headstrong. Still impetuous. He will do as he wishes. And I know in my bones it will end in the Tower.'

Will returned to the servants' wing, where a groom at the foot of the stairs said, 'Your printer's apprentice brought a packet from Stratford-upon-Avon.'

It was wrapped in strong paper and sealed with wax. Will recognized his mother's hand. She penned letters for his wife Anne who could not read or write.

He broke the seal as he climbed to his room. The packet contained a fresh table-book exquisitely bound with goatskin boards, and a letter on a sheet of paper folded twice. He read by the light of a landing window, fearing for his children's health and his father's. Anne reported that they'd had a terrible fire. God-sent rain helped extinguish it, and none of the household were hurt, but they would have to patch many holes in the roof and shore a wall and a chimney before winter closed in.

His mother added in a postscript, *Your father is back at work, as you can see. Your table-book is the first thing he's made in a while. God keep you safe.*

Back in his own room at his table, Will reached for a sheet of paper to promise money for the fire repairs and stopped dead. His hand froze in the air. A Bacon spy with access to the house had entered his room and dipped his quill to scrawl across his notes, 'The Moor.'

It made ridiculous Will's hope that he was safer within Southampton House than without or had any choice but to venture into Bacon's world. Heart pounding, he ransacked his resources for any possible advantage. He found, with the thinnest of ironic smiles, a slight one from Bacon's own brother.

He detached the title sheet from Francis Bacon's pile of pages and folded it small enough to hide it inside his new table-book. Were any authority to challenge him, he would brandish the link to Queen's Counsellor, Francis Bacon – a famous courtier licensed to arrest anyone he deemed a traitor – like a passport or a seal of authority. Slight, perhaps, but enough to collect cloak, purse, and courage and hurry into the city to find the Moor.

FOUR

The Bel Savage stood west of St Paul's Cathedral just outside the city wall. It was hot, blue with tobacco smoke, loud as an iron mill. The same shrill ballad-monger Will had heard hawking the news yesterday contributed to the din, imagining Father Valente's regret.

> 'My soul doth sorrow for words I said,
> For which offense my body hast now bled;
> But mercy, Lord! for mercy still I cry:
> Save thou my soul, and let my body die.'

Will saw no black men. He asked an alewife if the inn housed a Moor.

'You'll be wanting Isobel,' she smirked.

'A woman?'

'Black as sea coal,' said another. 'Upstairs.' And laughed a third, 'You've a long wait. She burns like coal, too. You'd better have me set you another.'

He climbed the narrow stairs to the stews. An apple-squire blocked the dark hallway and told him that the girl at the first door was available.

'Isobel.'

'She'll cost ya.'

'Tell her the playmaker is here. She's expecting me.'

'Tell her yourself. After you've paid.' The apple-squire held out a grimy palm. 'Three shillings.'

'*Three?* I pay my apprentice three for a week.'

'If it's boys you want you're under the wrong roof.'

'Who is she, Venus?'

'There's others for the smaller purse.'

'They said there was a wait.'

The apple-squire shrugged. 'The wine that made the gentleman stand to made him not stand to.'

Will counted out three shillings from his smallest pieces, and made his way into the darkness, wondering if he'd be knocked on the head for the remains of his purse. He found her door by bumping it with his nose and knocked.

'*Entrer!*'

French? Traffic known for nimble capers and the pox. He squared his shoulders and pushed in. Three shillings bought a room remarkable for its light and the comfort of a fireplace. The afternoon sun flooded through a glassed window and burnished the skin of the girl on the tester bed like polished walnut. In the warmth of the fire, she wore a thin white smock. Her feet were bare. A sprite, Will thought, small and finely formed, with dark, dark eyes and a tumbler's supple limbs.

Hers was not a comely face. No three shillings' worth to cast eyes on her harsh hawk nose. But pounds for shillings when she cast back a smile as dazzling as broken seas. A smile that could turn as cold, Will Shakespeare thought, gripping tightly his shreds of reason.

A clay pipe smoldered beside the bed and the room stank of tobacco smoke, despite a dish of sweet herbs. The fine furnishings – the canopied bed and feather quilt, a joined chair with back and arms, a pewter pitcher, and a Nonsuch linen chest inlaid with bog oak and holly – indicated this was the chamber of the tavern landlord. On a table sat a battered old three-and-a-half-octave virginals – a musical instrument more likely found in a lady's chambers – its keys beaten smooth by many fingers.

Entrer, it turned out, was the extent of her French. Her English was raw as Bankside. 'And who might you be, squire?'

'A gentleman told me to see a Moor.'

'The cripple?'

Will nodded. 'He said you would tell me a story.'

'Did he tell you to pay me five shillings?'

'I paid your apple-squire three. Which was more than enough.'

'You've been taken, squire. I'm no trull.'

'The alewives said you traffic.'

'They're jealous,' she retorted, with a proud, self-glorious nod for the well-appointed chamber.

Ten years in London, and he'd let the apple-squire gull him like a country bumpkin.

Isobel extended a small and astonishingly pretty hand, palm out, and left it there until Will had emptied his purse. She clicked the coins, laid them casually beside her pipe, which she picked up and puffed rings of smoke.

'He said you know of a letter from Queen Mary.'

She patted the bed. 'Sit.'

Will sat warily, wondering if the innkeeper was a jealous man. 'May I see the letter?'

'I don't have it. I only seen it once.'

'When?' he asked.

'Summer of the year 1586.'

She was not the young girl she looked. Ever more skeptical, he asked, 'How?'

'I was laundry maid at Castle Tutbury where Sir Amias Paulet imprisoned Mary the Queen of Scotland.'

Will nodded. A bleak prison. Whipped by wind and storm, the half-ruined stronghold built by John of Gaunt, whose son deposed Richard II, crouched on a Staffordshire hilltop like a winter-starved bear.

'Sir Amias was a hard, cruel man. He wouldn't allow poor Queen Mary to cross the moat.'

Isobel's gamine face grew animated and she spoke with a hollow sentimentality that reminded Will of the news ballader whose verses were drifting up the stairs:

> 'God's Queen, who saves us strife,
> Herself holds only mortal's life,
> And she who lives like you and me,
> The knife to her heart holds the key.'

Admirable lines, Will had to credit the monger. No base drudge, but sharp as a needle. A summary in three words of all the years of Queen Elizabeth's calming rule. Then, reminding those who loved her that she was one day doomed, as they all were. No God, but a fellow Briton, who had run her course. Unless a usurper – a murderer – suddenly accelerated their return to the chaos she had fought to tame.

'A prison,' Isobel cried. 'Tutbury was more Clink than castle.'

'With an extraordinarily young laundry maid. How old were

you, ten, twelve?' She looked no more than sixteen now, but if she were telling the truth, must now be well into her twenties.

'It was my first position. My last upright,' she added with a cockapert smile. 'One day a handsome young man came to see me. Very grand, he was – valet to the Spanish Ambassador. I let him woo me.'

'How did the Spanish Ambassador's valet happen to venture all the way to Tutbury?'

'He was sent to tempt my will.'

'You would have me believe,' Will asked gently, 'that a diplomat's servant was sent from London's royal court to *seduce* a laundry maid that was but a child?'

'I lived outside the castle.' She stared hard at him, measuring his wit. 'I walked home every night.'

'Marry! You smuggled letters.'

'From Herself. Mary Queen of Scots.'

Will's interest quickened like a startled heart. 'Go on.'

'Once they stripped me to my smock, but I hid it where even they dared not look.'

'But *you* looked at the letter.'

'No!'

'But you said you saw it.'

'That wasn't the letter I saw. It wasn't at Tutbury. I saw the letter later. After Sir Amias moved the Queen to Chartley. They stole her money from her cupboard when she was ill. She told Sir Amias she was left with two things which could never be taken from her, her royal blood and our Catholic faith.'

'And again,' Will prompted, 'you lived outside the house.'

'No. No one at Chartley could live outside the house.'

'Then how did you smuggle Queen Mary's letters?'

'I gave them to a man in the buttery.'

'Was he allowed to leave the house?'

'No.'

'Then who carried the letter to the Spanish?'

Isobel shrugged, uninterested in what she didn't know. 'Poor Queen Mary. She thought the bairn would save her.'

'The bairn?'

'Her son. King James of Scotland.' The girl's face darkened with anger. 'He sold his mother for four thousand a year.'

'How do you mean?'

'He struck a bargain with Queen Elizabeth. Four thousand a year.'

'For what?'

'For not saving his mother from the ax.'

Will nodded. But as he understood it, Mary had abdicated the throne of Scotland in favor of James years before she was executed. Every Protestant in England had sighed relief, believing that Catholic Mary's son had renounced the Pope.

'Queen Mary prayed every night that the bairn would march on England.'

Will remembered the invasion fears. Would the Scots King rouse the northern English earls, Catholics all? Would the French sail into Edinburgh? Would Scots and French and northern earls march on London?

'Queen Mary thought they would share the throne.'

Will imagined the depth of Mary's anguish when she learned her son had turned Judas for a pension from her arch enemy. *The woe of queenly care.* Loss of hope. Loss of her son. Did it shake her faith?

'I prayed with her,' said Isobel. 'Outside her door. All the women prayed for her deliverance. She was sore used and sore betrayed.'

'How did you see inside her letter? Wasn't it sealed?'

'Folded, stitched, and sealed. But this time The Mary—'

'"The Mary?"'

'The Scots ladies who waited on Her Majesty were called Marys.' Isobel was, Will noted, recklessly unafraid to call the traitor-queen Her Majesty. 'The Mary told me to bring the sealing wax and I saw the letter open on the table before she folded it.'

'What did it say?'

'There was no postscript.' She tested him, again, with a hard stare.

'I know not your meaning.'

Isobel drew her legs up and folded her arms around her knees. 'When they called Queen Mary a traitress, they said she wrote a postscript that commanded Master Babington to name what gentlemen he'd engaged to murder Queen Elizabeth.'

People still remembered, with whispers and averted eyes, the ferocity of Thomas Babington's execution. Queen Elizabeth had personally ordered his slow death, a benchmark by which Father Val's would be judged mild.

'Your meaning still eludes me.'

'There was no postscript.'

'What do you mean?'

'They added that later.'

'A forgery?' Hardly fodder for Bacon's play about 'the triumph of Elizabeth our Sovereign Queen over the traitress Mary Queen of Scots.'

He asked Isobel, 'Did you tell the cripple that Mary was wrongly accused?'

'He did not listen. What else was forged, squire? If you get my meaning. What other lies did they add to her letters?'

'You may have seen a different letter.'

'No! It was her last. False accused, she was. And false beheaded.'

Will wondered. He'd already been gulled by the apple-squire: was he being gulled again? He unfolded the title sheet of *The Tragical History of the Anointed-Sovereign Queen Elizabeth and the Traitorous Catholic Mary of France and Scotland.*

'Know you who this speaks of?'

Her face gathered in walnut wrinkles as she traced the ink with her finger. 'No,' she said slowly.

'You might if you could read.'

Her beautiful hands closed on the paper like claws. 'What does that prove?'

'You can't read. You didn't read a postscript.'

'I know a postscript when I see one!' she shouted back. 'There was no writing under Queen Mary's signature. They added it later.'

Will wondered who had taught an illiterate wash-maid words like postscript, engaged, and signature. Someone who had prompted her to tell him this tale more sympathetic to Queen Mary and less to Elizabeth, the opposite to what Anthony and Francis Bacon wanted him to hear? Were others in on the play plot? Rivals the Bacons didn't know about? Did this mean that his hope that Essex didn't know about the plot was true? Or that Essex did know but did not trust the Bacon brothers and had recruited new allies?

The Moor snatched up her pipe, stalked to the fire, and re-lit it with an ember. Her fury frightened him. But when she turned to him, her eyes were wet with tears, and Will Shakespeare suddenly felt like the hound from hell. 'I'm sorry,' he said. 'Certainly, you know a postscript when you see one.'

'And I'll learn reading one day.'

'I *know* you will . . . If you like, I could teach you.'

'Marry!' Her eyes got big and her smile flashed like the sun. 'Would you?'

'By my troth.'

'But someone told me I'm too old to learn.'

'No! Not a day too old. My mother taught my father to read when he was at least your age. He can read aloud proclamations at the fair.'

'Your *mother* can *read*? How did she learn?'

'She was a very lucky little girl – probably the only farmer's daughter in the shire so lucky. Being her father's favorite, he asked a cousin who could read to teach her. When she read the Bible, they gave her a pony.'

'When I was a little girl, God gave me Queen Mary. Where did your mother keep the pony?'

'In the barn with her father's oxen.'

'Could I read the Bible?'

'In time.'

She leapt to the bed, crossed her legs under her, and leaned forward expectantly, her back arched, her buttocks rounding her thin garment. 'Now!'

'First, tell me how you know it was Queen Mary's last letter.'

She gave a little whimper of frustration but plunged back into her tale. 'The next day Queen Mary went hunting. Sir Amias hadn't let her out in weeks and she was so happy. The last I saw she was astride her horse. What a beautiful sight she was, prancing over the moat and galloping down the road. She was a grand rider, so tall and straight. She used to ride at the head of her armies. Did you know she led her armies?'

'No.'

'Oh, she loved riding. But they tricked her. It was all a trick. The instant she was gone, men burst in and searched her closets. They took all her papers. Out on the heath she was tricked again.'

'How?'

'Queen Elizabeth's gentlemen galloped up to arrest her. Poor

Queen Mary, she thought Catholic gentlemen had come to rescue her.'

'How do you know that?'

'My bedmate was the gamekeeper's bastard. He said her face crumbled like old bread.' Isobel crossed herself, then reached under her mattress and took a bejeweled crucifix from its hiding place. Will's eyes widened. The piece was as dangerous as it was precious – a Catholic 'idol' that could get its owner imprisoned for recusancy.

'Where did you get that?'

Isobel kissed the cross. 'Queen Mary,' she said with defiant pride, 'gave me this when I converted to the true faith.'

'You speak too freely, child.'

'Gave me that too.' She nodded at the virginals. 'And taught me to play on it.'

Isobel hopped off the bed, ran her lovely hands over the virginals' keys, and played softly a sweet string of notes. 'Queen Mary taught me English words for Scotch songs of the olden time.'

She repeated the melody – newly adorned with notes like rubies – repeated again, doubling them all until the little instrument rang like an orchestra filled with a band of musicians. Then she re-stated the simple melody, closed her eyes, and sang an air as sweet as its words were perilous:

> 'Hail, O star of the sea,
> glorious Mother of God
> Oh Holy Virgin, Mary,
> O wide-open gate of heaven!'

'*Hush!*' Mariolatry – the Catholic veneration of Jesus Christ's mother – was forbidden.

Isobel smiled over her shoulder, 'You won't tell the priest hunters,' and sang,

> '*Salve, regina, mater misericordiae,*
> *Vita, dulcedo et spes nostra, salve!*'

Will shuddered. She had just sung, in total ignorance of the Latin, the 'Salve Regina':

'Hail Holy Queen, mother of mercy. Hail our life, our sweet-
ness and our hope.'

Overheard by the wrong ears, it would get both of them clapped
into Bridewell as fast as if she had opened the window to shout
to the streets, 'The Queen be damned!'

'I will not hold your secrets,' he protested.

'Then why all your questions?'

'Hide your cross. Put it away!'

Instead, she dangled it, teasing him.

'I'll teach you to read this instant, if you'll put that away.'

She clutched it to her breast.

Will said, 'I believe you will learn quickly. Musicians are clever
with new things.'

Isobel hid her cross under the mattress.

Will opened one of his table-books and scored its leaves with
the letters of the alphabet. He pronounced each as he wrote and
left space for her to copy them. He guided her hand through the
shape of each. When she rendered the letter J backward, he showed
her how to erase mistakes by wiping the leaves clean with a piece
of linen.

Isobel followed along eagerly and kept him there until she
extracted his promise to return for another lesson.

'Are you married, squire?'

'Yes. My wife is home in Warwickshire.'

'What's her name?'

'Her name is Anne.'

'How many children have you?'

'Three children. Hamnet, Judith and Susanna – Hamnet died
four years ago. Judith is his twin. As alike as a face in a glass.'

'Do you see them often?'

'No. It is a ways away and I am busy in London.'

'Do you miss them?'

'Yes, I do.'

'Do you miss your wife?'

'Certainly.'

She gave him a smile and a small laugh. 'All you busy come-
to-London men miss your wives. Certainly. Do you keep a mistress
in London?'

'I cannot afford a mistress,' he said, thinking to forestall an offer. But he felt like a callous fool when she said, 'You could find a handsome widow. You're not so old— You're smiling. You already have one, don't you?'

'No.'

'Yes, you do. I can tell.'

'I do not.'

Eyes like midnight bored mockingly into his until he dropped his gaze. 'If you don't, you have one in mind. I'll wager she's rich and beautiful.'

Will hung his head, half to hide his own small smile, half to hide his heart. 'She is all you say. But, sadly, married again.'

Isobel laughed. 'Oh, yes. You're a man who loves women.'

'How would you know?'

'And a fool for us, too.'

'You're but a child.'

'A wiser child than you, squire— Hold! You mazed me with reading. I forgot. The cripple left this to give you.' She pulled from under her pillow a folded paper. 'What do the words say?'

When he broke the seal, she made him sit on the bed again to spell out the words with the letters from her alphabet.

'Niles. The. Brewer. The. Queen's. Hart.'

FIVE

The Queen's Hart was a new-built tavern near the busy corner where the broad thoroughfare of Gracious Street crossed Eastcheap. Decorated plaster ceilings and glass in the red lattice windows warned a thrifty man that its landlord had spared no expense and would charge for it. Will Shakespeare favored the less dear Boar's Head in Doolittle Lane, the Mermaid, or the Cross Keys just along Gracious, where used to play the Chamberlain's Men.

The guests were prosperous merchants, unattended gentlemen, squires up from the country, and foists eying their purses. When he asked a perspiring drawer filling cups of ale to point out Niles the Brewer, the serving-man corrected him. 'You mean the landlord. Niles Roper. Over there.'

Will approached the swag-bellied, middle-aged fellow beaming at the busy room and handed him the paper Anthony Bacon had left with Isobel.

'The cripple?'

'Yes.'

'There's a piece of work.'

'By my troth,' Will agreed. 'He says you have a story to tell.'

'You've seen Isobel?'

'I have.'

'And had her too, I'd warrant.' The fat man smiled.

Will was startled how sharply the familiarity stung. Roper's assumption aroused hostility toward every man the girl had known. He had not 'had her.' She was hardly innocent – no child, but she was childlike, and had put a trust in him for helping her learn to read. He had no doubt she would do anything to please him. But he would hate to see a shadow in her brilliant eyes that said he had violated that trust.

The landlord clapped him on the shoulder. 'Another piece of work. Go softly there, young fellow, 'ere she cuts your heart out.'

'What were you to tell me?' Will asked coldly.

Roper beckoned a serving-maid who hurried over with a bottle
of Burgundy wine and a plate of marzipan. The landlord poured
two glasses. 'I've heard your plays, sir. And read your poems. You
honor my tavern.'

Will nodded his thanks and touched the wine to his lips. He
was growing accustomed to being recognized by strangers and
enjoyed it mightily. 'How is it you know Isobel?'

Roper lowered his voice. 'She came to Chartley House with
Mary of Scotland. I had my brewery in the town that victualed
Chartley. 'Ere Mary was there a week, a gentleman from London
ordered me to secrete a wooden box in my cask . . .'

Niles Roper winked dramatically as if he reckoned William
Shakespeare would write him into a lofty part for Dick Burbage
to play at the Globe. But Roper appeared so happily awed by his
own handsome tavern that he put Will much more in mind of
his comedical character Sir John Falstaff – the bane of the virtuous,
except for those persuaded to change their habits by Falstaff's
example. If he ever tried to write Falstaff again, Sir John would
wake from drinking hard all night to discover himself somehow
landlord of his favorite tavern.

'Well, sir, Niles Roper – late of Her Majesty's expedition to
France, home from the wars surviving sword and pestilence – had
not been born yesterday.'

Will nodded. Falstaff was an old soldier, too, if occasionally
late to battle.

'"Begone!" I told him, plenty loud to be heard two hundred
miles to the Tower of London. "Begone, or I'll set the dogs on
you. Niles Roper is no lover of Catholics, nor traitor to our
Sovereign Queen."

'Well, sir, what does the rogue do but he produces the seal of
Sir Francis Walsingham his bloody self. Commanded me to do
his bidding. Principal Secretary of State was Walsingham – long
before your time, young fellow – and king of all the Queen's
spies.'

Will had thought Kit Marlowe's claim a false boast, that
Walsingham's spy service had recruited him when he studied at
Cambridge. 'What was in the box?'

'I didn't ask. Would you?'

'Yes, I would have. What was his name?'

'Gifford. As three-faced a cozening rakehell you ever saw.'

'Bearing Secretary Walsingham's seal?'

'Which I already told you,' the landlord replied. 'When next the barrel returned empty from the Chartley, the box was in it, which Gifford took and gave me another to put in the beer going back.'

'In other words, Mary smuggled letters out of Chartley, not knowing that Queen Elizabeth's Secretary of State would read them.'

'In the same words, sir.'

'And when others smuggled letters to the Queen of Scots by the same means, their letters, too, were intercepted.'

Roper shot a warning glance at the nearest tables. 'If you must think aloud, think alone. I hear you not.'

'But surely Queen Mary's letters were sealed?'

'Would were your lips, sir.'

Will looked at the fine plaster ceiling, the several windows, and the fireplace. At the Keys, the beef roast was turned by a filth-spattered kitchen boy. Here in the Queen's Hart, the joint turned like magic on a spit moved by shiny clock wheels.

'You were well rewarded.'

'I obeyed the Queen's warrant.'

A legitimate name for a royal conspiracy, thought Will. Or at least Walsingham's. 'I wonder,' he said, 'they didn't slit your throat instead.'

Niles Roper sighed. 'I wonder, too. It makes for rough nights.'

But Roper's smooth round face showed no suffering lack of sleep. 'Do you wonder, too,' Will asked, 'why Her Majesty gives you warrant to talk to me?'

'I see no Queen's warrant,' said Roper. 'Who knows who the cripple serves?'

Will said, 'I've heard he serves the Earl of Essex.'

Niles Roper stared at Will for a long moment. When he spoke, his tone was not unkindly, as a long-time come-to-London man might advise a lad arriving fresh from the countryside. 'If you are going to mingle with the likes of that cripple, Master Playmaker, I suggest you learn to distinguish between open-hearted bluntness and cautious discretion.'

'I hear your meaning, sir,' said Will. 'And I thank you.'

Beaming with pride and pleasure, Niles Roper re-fashioned lines from *Richard III* to warn in doggerel: 'Wrens should be aware where eagles dare.'

Will nodded bleakly. 'But what's the wren to do when the cat's in her nest? I ask again, Good Landlord, did not Queen Mary seal her letters?'

Niles Roper murmured back, 'Look for Arthur Gregory at Paul's.'

'Who is he?'

'A seal-cracker.'

'Where at Paul's?' Will pressed. All London went to St Paul's Cathedral. The precinct walls encompassed church, burial grounds, homes, and shops.

'He dines with Duke Humphrey.' Which told Will that the seal-cracker was a hungry man without a home.

He left the Queen's Hart deeply confused and stood outside in the dark. Anthony Bacon would have a play that heralded Queen Elizabeth's triumph over Mary Queen of Scots. Why, Will wondered again, send him to witnesses who proved the Scots Queen wrongfully convicted and Queen Elizabeth an instrument of corrupt betrayal?

Should he head across Eastcheap to St Paul's? By day, the cathedral yard bustled with lawyers, printers, booksellers, and thieves, gallants hunting fortune, gentlemen seeking amusement, and servants soliciting work. By night, it was not safe.

Even here on broad Gracious Street, best to examine all shadows and dark patches where cutpurses and cutthroats vied for trade. Prudence counseled waiting for morning and to find a bed nearby rather than risk the long walk to Southampton's mansion. The watch had shut the gates and while there were places to breach London's wall, his fellow breachers weren't likely to be gentle souls with peace in their hearts. His mind leapt to Isobel's warm room. If she was too *slimp* for his taste, too slender like a boy, and if her breath was stale with tobacco, why did a moment's remembrance make him stand? But he had already made up his mind on that question. Teaching her to read, as he had his apprentice for the Chamberlain's Men – as he would have taught his wife had he ever been home long enough – would be its own satisfaction.

True prudence demanded that he never go to Paul's. Were it not for the threat to his mother he might decamp to Warwickshire for some months in hopes the cripple's enthusiasm might wane. If they came after him, he'd hide in one of Warwickshire's undiscovered priest holes. A smile bent his lips. A poet hole, as it were.

Except, where would his exit leave the Chamberlain's Men? Waiting for *Hamlet* while hired men spoke his parts and losing the Globe to the lease fine. And what of Southampton? Treason, even by the feckless, warranted the headsman. And the threat to his mother was all too real. He felt like an oarless coracle, tugged and pulled by rival currents.

The flicker of firelight lit eyes in a shadow across the street – a footpad wondering whether Will was so drunk he could be taken easily. Or signaling a brother in the trade to lend a hand if he were not. Will reached into his cloak as if to unsheath a dagger. The footpad inched deeper into darkness, cautious, if not yet intimidated.

Veterans lurched out of the Queen's Hart with cups in their hands and staggered arm in arm down the street. Will backed hastily into a doorway. London was thick with volunteers home from the Netherlands and Ireland, and English and Welsh mercenaries back from European wars as military campaigns broke for winter. Drunken soldiers wreaking wrath could be worse than footpads.

They raised cups and thundered a toast.

'Noble Lord Essex. Fucked the Irish and broached 'em on his sword!'

Oblivious that the earl had in truth fled Ireland in disgrace, or caring not a damn, several glared at Will pressed in his doorway. Informing them they had lifted their toast from his *History of Henry V* would not spare him a beating if he insulted their hero. More sensible to echo it loudly while correcting it to, '"From Ireland coming, bringing rebellion broached on his sword."'

It satisfied the veterans. They lurched on, singing mightily.

> 'A soldier's a man;
> A life's but a span;
> Why, then, let a soldier drink!'

Will took their cue, squared his shoulders, and affected a bellicose swagger toward the Cross Keys Inn. The footpad did not follow.

Just when he got to the Cross Keys, men burst from the tavern door and ran into the dark as if fleeing demons. Behind them roared an actual veteran – enormous, disheveled, scar-faced – slashing the air with a sword. He shoved past Will, scowled at his vanishing prey, gave a loud belch, planted his hands on his thighs, and vomited in the street. Then he wiped his mouth and shifted his scowl. 'Gentle Shakespeare.'

Will turned an affectionate smile on the younger man.

'Gentle Jonson.'

'What brings Southampton's pet to the lowly Keys?'

'Ease in the Keys will ever please.'

Ben Jonson glowered, truculent as a bear with a taste for dog. Hot-tempered, hasty to duel, and highly educated – which accounted for his habit of referring to his plays as 'works' – Ben was, Will thought, a terrible actor. But he was proving a writer of rare mettle who would make many a good play if the hangman didn't get him for murder in a drunken brawl. Less prone to explosion since his *Every Man in His Humour* earned money, perhaps tonight was a back-sling.

'Ale or oysters?' Will asked, indicating the midden to which Jonson had contributed the contents of his gut.

Ben got his sword back in its hanger on his third try, without removing any fingers. 'Bad herring. Let's drink.'

Ben threw an arm around Will's shoulders and the poets pushed into the tavern, Ben bellowing for ale, Will suddenly hungry.

'There's a gallant been asking for you.'

'What gallant?'

'With the tall cap. Full of questions.'

Will spied the gallant, who was tricked out in a velvet peascod-belly doublet that protruded from his stomach like a cannonball, extravagant piccadills that plumped his shoulders, and silk knee breeches padded with bombast. A tall velvet cap sprinkled with jewels and the gleaming poniard sheathed at his waist indicated a gentleman of considerable means, but at the sight of Ben Jonson glowering his way he shrank on his stool like a dry apple. 'He looks not gallant. Were those his friends you routed?'

'They insulted me.'

'How?'

'I do not recall.'

By the time Will had called for the ordinary and had the spoon in his hand, Ben was in a shouting match with a coven of Gray's Inn student lawyers on the subject of reforming the law, the students arguing that lawyers were the most qualified to reform the law, Ben bellowing that statesmen, poets, or even the most vulgar sort of bloodsucking market men knew better the principles of natural equity – principles of which practicing lawyers, bound by their lust for Roman law, were as ignorant as blind bears.

Will moved further down the table.

The tavern's door opened and in crept young Marc Handler. The slight, handsome apprentice player looked around anxiously. He saw Will beckon. Relief blossomed in a nervous smile. He ran his hands through his long, dark hair and hurried across the packed room, turning men's and women's heads in equal number.

A gentleman with the swagger of a born bully gestured to his friends to watch, and fell in behind Marc, mincing in a mockingly effeminate manner. Marc did not notice. The bully caught up at Will's table and tossed an insult.

'What a pretty piece of flesh.'

Will rose to his feet. 'This is my apprentice. You will kindly leave him be.'

'Apprentice?' drawled the bully, and confirmed Will's suspicion that a wealthy merchant father had sent him to university long enough to imitate a wit. 'Who knew that catamites apprenticed to their trade. And you must be the sodomi—' His voice shrank to a startled squeak when the tip of Ben Jonson's dagger pricked his throat.

The mingled din of tavern shouts ceased abruptly. Tomb silence cloaked drinkers, drawers, and alewives. A bead of blood trickled down Ben's glittering blade.

He asked, 'You would bandy lines from *Romeo and Juliet*? Here's another for you, jacksauce: "My naked weapon is out."'

The bully shriveled. His friends trembled.

Ben roared, 'You will exit this tavern as if pursued by a bear! And every tavern where you see me for the rest of your miserable life. Filthy knave! You, you . . . prating . . . you—' Livid he'd run out of words, Ben began to froth at the mouth.

Will whispered, 'Boiled-brains.'

'Thank you, Will. *Run,* you boiled-brains toad!'

The bully ran for the door. Ben said, 'Good evening, young Marc,' and resumed shouting at the lawyers.

Will asked Marc, 'Why your long face and dark eyes?'

'I am so sorry, master.'

'Why?'

Marc hung his head.

'Sit,' said Will. 'Take that stool. Have you eaten . . .? Now what is the matter?'

'There's a girl with child.'

'*Another?*'

'Her father wants money, again.'

'Again? The same girl?'

'No! Same father. Her sister. I am so sorry. I will pay you when—'

Will silenced the boy with a single raised finger. It was four years since his son had died. Three since he found Marc singing in the streets and made him his apprentice, which required teaching him to read because a player had to read his parts. It had become clear to both that Will could deny him nothing, even if Marc wasn't endowed already as if by a divinity with talent for the stage. 'Go ask Master Burbage to advance ten pounds from my share. But I warn you, Marc, if you do this again, do it with a girl who possesses great beauty and a kind heart. Because – I swear by God's wounds – next time you will marry her!'

He was about to resume spooning up his stew when the gallant who had been asking about him sidled over and sat tentatively on the stool between Ben's and his.

'Master William Shakespeare?'

'Your servant, sir,' he answered politely. The days were passing when only gentlemen wore gentles' garb, and Will mourned the loss of order. But if this sorry fellow, his clothing somewhat worse for wear when seen close by, desired to seem gentle, Will Shakespeare could not bring himself to challenge a humble's fantasy.

His kindness was rewarded with a flood of compliments. The gallant had heard all his plays, which he had thought unparalleled until he read Master Shakespeare's poetry.

Down the table, shifting metaphors as ponderously as a Spanish galleon struggling to windward while firing cannon, Ben abandoned his blind bears to liken the lawyers to crippled mastiffs at a bull-baiting. Next, they were beadles whipping whores through the town, the grievously abused women representing a benighted citizenry groaning under the weight of misconstrued ancient tradition.

Will's admirer climaxed in an explosion of praise that grew tedious: 'In truth, I believe, sir, that your *Venus and Adonis* will live a thousand years. My very sleep is sweetened by the copy I keep beneath my pillow. It is a poem for the ages. The imagery so, so—'

'Overwrought?' Ben Jonson shouted in his ear.

'No, sir! The passion is so—'

'Comic?'

'It is the last word on seduction, sir.'

'Pray so.'

The gallant, undeterred, quoted lustily:

> '"Graze on my lips, and if those hills be dry,
> Stray lower where the pleasant fountains lie."'

Ben hurled back,

> '"No dog shall rouse thee, though a thousand *bark*?"'

Will's admirer gripped his courage and his gilt poniard. 'If you would have a graver poem, sir, read you the all-praiseworthy *Lucrece*.'

'I would rather read headstones.'

The shabby gallant protested. Ben fumbled for his sword.

Will laid his palm firmly on the broad and hairy fist that gripped the pommel. Ben leaned around him to shout at the gallant, 'Shut your gob, sirrah. The playmaker should stick with his plays.'

'My poems have met with success, Ben.'

Jonson closed both big hands around Will's head and stared into his face. A veil seemed to lift from his eyes and for an instant he appeared sober as stone. 'They're not *terrible* poems, Will. Not even bad. But they're ordinary.'

Will could say that himself about his latest *Hamlet*. When he spoke it aloud, much of it sounded as good as his best writing. Some sang, and the parts that could do with improvement he would improve, and his brother players had no complaints with the earlier drafts he was trying to make better. But even improved, was it not still ordinary?

'*Write plays!*' Ben roared in his ear.

'When a poem brings two hundred?'

'The Reverend Henry's sermons bring two *thousand*! Would you write sermons? God's wounds! And if you would live a thousand years, you'd quit Southampton's lush chambers while you still know how to write.'

Will answered Ben with quiet surety. 'I do not forget that I was once a shilling-a-day player. I do not forget that my Lord Southampton (of your "lush chambers") advanced me one hundred pounds to buy my player's shareholding in the Chamberlain's Men which made me partners with Burbage and Condell and Kempe and the rest. I do not forget that if I hadn't my share, I'd have to scramble like every scribbler in London, new-working other men's plots, begging players to hear mine. Now, no matter what I write, I at the very least earn my living as a player-shareholder. Thanks to my Lord Southampton.'

Ben, who would give his eye teeth for a player's share of a company's profits, said, 'Write more plays.'

'I *am* writing more plays. But what makes you a sudden lover of the spectators?'

Ben had been shocked and sorely disappointed when his last year's play had earned far less than his great success of the year before.

'I love them not. The farther it runs from reason and possibility, the better the nutcrackers like it. And if you don't give them a jig or a bawdy on a regular basis, they'll fall asleep. But I love courtier-critics less. At least garlic-stinking groundlings don't perch on the stage like vultures. Fastidious impertinents, feathered ostriches bred in Hell.'

Will uttered his first full-blown laugh since Anthony Bacon laid a trap for him at Tyburn. 'You rail like a Puritan.'

Again, the veil seemed to lift from Ben Jonson's eyes. His voice dropped to a whisper only Will could hear. 'If you won't save your plays, save your life.'

'What are you talking about?'

'Beware Southampton.'

'He's my patron,' Will shot back, defending him as if by rote, despite the earl's refusal to see him. 'I just told you. And, my friend . . . in some ways.'

'But *his* friend, his nearest friend – you know of whom I speak?'

Will nodded his understanding. 'Yes. The Earl of Essex.'

'Is a fool. The worst sort of fool, the impatient fool.'

Again, Will nodded. He had seen as much from the Queen's stage, though he would argue that worst was the arrogant fool. Which defect, too, he had seen from the Queen's stage.

'I learned in prison,' said Ben, 'that the Queen's spies are as patient as the tide – did I ever tell you that when Topcliffe got me locked in Marshalsea for *Isle of Dogs*, they tried to catch advantage of me with that damned villain Poley cozening me to admit that satire was sedition?'

'You've mentioned it,' said Will. Usually while drinking. A friendly jailer had warned Ben that Poley was a spy and Richard Topcliffe had lost his Privy Council commission, luckily for Ben who was soon set free, though branded on his thumb. Ben was also too drunk to remember that Poley was one of Kit Marlowe's acquitted murderers strutting up Gracious Street.

Ben glanced about and lowered his whisper. Will was mildly astonished that even he avoided offending friends of Essex in a crowded tavern.

'So when the executioners come for the earl – when, not if – they will snare Essex's fools in the same net. Southampton is the fool's fool. If you stay with Southampton, they'll make room in their net for the fool's fool's fool.'

'What executioners? What do you know, Ben?'

'I know what is known at court. And I know what is known in the street.'

'What is known at court?'

'Essex is twenty thousand in debt.'

'*Twenty thousand?* Do you know how rich you have to be to fall twenty thousand pounds in debt?'

'In his case, not rich enough if the Queen continues to refuse to renew his sweet wine monopoly. He'll be ruined.'

'What do you know in the street?'

'Essex swaggers on the razor's edge – which he could get away with when he was the Queen's hero.'

'Before his army failed in Ireland.'

'Before his enemies *betrayed* his army in Ireland.'

'Betrayed? What do you mean?'

'I'm no lover of Essex, nor would I dub the Irish warrior a dull fighter, but I know what every veteran knows: his soldiers were starved, clothed in rags, and short of gunpowder. Essex's foes at court and in Parliament made sure supplies never reached him. I don't excuse his foolishness, his impatience, and his arrogance – good men died for it – but his army was betrayed.'

Will said, 'I'm surprised he didn't fight his foes at court.'

'I doubt he even noticed until it was too late. He absolutely failed to honor his duty to protect his men.'

Will nodded. Feckless and selfish was the man he'd seen from the stage.

Ben turned away to harangue the lawyers. The gallant grew familiar, leaning close to address Will in a voice thick with insinuation. 'It is said you raise questions about a letter.'

Will felt a chill as if the Cross Keys had suddenly opened all its doors and windows to the river wind. 'Who says?'

'It's heard about the town.'

'By whom? Where? What did you hear?'

'That you say Mary was false accused.'

'I say nothing!'

'Many agree with you.'

'I offer no judgement,' Will protested. 'And if you love my poems, you will answer loose talk so.'

'On my honor, sir . . . Though there are men of high station who appreciate the honor you pay the Scots Queen.'

'I honor no queen but my Sovereign Elizabeth,' Will retorted. 'England's Queen is my queen. Tell your "high-stationers" that Will Shakespeare pledges his heart and soul to Queen Elizabeth, long may she reign.'

'Long may she reign,' the gallant echoed. 'As long as she may reign . . . May I tell you a most interesting tale?'

'Good night, sir. I would finish my supper.'

'It will prove inspiring to your writing.'

'Good night,' Will repeated, a rare flash of anger in his eyes.

The gallant scrambled from the stool. 'Forgive my presumption. Perhaps another time.'

Will bent his head to his trencher. But his throat had closed, the mutton dry as ash. Anthony Bacon had dragged him into quicksand. And all he could do was prop an elbow on the table, palm his chin, and squint at the featureless fog like a blindman.

He heard Ben from afar. 'Will . . . Will! Where go your thoughts?'

Isobel had crossed his thoughts, and something she had said about Queen Mary. What had the Moor girl said of James? 'He sold his mother for four thousand a year.'

Suddenly, he heard his quiet voice murmur, a steadying sound like the measured beat of a clockwork. It spoke for Mary Queen of Scots – the child-deceived mother. She buried her sorrow in mocking thanks:

> 'Now mark how my good son serves me so:
> He will lift this heavy crown from off my head
> And this unwieldy scepter from my hand,
> The woe of queenly care—'

'Will?' Ben Jonson was nudging him hard.

The lines threatened to escape. Quickly, he opened a door in the memory castle he had built when a schoolboy and locked the verse inside. Only then did he look at his friend, looming big as a rhinoceros.

Carpe diem! Half drunk, Ben Jonson was quicker and stronger than most men sober. Why waste the night waiting for light when he had a tiger-hearted veteran to escort him to St Paul's?

SIX

'Would you walk with me to St Paul's?'

'Now?'

'Now.'

Ben Jonson lurched to his feet. His stool fell with a crash.

'Pestilence rides night vapors like black bats swooping o'r snow. But I'd brave worse to quit such places where the air is thick with lawyers farting from their faces.'

They started across the dark city from east to west, Eastcheap to Candlewick Street, past Budge Row. No need to play the veteran's swagger with Ben Jonson beside him. That Ben had put cruel Spaniards to the sword was writ in the scars on his face and a lunatic gleam in his eye. The few good citizens still about at this hour scattered at their approach, blackguards trembled in the shadows, and even a link boy – a 'moon-curser' who would light their way for a farthing – fled with his torch of pitch-soaked rushes. It was, Will thought, as if he had commissioned a vigilant archangel to convey him through Hell, a wary esquire who stopped repeatedly to cock his ear to behind, as if they were being followed.

'What think you of my bats?' Ben asked, after one of those sober pauses.

'They would make a pretty picture flying over snow, if they weren't fast asleep in winter.'

Windows winked out as the hour lengthened. Fewer and fewer cast flickers of fire or lamplight on the muddy cobbles. Where breaks between houses offered longer glimpses, Paul's square stone steeple loomed blacker than the sky.

'You know Old Stow?' Ben muttered.

John Stow, a cheerful old tailor who chronicled England's history. Tall, skinny Stow was a familiar sight as he wandered London and the countryside collecting material to write true annals of the past. Once traveling with players in Kent, and another time in far-off Wiltshire, Will had found Stow poking about ruined abbeys and bent among headstones, earnest as a stork.

'Stow told me they've raised the money for the spire, but God knows when they'll build it.'

Lightning had fired Paul's wooden spire before he and Ben were born.

They crossed Bread Street. A wet wind bore the dank of the Thames.

A dog barked.

'The watch!'

'Around him,' whispered Ben. 'Or we'll spend the night expounding to a dolt.' Ben pushed him behind a stack of firewood in a stinking alley. They stood still, ankle-deep in muck. A dim lantern bobbed toward them. Above it floated the pale face of the constable peering reluctantly into shadows.

His dog barked again. Will felt Ben move and, when his hand emerged from his cape, saw to his horror the gleam of his dagger. 'Don't.'

'I would kill the dog,' Ben muttered back, 'before a man with any honesty in him.'

The constable jerked his chain and dragged the dog along Watling Street in the direction they were heading.

Glancing over his shoulder, Ben nudged Will into Bread Street. They crossed to Pissing Alley and up Maidenhead Lane. The great bulk of the cathedral's nave and transept darkened the night and dwarfed the sleeping houses.

'Where now?' asked Ben.

'Humphrey's tomb.'

St Paul's was enclosed by a wall, which was hidden behind houses and shops. Ben studied the darkness, loosened his sword, and took Will's arm. They edged across Old Change and up Carter Lane and turned on Paul's Chain. Within the yard, the cathedral towered like a cliff.

The doors were shut and barred.

'No Humphrey's tomb tonight,' said Ben. 'Now what?'

Light and shadow danced in the distance. They approached and found a group of masterless men huddled about a smoky fire. The wide-eyed farm maid with them looked so hungry she'd soon be whoring in the streets, and none were likely to know a seal-cracker, but Will asked anyway, 'Have you seen Arthur Gregory?'

Their eyes filled with Ben Jonson scowling beside him. The

out-of-work mercenary in the oft-patched cloak and empty hanger looked like he regretted more than ever selling his sword. He signaled for reinforcement from an out-of-sorts gallant shabby in once-stylish slashed sleeves with tattered elbows. They were joined by a laborless serving-man in a quilt work of cast-off livery, and a ragged vagabond, whose shirt was spattered with dried blood from a whipping.

Suddenly, behind him, Will heard the broad accents of Devonshire as a tall, big-shouldered sailor spoke from the shadows. 'What does he look like?'

'I know not. Only his name. Arthur Gregory.'

'Is he a seal-cracker?'

'Do you know him?'

'Of him.'

'What's a seal-cracker?' asked a dispossessed countryman, who was standing close to the wide-eyed farm maid.

Will turned to them. 'Such a man as can open a letter and seal it closed again as if he never had.'

'He poaches words?'

'Like a poacher of words,' Will agreed. 'Have you seen such a man?'

'He'd look like any man,' said the gallant.

'Or any thief,' said the mercenary.

'No hungry poacher is a thief,' argued the countryman, with a look at Will as if he sensed that the poet, too, had known the pinch of the bad harvests that plagued the land.

'This one won't eat his prey,' Ben growled. 'Have you seen the varlet?'

'We know him not,' said the gallant. And the mercenary said, 'Begone.'

Ben swelled, ominously. Will seized his arm.

The farm maid murmured, 'There's men sleeping by the ghosts.'

'What ghosts?'

The farmer cuffed her sharply. 'Speak of the Devil.'

Will pushed him aside. 'What do you mean, girl?' He pressed pennies in her hand.

'I seen the ghosts,' she pointed to the north, toward the tombs and stationers' shops of Paternoster Row.

'*Ben.*'

Ben lumbered after him. 'What ghosts?'

'Old Stow told me there was a charnel house where the shops are. They moved the bones. Perchance they left the spirits?'

Ben snorted derisively, but stuck close.

The way was blocked by builders' scaffolding, which tumbled helter-skelter from the walls of one of the printers' shops. Beyond it lay a glow of light, spread by dormer windows above the shop. Will knew this place well by day. By day his printer sold his poems at the White Greyhound. Those could be his house lights shining down. But Paternoster Row seemed another place in the dark, mysterious and confusing where the houses crowded close. He shifted course around the scaffolding, into an ancient burial ground, whose mossy monuments cast tilted shadows.

'Stay here,' Ben ordered. 'I'll scout.' He vanished in the dark.

Father Valente rose from behind a headstone.

Will felt the hairs on the back of his neck start up and stand on end. 'Are you an angel?' he whispered. 'Or the Devil?'

Val's severed head and quartered parts were re-assembled in his familiar face and gait, like a dismantled puppet made whole again. It looked as much like Val as the ghost in his *Hamlet*. But Hamlet's murdered father fled at dawn, forced to plunge back into the fires of Purgatory before the cock crowed morning. Here in St Paul's it was dark, deep night.

'You are you, Val.'

It turned away.

'Stay! Speak.'

'*I'll come again.*'

'Where? When?'

'*Alone.*'

Ben rumbled up behind him. 'To whom do you speak?'

Will pointed at Val, slipping among the tombstones. 'Do you see nothing there?'

'Who do you see but ourselves?'

Val was gone.

'This . . . this thing appeared.'

'What thing?'

'I thought I saw my priest.'

'Your *priest*? What priest?'

'The Jesuit hanged at Tyburn.'

Ben peered among the stones. 'I see nothing but ourselves. Why do you have a priest?'

'Only a friend.'

'Did you question it?'

'It wouldn't answer.'

''Tis but your fantasy.'

'It said it will return,' said Will, sure it would. What he didn't know was what it wanted. Surely Val would never demand revenge like Hamlet's murdered father.

Ben laid a hand on his shoulder as if comforting a frightened dog. 'Come, Will. Let's find this seal-cracker.'

They had just emerged from the churchyard when Will sensed more than saw a rush from the shadows. Ben lunged ahead, drawing his sword. But before his weapon had cleared its hanger, an eight-foot staff with a tip of iron swished out of the dark and fell like the crack of doom on Ben's skull. His sword clattered on the slates, and the sturdy veteran plunged face down among the tombstones.

SEVEN

Were Alexander the Great unhorsed from Bucephalus, his earth-kissed body would not conjure a more bewildering vision than fierce Ben Jonson huddled on the ground. Will jumped back. The staff parted the air where his head had been. He turned to run, but sensed more danger behind, and leapt instead for Ben's sword. Bending to seize the pommel, he felt the cudgel brush his hat. He brought his guard up to meet a leaping shadow.

Ben's weapon was much heavier than a stage sword, for which God be thanked. When the staff crashed down at him, steel lopped oak as if it were straw. Will bared his teeth, flared his nostrils, roared like a hellish King Richard III, and slashed with broad strokes. Spectators who loved the modern rapier might mock old-fashioned clownish stage fights. But the holder of half a staff, a huge man in a rough wool cape, fell back frantically. So intent was Will's attack, he didn't notice the second figure until another staff smashed his wrist and swept the sword from his hand.

'Take him!'

Ben Jonson lay silent and unmoving as the tombstones. A hand reeking the stench of death clamped Will's face. He struck out with elbows and feet. Surrounded, he felt his every jab and kick sink home. But to no avail as a multitude closed in, pinning his arms and legs.

Ben's dagger was as long as some men's swords. Will wrenched free and threw himself on the insensate heap, grasping for the weapon. They fell on him again, thick as mud.

A deep-throated yell shook the air. He felt thumps through his attackers' bodies, heard startled grunts, cries of pain, then screams and the desperate pounding of running feet. A big hand hauled him to his own feet.

'Have they hurt you, sir?' It was the sailor with the Devonshire accent. He hurled the broken staff after the fleeing men. 'Best we run before they rally.'

Will tried to lift Ben. 'Pray, lend—'

The sailor knelt like Atlas, slung Ben's bulk over his shoulder and straightened up with a grunt. 'This way! Yarely, sir. Be quick!'

Will felt on the stones for Ben's sword and ran after them, out of the churchyard onto Paul's Chain. The sailor broke into a brisk trot, running the dark lanes as if Ben Jonson were a feather pillow and he had the night eyes of a cat. At the glow of the watch's lantern, he slipped into a maze of alleys and ran faster. Will followed the heavy pad of his steps and the bellows of his breathing, lost but for a sense that they were bearing ever down the slope toward the river. At last, on Thames Street, the sailor ducked into an all but invisible close. It led through a kitchen garden, past a midden and a jakes, to the scullery of one of the great mansions that lined the riverbank.

The sailor pounded the door.

A Judas hole opened. A woman cried out. The door swung inward. Rows of archways led under the vaulted stone ceiling of a vast kitchen. The sailor laid Ben on the hearth, and the kitchen maid threw twigs and rushes on the coals. They kindled bright flames, and Will saw she was but a girl.

'Water,' commanded the sailor.

He washed the blood from Ben's face and felt the bump on his skull. 'Bloodied and bruised, but not harmed.'

'He's scarce breathing,' Will protested.

'Most parts drunk.'

As if prompted to illustrate his condition, Ben opened his mouth and began to snore. The sailor looked up and Will caught his first clear sight of him as the firelight fell upon a strong face furrowed with scars and split by a conspiratorial gap-toothed jester's grin.

'I half know you, do I not?'

The sailor touched a knuckle to his forelock. 'Aye, sir. Jim Mapes, am I. Work ropes at the Globe.'

'Coxswain Mapes! The new stage-keeper! Sure, I'd have remembered, but I've only seen you aloft.' Swooping over the stage like great-winged sea birds, mariners skilled in sail-hoisting trimmed the ropes that lowered players from heaven.

'I thank you, Coxswain Mapes. You saved our lives.'

'God's will found me in the churchyard,' Mapes replied

modestly. And then, grin darkening to a scowl, 'It seemed the brigands laid in wait for you, sir.'

'For our purses.'

Mapes shook his head at the snoring Ben. 'No cutpurse would challenge a fellow his size. Nor are you a meager man. No, they set their course for you.'

'Ben's made enemies,' Will ventured, but the plain-spoken sailor would not be put off.

'It's that seal-cracker, methinks. Perhaps you're not the only one who seeks him.'

'Perhaps,' Will agreed reluctantly, all too aware that the kitchen maid was hanging on their every word. Mapes noticed and took her plump red hand in his. 'These gentlemen would sleep in the stable. Can you find them clean straw?'

With an adoring smile, she hurried off down a dim corridor. The sailor turned back to Will. 'Were you needing to employ the seal-cracker?'

Will greeted his boldness with a haughty look that would have done Anthony Bacon proud. The sailor knuckled his forehead again and, with downcast eyes, elevated him another notch in the order. 'Begging your pardon, Your Worship.'

His dissembling manner told Will that Mapes had something to hide. 'What,' he asked, 'lured a seafaring man to the Globe?'

'I'm stranded, sir. Fleetingly. My captain stood for Parliament.'

'In whose fleet did you serve?'

Mapes stood taller and Will was put in mind of a powerful swan. 'I am Sir Walter Raleigh's coxswain.'

Raleigh, the Armada hero, sea explorer, courtier, projector of New World expeditions, a strong Protestant, and a poet, had long ago been one of Essex's several rivals for the Queen's goodwill. What caused this link?

'How is it a sturdy mariner isn't fighting in the war?'

'The war, I wager, will come to me. What is it they say, sir? When the Ethiopian is white, the French will love the English? Well, when the French loveth the English, God will grant the Spaniard a gentle soul. It won't be a *French* armada we see darken the horizon. Bloody Spain's the enemy.'

Will nodded impatiently. Everyone knew that Europe's endless wars were Spanish wars. The great Empire was restless. Even as they savaged the Low Countries, Catholic Spaniards advanced against Protestant England. He said, 'God blessed *us* with his tempest. Let us pray he saves England with another great storm.'

The tall mariner laughed. 'The storm *saved* the Spaniard, begging your pardon, sir. The so-called Protestant Wind every landsman thanked God for was the Devil's curse on England. We'd have harried the Armada to bits, sunk their fleet ship by ship. But in God's terrible gale it was all we could do to swim, much less fight our ships. The Spanish fled. The tempest sank some, but it saved their fleet. They've come back twice already, and as the God you thank raises stars in the east and sinks them in the west, they'll come back again.'

Mapes bore off from his questions by filling his sails with a wind of words. Indeed, before Will could query him further, the sailor was blowing up another gale, his great brows beetling ominously. 'Storms did save us in '96 from the second Armada and from the third in '97, when the Spaniard tried to avenge Cadiz. But we can't count on God brewing storms forever. And when God is preoccupied, England won't be so rich in Spanish mistakes. I was there in '88, sir, under Raleigh, saw with mine own eyes. By God's wounds, sir, it happened like this.'

Will had cocked eager ears to many stage-keepers' tales of sea storms and sea battles and sea monsters. The boundless life of sailors – near-endless solitude, long idle waits upon wind and tide, sights earth-bound mortals never imagined – bred natural story-tellers. But every sea story he ever heard began as Mapes' 'By God's wounds, sir, it happened like this.'

He spread breadcrumbs on the kitchen table representing the opposing fleets of the sea battle twelve years ago. Twigs from the kindling basket defined the French coast. And soon Will was hanging on every word, so real did Mapes make the great horned crescent of the Spanish Armada pursued by a ragged line of nimble English ships.

'No seaman on either side had ever seen a fight like it – fleets of massed cannon, like wind-driven castles, the Spaniards linked tight as chain mail, ours swift and bold as terriers. We've both had years to consider our faults. But the Spaniard's used his time better than we have. In short, sir, we fought a new kind of war we had to invent as we battled.'

Mapes swept the crumbs to the floor, and Will surfaced from the sea of words. That Raleigh's garrulous coxswain had materialized out of nowhere had to be linked to his search for a seal-cracker recommended by a follower of Raleigh's rival Essex. Will was caught in the middle.

'Mapes,' he said, 'help me carry Ben to the stable.'

As they knelt to pick up Ben, Will heard a clatter of boots from the door to the upper stories of the river mansion.

Down the steps came a hunchback. He was as young as Will, plainly garbed, and leading two stern retainers with rapiers at their sides. He wore the almost-pleasant, neutral smile of a mild-mannered clergyman who might preach in a peaceful country parish untroubled by Catholic recusants and Puritan zealots. But his formidable escort gave the lie to the notion, as did the depths the hearth light revealed in his enormous hazel eyes.

EIGHT

'Coxswain Mapes,' Will Shakespeare asked quietly. 'Whom do you serve?'

'The Chamberlain's Men, sir.'

'Not here. Not tonight.' *Were I penning this entrance myself, I wouldn't believe my direction for the stage:*

> [Enter SIR ROBERT CECIL, the Queen's Secretary of State, in sober apparel, leading two Armed Guard cloaked in beaver pilches.]

He could not imagine how Cecil had discovered *The Sister Queens*. But why else would he be here? Cecil had to know that Southampton was Will's patron. And that Southampton worshiped Essex. Which, in his mind, would place Poet Shakespeare in Essex's circle, too. Nor could Will's *Henry V* chorus applauding 'the General of our gracious Empress' for bringing rebellion broached on his sword when Essex led her army to Ireland have escaped the secretary's attention, whether he heard the play at the Globe or reports from spies.

Cecil descended the stairs carefully. The steps were steep, and he made a strong effort to walk as if he were not humped, but a hearty man who sauntered like a knight. A hunchback who clashed with the glamorous Essex couldn't be proud that the Queen was said to call him her little elf. Or that the earl's retinue nicknamed him 'the camel.'

Will doffed his hat.

Cecil glanced a silent command at Coxswain Mapes. Mapes scooped up the snoring Ben Jonson and carried him from the kitchen. Will saw that he had wrongfully estimated Cecil's guard. Though dressed as armed gentlemen, fine cloaks tied and thrown over their backs to speed access to rapiers and bollock daggers, they were first and foremost war veterans – mastiffs bred to kill first and let their masters discuss the finer points later. They were of short stature, in proportion with their elfin master, but no less formidable for it. Cecil stepped closer to Will and raised his head to look him in the eye.

'Master Shakespeare, I am not inclined to teach a poet his business. But I ask you to recall the equal-matched antagonists you wrote for *Richard III*. You had me perched on the edge of my stool, head cocked like a raven, straining to hear who might prevail – Richard or Richmond. It made the highest entertainment.'

Will bowed. 'Thank you, sir.'

'I thought it ingenious how very much we heard of Richmond before he appeared on the stage. Richard first called him a "little peevish boy". Then we heard that "Richmond aims at young Elizabeth".'

Will had long ago learned not to interrupt when an admirer described his play as if the poet was hearing the plot for the first time. But in this instance, he sensed that Cecil was laying his own plot.

'Threat upon threat upon threat, the storm of Richmond gathered – "Richmond troubles me more." "Richmond is on the seas." "Richmond is with a mighty power landed." "Where is princely Richmond now?"

'At last Richmond entered. "Look on my forces with a gracious eye," he prayed. Then – sudden as thunder – you presented the warrior you so long made us anticipate.'

The bantam Cecil gathered breath in his lungs and loosed a lion's roar: 'Put in their hands thy bruising irons of wrath!

'How fitting that in victory, Master Shakespeare, you had Richmond unite England in everlasting peace. What were his words?' Cecil asked, and continued quoting lustily, cropping Will's twenty-seven lines to a neat six.

'England hath long been mad, and scarr'd herself;
The brother blindly shed the brother's blood.
O, let Richmond and Elizabeth conjoin together!
And let their heirs,
Abate the edge of traitors
That would make poor England weep in streams of blood!

'You demonstrate, Master Shakespeare, that you are a poet who worships order.'

Will produced an appreciative smile to mask his alarm and spoke the truth. 'I cannot make plays without it.'

But not your government order, was his mute aside. *True, I fear chaos, the hammer of war. But I fear more when authority binds spirit, life, and audacity in tight bundles. I prefer groundlings cracking nuts in the pit, rather than seat them row by row, hands folded like schoolboys whose master can beat them with his rod.*

Cecil said, 'Order is what I ask of you, that our government might continue England's everlasting peace.'

Will spoke one of Richmond's many lines that Cecil had hacked. '"Peace makes smiling plenty and fair prosperous days!"'

Robert Cecil's was a gentler manner of command than Anthony Bacon's, but no less strict. His was the government that slaughtered Father Valente on the gallows. His authority left Will with no choice but to ask, 'What would you have of me, Mr Secretary?'

'I would have your "Sister Queens" be equal parts heroic.'

'How do you mean, sir?'

'I would have your warring queens leave equal heirs, equal successors.'

'Do you mean a strong King James and a strong Earl of Essex?' Will asked.

'Yes! You must coin different names for a king who is the legitimate son of an illegitimate queen, and an earl who is no longer a favorite of our sovereign queen.'

'Yes, Mr Secretary.'

'Do not underestimate the risk of presenting your play while Her Majesty still lives.'

It is not my play, Mr Secretary. At least not yet. But I am even beginning to doubt that it's Francis Bacon's play.

'May I ask . . .'

'Yes! Ask anything. We must make this work for fair, prosperous days.'

'Lord Essex is noble not royal. King James is royal only to Scotland and to Catholics who hope James will restore their faith to England. Which heir do you choose?'

'I dare not choose. Civil war looms.'

'But, Mr Secretary, a playmaker must choose what he would

have the spectator see, the audience hear. And if I may be so bold—'

'Be bold!'

'It is no secret that you and Lord Essex are rivals. You must know that if one heir triumphs you will likely remain Secretary of State, but if the heir with whom you are at odds triumphs, you will have no place in the new monarchy.'

Robert Cecil shook his head violently. 'I cannot permit myself to serve only myself. And I will tell you why.' He took a deep breath – much as he had filled his lungs to roar Richmond's prayer. 'It was neither long ago nor far away that Frenchmen put their fellow countrymen to the sword in the St Bartholomew's Day Massacre. Not the Ancients, but modern Frenchmen. Nor did their blood drench distant shores. Only one hundred miles beyond the Narrow Sea – near to London as Stratford-upon-Avon. Only twenty-eight years ago when you and I were schoolboys, Catholic Frenchmen butchered their Protestant neighbors by the *tens of thousands.*

'We cannot choose. We can only stand vigil and watch events unravel until one heir is clearly ahead. Then we will try to stop the other before civil war sees the heavens on fire. Certainly, I *hope* for a sovereign as benevolent as Queen Elizabeth and as clever at keeping the more lunatic of her subjects from each other's throats. And naturally I would prefer one who will permit me to continue serving our nation. But I would be a terrible servant of my nation if I let that color my choice of our next sovereign.'

Will said, very carefully, 'You maze me, sir, by how deeply you confide.'

'Why shouldn't I confide? You have written play after play about civil war. God's wounds, man, you are the *poet* of civil war. Clearly, you fear it as the anathema I do. But *I* couldn't write "Where civil blood makes civil hands unclean." Nor could Marlowe or Kyd or Greene, and surely not that scoundrel Ben Jonson. Only Master William Shakespeare has written, "Where civil blood makes civil hands unclean."'

Cecil looked away as he flattered. That falsity gave Will the truth he feared. *This confidence is temporary.* Cecil's gaze drifted toward his guard, out of earshot, but poised to spring at a gesture.

If I in any way disappoint their master, how long before rapiers
dust my doublet front and back?

Cecil fixed him again in strong regard. 'Now I want you to
write your play fast as you can. How long will it take you?'

'Foul copy in half a year, I would think. Writ-new another
month or two.'

'I'm sure you pleaded difficulties with the muse, but I can't
believe Anthony Bacon accepted such a delay.'

It was already clear to Will that Cecil knew more than most
about the theater. He said, 'Bacon demanded three months to
performance.'

'Two would be better. It is Mercury setting the pace.'

'I will write as fast as I can,' said Will.

'At the same, I will need every pair of eyes I can muster to
defend the Queen. You will help me watch. You will report who
Anthony Bacon sends you to. So far I know only of the Moor girl
and the brewer Niles Roper. In addition, you will report approaches
made by Essex and Southampton.'

Will leapt to his patron's defense. 'My Lord Southampton is
out of all suspicion.'

'We shall watch. And we shall see. Won't we?'

This was the moment to ask Cecil to protect his mother. But
three fears stopped him. He would expose her recusancy to Cecil
and anyone Cecil conspired with. Anthony Bacon would be 'disappointed' if Cecil tried to protect Will's mother. And, besides, Cecil
never would oppose Bacon on Will's behalf if opposing Bacon
endangered his own plots. The best Will could hope from Secretary
Cecil was to keep him as 'troops of reserve' for a desperate last
charge if Will could not save her any other way.

Will lay down on the sweet straw beside Ben Jonson. Cecil had
gone with his guard. Mapes had disappeared with the kitchen
maid. They were alone but for some horses snorting content-
edly, the stable lit by flickers from the kitchen fires across the
yard. He nudged Ben with his elbow repeatedly. Finally Ben
woke up, held his head in both hands, and groaned, 'What
happened?'

Will related in whispers their rescue by Coxswain Mapes.

Ben interrupted, 'How did the Globe's new stage-keeper,

coxswain to Sir Walter Raleigh, no less, happen to be at Paul's in the middle of the night?'

'I wonder, too. But let me finish.'

Within moments, Ben interrupted again. 'Robert Cecil? Are you quite sure, Will?'

'Why do you doubt?'

'Earlier, at Paul's, you saw the ghost of a freshly drawn-and-quartered priest. Now you've encountered the Queen of England's principal secretary in a scullery. Your imaginings are moving up in the world, Will. It'll be the Archbishop of Canterbury waylays you next. Or the Pope.'

'I am not "imagining" Robert Cecil. I will illustrate him for you. He was small. Elfin. He had a slight hump. His attire was modest, more like the chief clerk in a counting house than the sorts of gallants his armed guard appeared to be in costly black capes lined with beaver fur.'

'You recognized beaver fur by dying firelight?'

'My father is a glover. I know my skins. Let me finish!'

Will related his conversation with Cecil, word by word. He left nothing out, in order to harness Ben Jonson's broad experience, vast hoard of court gossip, and sharp brain of a natural intelligencer. Ben soon stopped interrupting, grew solemn, and when Will was done nodded gravely. 'Robert Cecil has made you his spy.'

'Exactly! But how did he learn what Bacon is hatching? I know that Cecil and the Bacons are cousins, but—'

'Cousins who will slit each other's throats when it suits their schemes,' said Ben. 'In truth, Cecil knows his business. Beagles are the wellspring of power. Spies, intelligencers, and projectors enrich themselves by making their masters great, and Cecil knows better than all where to dip the bucket to draw sweet from foul. Never forget that he inherited Walsingham's spies from his father – the best in England, the best in Europe – except those like Anthony Bacon that Essex poached.'

'Sure, it didn't take him long to discover *The Sister Queens*.'

'But,' said Ben, 'I believe not a whit Cecil hasn't chosen whom he prefers to succeed. He's licking his lips for a chance to destroy Essex, who, let us not forget, has never missed an opportunity to try to destroy Cecil. This is also Cecil's opportunity to ensure a peaceful succession from an aging Elizabeth to a vigorous young legitimate King James. Far more legitimate than Essex. James is royal, Essex merely noble.'

'Countess Southampton put it neatly: "Noble Essex would be burnished regal. The peer would make himself peerless."'

Ben said, 'Put those in your play. Before I put them in mine.'

'Consider both spoken for.'

'Don't you see, Will, that's exactly what Cecil wants in *The Sister Queens*. Despite his "not for me to choose". To champion Mary Queen of Scots is to champion her son King James. To champion James is to destroy Essex.'

'Let me ask you something,' said Will. 'Is it possible that Cecil planted the seed for the play in Francis Bacon's brain?'

'What?' Ben Jonson sat up and stared at Will Shakespeare.

Will said, 'You heard me. Could the play plot be Cecil's plot?'

'Will! You could tutor Machiavelli in deceit – I didn't know you had it in you.'

'It explains things that have been making me wonder. Did someone prompt the Moor to tell me a different tale than Anthony and Francis Bacon wanted me to hear? Are others involved in the play plot?'

'Who?'

'I don't know. Rivals the Bacons didn't know about? I've hoped that Essex doesn't know about the plot. But what if he did? What if he didn't trust the Bacon brothers and recruited new allies?'

'But Bacon is Essex's own spy master.'

'I know. That's why I incline toward Cecil as the actual plotter.'

Ben said, 'Cecil was wiser than he knew when he dubbed you poet of civil war.'

'Which takes me back to your first question. How did the Globe's new stage-keeper and Raleigh's coxswain happen to be at Paul's when we were?'

'And what is your answer?'

'Everything that happened to me tonight feels staged. Attacked by a crew at St Paul's. Saved by Coxswain Mapes. Led to this scullery by Mapes. And presented to Cecil like a goose in a basket.'

Ben said, 'My aching head doesn't feel staged. But I will admit to being somewhat impaired by drink. Earlier in the evening I would have seen that staff before it brained me.'

'But *I* was *not* brained,' said Will. 'Is it possible that crew was commanded not to injure me so grievously that I couldn't write the play?'

'To what purpose?'

'To present me to Cecil off-balance and afraid. Which is exactly what happened. Cecil received an off-balance and afraid goose in the basket. But I was not afraid of Cecil. I still blamed Bacon for extorting me to make his play. Cecil seemed to be my rescuer, my hero.'

Ben nodded, causing him to groan and grip his head. 'Plus, by slipping it into Francis Bacon's brain, Cecil gets the play that serves him without enraging the Queen. Cecil's the fiddler calling the tune, the puppet-master – my word, by the way.'

'Except, could Francis Bacon be so credulous as to be cozened into thinking the plot is his? That's where my theory breaks down.'

'Not necessarily,' said Ben. 'Francis Bacon is not only Queen's Counsellor, but a famous scholar with a boundless belief in his selfhood. Having lectured multitudes in the method of science and the joys of skepticism, and having heard much sincere applause for his wit and his aphorisms – "Every honest man will forsake his queen rather than forsake God, and forsake his friend rather than forsake his queen," etcetera, pompously etceteraly – Francis Bacon is convinced he can do anything he puts his mind to. Why not write a play? Invite his friends to the Globe and install Essex on the throne the same afternoon. Fear would be the only thing holding him back. He's a man with a lot to lose.'

'If I'm right, then I am not Bacon's tool. But all the more Cecil's tool.'

'A *useful* tool,' Ben yawned. 'Because the nutcrackers listen to you. But as I go back to sleep, my friend – with the strong expectation of not being untimely awakened again – I leave you with a thought to sweeten your dreams. When the blacksmith's tongs wear thin, he hammers up new ones on his anvil and throws the old tool in the fire.'

'I have to ask you one more thing,' said Will.

'*What?*'

'What do you know about Topcliffe?'

'Topcliffe got me arrested and locked in Marshalsea. Saw to it that my "Isle of Dogs" was destroyed. With Cecil's help, by the way. Topcliffe gave false evidence against me to Cecil. Cecil brought it to the Privy Council.'

'You've told me all that.' Ben had written a satire, *Isle of Dogs*, with Thomas Nash. The government charged it was seditious, Ben protested it was satire, but the play was banned, every copy destroyed. 'What else do you know?'

'Topcliffe never regained his commission. And he's feeling the pinch of paying his priest hunters. He still takes no government money. Pays his own way so they can't tell him how to persecute Catholics. And I hear Topcliffe gets work as a mercenary inter-rogator in the Tower – God knows if it's for money or the man's idea of pleasure.'

'Thomas Kyd told me years ago that Topcliffe cared little about recusancy, that he's like the rest and cares only about succession.'

Ben's reply was a dubious, 'It is likely that Thomas Kyd got confused while encountering Topcliffe in the Tower. Why do you ask?'

'Anthony Bacon threatened that if I "disappoint" him, he would betray my mother to Topcliffe.'

'Your *mother?* On what charge?'

'Recusancy.'

'Recusancy? Your mother's no Catholic.'

'She is,' said Will. 'When they were young, she converted my father.'

'Oh, my friend . . . God, we've got to find some way—'

'Yes, I know, find some way to save her.'

'Hold! What about you, Will? Are you a secret Catholic, too?'

'No. She let me go my own way. She told me that she did not believe it was a safe decision to be made by, or for, a small boy in England.'

'Sensible, all things considered.'

'I've always remembered she had tears in her eyes.'

'But you, too, did the sensible thing. You were wise to leave the Roman Church, all things considered.'

'Not as you mean, Ben. I left because I had made up my mind about the Pope.'

'At age five or six?' Ben scoffed.

'Six.'

'How?'

'I had begun to imagine God . . . Don't laugh. It just happened.'

'Did you like it?'

'Very much. Imagine a whole new world on top of the old, which I already very much liked. My mother had taught me to read, and I found the English Bible at the grammar school.' Will shook his head and smiled. 'I think it led to my friendship with Father Val. He tried so hard to bring me back to Rome. We had arguments. In the course of them, he taught me how to think.'

'Which one expects of a Jesuit.'

'Indeed.'

'Your mother sounds like a particularly interesting mother.'

'She is.'

Will's dreams were often sweet. Many occurred in the house where he was born. There was extra room in the dream-house for all his family, living and dead. As Ben resumed snoring, Will was sliding gratefully into one that was half-fantasy, half-memory. His sisters who had died before he was born were laughing children. So was his little sister Anne, whom the plague had taken when he was fifteen. His brothers were schoolboys. His father was robust. His son Hamnet was his lively, cheery self. And his beautiful mother was young.

'*Tell no one!*' she said, gripping his hands so hard they hurt and staring into his eyes, and he knew there would be no flash of merriment in this dream. He was four years old. A stranger and his servant were hiding in the stinking back room where his father cured calfskin.

'If you ever tell, we will be . . .' She hesitated for the blink of her eye and he could hear the next word forming on her lips. *Killed.* But she didn't say it. Instead, she said something a little boy would imagine worse than death. *Driven from our house. Cast out to lie in the street.*

'What is his name?'

'He is Father Val. His life, and our happiness, are in your trust. Promise you'll tell no one.'

'I promise. Where did he come from?'

'He crossed the Narrow Sea in a boat.'

Will's dream moved out of doors to the street that the town

hugged closely with houses. He saw hay fields and corn beyond
the houses, and the river. In the river was a shallow pool
below the Clopton Bridge. The bridge was enormous to a small
boy, a chain of arches that seemed to stretch forever, arch after
arch after arch. Everard – an open-hearted Cambridge student and
Father Val's acolyte – was teaching Will to swim. A dark figure
stood in the shadow of an arch as if guarding them. And Will's
mother smiled in sunlight.

'Is the Narrow Sea like the river?' he asked Everard, who, Will
had been astonished to discover years later, had gone on to write
a book called *The Art of Swimming*. The copy he had stumbled
upon in Southampton's library had been translated from the Latin
and included the original woodcut illustrations of the frog-copying
strokes Everard had taught him in the Avon.

'The sea is not at all like the river.' Everard laughed. 'The sea
is bigger than the sky.'

'Like Heaven?'

Everard – who had eventually broken with Father Val to preach
for the English Church – crossed himself. 'And Hell.'

'The sea can't be both.'

'You haven't seen it.'

Will's memory dream moved back into the house, deep in a
dark cupboard while a tempest roared outside. He watched
through a hole in the floor. He was breathing hard, his cheeks
burning with excitement. Neighbors and cousins crowded into
the cellar – risking their lives to celebrate a Catholic mass. He
had never seen anything so beautiful, and he never forgot the
candlelight, the gold cross, and Father Val's red robes. The stern
priest whispered a foreign language that Will was soon to learn
in school was Latin. The miracle, as he dreamed it, was that his
father and his mother were both afraid and happy. He was
wondering how that could be when Father Val suddenly looked
up at the hole in the ceiling, locked gazes with him, and said in
English, 'You are no man's tool.'

He started awake in daylight. Rain was spattering the stable
yard.

Not Bacon's tool. Not Cecil's tool.

He left Ben asleep in the straw and set out for Southampton
House. Half-entertaining a fantastical thought that Val's ghost

would reappear at the Tyburn Tree, he walked out of his way on a roundabout five-mile route.

He was having second thoughts about it, as would Prince Hamlet for the ghost of his father. In reality, was all he had seen merely a vaporous confection of the night mist in Paul's churchyard? Ben had not seen the ghost. But Ben had never known Father Val. He had no personal bond with him, no connection to Val's spirit. Besides, Ben had little notion of spirits at all.

The scaffold stood empty. They would have burned the body by now – Val's head destined for London Bridge – and the only sign that blood had spilled were crows racketing to peck the boards before the cold rain washed them clean. Will sheltered under the scaffold from a heavy gust. He roved a doubtful eye up the triple pillars that supported the gallows' cross trees. He was not likely to see Val here or now. Ghosts walked by night. Although if not an honest ghost – but the Devil in disguise – nothing could prevent it from appearing in sunlight, much less a gray morning like this one with a bleak wind and bursts of rain and thunder.

Would he have seen any ghost at all if he weren't writing *Hamlet*? But he wasn't writing *Hamlet*, was he? Not while he was consumed by *The Sister Queens*. Once again, his tragedy of *Hamlet* had fallen by the wayside. Or, worse, had stepped aside.

NINE

'Death to Papists that taketh away the life of the soul!'

The Reverend Charles Mills preached with great passion to a dwindling congregation. Cold shadow crept across the open-air St Paul's Cross pulpit. Shivering citizens skulked off in search of the sun. They found it south and west of the cathedral, where bookstalls basked like ripening corn and the yards bustled with trade, gossip, and news.

Will Shakespeare stopped at his bookbinder, who greeted him warmly, his hands busy the while, stuffing calfskin covers with scraps of manuscript paper monks had labored over before the invention of the printing press. But his bookbinder did not know Arthur Gregory, had never heard of the seal-cracker.

Will's printer in the next stall was busy mollifying a customer who was complaining that his name had been misspelled. 'Surely you see, sir, that had I not added a letter at the end of your name that there would be a blank space in the line where none was called for.'

'But my name has no "e" at the end.'

'Except here, where it looks rather fine. Would you not agree, Master Shakespeare?'

'Good morrow, sir,' Will greeted the customer and commiserated that 'Someone added an "e" to mine and it stuck ever since like an arrow in the butt. But as with yours, it looks quite fit.'

The grateful printer did not know Arthur Gregory, though he had heard the name.

At the last book stall, he chose a translation by the Countess of Pembroke, *The Tragedie of Antonie*. The seller closed his hand around Will's coins – twenty times over the value of the sum he owed for the book – and his eyes widened with surprise.

Will murmured, 'For Father Val.'

'Bless you, Master Poet.' The bookseller was a secret Catholic and a courageous man to break the law for his faith. This was the first time Will had ever hinted he knew, much less risked conspiring with him. His money would pay for clandestine masses to speed Father Val's time of punishment in Purgatory. Or so Val and the brave bookseller would believe.

He plunged into the crowd searching for faces he knew. Knights, gallants, roving gentlemen, thieves, and strutting upstarts mingled – flushed with prospects of opportunity. Unemployed servants scanned the notices at the *Si quis* Door: 'If anyone' sought employment as a cook, footman. Servants had posted their own broadsides advertising their talents and experience. Lawyers huddled with so-called knights of the post – respectable-looking gentlemen they could hire to give false witness. Beggars thrust filthy hands toward the sky. Clowns gamboled for pennies. A country lad looked overwhelmed by the noise of so many people, an initial assault Will still remembered.

Usurers prowled the tombs. Will's father had lent out money, and he knew the business. But at St Paul's the usurers had perfected a fraud. He watched a lender offer pen and paper to a borrower, divide the contract with a wavy cut and give half back. But instead of money changing hands, the borrower received a packet of lute strings, which the poor gull had to sell to raise the actual coin before he ended up a *bankerout*, kneeling with the beggars.

There were foreigners aplenty, delft- and glassmakers from Belgium and Holland, coach-builders from Germany, a startlingly black Moor, swarthy Italians – music teachers, translators, fencing instructors like the fellow Dick Burbage had hired to teach the rapier. Will skirted a huddle of French Protestant refugees who had caught the attention of a burly high-man scouting for gulls for his gang to fleece, and entered the cathedral.

He wandered briskly through the great pillared nave asking for Arthur Gregory. Some knew the name. None had seen him. As the noon hour approached, and his hopes faded, he went to Duke Humphrey's tomb. All he saw there were a couple of thieves, Charles Post and Wesley Little, tempting the gallows to be hunting in daylight, and David Hope, one of many gentlemen attendants beggared when their patron died.

Will decided to wait. If a hungry Gregory came along, he would be grateful and perhaps talkative when stood to dinner at an ordinary. But the crowds thinned as dinner time drew near. Finally, even the thieves prowled away. Will was preparing to leave himself, when he saw a splendidly attired gallant approach, a big man, broad of shoulder and massive of belly. His doublet was undone to allow breathing room, and he had broad pink cheeks and a spirited smile that owed much to *bouse* as did his red-veined nose.

The gallant eyed the monument with pleasure, then turned his beaming countenance on Will. 'Half London ventures here to gawp at Duke Humphrey's tomb. Yet the good Duke's buried at St Albans. This here's John de Beauchampe. Have you dined, sir?'

'I beg your pardon?'

'Have you dined? Are you hungry? Would you join me for dinner? I've in mind a tavern feast. A chine of beef and some guinea fowl. Plover's eggs and oysters to begin.'

Will felt his stomach juices stir. 'You are generous, sir, but I'm meeting—'

'A seal-cracker, perhaps?'

'Yes!' He'd been asking all morning and the word had got around. 'Do you know him? Arthur Gregory?'

'As I know myself.'

'Where is he?'

'He stands before the tomb of John de Beauchampe that others call Duke Humphrey. And he stands before you, Master Shakespeare, whom all London calls "Poet!"'

Will regarded Arthur Gregory's fine embroidered cape with surprise. And when Gregory turned, swirling it off his sleeves, Will saw that his doublet, too, was quality: rich brocade slashed to reveal gorgeous red silk beneath. He wore silk hose; an Italian rapier with gilt pommel; a similarly decorated bollock dagger on the back of his sword belt; and an extravagantly feathered soft bonnet.

'I was led to believe that Arthur Gregory had fallen on hard times.'

'It is an up and down world, sir. Come, let us discourse upon its vagaries in a happier setting than a tomb.' Gregory swept an expansive arm over the monuments. 'The gentlemen who live here have no doubt settled such questions that are still our task to answer. And lost their appetites, too. Come, sir. The dinner hour's chimed.'

They walked toward the river, weaving their way through wheelbarrows and carts heaped with goods that had been landed by boat.

Gregory turned into Fleet Street and into a tavern. The host greeted
him with bows and curtsies and led them upstairs to a private room
where two places were already laid with silver plates and drinking
cups.

A serving-man ran in with bowls of oysters, another bearing
plover eggs. The host brimmed the cups with claret wine, and when
he had bowed his way backwards from the room, Gregory drained
his wine in a single gulp and turned on Will with glittering eyes.

'Out with it boldly.'

'I beg—'

'What would you have me do? Who sent you?'

'Niles Roper. He keeps an inn in Gracious Street.'

'Roper's a damned meddling fool.' Gone was the fat man's
cheery smile, gone his merry eyes.

'Methinks,' said Will, 'that Niles Roper had no choice. It's
Anthony Bacon who calls his tune.'

Arthur Gregory reached for more wine. 'Bacon? What does he
want with me?'

'He wants you to tell me about cracking the seal of a letter sent
by the Scots Queen to Thomas Babington.'

'I cracked no such seal.'

The quick denial was, Will saw, borne of the fear that paled
Gregory's face. He said, gently, 'But Anthony Bacon thinks you
did, which is much the same thing. Or could be, in effect.'

'Why? Why does he ask you?'

Will shook his head. 'I know not.'

'But you bandy my name about the city like a tennis ball.'

'As I was commanded. I have no choice. Did you read the
letter?'

'No!'

'Did you read what was added? The postscript?'

'Certainly not!'

Will rolled a plover egg under his fingers, cracking the shell.
He peeled the egg, popped it in his mouth and reached for another.
'You were not curious what Gifford wrote?'

'How do you know about Gifford?'

'I know more than I want to. But I know not what he forged.'

'Why don't you ask him?'

'Niles Roper called him a cozening rakehell.'

'None would disagree.'

'I'd not speak with a cozening rakehell if I could speak with you.'

'It was said at the time that Gifford recruited Sir Walter Raleigh's followers to assassinate the Queen. To make room for Mary Queen of Scots.'

'Absurd,' said Will. 'Raleigh's no Catholic.'

The seal-cracker held up his hand and crossed two fingers. 'Raleigh and the Queen were like this back then. Gifford believed that Raleigh's people could get inside her guard. Then in a flash Her Majesty meets her misery.'

'Absurd,' Will repeated. 'I ask you again. What did Gifford write in that postscript?'

'I have nothing else to say.'

'Gifford will ask me how I know he added to Mary's letter. I'll have to tell him how I know.'

'Gifford is dead.'

'No. Roper said nothing about Gifford dying.'

'Dead ten years. Roper doesn't know or doesn't give a damn. Gifford fled to France when Babington was exposed. Got arrested for being anti-Catholic or not Catholic enough. Landed in the Bastille. Starved to death.'

'Then it is up to you. For the last time, sir, tell me what Gifford wrote.'

Arthur Gregory poured again and downed it in a swallow. He looked at Will's cup, which the playmaker had not touched, and downed it too. Color rose higher in his cheeks. 'You would condemn an innocent?'

'*I* am innocent,' said Will. '*My* life and *my* fortunes are at risk. You can save me. I know you saw it. No man alive would avert his gaze. *What did the forger write?*'

The fat man took a deep, trembling breath, and when he finally capitulated, he looked as gray and hollow as a dead hornets' nest. 'He forged a postscript wherein Queen Mary asked Thomas Babington to name his fellow conspirators.'

Just as Isobel the Moor insisted. The letter that John Hooker had written of in the last pages of Holinshed's *Chronicles of England, Scotland and Ireland*. The letter that had condemned Mary Queen of Scots. False accused and false beheaded.

Will stood up, went to the window, and stared down at the busy street. He knew too much. What he carried in his memory could kill him, like a smugglers' vessel overladen in a rising sea. The notes in his table-book could land him in the Tower. Even if he erased them, wiped them from the soft gesso page, interrogators schooled in intelligencer practices might hunt out traces.

Gregory swallowed more wine and his voice grew big with drink. 'I'll give Gifford this,' he boasted. 'He hired the best seal-cracker in the business. You want to see how I do it? Look here!'

Will turned back to the table.

Gregory drew a letter from his doublet and smoothed it on the table. Then he took a thin-bladed knife from his penner and held the point in the candle flame. The paper, thrice folded, was sealed shut with a flattened blob of hard red wax in which the sender had pressed his mark.

Drunk or no, his hands were quick as a sparrow. Will smelled a sweet whiff of melted shellac and in seconds Gregory spread the letter gently open. 'What have we here?'

The blood rushed from Will's face.

Too late to avert his eye from Latin fair-copied in a clerk's hand clear as crystal. The letter had been sent by Lord Burghley, Queen Elizabeth's Lord Treasurer and Secretary of State. The intended recipient – before Gregory laid his hands on it, God knew how – was King Philip II of Spain. A single sentence leapt from the onion layers of decorous greeting and ceremonious farewell: Secretary of State Burghley begged King Philip to allow his daughter – the Infanta Isabella – to succeed Queen Elizabeth on the English throne and urged that they move quickly to circumvent the Scots King James VI.

Allow? The Spanish King had plotted little else since Mary Queen of Scots was beheaded. He had sent three Invincible Armadas, so strenuously did he 'allow' the Infanta Isabella anointed Queen of England.

Will retreated again to the window. Porters were shuttling barrows from the wharfs, apprentices were hurrying back to work from their dinners, and a ballader was singing the praises of the noble contestants preparing for the Accession Day tilts.

Had anointing the Infanta Isabella been the Queen's wish? Or had Burghley plotted behind her back? Had King James known he was being undercut by Elizabeth's chief courtier? *I do not know and I do not want to know*. But why had Gregory let him see it? Was the seal-cracker that drunk – that needy of a boast?

'*Not a word!*' Gregory hissed like a punctured bladder. 'You should not have seen it.'

Will answered without turning from the window. 'I saw nothing.' *You are no man's tool.*

He imagined this was the sort of shadow battle Queen Elizabeth had fought her entire reign – starting as a young woman alone, besieged by foreign kings and English nobles who would marry her crown, always steps behind grizzled courtiers like Lord Burghley. No! Rarely steps behind. She was steps *ahead* or she would never have survived so long.

He whirled from the window. 'Did the King of Spain return this letter?'

'What do you mean?'

'After he read it?'

Arthur Gregory had a look on his face that the playmaker knew well: fiercely determined, gapingly vacant – a bad actor made to speak ghastly lines.

'Ah, no. I mark your meaning. No! This is a copy. The message being so important, two were fair-copied in the event the ship conveying it went down.'

Will strode to the door.

'Stay! Stay! Where are you going?'

The letter was a lie; the postscript, the broken seal, the drunken seal-cracker and his costly dinner, all lies. Why, he did not know. Had Anthony Bacon instructed Arthur Gregory to gull him into believing that Burghley had sought a Spaniard on the throne? To turn the play against Burghley's son Robert Cecil and Queen Elizabeth? Or, had Cecil himself ordered the seal-cracker to deepen the crumble-edged pit that yawned at Will's feet for some reason he could not yet fathom?

Who was left to turn to? Southampton was still 'closeted,' still wouldn't see him, for reasons Will might never know. In ordinary times, a playmaker worked with collaborators, and he would naturally ask his fellows in the Chamberlain's Men for suggestions and advice. But he couldn't inflict his misfortune on innocents; he'd get the entire company locked in the Tower. A mirthless smile wracked his lips. What I am in need of, he thought, is a champion knightly clad and armed with high courage and low cunning. If only Marlowe were alive. *But Marlowe is dead, and I am alone.*

Though no innocent. He was no fledgling. Secretary Robert Cecil had dubbed him 'poet of civil war.' Flattery aside, he *was* a poet of civil war. History play after history play imagined how the political upheaval of corrupt ambition flayed civil peace. He did not need Kit Marlowe to tell him that the Bacons wanted his play to gull Catholics with false tales of betrayal by Queen Elizabeth and her corrupt courtiers. Or that their beloved Mary Queen of Scots' son James commanded Scotland's armies. Or that Mary's raging worshipers would embolden King James to march on England and inflame an uprising of the Catholic north.

It was, Will thought, as if the conspirators had memorized his plays.

Who would save England from that double invasion? Triple, in truth, as the French were certain to attack from the sea. Who could defend the realm? Surely not an old woman forty years on the throne.

Only a young war hero could save England. Only the noble Earl of Essex could, with God's help, send the knaves of court packing, sink the French fleet, rout the Scots, and destroy the northern earls.

A grateful nation would crown the Earl of Essex king.

Will hurried back to Southampton House and cleared away Holinshed.

Where the volume had lain on the table he found a folded sheet of paper with a simple wax seal. Breaking the seal and unfolding the paper, he read a vicious writ in the anonymous hand of an amanuensis that could only have been dictated by Anthony Bacon: 'Chess players hear "Check" when their king is menaced. Hear this: "*Check-Mother!*"'

Will knew only one way to quell the helpless anger shaking his hands before it overwhelmed him. He laid out paper, sand, and ink pot. He stripped the vanes from a feather with his pen knife. He sharpened the tip of the quill.

He was writing mid-morning, days later, fast as he could move his hand, when a blue-coated porter dashed in.

'Master Shakespeare! The earl will see you now.'

TEN

There was in Henry Wriothesley, 3rd Earl of Southampton, a star-bright beauty that promised the world was ever fresh, forever boundless. For Will to look upon his face was to remember his own youth with a clarity youth had never known. And to know its loss: for while in his brain and his heart he felt younger than when he had finished *Venus and Adonis* – younger still after *Lucrece* – the glass reflected furrows in his own brow that only death could smooth.

He found Southampton reclining on a daybed, eating sweetmeats and crystallized fruits off beechwood roundels. An affectionate kitten, black with white chest and paws, nuzzled him. 'Would you have it when I'm done?' he murmured, and fed the animal a morsel on a silver fork.

'Will.' He smiled. 'You gawp like an apprentice. What's the matter?'

'Forgive me, my lord. But I could not help notice your mustache new-grown.'

'And you don't like it.' Southampton laughed.

'Very gallant,' Will assured him, wondering why he felt such aversion to any change in him. 'Most military, as befits Lord Essex's General of the Horse.'

'No, tell me what you really think. I don't believe you admire it, and I know you dislike change.'

His golden hair, which had always fallen like sunlight to his shoulders, was even longer than when Will last saw him months ago as he left for Ireland. But the mustache was a shock, even taking into account that he was no longer a boy and that his promotions in the Irish war were a man's achievements, as were marriage and fathering two children. Possibly, it announced that the soldier home from Ireland was not the unfledged youth for whom his mother had commissioned Will to write love poetry, and who confided that refusing to marry the Lady De Vere had nothing to do with the lady, but everything to do with his dreams of following the Earl of Essex into glorious battle for the Queen and England. Dedicating *Venus and Adonis* to him had been as strong a warning against war as Will was allowed to voice, and it had fallen on ears deafened by hero-worship.

'Well? Tell me the truth.'

Will returned his smile – a smile that sent an unmistakable signal that the earl would address Will's 'thorny matter' only after they engaged as lord and poet. Which meant, in this instance, games of word play upon his mustache.

'In truth, sir, it is a violation.'

'A violation?' Southampton mocked. 'Would you liken me to a looted monastery? "Bare ruin'd choirs?"'

'I fear I may have overspoke, my lord,' Will replied, and they fell naturally to it. '"Ruin'd choirs" implies change as unchangeable as losing a footrace to a panther.'

'A mere de-consecration?'

'Not quite a dissolution.'

'A stripping of the altar?'

'We are getting closer, sir. But perhaps more like a portrait sword-slashed.'

'Ah, like a Vandal laying waste to the beauties of Rome?' Southampton asked with a superior smirk.

'Vandals knew not what they Vandalized, my lord.'

The earl laughed so loud the cat jumped. 'What a word, Will! *Vandalized!* Did you just make that up?'

'It was you who spoke of Vandals, sir.'

'Yes, I did! An excellent word.'

He turned to one of the glasses situated about the chamber, studied his mustache. That he could teach Narcissus about self-love seemed only natural. Filled with grace, he stole men's eyes and captured women's hearts. But his early boyish taste for boys – Marlowe's hope – seemed by all accounts to have waned. God alone knew whether he would always enjoy women with a voracity that rivaled multi-jawed, thousand-fanged Scylla's appetite for Odysseus's shipmates, or would never again in a long life sample 'masculine love.' More important was that Southampton – encouraged by his poet's praise of a man 'pricked out by Nature for women's pleasure' – would continue to perform his noble duty to spawn sons by the squadron to guarantee their family line continued through war, accident, and plague.

Southampton reached into the pocket in his sleeve where resided the purse from which he'd poured clinking gold for Will's share in the Chamberlain's Men. He extracted a perfumed handkerchief embroidered with the Wriothesley arms – four hawks within a cross – touched his nose, ruffled his cat, and smiled warmly at his poet.

'Out with it, Will. Tell me what has happened. What can I do for you?'

This, thought Will, was Southampton at his best. At his worst, Narcissus, dying 'to kiss his shadow in the brook', but at his best a man who could slip the bonds of self-regard. This was the man Will was proud to have tutored to project his presence into the mind of another and ask with genuine sympathy as Southampton did now, 'Why your long face and dark eyes? Trouble with your players?'

'May I ask, sir, do you know Anthony Bacon?'

'Surely. Anthony Bacon advises my Lord Essex on matters of intelligence and . . . such things.'

Will was still crafting his next question when Southampton suddenly laughed out loud.

'Yes, my lord?'

'Did you know, Will, that Anthony Bacon's mother writes Essex letters of advice?'

'Bacon's *mother*?'

Southampton smiled. 'That it never occurred to you that the man has a mother suggests you've met him.'

'I have. Only this week.'

'Did you really . . . Well, his mother, Lady Ann, is a lively old lady, famous scholar of religious things – translated that defense of the Church apology from the Latin – fiercely Puritan, but still quite charming, and very close to her sons. Showers Francis with letters on spiritual matters. Showers Anthony with curative herbs for his various ailments, leeches for his gout, etcetera. No wonder he dotes on her.'

Will interrupted, something he never did with his patron. 'Forgive me, my lord, did I hear you say that Bacon's mother translated from Latin Bishop Jewel's *Apologia Ecclesiæ Anglicanæ*?'

'Absolutely from the Latin,' Southampton snapped. 'That's what Jewel wrote it in, so Europeans could read it – anyway, having delighted both Queen and Archbishop with her defense of the Church of England, she now counsels Essex against what she dubs, "carnal concupiscence".'

Southampton laughed again, and Will worried that, like Coxswain Mapes, his patron was ducking a question under a wind of words.

'My Lord Essex has shown me her letters. The old lady warns that Essex is "blackslinging" into fornication. Or at least "carnal dalliance," whatever she means by that. To give Lady Ann her due, she seems less troubled by actual acts of "carnal dalliance" than by how Essex might endanger his friendship with the Queen. The earl protests he is as chaste as unsunned snow. But gossip, Lady Ann warns, has reached Her Majesty's ears that Essex is "inflaming" a certain nobleman's wife – why do you ask whether I know Anthony Bacon?'

Of a sudden, the young earl was watching him shrewdly.

Will told him how he was waylaid at Tyburn.

'You never told me you loved the gallows,' Southampton replied lightly.

'I do not love the gallows. I love the hangman less. But all London turns out for executions. It is an opportunity for a poet to observe men and women with their reason excited.'

'What did Bacon want?'

Will had pondered at length how to answer this. He could not save Southampton from the consequences of Essex's ambitions if he appeared to get between friends. But, delicately as parting layers of an onion, he had to open some possibility of separation before Essex dragged Southampton down with him. Toward that hope, he described *The Sister Queens*.

'Are you telling me that Anthony Bacon commands a *play* to rouse the groundlings?'

'Bolstered by witnesses he dubs "living Holinsheds." People linked to Mary Queen of Scots.'

'My father—' Southampton started to interrupt, but reconsidered before he concluded the thought, and gestured with his fork instead. 'Go on, Will. Continue your tale.'

Gingerly, Will repeated Anthony Bacon's claim that people said Lord Essex possessed the domestical greatness of a princely successor to Queen Elizabeth.

'What did you answer, Will?'

'I said, "Not I."'

'Why?'

Will was taken aback by what seemed an odd question with an obvious answer. He said, 'I thought it sounded of treason.'

'I do not believe for one minute that mere observations of Essex's princely qualities fall into the realm of rebellion. Not one minute! What else did Bacon demand of you?'

'He bade me speak of Mary Queen of Scots with a Moor at the Bel Savage.'

'His "living Holinshed?" Did you?'

'I did, my lord. She told me that Mary Queen of Scots was falsely accused.'

'Many said so at the time – my father among them. According to my mother, he was nearly beheaded for the Scots Queen. Did the Moor offer proof?'

'She claimed to have seen a forged letter.'

Will noticed a troubled shadow he'd never seen in his patron's eyes. Fear? But Southampton was as fearless as any noble who lived like a god. And, indeed, in an instant his eyes lit as if a blazing sun had driven the shadow back to night.

'I'll speak with Essex!' he said staunchly.

'Yes, my lord?'

'The Earl of Essex is, in truth, destined for domestical greatness. He would never allow such behavior by his people. Anthony Bacon must answer to him.'

'Yes, I saw Bacon wore the orange ruff.'

'Do not worry; your cares are ended.'

'Thank you, my lord,' Will answered.

'But you still look troubled. Be not. Essex – and I – will protect you.'

'Yes, my lord.'

'The earl is my great friend. Did I ever mention how you pleased his lordship with your salute in *Henry V*?

'"Were now the general of our gracious empress,
As in good time he may, from Ireland coming,
Bringing rebellion broached on his sword."'

'It delights him. More than once, in Ireland, I have heard his officers raise glasses in hearty toast, "Broached on his sword!"'

'Yes, my lord. Veterans toast him in the street.'

'I will remind the earl that you are *my* friend and that will be that!'

'I thank you, my lord.' But if his patron openly espoused that Essex was 'destined for domestical greatness', he had failed to separate Southampton from his 'great friend.'

'The earl particularly admires the common touch in your plays. He too has a common touch – from a loftier angle.'

Southampton put his cat aside, stood up, and clapped Will on the shoulder.

I fear, Will thought, *what you are about to say, my lord.* It lurked in Southampton's eyes like a fox inching from forest to meadow.

'You know, Will, your *Sister Queens* is an excellent idea for a play.'

Will could barely conceal his disappointment. The soldier, the husband, the father, and the man Will hoped he would become, was still the boy. 'Do you mean that, sir?'

'Would I have said it if I didn't mean it?'

'Certainly not, sir.'

'You should turn your mind to it! Straightway!'

'My lord, I must tell you that Bacon threatened me not to discuss this with you.'

'But you did, regardless. As a friend should. I thank you, Will. Bacon will not hear of this from my lips. And I will persuade the Earl of Essex to remind Bacon – subtly and discreetly – of the esteem of which I, and through me Essex, hold you.'

Will doubted that Essex's 'esteem' would not stop him from confiding in Anthony Bacon, his trusted chief intelligencer of many years. But Southampton smacked his shoulder again before he could think of a way to voice his concern.

'Now take yourself down to the buttery. Tell them to stir your poetic brains with a bottle of my best sack. Off you go!'

Will headed first to the library for a look at the *Apologia*. He was almost there when he finally admitted what he knew to be true. Every instinct, every ounce of his imagination, told him that Southampton had known about *The Sister Queens* before admitting him to his chambers.

He turned on his heel, rushed back up to his room, and wrote a note to Frances Mowery. The waiting gentlewoman sent a page for him within minutes, and he was ushered quickly into the countess's chambers.

'What is so urgent, Will?'

'I am wondering, Lady Mary, whether my Lord Southampton might find an ally at court. Someone to speak for him, even steer him through difficult waters.'

'You said as much when we spoke last. Whom do you have in mind?'

'Perhaps the Secretary of State?'

'Cecil? Robert Cecil?'

'Cecil and the Bacons are at odds.'

'Where did you get such an idea?'

He would not confide that he had gathered as much from Sir Robert Cecil's own lips. The less she knew if interrogated, the better. A fiction would suffice, if simple truth were artfully embellished. 'A poet's ears are his sharpest tool, my lady. They convey private thoughts whispered at a distance. God blessed me with ears that hear farther than people know.'

'You play at court for the Queen.'

'Thrice this year, my lady. And we will again at Christmas Revels.'

She looked at him, taking his measure as if anew. 'Then you must be aware that the depth of "odds" between courtiers rises and falls like the tide, dependent upon who needs what from whom.'

'Yes, my lady.' A fact to keep in mind when caught between them.

'That said, Sir Robert Cecil is patient as a spider. A patient spider will not attack until it finishes weaving a web stronger than its prey. My second husband, Heneage, admired and trusted him. Can you guess why, Will?'

'The Secretary of State loves the Queen.'

'Robert Cecil does love the Queen. But he loves England even more. Which is good for the Queen and good for England.' A bleak countenance furrowed her brow and tightened her eyes and lips. 'But Robert Cecil is not good for a noble with mad thoughts of stately schemes. And not good for his credulous followers.'

Where in the countess's lists of 'credulous followers' did she place her new husband, knighted by Essex? Will wondered again if she had cautioned him to stay in Ireland when Essex returned to London. She was too clear-eyed about Essex not to.

Why had the soldier obeyed his wife when her own son had not? Ambition. He had already married well above his station – his knighthood being neither a hereditary rank, nor as honorable as being dubbed Knight of the Realm by the Queen. He had stayed in Ireland, and out of Essex's plots, because he was an ambitious man who saw better chances in order than chaos. Like I am, Will thought, and also see.

The countess shook her head. 'That will be all, Will.'

And yet, he was halfway out the side door to which Frances escorted him, when the countess called, 'Will! Come back here!'

He hurried to her side. She dismissed Frances with a gesture.

'Will, you are correct. My son needs an ally. And so do I.'

'Yes, my lady,' said Will, deeply relieved that she was admitting the danger in time to thwart it.

'I ask you again, why did you suggest Robert Cecil?'

Will hesitated, unsure of his course.

She said, 'Do not play false. Give me the honor I am due and the respect you owe me by answering me honestly.'

'Forgive me for dissembling. I thought it best to try to shield you from knowing more than it is safe to know—'

'If you would shield me, arm me with *truth*, not ignorance.'

'Yes, my lady. I suggested Secretary Cecil because he learned somehow that Anthony Bacon suborned me to write a play that will excite popular support for Lord Essex's stately schemes.'

She stared, silent. Eventually she said in a cool, level voice, 'A play to inspire a rebellion?'

'Yes, my lady.'

'What is this treasonous drama named?'

'*The Sister Queens.*'

'Naturally. The Scot . . . I am astonished that Cecil didn't lay you by the heels into the Tower.'

'He commanded me to spy on Bacon.'

Her ladyship nodded. 'The patient spider . . . Dare I ask, did he speak of my son?'

'I am sorry, my lady. Cecil is watching him.'

'Is my son involved in this . . . this lunacy?'

'I don't know. When I turned to him for protection his lordship promised to speak to Essex.'

Hope fired her eyes and Will thought in that moment he would give his life to keep it burning. But he could not forget the shrewd look the earl had leveled at him when he asked about Anthony Bacon, nor his own shock and disappointment when Southampton suggested that he should put his mind to writing *The Sister Queens*.

He said, 'Forgive me, my lady, but you did ask me to be honest.'

'Yes! Yes! Go on! Out with it!'

'I imagined – rightly or wrongly – that his lordship encouraged me to write the play.'

She sagged deep in her chair. 'Good God.'

'*I* will be your ally, my lady, if you let me. I will do my best to serve you.'

'Serve me by speaking sense to my son.'

'But I fear – again, in honesty, my lady – that the earl is already allied with Lord Essex.'

'Un-ally him!' she shot back. 'Will, only you can do it.'

Was she so desperate that she had forgotten his abysmal failure to convince Southampton to marry Lady De Vere? What on earth could he say to the earl to re-capture his attention, much less convince him to veer from a course he was bent upon?

'We spoke of this only today. Nothing in what he said or his manner invited me to speak again. Yet I will do my best,' he added hastily, when he saw her eyes moisten. But he knew he was offering false hope. Essex's fate would be Southampton's fate, unless Essex himself could be somehow persuaded to change his course.

'Do you intend to write the play for Bacon?'

Will decided not to voice his theory that Cecil had secretly put Bacon up to it. 'I have no choice. Secretary Cecil demands it, too.'

'Surely not to advance *Essex*?'

'More likely to destroy him.'

'And those in his thrall,' she whispered, and turned away.

Will bowed low and withdrew. In his mind he heard Ben Jonson's warning not to become the 'fool's fool's fool', and he recalled the lament that Kit Marlowe had penned in *Edward II* when conspiracies whirled out of control – four words of such icy exaction that they gleamed hard and bright as sharpened steel.

'Now begins our tragedy.'

He hurried straight from the countess's chambers to Southampton's library and traced by beeswax light the many shelves of books on religion. Bishop Jewel's original Latin *Apologia Ecclesiæ Anglicanæ* stood side by side with *An Apologie or answere in defence of the Churche of Englande*. Neither the translator, nor the author, was noted on the title page. But the Archbishop of Canterbury had introduced the book with a letter of gratitude addressed, 'To the right honorable learned and vertuous Ladie, A. B.'

Will had first seen the books when he was twelve years old, learning Latin in the King Edward VI grammar school. It was unlikely that anyone in the school, or the entire town, knew that A. B. was Lady Ann Bacon, mother of both a future Queen's Counsel Extraordinary and a future spy and nemesis of a Stratford boy who would one day make plays in London.

Published only ten years before he was born, the *Apology* had done double service in grammar school – guiding students in the art of translation, while persuading the boys to conform to the new English Church and leave the old Roman Church behind. Re-reading it now by beeswax light, Will jumped quickly from section to section – scratching lines and phrases in his copybook. Lady Ann Bacon had served Bishop Jewel well by projecting a lively tract with doses of wit and sarcasm to charm the English reader into accepting that Queen Elizabeth's 'new' English Church was not at all new, but a return to the original gospel church founded by Jesus Christ's disciples.

Thanks to Southampton trying to distract him with amusing tales about Bacon's mother, Will left the library with reason to hope that he might be armed to parry Bacon's taunting 'Check-Mother' with a 'Mother-Check.'

ELEVEN

Celebrant bells rang all morning from the city to Westminster. A cool sun shone through rain clouds upon the yards of Whitehall Palace where thousands seated in a stepped gallery of planks and timber watched a tournament marking the forty-second anniversary of Elizabeth Tudor's accession to her throne. Broken lances and shattered swords littered the trampled mud of the tilting ground. A feathered helmet crushed by an iron-shod hoof had fallen beside the center barrier.

Seen from the highest, farthest benches, the Queen of England appeared as a faint red coal. Will Shakespeare, who sat close beside Ben Jonson on the topmost bench of the gallery, could fix this ember in a distant hearth by the flickering around her. Everywhere she turned her face, a hundred courtiers bowed their heads.

Trumpets shrilled. A black chariot drawn by three dark horses stormed into the tiltyard. Its passenger was a knight in armor that shined like jet.

Will nodded toward the court and asked Ben, 'Do you suppose that our modern knights are strong enough to fight actual battles in all that iron?'

'The Knighthood nowadays clank softer than the Knighthood of olden time,' said Ben.

The black knight's shield bore a picture of a blind crusader tapping his way with a stick, and the legend 'Struck Blind By The Infidel!' The sightless veteran pawed the air with his gauntlets of mail while the chariot made a slow pass along the gallery and stopped before the Queen's viewing stand. Her marshal's challenge carried to the highest benches.

'In God's name and Queen Elizabeth's, say who thou art
And why thou come thus knightly clad in arms.
What's thy quarrel? Speak like a true knight!'

Of the knight's answer but a few words rose on the wind: '. . . and to prove by God's grace and my body's valor . . .'

'But thou art blind, brave knight,' roared the crimson-clad marshal.

Queen Elizabeth rose with a flourish of her warder, a golden staff that reflected the cloud-sparsed sunlight. Her courtiers fell to their knees. A hush swept the packed galleries. Silence deepened. Not a dog barked, nor a crow cawed. She banged her warder three times and swept a majestic arc over the blind knight's helmet.

He opened his arms, spread them heavenward. His voice grew huge with astonishment. 'I can see! I can see. Our Virgin Queen – sovereign bride of England – has restored my sight. Thank you, Great Lady and Beauteous Prince.'

Cheers echoed from the palace walls – a proud and joy-filled thunder.

The Queen raised her warder again. Grooms and squires led in a splendid charger and the Queenly healed blindman vaulted to its saddle. In galloped his opponent, an enormous champion astride an equally immense horse armored in gilded steel. Man and steed wore bright red apples dangling from their armored heads. A yellow wig of maiden's hair flowed from the knight's helmet.

'A pound on Apple Head,' growled Ben. 'Though if half what you've told me be true, you'll not be around long enough for me to collect.'

'I've told you but half,' said Will. 'All true.'

Ben glanced warily over his shoulder – as he had done all morning – even though the playmakers had little to fear behind them as no living thing perched higher, except the crows on Whitehall's turrets.

Trumpets called. The Queen flourished her warder. If her voice was attenuated by age, it still carried to the top of the gallery, firm in spirit and rich with mirth. The voice of a woman, thought Will, who liked to laugh. A woman who knew she had earned the right to savor the vigorous nation that she inspired. A woman who would defend it forever against the foreign empires that would slaughter every Protestant in it.

'God in thy causes make thee prosperous, gallant knights . . . Order the trial, Marshal. *And begin!'*

The horsemen lowered their helmet beavers, covering their faces, and trotted to their stations at the opposite ends of the jousting course where the tilt, a low wooden barrier, separated two long, straight parallel tracks.

'Will you take my bet?'

Will rarely risked his money in wagers and never the sum so large as a pound. But he had noticed that Ben's champion had arrived already mounted – signifying that the armor-burdened knight was too old to horse himself unassisted. Yet the 'blind' knight, as heavily clad in chain mail and steel plate as Apple Head, had vaulted easily from his chariot onto his horse – a high-spirited animal that seemed to take mettle from his rider.

'Two pounds.'

'And dinner,' Ben blustered back.

'I can taste it already.'

The marshal commanded his mounted heralds: 'Go bear this lance . . .' and the heralds hurried out to deliver fourteen-foot lances with the pennants of the champions' colors, red for Apple Head, black for the former blindman.

Ben rumbled gravely in Will's ear, 'Accession Day starts the season. Everyone comes to London. Imagine how many high-stomached county gentry your *Sister Queens* will offend.'

'I have imagined little else. Of what I've written, even the worst cowardly, bloodless, lily-livered pap will offend someone. The best will inflame them all.'

'That's Anthony Bacon for you: write an impossible play that can't help but offend everyone. Cunning as Caesar. In Paris he played fast and loose with all sides of the wars. Catholics, Protestants, bloody Spanish spies, perfidious French, Dutchmen, Flemish, Netherlanders, Italians. Bacon was "friends" to all. Played 'em like puppets.'

'I didn't *choose* him. He chose me.'

'Bacon chose well. Unless you're right about Cecil inventing the scheme, in which event, Cecil chose well. You love all that princely conflict.'

'God-a-mercy, Ben!'

'Try not to annoy any northern lords,' Ben gloomed on. 'They'll have your guts for bow strings if you fail to put their beloved Mary in a worshipful light.'

'Which would alight me in the Tower.'

'Charybdis and Scylla, my friend, drown in the whirlpool and smash on the rocks.'

Will decided to voice an idea that was growing large in his mind. 'Let me ask you, Ben.'

'Go ahead.'

'If I had to suddenly flee England for France or Italy, would you know any veteran comrades who traffic in such things – slipping fugitives past the authorities?'

'France and Italy are Catholic. You're a Protestant Englishman. Would you expect a warm welcome?'

'Alone, I would not,' said Will. 'The seal-cracker told me about someone arrested in France for being "anti-Catholic or not Catholic enough". He starved to death in the Bastille. But I'd be escorting a recusant fleeing priest hunters.'

'Your mother. Surely! That might open doors. Would you stay away long?'

'I hope not,' said Will. 'But returning home would depend on *The Sister Queens* resulting in Queen Elizabeth safe on the throne, a legitimate successor ready to be anointed, and Bacon and Topcliffe and Essex no longer a threat.'

'That's asking a lot of one play.'

'In truth, she may refuse to leave my father. He's not well.'

'Slipping one out of England is less dangerous than two,' Ben cautioned. 'Three people would make it very dangerous . . . But there are other difficulties. Yes, to answer your question, I do know veterans who spirit people in and out of England. We who fought in Holland called it "smuckling". But I know none who I could promise would be trustworthy traveling companions. It is a nasty business and you and your mother could find yourselves sold to the highest bidder – especially if Bacon or Topcliffe were hot on your scent.'

'Would you put your mind to how we might find a trustworthy one?'

'I will think hard on it and ask around the town.'

'And I will think on a way to hold Bacon at bay. I'm most worried about what he does after I finish the play. That may be when I most need to get her out.'

Ben said, 'Be aware of yet another difficulty. You could run afoul of French designs on Scotland. Mary was also France's queen until her husband died, and perfidious French love any Scot who'll open a back door to England.'

'The poet of civil war is aware of that, Ben.'

The trumpet sounded. The knights cantered at each other, head-on but for the narrow tilt rail between their tracks.

'Perhaps I should go alone to the Netherlands. Disappear. If I vanish, I won't exist, and there will be no play. But would Bacon seek vengeance on my mother?'

'I don't know,' said Ben.

'Maybe I should just go home.'

'And single-handedly protect your poor mother? Three for one they'll be in Stratford afore ye—'

'If they come we'll retreat to a priest hole. Warwickshire's riddled with them.'

'Not being unearthed would depend on how hard you're hunted.'

The champions closed, charging at full tilt, leveled lances at each other's shields, and struck hard. Apple Head's yellow wig took wing. Will's blind knight lost a stirrup and nearly fell off his horse. But both had struck true and both their lances shattered, which meant no winner yet.

'I envy you,' said Ben, as the heralds sallied forth to replace their weapons.

'*Envy me?*'

While pretending to listen to Will's troubles, Ben had managed to talk most of the morning about Ben Jonson. The boy actors at Blackfriars were showing his *Cynthia's Revels,* a witty satire, to solemn spectators. Will cheered him by quoting Ben's *Cynthia* Prologue on the subject of criticism: '"Then cast those piercing rays round as a crown!"'

Ben repeated a theory he held dear, that most powerful men, and all critics, secretly hated poets because the poets' ability to deliver the muse's merchandise made them noble as gods. 'The dismal fools can't imagine what it's like to thank God at the end of an endless night for a short row of words that come vaguely close to what you had hoped to say the day before.'

'It might be bull-headed,' said Will, 'to write that in your next Prologue.'

In fact, he knew no one as widely read or better educated than Ben had been at Cambridge. His adventuresome curiosity and the cold-eyed wit he had acquired in the foreign wars had honed his mighty learning to a steely edge. Little wonder he drank, if only to still wild swirls in his brain. Nor did it escape Will that Ben sat protectively close. His fierce eye roved everywhere, his hand strayed rarely from his sword. While he had none of the noble influence Will had hoped Southampton would wield in his defense, Ben had appointed himself Will's personal squire of the body and would fight to the death to protect him. If only a choleric, still-bellicose war veteran could hold scheming courtiers at bay. He knew court gossip better than most in the court but knew few if any who would listen to him.

'Sure, I envy you. Impossible or not, you've got a story for the gods.'

'I'll not deny that,' Will admitted. 'But so intricate, my head swims. And these two warring women make gods look like babes in the wood.'

'Why do you suppose the Queen was so long gentle with her enemy Queen?'

'Here lies the rub,' said Will. 'For that matter, why's she been so gentle with Essex?'

'That is the better question,' said Ben. 'I thought she would clap him in the Tower when he snuck back from Ireland and leave him there to rot. She's not famous for tenderness.'

'Do you think they were lovers?'

'Another good question. I don't know. No one knows.'

Will said, 'I would think that if they were and if he betrayed her, she'd have dealt harshly with him.'

'We should not expect consistency from a monarch who's of womankind. Not to mention constancy.'

It occurred to Will Shakespeare that Isobel the Moor would never tell Ben Jonson that he was a man who loved women.

Ben asked, 'What causes your sudden self-regarding smile?'

'I was thinking that if her ladyship the Countess of Southampton heard your view of womankind, she would summon her halberd men to cleave you to your girdle But in truth, the Queen is remarkably consistent in letting Essex get away with things repeatedly that she would punish anyone else for. As for constancy, why would most agree she is the Virgin Queen if she was inconstant?'

The tilts rumbled below. Will resumed his account of the scenes he had written thus far from events reported by Anthony Bacon's 'living Holinsheds', from reading the actual Holinshed's *Chronicles of England, Scotland and Ireland*, and from long walks about London with Holinshed's successor John Hooker, and old John Stow, in whose prodigious memory thirty years past were as recent as breakfast.

'. . . I have Her Majesty's courtiers demand Mary's head, arguing that Mary had challenged Elizabeth all their lives. One courtier howls that when she was Queen of France she blazed English arms on her plate – signifying that she was England's rightful queen as well. Another fulminates that Mary refused to ratify the Treaty of Edinburgh, thus denying Elizabeth's right to rule. Others remind Her Majesty that when the King of France died, Mary was suddenly available to marry again, stealing the thunder from our Sovereign Queen – who in those early years was supposed to be the best catch in Europe.'

Ben said, 'Your play is taking a long time to say that Elizabeth seized the allegiance of Mary's subjects and forced on them her religious and political rule.'

'I have European princes who say they would marry Mary – Don Carlos of Spain, Archduke Charles, the King of Sweden, the King of Denmark – snatching at the English throne like sweetmeats—'

Ben interrupted again. 'Mary's claim to the throne is as good as the Queen's.'

'If you must speak treason,' Will muttered, hunching his shoulders, 'could you at least whisper? You'll get us arrested.'

'It must be in your play.'

'I have put in my play that the English court feared that if Mary married a foreign king they would raze the national boundary between England and Scotland and enfire civil war between Catholics and Protestants both in Scotland and England.'

Ben, who felt his blood roots strongly in Scotland – though as far as Will knew he had never actually been north of the Roman wall built by Emperor Hadrian, much less the Borders – declared, 'Such might happen.'

'Then Elizabeth falls near death with smallpox. Succession is suddenly in doubt again, making whoever Mary marries even more of a threat to English sovereignty. But instead of another king, Mary marries Lord Darnley.'

'Rakehell,' muttered Ben.

'Rakehell he was,' said Will. 'Mary tires of his cruelty and turns from one fool to another, taking her secretary as advisor. An Italian.'

'I don't trust Italians,' Ben broke in. 'They serve all princes at once, and with their perfumed gloves and wanton presents, lick the fat even from our beards.'

'Darnley didn't like Italians either. I have him murder Mary's right before her eyes.'

'That should delight your spectators. More gore than *Tamberlaine*.'

'Shades of Kyd's revenge, too,' Will answered. 'Hear this: Mary's great with child. "No more tears now," she says over the bloody corpse. "I will think upon revenge." She points to her belly. And who does that baby grow to be? King James! Such riches! Do you know what our Virgin Queen said when her cousin had borne the child? "The Queen of Scotland is lighter of a fair son, and I am but a barren stock."'

Ben said, 'She's reigned so long, we forget she was once a young woman. A girl.'

'And how much she gave up to keep her crown. Love. Marriage. Children. Not to mention how hard she had to fight to keep it. Parliament and the nobles begged her to marry. Lord Treasurer Burghley concurred.'

'Anthony Bacon's uncle,' Ben noted darkly.

'Cecil's father,' said Will. 'I'm working on a scene where Elizabeth imagines she will lose her crown to a husband.'

Quickening hoofbeats announced another pass down in the tilt yard. The formerly blind knight and Apple Head, surprisingly lithe for such a big man, were proving equally matched. Though the horses, Will noticed, were tiring, particularly Apple Head's, straining under his great weight. Again, shattered lances left both knights still in contention.

As they trotted back, Ben asked, 'Then what happened?'

'Mary Queen of Scots was raped by Bothwell—'

'*Raped?* You didn't find that in Holinshed.'

'The Moor told me – I went back to see her.'

'For antiquarian purposes, I presume?'

Will ignored Ben's laughter. 'She told me much of what I'm telling you now.'

Isobel had poured out stories of Mary Queen of Scots that she'd garnered from kitchen gossip. But she swore that Mary herself had told the tale of her rape during their long, cold afternoons at Tutbury and Chartley. Between her stories, Isobel had played hymns for Will on her virginals. Will had stood behind her, entranced by her fine hands walking music from the keys. She turned her neck like a dark swan, raised her lips toward him. He stepped back. She laughed at him and changed her music to the merry notes of Apollo's lyre.

'We were discussing rape,' Ben interrupted.

'Bothwell was a Protestant earl. He became Mary's lover.'

'Did your "Mooress" happen to explain how Bothwell metamorphosed from beast who ravished to Mary's cherished?'

'They plotted to murder her husband, Darnley.'

'Edinburgh's a great town for killing,' said Ben. 'Murder's in the air.'

'Some say blown up with gunpowder; some say stabbed.'

'The nutcrackers would prefer gunpowder to a quiet stabbing.'

'Needless to say,' said Will, 'I chose gunpowder.'

'God, don't you loathe the theater? Why do you keep playing?'

Will said, 'How many poets can stand on the stage and feel the nutcrackers take to their verse? When I play for them I know what boils their humors. I hear how they thrill to the sound of a word.'

'They have to thrill to the sound, they can't read.'

'Read or not, they can all feel and think. I can try new work, re-work it, and work it again. How many new-writ versions have I presented of *Hamlet*?'

'Enough, say some.'

'Say what they like. It's mine to plant, mine to prune, mine to nurture.'

'Burbage prays you'll declare the harvest reaped.'

'Dick tires of "A Horse, A Horse." No, I shan't quit playing, if only to know my listeners.'

Ben Jonson said, 'May I ask you an appropriate impertinent question?'

'Another?'

'Do you know what it is your *Hamlet* is about?'

'Death, and purposes mistook.'

Ben nodded with grudging admiration. 'You are clear.'

'Except for one essential thing missing that I can't yet lay my finger on . . . Is there anything else appropriate you would know?'

'I would know the remainder of your Scots adventures before my man knocks your man off his horse.'

'When Darnley is gunpowdered to the moon, the Scots nobles revolt. They capture Mary and force her to renounce her throne in favor of son James. But back in England, Elizabeth is outraged at the overthrow of a sovereign.'

'As well she might be,' said Ben. 'When subjects unseat one Sister Queen, how long before it becomes a habit? Lopping heads in the process.'

'Loyalists free Mary, and her armies attack her son's regent. He crushes her armies. Mary escapes to England, and Elizabeth offers sanctuary. But the Privy Council insists she be imprisoned before she stirs up trouble. And, indeed, it isn't long before Mary charms the Catholic north.'

'Surly savages. They suck mutiny with mothers' milk.'

Will said, 'Mary stirs the north to rise. Messengers report a thousand foot. Two-thousand horse. I show the rebels casting out the Bible and communion table at Durham and saying a Catholic mass. But they fail to rescue Mary. The Queen commands Mary be kept in "humble custody". So ends the first part of the play.'

'The *first* part? You've got four plays already.'

Will said, 'These are events of forty years.'

'*Forty?* Even the Old Queen can't sift forty years.'

'Mary's twenty more years prisoner before the ax falls.'

'Write the last week when they chop her head.'

'It is too intricate,' Will countered. 'I've not even begun to explain the betrayals.'

'Don't,' said Ben. 'Heed the ponderosity of Francis Bacon's *Tragical-Anointed-Traitoress, etcetera, etcetera.* Confine your play to Mary's last day on earth. Make the clock stroke every minute on the stage.'

Will shook his head. Brash Ben had a point, though taken, as usual, too far. Ben Jonson's clock stroked louder for Ben than the characters in his plays, who were run ragged chasing after a creator who bore a disturbing resemblance to Narcissus.

'That wouldn't be a play,' he explained, not unkindly. A mind with such lively contradictions as Ben's should be encouraged. 'The players would have to make a hundred declamations about events past – tumbling backward, rushing ahead – trapping the audience betwixt and between, unable to endure. No. For example, how do I show the torture of Throckmorton?'

'Poetry.'

'Or write Queen Mary's Jesuit conspirator, tearing up an incriminating letter and throwing it overboard only to have the sea blow the shreds back to the mariners guarding him?'

'"Snowflakes."'

'*The Sister Queens* must at least span from Mary's trial to her execution. Queen Elizabeth resists signing her death warrant. Does love for her sister queen stay her hand? Or reluctance to spill royal blood? Or a longing for peace? Or a practical desire not to make a martyr of her?'

Ben turned suddenly from the tilts, clasped Will's head in his big hands, and glared into his eyes. 'My friend, hear these words from the Prologue of a rousing play you named *History of Henry V*:

> "jumping o'er times,
> Turning the accomplishment of many years
> Into an hour-glass."'

Will's pulse quickened as opportunities galloped through his mind.

'I'll start with the Babington plotters drawn and quartered – Walsingham's forgery linked to Mary. Then shift between Mary's dungeon and James's palace, the imprisoned mother longing to be rescued – sure of deliverance – and her son the Scots King reluctant to risk losing four thousand pounds a year, not to mention his chance to succeed Elizabeth. Shift, again, to Queen Elizabeth in her Privy Council, mired in quandary. Perhaps erect a wall between the women – a wall of stone – Hadrian's wall.'

'Bombast! You say you're a poet, Will. Write words.'

Sound advice again from the younger man, said Will's quiet

voice. But he heard it from afar. Others vied for his ears. 'King James will justify his cowardice: "There is no virtue like—"'

'You know what this play could use? A visitation by Sir John Falstaff.'

'Sir John left me in *Henry V.*'

'*You* left *him* in Abraham's Arms with Mistress Quickly inspecting his privates.'

'But *Sister Queens* is one-hundred-and-seventy years later.'

'What's to stop Falstaff from descending from Heaven? Or his ghost rising from Hell like your priest. Or let him invade a sister's dream – that's it, arouse the Virgin Queen.'

'Sir John left me. Perhaps I wore thin my welcome.'

Ben laughed, 'I wondered why you killed him off.'

Will had mulled upon that often. He had an eerie feeling that Prince Hamlet had killed John Falstaff. Or had given him the courage to do the deed.

Ben looked at him intently. 'Do you miss him, Will?'

'Like a brother.'

'Hold!' Ben aimed a malevolent scowl at a grizzled blue-clad servant who was climbing toward their high corner. 'Who's this knave?'

The man climbed purposefully, more like a soldier than a lackey, driving a path through the spectators, splitting them like green timber and ignoring the complaints of the jostled. Ben reached under his cloak to scratch a flea bite beside his dagger.

Will said, 'I half know him. Though I cannot think from where.'

The servant doffed his cap and bowed to Will. 'Good morrow to you, Master Shakespeare. My Master Roper begs you dine at the Queen's Hart.'

The landlord's ale drawer. 'How did you find me here?'

'They told me at Southampton House I'd find you at the tournament. All London's here. I've searched the morning.'

'Tell your master I will wait upon him after the tilts.'

The servant knuckled his forehead and clumped back down the wooden benches.

'The tavern-keep who hid Queen Mary's letters in his barrels?' asked Ben.

'Niles Roper. Passed to him by the Moor. He's probably decided to tell me more about the forged letters. He left a few things out first time we spoke . . . I liked him. Reminds me, a little, of Falstaff.'

'Tell me more about the Moor. You galloped around her earlier.'

'There's nothing to tell.'

'You devil.'

'Nothing,' said Will. 'She is a child. She could be my daughter . . . almost. I have not touched her and I will not.'

'Most Platonick is your love – or do I mean Socratick?'

'Each.'

'Is the "child" married?'

'No.'

'Too bad. Married women make better mistresses. Parcel out their wants between their cuckold and cuckolder. Your countess married again, did she not?'

'She is not my countess.'

'But married thrice.'

'Twice widowed.'

'This third husband is a betting man?'

'The second was old Heneage. Sixty if he was a day.'

Ben laughed. 'Standing largely in memory. Shall I walk with you, Will?'

'No. I'll be safe enough in a busy tavern.'

Hoofs thundered as the heavily laden animals charged again, commencing the knights' fifth pass. In the instant before they collided, the apple knight's horse stumbled, causing the bigger man's shoulder to drop. The blind knight's lance slid harmlessly over it while the apple knight's smashed soundly into the smaller man's shield, flinging Will's champion off his horse into the mud.

'Two pounds!' Ben laughed, and held out his hand. 'Pay up.'

Two pounds? He was a fool. 'I don't carry so much. I'll pay you tomorrow.'

'You thought my man old and decrepit? And the smaller fellow a better rider? Did you not, Will?'

'Perhaps I did,' Will agreed sourly.

'But my mine was bigger and wiser. Did you not see his gnarly wrinkles before he lowered his beaver? A champion that old could only be wise. If he were reckless he'd never live so long.'

'I'll pay you tomorrow.'

'At dinner?'

'At dinner,' Will conceded, standing up to walk to the Queen's Hart.

Ben said, 'Mind you don't lose your head before you reckon your debts.'

TWELVE

B y daylight, the Queen's Hart looked fair built – the timbers new-tarred, the plaster freshly white-limed. The gates were flung open on a commodious yard where servants were helping guests alight from their coach and ostlers unhitched the weary team.

Inside was a tumult of new arrivals from the country – some in high dudgeon and shouting at the servants because horrid roads had made them late for the tilts, others palpably grateful to be back after an endless summer and autumn in the countryside.

But Niles Roper was nowhere to be seen. Will sought out the servant who had come for him. He too was missing, but a porter had a message. Would Master Shakespeare meet Master Roper where his new house was abuilding near the Pewter Hall in Lyme Street?

It had begun to rain, but Will set out for Lyme Street, heading up Gracious, and wondering how Roper managed to get builders to work on Accession Day. And indeed, as he turned onto Lyme from St Denys Street, he heard neither banging hammers nor the anxious rasp of the joiners' saws.

The house was abuilding around the ruins of an old abbey, with fresh timbers rising from ancient stone like cowslips on a dung heap. The first story of walls was already closed to the weather. The scaffolding around the second stood empty of workmen. Barrows were tipped to cover lime and sand heaps. He walked under the staging, up the low incline on a board plank and peered into the dark within.

'Holla!'

A slender figure, cloaked to the eyes, pushed through the doorway. The brim of his low-pulled bonnet shielded that of his face which the cloak did not. A rapier was scabbarded from his girdle.

'Good day, sir,' Will began. But the man shoved past so hard that Will fell from the narrow plank into the mud. He caught his balance, but one knee was soiled and his cloak splashed. The man ignored his angry protest, hastened up Lyme Street and disappeared around the corner at Cornhill.

Will started into the street after him, then thought upon the fact that he, unlike the fellow who had bumped him, was not armed with a sword, much less a rapier, and tried to clean his clothes instead. His hand came away sticky and when he looked he saw blood mixed with the mud.

'Master Roper?' Will called tentatively. No answer. He stepped further into the shell of the building. 'Master Roper?'

Cold light slipped between the planks that were scattered atop the ceiling beams. He smelled the sharp, clean odor of wet plaster, layered over a sweeter smell from the ancient stones of the former abbey. 'Master Roper?' he called loudly.

'Below,' a voice called from under the floor. 'In the cellar.'

Will spied an opening and hurrying to it found a ladder. He climbed down into the dark. 'Master Roper?'

'Here, lad.'

There in the light from cracks in the ceiling he saw Niles Roper on the stone floor, half sitting with his back to the wall. A massive English sword lay beside him, the pommel by his hand. Across his knees was a thick leather buckler studded with steel rivets. It had proved a poor shield, for a dark stain of blood had soaked Roper's waistcoat beneath his open doublet.

Will saw immediately what had happened. The old soldier had fought proudly with his heavy sword and shield, hacking away with wide, plunging slashes, until his opponent had slipped under his guard and skewered him with a rapier. There'd been any number of such contests as the needle-pointed stabbing steel grew in favor. More often than not, the new science prevailed over the old.

'Who did this?'

Roper turned his face in shame. 'A foreigner.'

'I'll bring a physician.'

'Don't. Not even a ship's surgeon could tar this deathful hole.'

Will knelt beside the dying man. Roper was shivering. Will whipped off his cloak and spread it over him.

'Don't be found here with me,' Roper gasped. 'They'll throw you in the Clink.'

'I've done nothing.'

'All *I* did was obey Master Bacon.'

Will rocked back on his heels. 'But did not Bacon tell you to speak to me?'

'It seems his enemies would rather I not.'

Will thought of Isobel. Was she in the same danger? Not likely. Roper had been recruited by the government. He was a witness and a participant in Walsingham's conspiracy to intercept Queen Mary's letters and alter them.

Roper clutched Will's arm with a failing hand. 'Did I ever tell you?' he asked, as if they were old acquaintances. 'Did I ever tell you . . .' His voice faded.

With a long-time acquaintance at his side, the old soldier wasn't dying alone, and Will answered, 'I'm here, Niles.'

Roper swallowed hard and closed his eyes. 'Did I ever tell you what I loved in your Falstaff?'

He had not, but Will said, 'I believe you did. But tell me again, Niles.'

Will heard shouting nearby.

'Run!' Roper whispered. 'Run, young fellow. Take your cloak. I'll not need it long.' He shoved it into Will's arms. 'Run!'

'Tell me again, Niles.'

Niles the Brewer whispered words of Sir John Falstaff, who had recruited for a bounty the halt, lame, and hopeless.

> '"I have led my ragamuffins where they are peppered:
> there's not three of my hundred and fifty left alive."'

'Do you know what that means, Master Shakespeare?'

'Tell me, Niles.'

'He is not as bad a fellow as Puritans think. Surely, Falstaff recruited the dregs for the King's press. But he led them into battle, personally. Chanced his life beside them.'

A dog barked.

'Run! Run while you can.'

Will jumped to his feet, bounded up the ladder, ran toward the street, and stopped abruptly. Two rapier-and-dagger men blocked his way. They drew their weapons, swords in their right hands, knives in their left.

THIRTEEN

The rapier's speed shocked him.

He saw it flicker and jumped back. It darted the distance like a shooting star and pierced his doublet. For some reason, he felt no pain. The long whippy blade bent like a drawn bow. His attacker looked astonished, and in that moment when all motion stopped, Will realized that his father's goatskin-bound table-book, pocketed inside his doublet, had taken the thrust.

Tick-tick. Tick-tick.

It was so quiet Will could hear his heart beating and the rustle of his attackers' shoes as they recovered, exchanged looks, and advanced again.

Tick-tick. Tick-tick.

Not his heart. The clack of steel on brick.

The rapier-and-dagger men whirled to see behind them a slight, compact figure tapping the wall with his sword. *Tick-tick.* Quickly, they spread apart in the open yard. The challenger stepped from the shadows and Will recognized the Italian Dick Burbage had hired to instruct the Chamberlain's Men in the art of stage duels. Eyes on the swordsmen, he addressed Will. His accent was so slight he must have learned his English young.

'I ask you to walk quickly to the street.'

Up close, when he glanced at Will, he looked middle-aged. There was humor in his eyes, and a veil of sorrow that did not extinguish it entirely.

Will picked up a board the length of a fighting staff. Between the two of them they could try to get away.

The Italian said, 'Put that down.'

Will refused.

'Young Master Poet-Player, were I to strut a comedy upon your stage, I would move the spectators to tears. If a tragedy, they would laugh. If you strut on *my* stage, you will die. Go!'

'They are two. You are one.'

'Two against one makes all sorts of trouble for the two.'

'They are twenty years younger.'

The Italian touched his pommel to his forehead. 'What age loses of speed it gains in scheming. Please wait for me in the street.'

One of the rapier-and-dagger men staggered out of the half-built house, sword hand empty. White-faced, clutching a blood-soaked sleeve, he saw Will and ran. In several minutes, the second appeared, swordless as the first, eyes downcast, a hand pressed to a red stain on his shoulder. He ran.

The Italian strolled out next, returned his rapier to its hanger, and said to Will, 'I am Stefano Fogliaverde, Master Poet-Player. What say you to a cup of wine?'

Will invited Fogliaverde to the Mermaid and ordered the best claret they sold. Fogliaverde raised his cup with a hand steady as iron. 'Your continued good health, young master.'

'I am deeply in your debt.'

'You owe me nothing.'

'I'm most fortunate you came along when you did.'

'It was not fortune. I followed you there.'

'What? What do you mean?'

'I noticed the two of them following you. I did not love their appearance. I followed them.'

'Then should I say it was my good fortune you happened to be where you noticed me?'

'In truth, I was following you already, from the tilts to the Queen's Hart.'

Bacon's man? Cecil's? Essex's? 'Why?' Will asked.

'I have an interest in your continued good health.'

'You are too mysterious, sir.'

'Among my reasons for wishing your continued good health are the plays I hope to hear that you've not yet written. Please, forgive me, that is all I can say now.'

'Who do you serve?'

'Myself.'

Will studied the older man at length. Fogliaverde gazed back placidly. He seemed as self-contained as a falcon or a warlord. Yet, he was not remote so much as content, proud that he knew himself, humble he had survived to his present age. Will saw again the humor in his eyes, and a veil of sorrow, and he acted on a strong sense that this was a man he wanted to know better.

'Would "Fogliaverde,"' he asked, rolling the name on his tongue, 'translate to "greenleaf?"'

'You speak Italian?'

'Backwards from Latin and only *molto poco*. I believe that figuratively, "Fogliaverde," "greenleaf," could imply "*new* leaf."'

'"New leaf" indeed.' Fogliaverde smiled.

'With no offence, sir, until you tell me more, I will think of you as the mysterious Master Greenleaf.'

'I could never take offence from you.'

'May I ask what did those rapier men tell you?'

'The first, nothing. The second was a weakling. He claimed they were paid to intimidate you. They were to wound you and chase you away.'

'I'm not sure I believe that.'

Will pulled the table-book that had stopped the rapier thrust from his doublet and handed it to the Italian. Fogliaverde examined the dent in the goatskin board. 'Perhaps he feared I would be strict if he admitted he meant to kill you. Or, perhaps, more likely, he missed his intended thrust to wound you lightly. In which event, your good fortune of a strong table-book saved him from having to report to his master a terrible accident.'

He handed back the table-book, noting, 'This is finely fashioned.'

'My father made it for me.'

'I imagine he will be happy to hear that you are in his debt.'

Will saluted him again with his cup. 'Why did they kill Niles Roper?'

'It wasn't they. It was the man who pushed you in the mud – no man they knew.'

'Who is their master? Who hired them?'

'The second named a thief I've heard of, but do not know.'

'Did he answer why?'

'He didn't know why.'

'You believed him?'

Fogliaverde smiled patiently as a kindly schoolmaster would for a slow student. 'As the amount the thief paid them was substantial, I assume he was a go-between, working for someone who is himself hired by another go-between, etcetera, each higher and higher placed. None know why but the highest, and the highest will never be here to tell. Which is the point of go-betweens. And that, sir, is all I can tell you. I thank you for the cup of wine. It was a pleasure to be in your company.'

Will said, 'I look forward to your rapier lessons, Master Greenleaf.'

'As do I, Young Poet.' Fogliaverde touched his bonnet in a friendly salute and glided away.

Young poet? thought Will. *Strange he would see me that much younger than he.* Perchance the swordsman was even older than he looked, closer to sixty than fifty?

Will found Dick Burbage in the Cross Keys Inn.

No actor in London was loved more, and Dick was surrounded by his usual flock of theater followers – an uproar of bedazzled men and adoring women who bellowed laughter at his jests. Will pried him loose with a cryptic, 'We must talk,' and Burbage, a sharp man when it came to shareholder business, joined him in a private corner.

'Where have you been, Will? You sweat like you've lost a foot race. Either you've finished another *Hamlet* or run short of quills. Your brother shareholders dependent upon you for their livings pray it is the former, so we may pay our lease fine on the Globe and buy the Blackfriars Theatre. But you won't finish *Hamlet.* You won't write me a *Henry VIII. A*nd you won't put money in the Blackfriars because you hoard every penny to buy some Warwickshire farm on the far side of England.'

Will occasionally likened their business differences to the smoldering disappointments of a bad marriage. But at this moment, shivering in clothes soaked with fear-sweat, he felt rescued by the mundane from the twin horrors of Roper dying before his eyes and a murderer's rapier jumping at his chest, and he was grateful to take up the argument. 'I know the value of a farm.'

'I know the theater,' Burbage shot back. He was the son of London's leading theater manager, and, like Will, a shareholder in the Chamberlain's Men, though Burbage and his brother held double shares.

Will said, 'You also know I have daughters growing older. They will need homes to live in. Dowries to bring to suitable marriages.'

'Put your money here in London theaters and they'll have dowries that draw suitors like flies.'

'Dick, you're London born. You are home. I'm from the countryside. There will come a day when all this is over and I will go home.'

'All over? What will be all over?'

Will gestured at the bustling taproom. 'Plays. Theaters. London.'

'London's been here *a thousand years*!'

'Players inhabit shorter parts.' That was rapier-thinking, spoke Will's quiet voice. There was nothing like a whippy length of stabbing steel to focus the mind on eternity. 'Besides,' he reminded Dick, not for the first time, 'the Blackfriars seats only five hundred.'

'*Indoors!* Year round! Day and night! Winter and summer to spectators paying three times more to listen warm and dry.'

'No pit for the groundlings!' Will shot back. 'What sort of theater only has room for nobles and gentles?'

'The nutcrackers are welcome at our Globe on warm winter days and all summer.'

'We won't have a Globe if we don't pay the rent and lease fine. Shouldn't we settle that first, before the landlord sweeps the ground out from under us?'

'Let *Hamlet* pay the landlord,' Burbage shouted.

All in the Cross Keys took notice.

Burbage whispered, 'Why can't you finish *Hamlet*?'

'I am trying to see light from dark,' said Will slowly, as if reciting his dilemma might solve it.

'It's making you blind. Can't you see the Blackfriars promises time for you to keep trying – constant money, Will, money we can store up against bad weather and the plague.' Burbage lunged close and glared in his face. 'You may dream that your beautiful countess will rescue you when times grow hard. No countess will rescue me.'

'You are spouting boiled-brains nonsense! You know damned well I have no "my countess" to rescue me. I never have, and I never will.'

'Then why won't you put your money in the Blackfriars? Don't you want a better theater?'

'I want a better play.'

'I want a *finished* play. God's wounds, Will, finish the bloody thing or give me a *Henry VIII* we can sell. Didn't I offer to pay hired players to give you the time to write?'

Will felt suddenly cold. His legs were shaking. The back of his hand was pale as paper. The rapier hit repeated in his mind, again and again. 'I must go,' he said, longing to escape the din of the Cross Keys for that bottle of Southampton's best sack in the warmth of the buttery. 'I must go. But, first, I have a question for you.'

Burbage said, 'First, I've unriddled how you can finish *Hamlet* this very day. My answer is inspired as if from heaven. Let Prince Hamlet call upon the gods of Greece and Rome to resolve his dilemmas.'

'That's a Kit Marlowe dodge. I'd still have to unbind his knots – Dick, how did you happen to meet Stefano Fogliaverde?'

'Who?'

'The rapier-and-dagger man. How did you meet Fogliaverde?'

Burbage shrugged. 'I don't know. We got to talking at the Mermaid.'

'Did he approach you or you he?'

'Why would I approach an Italian I didn't know?'

'What was his purpose?'

'Admiration. What else? He came admiring my Hamlet.'

'Which one?'

'The last but one.'

'The August show? He heard us back in *August*?'

'Must have, to admire me.'

'What did he say?'

'Words of esteem. Some oddly chosen, Fogliaverde being Italian, but all lavish of praise, and filled with insight. Would that all the audience were as discerning.'

'Did he ask about me?'

'You? Why would he ask about you?'

'I am asking you, what did Stefano Fogliaverde ask about me?'

Dick Burbage's strong features contorted with bafflement. 'I played Hamlet. You played my Father's Ghost, under the stage as much as on it, howling "Swear!" "Swear!" – or some such, I can't remember precisely which in that version. How would Fogliaverde notice, with you there so little and me so much?'

Will said, 'I'm considering enlarging my part.'

'I wouldn't go that far, Will. You've written a poetic balance between your role and mine.'

'Dick? Is it possible that Fogliaverde had another motive for expressing his admiration with such zealous fervor?'

'I can't imagine what.'

'Perhaps to get paid to teach rapier fighting?'

'No.'

'How much are we paying him?'

'Cheaper than stinking mackerel.'

'*Nothing?*'

'Fogliaverde told me, "Silver for gentles, gold for nobles." I protested that we are neither gentle, nor noble, but mere players who can afford precious little silver, and less gold. He said that the opportunity to hear the Chamberlain's Men rehearse was payment enough.'

'That's no way to make a living.'

'I said as much. Fogliaverde said, "I will treat it like a feast day. Who makes a living on a feast day? Other than cooks and servants." Listen, Will, if someone gives me a horse, I do not examine its teeth.'

'He is a mystery.'

'No mystery,' Burbage said. 'He is smitten by the stage. For which I, in all modesty, feel responsible. You should have heard him go on about my Shylock – not to change the subject, but he did admire *Merchant of Venice*. Thought it one of the best you've written. Said it was your answer to the Lopez execution. Was it?'

Queen Elizabeth's royal physician had been hanged for taking a bribe from the King of Spain to poison Her Majesty. The Earl of Essex had led the prosecution. Dr Lopez was exposed as a fraudful man with many cozening irons in the fire, but the poisoning charge against him hinged largely on accusations that he was a secret Jew.

'I saw Lopez at Tyburn.'

Burbage said, 'Needless to say, my Shylock touched a chord with the Italian. Said I played the Jew with great sympathy. Isn't it funny, Will? Since we have no Jews in England – haven't had a Jew in all this island for what, for four hundred years? – my Shylock stands for all of them.'

Will rose from his stool and covered his retreat with a promise. 'And soon your Hamlet will stand for all Danish princes.'

Burbage knew an end-of-scene exit when he heard one. And how to top it. 'I look forward to your prince. In our lifetime.'

'How pale and wan you are, Master Shakespeare,' said the moon-faced butler.

'Feeling the cold, Steven. Fortunately, his lordship requested some days ago that you "stir my poetic brains" with a bottle of his best sack. This would be the perfect moment for it.'

Steven showed Will to a stool in the pantry and returned from the cellar with the sherris-sack, promising with a smile that the Spanish wine would ascend into his brain, drive out all the dull foolish vapors, make his tongue nimble, and warm his blood. But as the butler closed a practiced hand around the knob of the cork stopper protruding from the bottle, a serving-groom burst into the pantry with panic in his eyes.

'Praise God, you're here, Master Shakespeare. They're hunting everywhere in the house. The earl would see you.'

'Now?' He signaled Steven to leave the cork in the bottle.

'Now.'

'Good God, Will, you look transfixed by ghastly fiends. Like that poor devil in the *Faerie Queene*, consumed, as if you'd lost a foot race with a panther. What happened to you?'

'I had a fright, my lord. I stumbled upon a man who'd been attacked. A brewer and a veteran.'

'How on earth did you happen to "stumble upon" a brewer?'

'I was seeking help from one of Anthony Bacon's "living Holinsheds." The poor soul died of his wound.'

'Did the watch take notice?' Southampton asked sharply.

'No, my lord. The streets were empty, everyone still at the tilts.'

'Well, your troubles are over. I promised I'd speak with Essex and I have. Essex will rein in Anthony Bacon.'

'Thank you, my lord.'

Southampton frowned. He rubbed his mustache. He toyed with his hair. He glanced at his cat, asleep in a corner. 'You do not *look* untroubled.'

Will did not know what or whom to believe. Nobles never

explained themselves. It was unlike Southampton to report, 'I promised I'd speak with Essex and I have.' He sounded as false as a player fumbling for forgotten lines.

'Well?'

Will held him off with the first bit of truth that entered his head. 'I am concerned about the girl.'

'Girl? What girl?'

'The Moor at Bel Savage I told you about, my lord. What they did to the brewer, they might do to her, too and she's barely grown from childhood.'

'What is this Moor's name?'

'Isobel, my lord.'

'I'll see to her safety myself, good poet. Be assured I'll keep Isobel out of danger. Now off you go to bed. You look desperate for a night's sleep. I want you well rested and hard at work hammering out your play. But stay close as I may call on you to meet with me soon. If not the next day, or two, then next week. I'm damnably busy. Off you go now!'

Will went to his room, wondering why Southampton would summon him. To meet Essex? To hear suggestions for the play? Or had it been merely 'off-you-go' talk?

The long day repeated in the dark. Ben's warning: 'Bacon was "friends" to all. Played 'em like puppets.' The strength draining from Niles Roper's hand. 'Run, young fellow. Take your cloak. I'll not need it long.' The rapier flickering in his face. He picked his table-book from beside the bed and felt again for the weapon's dent. He heard a dying soldier sing the virtues of an unrepentant rogue who stands by his ragamuffins where they are peppered.

If I could only disappear, would the threat to my mother disappear with me? No poet, no play? No play, no play plot? If a ship sailed this hour to Cathay, or a mile beyond the moon, would I sell my soul for passage?

FOURTEEN

'I am ready at last – at *long* last – for my lord's best bottle of sherris-sack!'

Will Shakespeare reeled down the buttery steps in the dying hours of an afternoon, lightheaded with exhaustion and mightily pleased with seven full days in a row of work begun early each morning by candlelight. 'Fetch my sack back from the cellar, please. I deserve it.' An excellent week – despite the plague of the Bacons – and if there was one lesson he had taught himself it was that a playmaker should celebrate small victories. God knew what would happen next.

Upstairs in the Great Hall, travelers had just arrived, tired and hungry from York, and the kitchens and buttery were thrown out of kilter. But the moon-faced butler took the time to show Will to a pantry table and ask the carver to slice him a heaping dish of the new arrivals' roasted capon. Then he ran to the cellar for the sherris-sack and repeated last week's promise as he gripped the cork. 'Spanish wine will ascend into your brain, drive out all the dull foolish vapors, make your tongue nimble, and warm your blood.'

'Bless you, Steven,' said Will, raising the cup to his lips. 'For each of those blessings I pledge eternal gratitude.' He drank deeply. 'And to our Lord Southampton's good health, and to your kind hospitality, Steven, thank you.'

When the sweetmeats had made their way upstairs, at last, the butler wiped his face like a plowman plodding home from the last furrow. 'Save me a piece of marchpane!' he called to Cook. And then through a mouth full of the marzipan, he asked the porter at the oaken door, 'Is Susan out there?'

'Nell, too.'

'Let them in! Let them in!'

The girls came in, soaking wet from the rain, and stood with their backs to the fire, raising their skirts to warm their legs.

The butler threw himself onto a commodious joined stool. 'Come here. *I'll* warm your bottom.'

He coaxed Susan onto his lap, and warned Nell with a wink at Will, 'Don't waste your time on Master Shakespeare, his heart is spoken for.'

'How would you know?' Nell asked.

'I've heard his plays.'

Nell gave Will a pretty smile. 'Then why does Master Shakespeare look surprised?'

Will said, 'I'm only surprised that Steven heard *that* in my plays.'

'Is he right that your heart is spoken for?'

Will took another sip and passed Nell his cup. 'I'm afraid so. But thank you for asking.'

Susan laughed. 'Tell us who speaks for it.'

A frantic boy ran into the pantry. 'Master Butler, sir, you are looked for and called for and asked for and sought for in the hall.'

The butler winked again at Will. 'Well, I can't be here and there too.'

'But more's come to sup,' said the boy.

'Now who?'

'Master Bacon.'

The butler shook Susan off his lap. 'No rest for the wicked.'

'Which Master Bacon?' Will asked the boy.

'Master Anthony, sir.'

'Here?'

The butler flung the back of his hand in the boy's face. 'Why didn't you tell me it was him? God's blood, that's no man to offend.'

'Does he come often to Southampton House?' Will asked.

'Once is too often,' the butler growled as he bounded up the stairs.

Will sat stupefied, the warmth of the wine slipping from his heart.

'He gave me a coin!' the boy whispered to Susan.

'And in what coin will you pay him back, simpleton?'

'What do you mean?'

She glanced at Will and said, 'He'll never give me a coin. Nor Nell.'

'Not ever!' laughed Nell.

'Now do you understand?'

The boy colored red to the roots of his hair.

'Go away,' said Susan.

Cook, who'd been listening, beckoned severely. 'Boy! Run to Goodwife Canning and tell her you're to sleep in her stable and come home at first light with two dozen goose eggs.'

The boy ran out of the kitchen.

Horsemen clattered into the courtyard.

'Essex!' a porter cried. 'The earl! The Earl of Essex!'

All work stopped. Cook, cook's boys, kitchen-maids, porters, and serving-grooms crowded to the high barred windows that admitted daylight from the courtyard. Will strained for glimmers over their heads. Magnificently appointed horses were milling about the cobbles. Astride the tallest was a dashing rider in plumes and silk.

'The earl!'

En masse, the servants raced to serve him. Will, suddenly alone in the kitchen, jumped onto a stool to view the courtyard from the window. Bacon and Essex together? Plotting in Southampton's house?

FIFTEEN

The proud seat on the prancing horse, the gold-scabbarded sword at his side, the diamonds that speckled the hat he doffed so graciously, the shimmering cloak, and the handsome, shining face could only belong to the thirty-four-year-old Earl Robert of Essex – victor of the battle for Brest, Master of the Horse, victor at Cadiz, Privy Counsellor, and erstwhile warm companion to his cousin the Queen of England.

Will glimpsed Sir Walter Raleigh in the rear ranks of the mounted retinue. Raleigh sat on his horse with gentry ease, but he looked more like yesterday's hero than when Will had last seen him at a court performance, and a bit worn down by time and cares. Or was it simply that a famous sea captain – who had roved the oceans sinking Spaniards, founded colonies and found treasure, courted the Queen, and whose service in Ireland had far out-shone Essex's – was embarrassed to be no longer the center of acclaim.

There was no denying that Essex eclipsed every looking glass in the realm. Anyone doubting the nobleman's popularity had only to see the courtyard fill and heads craning from windows, as house guests and servants alike pressed for glimpses of their champion. The earl saluted them with kind nods and warm gestures, and they cheered as if they would march on Hell with him the instant Essex asked.

Eager ostlers seized his horse. Southampton himself flew into the courtyard, his face aglow with worship. Essex's admirers fell back respectfully, thrilled by the honor he did their lord's house and the obvious warmth the nobles shared. Southampton bowed low in welcome. Essex swept his hat from his head again, and in a gracious gesture of friendship kept it off as they sauntered inside, arm in arm, trailed by the excited household.

The strangest thought prickled Will's brain like a briar. He had wondered whether the earl even knew that the play plotters were conspiring in his name. Today, watching Essex dazzle as naturally as crystal, Will imagined himself in the conspirators' minds: what a brilliant stalking horse to disguise their own ambitions; what a warship to fly their false flags. Will had sworn he was no man's tool – brave words yet to be proven. But was Essex – whether ignorant of the plot or beguiled to believe he ruled it – also the kingmakers' tool?

'How goes the play, Master Shakespeare?'

Will turned warily to the cold voice behind him.

The first time Will had seen Anthony Bacon, the cripple had been seated in his dark coach. In the bright kitchen, his flushed face and winces revealed a man plagued by pain. But his lame leg did not prevent him from moving toward Will with an insect gait that covered ground quickly.

Will stepped down from the stool and removed his hat. Even if Southampton could actually keep his promise of protection – and Essex's too – there were no earls here in the kitchen. Just a captive poet with enough sherris-sack in his belly to scramble his brain, or give him courage, and a master spy provoking rebellion. With a guard watching from the open stairs, Will realized belatedly, the veterans and footman who had dragged him into the coach at Tyburn.

Will said, 'May God smile on your endeavors.'

Anthony Bacon's eyes glinted like shards of ice as he probed the shadows. 'I asked you, how goes the play?'

'I cannot say your brother's work shows promise.'

Bacon exploded in a brimstone rage.

'*Dare* you sport with me? You, you fame-thirsting "new man" projecting yourself above your bounds. You impertinent – *dare* you?'

As Ben Jonson in his cups would marvel, some men hated poets. But Anthony Bacon's wild rage exploded from lower depths, Will suspected, as if something had gone crooked with his schemes, or he sensed his old enemy Cecil was on to him, pulling his strings? Surely a spy whose strength, and survival, demanded knowing more than everyone else would be driven mad by the threat of a mysterious new player. Might Bacon be so far off balance that he could be vulnerable to a flimsy Mother-Check?

'Your *brother's* play,' Will answered, 'is indifferent, sir. I had no choice but to discard it and start anew. But it goes slowly. I find it exceeding intricate.'

'Have not my "living Holinsheds" made it simpler? I expected you'd be near finished by now. I've made inquiries. You're said to be swifter of pen than you told me.'

'Swifter? I've been years on my *Tragical Hamlet*.'

'Eleven years,' said Bacon, 'beginning in '89 with that filthy scoundrel Kyd.'

'And still not done,' Will shot back to disguise his shock. Not even Dick Burbage knew he had written with Thomas Kyd. Kyd had wanted it that way and Will honored the agreement he had made – as an 'artless' young poet new to London – to write like Kyd's ghost.

'Well?' Bacon demanded like a whip-crack. 'Have not my "living Holinsheds" made clear the intricacies?'

'No, sir, they have not.'

Bacon's face darkened.

Will feared his answer would visit Bacon's wrath on Isobel. Hastily, he amended, 'Not from any fault of their own. Each gives me all they know. But they know not all.'

'That is precisely the point. It is for *you* to know all. And write all.'

Cook and servants clattered on the stairs, Cook shouting for marchpane and mulled wine 'for our noble guest, his lordship, the mighty Earl of Essex.'

Anthony Bacon seized Will's sleeve. 'News has reached me that your Lord Southampton spoke of you with my Lord Essex. Were I to learn that you ignored my strict warning at Tyburn not to address him on the subject of our discussion, I will be sorely disappointed. Do you forget who I can betray to Topcliffe?'

Will manufactured a look down his nose that was both weary and superior. 'Do *you* imagine, sir, that *I* could write a word of this play while fearing for my mother in the Tower?' When he saw doubt flicker across Bacon's face, he pressed harder. 'Or do you believe I could write a single syllable while mourning her death?'

Bacon tried to conceal his doubt with the cold smile of a man who was nursing a secret. 'I am informed that playmakers, more than any other sort of poet, are famous for their ability to ignore distractions. Apparently, you learn to keep charge of your thoughts while rehearsing in the natural chaos of the theater where players, stage-keepers, prop-men, and musicians all shout at once. It makes for fast scribblers undeterred by interruption. You will finish it immediately, or she will suffer.'

Will said, 'You are an intelligencer famous for ignoring distractions in the chaos of spying and conspiring both foreign and domestic. Could you keep charge of your thoughts while fearing for the life of *your* mother – or her torture?'

'Dare you speak of my mother?'

'She is a scholar to whom I would welcome your introduction some day if your plots haven't set the heavens afire.'

'Dare—'

'You've dared *threaten* mine. I'm *praising* yours.'

Will wondered would the spy set his guard on him. When Bacon hesitated, he charged again, full-tilt.

'Your mother is a charming lady, by the accounts I hear, and the pre-eminently languaged translator of the *Apology in Defense of the Church of England*. A wise, learned translator who knows when to unleash a critically chosen word and when to jest. Surely you smile when she quotes Pope Pius the Second who saw "many causes why wives should be taken away from priests, but many more, and more weighty causes why they ought to be restored them again." With that salvo for priests to marry, your mother converted multitudes to the Church of England.'

'Dare you ransack my mother's work!'

'Your mother's work deserves far closer reading than a ransack. She wrote of people "who wickedly wink at the injuries done in the name of God." I had that same thought when I met Thomas Kyd after he was racked in the Tower, but I couldn't find the words your mother chose so felicitously.

'Next, she demolished the Pope like a cannon flattening an out-of-date fortress: "Nobody is able truly to say his heart is clean. Christ alone is the prince of this kingdom."

'Your mother tells clear as crystal that since man so sorely misleads the Church of Rome, England's Church of the Gospel is best led by God. That we, His servants, should teach, but never rule. That God invites common people to act. That true faith is lively . . . I imagine your mother is a lively presence in your life. *As is my mother in mine.*'

It took Anthony Bacon a long moment to recover his poise and shoot back lamely, 'You are not the only playmaker in London. Others can take your place.'

Will required no acting prowess and no rehearsal to deliver his ice-cold response: 'The only playmakers who could even *attempt* to write *The Sister Queens* are dead – murdered by spies and conspirators.'

Bacon whirled away from him and slithered up the stone steps, hauling himself along the low bannister. At the top, he whirled again, as if to shout at Will, and lost his balance. Will saw what would happen next – the pitch forward, sudden and ferocious as a lightning strike, the desperate grab at empty air, the tumble over the low bannister, the skull-crushed thud on the stone floor. *Die and take your secrets with you!*

But the burly footman caught his master with a mighty yank of his flailing arm that saved his life at the cost of unbearable pain. Bacon shrieked at Will, 'Never disappoint me again, or you will be grievously abused.'

Will turned his back to hide the relief that lit his eyes like a sun. Anthony Bacon had just admitted with a new threat of 'grievous abuse,' that he dared not risk undermining Will's ability to write. He had admitted, too, that he had no poets in reserve to take Will's place, no playmakers sharpening quills. The spy could not harm Mary Arden Shakespeare before the play was finished.

A message from the Globe Theatre was waiting in Will's room.

No hired man tomorrow. Shrew. Sly. Blackfriars.

Will could not get out of it. Apparently, Dick had arranged temporary use of the Blackfriars Theatre he was angling for the company to buy and could not, or would not, honor his promise to hire a paid player to replace him. Fortunately, the part of Christopher Sly in his old comedy *The Taming of the Shrew* was short – two scenes in the Prologue and a couple of lines in Act One. That Will's head was spinning from the sherris-sack and would ache tomorrow would fit the part of Sly the drunkard. Besides, he had played it often.

He rehearsed the lines from memory. The third time he was mouthing *But I would loath to fall into my dreams again,* he started worrying that he would need a substitute if Southampton happened to summon him as he had promised a week ago. Ben

Jonson could play it. Burbage would protest. Kempe would side with Burbage. Will climbed into bed and blew out the candle.

Even bets he could persuade Heminges and Condell that a favor to Ben the actor might one day earn the Chamberlain's Men a good show by Ben the playmaker. For what, he wondered again, would Southampton summon him?

He drifted into sleep on a happy note. He had put to rest the threat to his mother, at least until after *The Sister Queens* played. He awakened wondering how to stop Bacon from betraying her to Topcliffe after the show out of spite?

SIXTEEN

'Who's in there?'

Will Shakespeare thought he was alone behind the stage in the Globe's tiring-house when he unlocked his trunk to find a hat for Ben Jonson, hoping the company would let Ben substitute for Christopher Sly. But he heard a rustle of stiff taffeta. He edged toward the nearest door in the stage wall, ready to bound onto the stage, jump down to the pit, and run like the Devil.

'I say, *Who's there?*'

Even in dim light, the costumes glowed as if scores of lanterns shone on scarlet and purple cloaks, feathered bonnets, rich farthingales for the boys, gleaming swords and daggers, and taffeta doublets. Little wonder they cost a fortune – even dead men's garb purchased from servants who'd inherited their lords' clothing.

A hoarse voice answered from the shadows. 'By your leave, sir. Begging your pardon, sir.'

An enormous man with the rough garb and harsh countenance of a town beadle hulked out of the costumes. All he was missing to complete the picture of a brutal enforcer of the law was a club and whip. But there was little menace in him: he held his hat in his hand and shuffled his feet and dared not raise his eyes.

'Who are you?'

'Grinner, sir. Walt Grinner's my name.'

'Who's your master?'

'I'm a warder at the Clink.'

Oh, God, thought Will. Ben was arrested. 'What's happened?' he asked. A brawl? Another duel? Sedition or drunkenness?

'Master Bacon sent me, sir.'

'What?'

'Master Bacon charges me to speak to you.'

Another 'living Holinshed.' So much for Southampton's protection. But another sign that Bacon was growing desperate. 'What about?'

'Well, you see, sir. I've not always been a lowly warder, if you get my meaning.'

'I do not.' And then, because the poor brute looked as worried as a baited bear, he asked, not unkindly, 'What does Master Bacon want you to tell me?'

'I was in service to the Queen.'

'Queen Mary?'

'Perish the thought! Her Sovereign Majesty Queen Elizabeth.'

'Go on, please. Quickly.'

Bacon's emissary hung his head and twisted a dirty hat in filthy hands. His crown was bald, his hands scabbed. A louse crept from his sleeve, turned around, and crept back in.

'How did you serve Her Majesty?' Will prompted. 'Speak, fellow. There's no one here. The players are at their dinner.'

'I was Her Majesty's headsman.'

Will recoiled. In his imagination, he saw the hard pig eyes gleaming inside a black mask, the sloping shoulders heavy with the ax. 'You are the Queen's executioner?'

'No longer, sir. Mary Queen of Scots, she was my last. After her, the Queen had me driven from her house. It was the kindness of Lord Burghley that found me a place in the Clink.'

Where, Will's quiet voice spoke, the banished headsman could spy on prisoners the Lord Treasurer had jailed there. The cynical thought had come unbidden; the relentless Bacon was honing a sharper edge on him.

'She forgave me.'

'Who forgave you?'

'The Queen of Scotland.'

'She forgave you for chopping off her head?'

'You'd be surprised how many do, squire.'

'Perhaps I would.'

'It squares 'em with our Lord, you see.'

'Well, yes, I can see that,' said Will. 'You were, after all, merely the instrument of justice.'

'A poor instrument. My hand trembled and my blow missed.'

There'd been a second stroke from the ax, Will recalled reading, but the headsman so amazed him with this confession that he could only stare blankly.

Walt Grinner shook his head. 'Many's the night, sir, I've wished to undo that terrible blow. She cried out, don't you see?'

Will opened a door in his memory castle and shut it on, 'A blow no less cruel for its poverty.'

'When I picked her head up, it rolled away. I held only her red hair. Don't you see, sir? Her hair was but a wig.' With that, the headsman fell silent. Will waited, wondering what he was supposed to do. A curtain swished open and Dick Burbage rushed in, gasping dramatically as the messenger from Marathon. 'Will! There you are. A message from the Earl of Southampton. And wherry men waiting at the Cross Keys.'

He finally noticed the warder and stared down his grand nose at him.

'Grinner of the Clink,' Will explained.

Burbage paled.

'On private-time,' Will reassured him, taking the folded, sealed letter.

Dick slipped away. Will nodded that the headsman should go too. He couldn't wait to open Southampton's letter. Grinner put on his hat and started through the curtain. There he paused, half in and half out, like a bear peering from a hedge.

'She was a brave lady, Master Shakespeare. More queen in death than ever she was in life.'

'Why did Queen Elizabeth banish you?'

'Because I chopped off Mary's head.'

'But the Queen signed Mary's death warrant.'

'Her Majesty preferred her murdered.'

'*What did you say?*'

A grave look passed over the man's face, then alarm, as if he had said too much. 'There was talk,' he mumbled. 'Would some fellow strangle Mary instead.'

'What talk?'

'It was whispered. But it came to naught.'

'Whispered by whom?'

The headsman shrugged. 'Whispers, sir. Sterling money offered, too. Mary knew.'

'Who knows that Anthony Bacon sent you to me?'

'None from my lips.' He pushed through the curtain.

'Hold! What else did Queen Mary say to you? What did you mean, Mary knew?'

Behind the curtain came the voice of the headsman. 'She said she had prayed for the kiss of my blade; better she said than a dagger at night.'

Will listened to his heavy steps fade. With trembling hands, he broke Southampton's seal. The letter he read soothed his heart and made him smile: *Pray meet with me at Greenwich Palace this afternoon.*

The earl had closed with lines from Will's own *Venus and Adonis*:

> '"For know, my heart stands armed in mine ear
> and will not let a false note enter there."'

Southampton's boatmen were waiting at the Cross Keys to row Will down the Thames to Greenwich. But first he had to persuade the company to allow Ben to stand in for him.

'*Ben Jonson?*' protested Burbage, eyebrows slashing the air. 'Why Jonson?'

'He's ready to rehearse,' said Will. 'He's just outside.'

'So's the ostler who holds the horses. And his horses.'

'He could use the money, Dick.'

Will Kempe grated in a voice sure to set three thousand laughing. 'The Queen could use the money to send another army to Ireland. Would you have the Lord Treasurer speak your part?'

Will looked to Harry Condell and John Heminges. The practical Heminges, who dealt with the Revels and helped Burbage look after business details, looked away. Will said, 'Harry, do you still want to borrow my mouse-colored velvet hose?'

'Will's bribing you,' said Burbage.

'At least Harry can be trusted to return my hose clean and mended,' Will said.

Harry Condell said, 'Let me remind the company that if Ben Jonson manages to write another success like *Every Man in His Humour,* it would be good that Ben remembered the Chamberlain's Men fondly.'

'Sly's part is small and over soon,' said Will, unfurling his sides, a short roll of paper that contained Christopher Sly's lines and cues when to enter, when to speak, and when to get off the stage. 'Besides, Dick, can't even the least imaginative friend appreciate the summons of an earl?'

Will had to press hard to worm through the crowds crossing London Bridge. Glimpses of the river showed the tide going out. Gallants were 'shooting' the bridge for sport, steering boats over the furious hills of water that tide and current squeezed between its arches – a dangerous game that Will had never played in all his years in London.

He found Southampton's wherry men ale-washed and fat-witted in the Cross Keys' taproom. Reeking and stumbling, they followed him out of the inn, along Gracious and into New Fish Street.

'This way, squire.'

They reeled onto Thames Street.

'Where go you?' asked Will. 'The river's there.' They were so close he could see down the narrow slot of New Fish the roofs of the houses that were built on the bridge.

'The boats are at Essex House, squire.'

'Well I should walk back to the bridge and—'

'Hurry, sir. We can't lose the tide if we're going to shoot the bridge.'

'But I'll take a boat from *below* the bridge.'

The wherry men – a breed who did not suffer fools gladly, even sober – exchanged hugely pained looks of *who is this pied ninny?* The elder and drunker chuckled, a sound like an anchor chain clanking from a galleon. 'And I suppose your lordship's wherry men are known to the palace guard? And know upon which stairs to land their boat? And what coin to slip which yeoman as a gift or gratuity so that your boat awaits your return? Or does your lordship call so regularly at Greenwich Palace that he's welcomed by open arms wherever he chooses to land and from whatever vessel?'

The younger shushed him.

'Begging your pardon, squire. John means no harm. The good earl always hires our boats for his friends.'

John belched. 'You might say we're of his retin-noo. Thames attendants, I calls Peter and me, sir. Thames attendants.'

'We've two boats,' Peter assured Will. 'John'll row ahead and shoot the London Bridge alone. John's the best hand on the river for shootin' the bridge. You and me, sir, we'll tie on above the bridge and walk around dry and meet him downstream. But the tide's ebbing fast, so we better hurry, or even John won't make it through alive.'

The oars stirred stink from the sewers. But pulling further from the bank, the boats broke into clear water and sweet-smelling breezes. Will sat on a rough cushion under an awning. For him, the River Thames was a second London, as spirited and mysterious as the first, but a fresh and open city with flat and airy expanses that comforted a country man, and yet in some ways, even more fantastical.

'There's a sight for English eyes!' bawled Peter. He jumped to his feet. 'Holla! Holla, Your Majesty!'

The Royal Barge was advancing upriver, rowed against the current by ten oars. Four boats crammed with armed gentlemen were stationed off its quarters, ax-and-spear-headed halberds gleaming like dragon teeth in the watery sunlight. Lute and pipe music drifted faint and fitful on the wind.

John stood in his wherry and, reeling drunkenly, hailed the distant procession. 'Holla, Your Majesty! God's Good Grace to England's Greatest Prince!'

All across the river hundreds of wherry men took up the chorus, 'Holla, Queen Elizabeth. Long live the Queen!'

The regal fleet rounded the river bend toward Westminster.

Will's boat neared the middle of the Thames and turned downstream toward London Bridge – whose twenty stone arches linked the city to Southwark's Bankside and the suburbs' theaters and bear gardens, but divided the river. Above it, thousands of small craft plied the broad waters. Below were anchored the tall-masted seagoing vessels that the bridge barred. There was a drawbridge near the Southwark foot. But its wheels had broken and it hadn't been raised in living memory, so great galleons and carracks that ventured to the Indies, roved the South Seas, and grappled with Spanish treasure ships, could not sail the last mile to Westminster.

'Where are you going?'

'We'll shift boats on Bankside, sir. It's safer.'

The bridge's arch footings were protected from the pounding

currents by stonework starlings that parted the rushing water like arrowheads. But falling tide and the powerful river current united were more torrent than could squeeze between them. Water backed up around the stone starlings, wild water that raced so like the fiercest rapids that even the gallants Will had seen braving them had given up the sport.

A verse for Isobel had been trickling through his mind, and now, quite suddenly, it coursed full as the river:

> In the old age black was not counted fair,
> Or if it were, it bore not beauty's name.

Moor skin or raven hair? He scarcely noticed the second wherry draw close, nor John straining at the oars.

> But now is black beauty's successive heir,
> While fair slanders—

They were near enough to the bridge for him to recognize a head on a pike. Father Val. Stuck there within the hour, so fresh the birds had not yet speared its eyes. So fresh it still contained thoughts, and Will imagined he could hear them as if he and Val were hiding in a priest hole and Val was whispering in his ear to comfort him. *I vowed to serve the Lord's true Church of Rome, and the Lord gave me this merciful thought: the worst they can do is kill me. He gave me the strength to stand firm, for I often prayed to give my life for my Lord.*

Will could not smother his own thought, *Look where that got you.*

An unworthy thought, he repented, more the dismal sort he'd expect of Ben Jonson. But it stood firm as the stone starlings and could not be denied until he asked the priest's skull what had he misunderstood about Val's motives, needs, and desires? What drove him beyond fear and pain? What did he really want?

I wanted the pain to end and even as the pain flayed my courage I remembered that if I died for the Lord's Church the pain would end with joy in His presence.

Good Christ! thought Will. What heavy tasks you demand.

I am sorry, Val, but Rome does not teach. Rome commands and

I am not the Pope's subject. Forgive, too, the sad irony when I
echo my answer to Anthony Bacon: my priests father English
heirs. I am an Englishman. I was never Father Val's acolyte,
only his friend.

The boat lurched from a shift in weight. Peter had jumped to
his feet.

'What's wrong?' asked Will. John's boat shot alongside and kissed
wood to wood. Peter took his oars and stepped nimbly into it.

'What . . .?'

'Let your Lord Southampton save you now,' Peter flung over
his shoulder as he hastily unshipped his oars and began pulling
for Bankside.

'Murderers!' Will roared at them. The bridge was closer now,
his abandoned wherry gaining speed as the current hurtled him.

'You can meet him in Heaven.' John laughed.

But the false wherry men had cut their escape too close. The
current took them first, spun John's little boat like a leaf. Will
heard them exhorting each other to pull harder. Their voices grew
shrill. So close that the buildings on the bridge loomed overhead
like cliffs, they abandoned the attempt to reach shore, and instead
steadied up with their oars and tried to aim for the narrow passage
between two starlings.

Will, drifting helplessly behind them, saw John's oar catch a
crab with a fatal splash. Their boat lost way, half-turned, and
instead of slipping like a needle through the narrow passage,
smashed into the stones and split with a cannon *crack*. Water
blasted shattered planks and buried John and Peter.

Flailing their arms, screaming for God and mercy, they grabbed
at the starling, and tried to climb the slippery rocks. But the fierce
current swept them banging and smashing, rubbed lifeless along
the stones, until the river spat their bodies downstream, raw as
butchers' barrows.

When the current dragged Will's boat under the bridge, his last
sight of the sky was peppered with the rotting heads of the traitors
spiked above Southwark gate. Father Val's wore a crown of crows.

SEVENTEEN

S alt tide roaring home to the Narrow Sea and sweet water from a thousand English brooks hurled Will Shakespeare's boat at London Bridge. It made no difference that the drowned wherry men had stolen the oars. Coupled and inseparable, the River Thames and its ocean consort were in command. They whirled his boat like a top and threw the frail wooden shell at a rock-girdled pier.

Overboard! said Will's quiet voice.

He ripped off his heavy cloak and jumped into the water on the instant the boat struck with an awful noise of splintered planking. The torrent swallowed him. It pulled him under, covered his head, tossed him in the air, and dragged him under again. Currents and cross-currents tumbled him so violently he could not distinguish the light sky above from the dark below. Water rammed into his mouth and his nose.

Curb your fear. You wrote what pain it is to drown.

What dreadful noise of waters in your ears!

Swim before you drown. You know you can.

He had been sure he would drown in the Avon when Val's acolyte taught him to swim. He could see his little boy self sniffling fearfully in a shallow pool below the Clopton Bridge, the dark sentinel shaded by its arch, and his mother smiling in sunlight.

'Will!' she called from the riverbank, laughing at the jest of a most obvious truth. 'Boys who swim in the water fly like birds in the air.'

His mother's jubilant fancy had filled his imagination forever. Now, mauled by the Thames, he located the orient-pearl glow of daylight above the water, and he thought he saw under him the dark shape of the riverbed. It was much closer than it possibly could be. But hadn't old John Stow written of a mud bar below the center arch of London Bridge – an underwater island cast up by the roiled stream – where the river was suddenly shallow? The

current shoved him deep into soft mud, trapping his foot like an
arrow stuck in an archery butt.

He had to breathe air. He had to rise, and if he couldn't he
would breathe the water and that would kill him. His other foot
landed on something hard and he saw the shape of a great anchor
– what could only be a holding anchor scattered from a fearful
wreck, lost when the cable broke. He pushed off with all his
strength. The mud released him and suddenly his head was in the
light. Gulping sweet air, he found himself atop the water, buoyed
up by his frog-copied swimming stroke.

He was far below London Bridge, swept free of the rock piers
and into the middle of the wide Thames. He was so far from
either bank, and so low in the water, the only landmarks he
could see were the bridge behind him and St Paul's square tower
far to his left. Too far to swim against the stiff current and the
icy chop. The cold was sapping his strength. How long could
he swim? Not long enough to reach the bank. He paddled in
circles, looking for help. He saw ships on the horizon, giant
slab-sided creatures too far to swim to or sailing too fast to
overtake. He turned more circles, growing weaker. A ship
loomed, a small merchant vessel with a high forecastle and high
afterdeck and two stubby masts – one of the many hard-working
freighters that plied the Narrow Sea between England and the
Low Countries.

It was close enough to see the steersman standing on the high
quarterdeck. He gripped with both hands the pivoted pole that
passed down through the deck, swinging the whipstaff left and
right to move the rudder. Will saw the mariner scanning the water
while he guided the rudder that guided the ship. He tried to shout,
took a mouthful of water that gagged him. He coughed, spit, and
tried again.

'Holla! . . . *Holla!*'

The pilot's eyes glinted in his direction. Then he was pushing
the whipstaff and shouting for his mates. The ship staggered, sails
banging like musket shots. It seemed to take forever to turn and
come back. At last it hulked aside him like a wooden wall. Strong
arms reached down and dragged him on board. He caught a terrible
glimpse of the Tower of London where a boat at the water stairs
was delivering shackled prisoners with black hoods on their heads.

His teeth were clattering and the sky whirling, abruptly dark as one of those Tower hoods pulled over his eyes.

He awakened in a low-ceilinged wooden cave, warm and clear-headed, propped half upright against a timber and wrapped in a blanket. A fire blazed in a little furnace under a soup caldron into which a cook in a canvas apron was dumping raw, fatty lamb. The cave was moving, rising and falling, lurching sideways. Marking its erratic rhythm, inhaling the cloying odor of warm grease, Will felt his gorge rise in his throat. His clothes were hanging from pegs in the ceiling, swinging in time with the lurching ship. They looked dry. He had been here for hours. He noticed his skin was deathly white and found himself disposed to eject the contents of his stomach.

'Seasick,' the cook said to someone in the doorway. 'Put him out on deck before he spews his guts all over my cookhouse.'

'Out we go, squire.'

A pair of sailors tugged Will to his feet, helped him into his clothes. Jake and Giles he half-recalled the two addressing each other when they hauled him from the river and up to the warm cookhouse. He felt for his table-books and discovered that everything he had carried in his doublet pockets was still buttoned safely within. Jake saw him patting his pockets. 'It's all there, squire. We don't rob shipmates.' Now they walked him down steep steps and out under the open sky. The clean, cold air felt sent from God.

It was late in the day, the light failing, and he saw only gray water and dusky sky in every direction. It glimmered darkest ahead, brightest behind where the vanished sun still lipped the clouds, and he surmised the ship was sailing eastward toward the night, down the Thames Estuary to the Narrow Sea. London, like the sun, had disappeared behind them in the west, and Will Shakespeare felt safer than he had since Anthony Bacon ambushed him at Tyburn.

Steadying him by his elbows, Giles and Jake guided him along a low deck toward the middle of the ship. Between its masts, they sat him down, nestled firmly in a coil of rope, and threw a square of canvas over his shoulders. 'Our *Eliza* capers less down here in her belly than up high in her forecastle,' said Giles.

Jake promised, 'You'll have your sea legs now that the old cow's stopped tossing you.'

'I am better already, thank you. And thank your *Eliza* – tell me, good fellows, where are you bound?'

'Brace yourself, squire. Here comes the master.'

The master bustled up, a short, squat man with a thunderbolt voice. By the scars on his face, he might well be clenching a pirate dagger in his teeth. Will rose on still shaky legs to look him in the eye. 'Thank you, Captain, for stopping your ship to rescue me.'

'No choice,' the master bellowed. 'Law of the sea – assist all, even fools who fall overboard.'

'I thank you nonetheless. May I ask, sir, where are you bound?'

'Antwerp.'

Safer still, in three or four days. Thank God. I am disappearing, he thought. Disappearing from the Bacons, from Cecil, from Essex. I will cease to exist in England because whichever of them conspired to drown me, they will believe I am drowned.

'I am strong, sir. I have vigor. I will work in exchange for my passage.'

'I'm putting you off at Gravesend.'

'Oh, no! No, sir. I'll *pay* you for my passage.'

'How did you fall in the water?'

Will conjured up a rake's proud smirk. 'The lady's husband returned early.' He gave the master a manly wink. 'A soldier. Famous for his duels.'

The master wasn't fooled. He stormed away, roaring, 'Your troubles won't be my troubles. I'm putting you off at Gravesend.'

Will sank down on the coiled rope and stared ahead, dreading the moment the ship veered to shore. Gravesend, only twenty miles from London and fortified with blockhouses to defend the city from Spanish and French war fleets, was a childbed of spies. Thick with them, foreign and domestic. News would fly to Bacon and Essex and Secretary Cecil that Will Shakespeare was put off a ship bound for Antwerp instead of drowning in the Thames. Whoever had ordered him drowned would dispatch new murderers. Whoever still wanted *The Sister Queens* would order him strapped over a pack-horse and galloped back to London.

EIGHTEEN

'Wake up, Playmaker.'

'Let us ask you a question.'

Will opened his eyes, surprised he had dozed off. Night had fallen. Jake and Giles had returned with their shipmates. They circled him, faces gleaming in lantern light, and it was easy to imagine waking as a terrified Spaniard captured by English privateers.

He said, 'The least I can do is answer the men who saved my life. Ask anything and I will tell you everything.'

The mariners did not smile back. 'What's all this about Sir John Falstaff?'

'What do you mean?'

'Is he dead?'

Will felt every sense come alive. This was a gift not to be squandered. The seafarers were hardly the first to ask. Niles Roper would have, had he survived. Ben, surely, was ever-angling for Falstaff. Most of the Chamberlain's Men expected to see the role continue. Kempe the clown had quit, briefly, citing Will's failure to bring him back, and might quit again after a disappointing Falstaff reappearance in *Merry Wives*. He had projected a lucrative show by dancing from London to Berwick; now Kempe was threatening to dance backwards to Scotland – which reminded Will how grateful he was to have a poet arrow in his player quiver.

'So you have been to the Globe?'

'And The Theatre by Shoreditch, before the Globe,' said Giles. 'Me, the swabber, the boatswain, and the gunner and his mate, and Jake, we all been. It's our right to put it to you.'

'Of course it's your right. But put what?'

'You killed Falstaff in *Henry V*,' said Jake.

'Had you returned to the Globe last summer, Jake, you'd have met him again in *The Merry Wives of Windsor.*'

'That wasn't Falstaff.'

'But he certainly was, from the moment you first heard him

speak. Recall: "Now. Master Shallow, you'll complain of me to the King?" Who else would speak like that?'

'*Anyone else* would speak like that,' said the gunner.

'Except Sir John,' said the gunner's mate, a short, heavy fellow near wide as he was tall.

Will said, 'But he *was* Sir John. The same Sir John Falstaff.'

'The name's the same. But not the man.'

'Not the man we knew.'

'Now, good mariners—'

The gunner's mate said, 'You can name any codswabble "Falstaff". That don't make the codswabble Falstaff. He's still your barbermongering codswabble! Not Sir John!'

'You killed the man we know in *Henry V.*'

The man whose words the dying Niles Roper spoke because Falstaff stood with his ragamuffins. The man who was not as bad as Puritans thought.

'All right, my friends,' Will answered carefully. 'Putting *The Merry Wives of Windsor* aside for the moment – which I am more than content to do – do you remember that in *Henry V* I recorded what happened to Sir John?'

'We never seen him die,' said the gunner's mate.

'Why didn't you show us Falstaff dying?'

Will had a ready answer, a tenet of stagecraft since the time of the Greeks. 'If I had let Sir John Falstaff die on the stage, you would not pay Prince Hal the attention that must be paid to your play's prince.'

'Who cares about Hal?' Jake shot back.

'Sir John is our prince,' said the gunner's mate.

'How do you expect us to know Falstaff's dead if you don't show us?'

Will asked, 'But don't you remember? Mistress Quickly said he parted at the turning of the tide?'

'We never saw his dead corpse.'

Will asked, 'What happened when she felt up his legs?'

'Cold as stone.'

'Wasn't that how Mistress Quickly knew he was dying?'

The sailors responded with a chorus of rebuke, dismay, and advice.

'Mistress "Quick-Lay" spurred too fast.'

'She gave up on Sir John too soon.'

'Or felt up too low.'

'You should have sent Doll Tearsheet to warm him up.'

'Doll would stand him lively.'

They left it to the gunner's mate to pose, 'Is Sir John coming back?'

'I don't know.'

Every face in the lantern light froze in disbelief. 'Playmaker! If you don't know, who would?'

'In truth, good fellows, I do know *where* he is. But I do not know for sure *when* he's coming back. Or even *if*.'

'Is he dead?'

Will said, 'As the wisest among you ask, how can Falstaff be dead if you haven't seen him die? So, clearly, Sir John Falstaff can't be dead. As for the rest, it is a long, long story, which I long to tell you. But your captain is about to put me off at Gravesend. I see its lights now.'

The sailors rose as one and marched to the back of the ship where the master had his cabin. Will sat still, listening anxiously. He had just played the performance of his life and all he could do now was hope to hear them clapping their hands. He heard shouts, angry retorts, more shouts. The mariners' chorus was loud, the captain even louder. Giles and Jake returned, crestfallen.

'What happened?'

'The master allowed us a sailors' vote.'

'What is a sailors' vote?'

'Our opinion.'

'What do you vote on? How to sail the ship?'

'No! God's wounds, Playmaker, what are you thinking? In sailing, the master is always master. We vote on comforts. A change of lamb stew to pig or beef; when to purchase cloth to sew new clothes. We voted our opinion to keep you all the way to Antwerp.'

'Thank you, my friends. Thank you.'

'But we can't hear what happened to Sir John tonight. Fog's coming in. The master orders lookouts tripled. Falstaff must wait to noon dinner.'

'In truth,' said Will, 'Falstaff is rarely out of bed before.'

*   *   *

At noon, the ship's company wolfed down lamb stew that Will's stomach was not yet prepared to digest and demanded what happened to John Falstaff.

Will beckoned them close. He lowered his voice to a penetrating stage whisper that could project an aside across London Bridge. 'Good mariners, among us – in private – the whisper, at least, goes so: Sir John Falstaff set out for Jerusalem.'

'No!' cried Giles.

'Fighting the infidel?' asked Jake, incredulous.

The gunner piled on. 'What would Sir John want with crusades?'

The gunner's mate crossed his arms. 'Crusades ain't his way.'

Will nodded. Off to a bad start. 'No question of that . . . My honest lads, I will tell you what I am about . . . The letters Falstaff writes home say he's sorely disappointed in his expectation.'

'What did he expect?'

'He expected to enjoy himself, as you would imagine.'

'Verily, and in truth,' several agreed.

'All the perfumes of Arabia . . . The phoenix . . . The harems, surely . . . Even the unicorn. But his hopes were dashed.'

'Why? What happened?'

'It seems the infidel adds lime to his sack-wine to make bubbles.'

His listeners nodded sadly for Falstaff. Lime-debased sack was abominable.

'No!' shouted the gunner's mate. 'No! The Muslim don't drink wine.'

All turned on Will, faces dusky with suspicion.

Will smiled warmly at the gunner's mate. 'You see, don't you, Jake?'

'See what, Playmaker?'

'You see that Sir John discovered why the infidel don't drink.'

The mariner's face lit like the sun. 'It's the lime. Lime in their sack. No wonder they don't drink.'

Two days passed, and Will was feeling himself again – though weary of debating the future of John Falstaff – when a harsh east wind swept them off their Antwerp course. By all that was right, Giles and Jake told him, they would turn around and run for The Downs, a sheltered anchorage between the Thames Estuary and the Straits of Dover, where ships bound for Antwerp anchored up until the wind turned favorable. Only the few ships captained by masters as hardfisted as *Eliza*'s tried to beat against such a wind.

'Nimble, sir, don't you see,' Giles and Jake explained. 'Here's your English master. Unlike your Muslim, who must sail with the monsoon wind, half the year south, then half the year north. Back and forth like clockwork. Your Muslim, he takes the easy way. Englishmen don't have the luxury of clockwork winds. We meet every wind known to God and man. But Englishmen sail everywhere because we sail against the wind.'

'Don't the Spanish sail against the wind too?'

'Oh, aye. So do the French. Or so they try to. But not near so close as we. Ask anyone who's met the Armada.'

'I have heard, at some length,' said Will, 'from Sir Walter Raleigh's coxswain.'

'Mapes! There's a piece of work, sir. But a right seaman, I'll give Mapes his due.'

'So we English sail against obstacles?' asked Will, thinking how profits would accrue when daring to act in the moment against the odds. 'Sail against wind, tradition, law.'

'We do our damnedest, sir – nimble ships and bold pilots.'

'Is that why now we're beating so hard against the wind?'

'We have the bold pilot,' said Giles.

Jake agreed with a dark mutter. 'Even if old *Eliza* was built for gentler ways.'

'Not that it's for the likes of us to say,' said Giles, 'that the master will run ourselves aground by keeping us out here too long to turn around and shape a course for shelter in the Downs.'

'Nor,' added Jake, 'would we presume to speculate that wiser souls than *Eliza*'s are already anchored safe in the Downs, having sailed west on this east wind we're beating our brains against before it started blowing this hard, and that when we arrive late we will have to navigate the Goodwin Sands in rain, fog, and gales. And if we somehow manage that, try to drop anchor in a pack of ships there already cheek by jowl.'

'Not to say,' said Giles, 'in the pitchy dark of night.'

The mariners grew quiet. They were watching the sky. And had been for some time, Will realized, belatedly. They had even stopped remarking on Falstaff, no more argument, nor any rebuke, as if

Sir John was only a figment of their brains. They were glancing aloft often – watching sharply, warily, as he, were he back in London, would *scrute* a shadowy lane for cutthroats.

The sun yet shone merrily in the west, but clouds were stacking in the east, hard-edged as cliffs. They grew swiftly taller and darker and pushed ahead of them a haze that thickened on the sea. It seemed as if the mariners' silence had somehow muffled the waves. The water grew oddly still and utterly quiet – a silence in the heavens as hush as death, thought Will – a silence suddenly broken by a strange hissing noise like a thousand serpents slithering ahead of a white line that swept toward their ship. The wind doubled its speed and turned ice cold. A sudden dreadful thunder pealed so loudly it hurt his ears.

'We'll be gifts of the sea before we know it,' Giles told him.

Jake explained that 'wreckers' waiting on the beach named their booty 'gifts of the sea' when they plundered ships that split on the rocks.

NINETEEN

'*Come on, you cow! Into the wind! Into the wind!*'
    '*Close to the wind,* Eliza! *Before these roarers throw us aground.*'
'*Out of our way, Playmaker! You assist the storm.*'
Eliza's master had finally given up beating east to Antwerp, turned the ship around, and fled west in hopes of anchoring safely in the shelter of the Downs. They ran before a shrieking gale, rolling wildly as the ever-stronger wind carved steeper and steeper seas. It was long after dark and the mariners were shambling like wakened corpses when they ventured at last to cross the shallow Goodwin Sands that protected the anchorage.

'Let me help. I'm strong. I can pull this rope.'
'*That is the wrong rope. Pray, go below. Touch nothing!*'
It was anathema for Will Shakespeare to do nothing when others worked, anathema to be useless. Even knowing the master was correct – that he would only get in their way. So as the ship tried to cross the Goodwin Sands, Will retreated reluctantly to the hold and found a nook by a ladder where he could listen and glimpse the sky – if dawn ever came. For relief from uselessness, he opened a table-book with waxed pages that might stand up to rain and spray and wrote every word he heard shouted. And he vowed that if he survived to finish *The Sister Queens,* he would open his play with Mary Queen of Scotland invading England in a tempest.

Again, and again, the ship touched bottom. The third grounding came so hard it shivered the deck under Will's feet. The fourth scraped so long that the mariners bawled prayers. At last, the battered ship and exhausted crew got across the Sands and into the Downs. But the wind shifted direction and howled stronger.

It churned usually protected waters into such violent seas that the master could not bring *Eliza* about to drop anchor, and it drove her through an endless maze of anchored ships. They were invisible in the dark until they were sudden shadows only paces off. The pilot, flinging his whipstaff side to side, skirting catastrophe repeatedly, was taken by surprise. A burst of rain and sleet shrouded an enormous galleon until the last moment. In that moment, *Eliza* dodged the galleon's castle-tall hull, only to sail under its mighty bowsprit and shear off her foremast, which crashed to the deck in a heap of broken spars and tangled rope.

The ship staggered with only its mainmast standing. At dawn, when the lurching grew sharper and their course more erratic, Will heard a fearful rumbling and cries on deck, *'The surf! The surf!'*

The rumbling could only be the sea dashing land. It was then he heard the master's bellow, *'All lost!'*, and he wrote what would surely be the mariners' last command: *'To prayers, to prayers!'*

TWENTY

The ship struck so hard it split her hull.

Stout planks parted, opening wide as a barn door on a sudden blaze of daylight. Will glimpsed a beach pounded by white surf, cliffs surmounting it, and a point of land – the cape the ship had failed to clear. He felt the sea grip *Eliza*'s hull to suck her back into the depths. She leaned hard over, too wearied to resist. Water tumbled through the hole in her side. Will clambered through it. He landed half in the foaming surf, half on a beach of hard sand, surged out of the water and tried to stand. The wind knocked him down. Before he found his feet, the sea had driven the sinking ship around the cape and he was alone on a wind-whipped, surf-thundered stretch of the Kentish shore.

Will couldn't see more than five paces through the rain.

The wind shifted suddenly and it blew from the land the sound of his shipmates shouting. He stumbled toward them. The shouting grew louder, and he suddenly realized that the tone was not of frightened sailors who had somehow escaped drowning, but more like hunters – fox hunters exhorting hounds and horses to the kill. How could there be foxes in this unholy storm? Or hounds? Or horses?

The wind slammed around again, blowing off the sea, and he heard only the surf until another titanic shift brought a new noise no man could believe. He could swear he heard music. Like birds singing. Music in the gale. *The storm is taking my mind. My wits have turned.*

Chanting. Chanting, faint on the wind that was tearing him in pieces. He crouched low and pushed into it. A break in the cliffs led to empty fields, flat ground, a blasted heath where neither a tree nor a bush was left standing. He pushed on, inland, into the wind, away from the surf, anywhere to get away from the sea. He heard the music again, and plodded toward it, using it to guide him to God knew what.

The wind slackened. Was the tempest ceasing to rage? Not a

whit, he discovered with twin bolts of pain when he crashed his shins against a heap of stones. The stones were fallen from a wall that was shielding him from the wind. It was a low, tumbled stretch of a ruin. From the little he could see through the murk of rain, the ruin had been a large building. The roofs were long gone, stripped of slates and lead, and many walls had fallen. Its enormous size suggested a rich abbey looted when King Henry dissolved the Catholic Church.

He heard music again, voices rising in song:

> *'Salve, regina, mater misericordiae,*
> *Vita, dulcedo et spes nostra, salve!'*

The 'Salve Regina' Isobel had played on her virginals and sung for him, *Ad te clamamus, exsules, filii Hevae.*

His wits were gone. Yet, somehow, the wind had left the Latin in his mind, and it took no effort to hear it as English:

> To thee do we cry, poor banished children of Eve,
> *Ad te suspiramus, gementes et flentes,*
> to thee do we send up our sighs.

If the wind had not taken his Latin, then the music he heard must be true. Which meant that somewhere inside the ruin or a cellar underneath, Catholics were worshiping secretly. Just as a Warwickshire tempest had shielded Father Valente's secret mass in his mother and father's house from the priest hunters, here in Kent, people were braving the tempest to pray in peace.

Voices behind him whipped his head around. Stealthy calls. Hunters signaling. Not fox hunters. They could only be priest hunters. They were approaching the ruin from the sea, which meant they had gotten lost and overshot and only discovered their mistake when they heard the surf.

Priest hunters were as relentless as Catholics were brave, whether lowly paid spies, frightened Catholic turncoats, pursuivants for the Crown, or justices of the peace. But what of the rest of us, Will wondered, in a flash of bitter reflection? What of we who can imagine the terror of hunters beating on our chapel door? What do we do in this storm?

He felt an odd smile grip his face. He surely did not expect the ghost of Father Valente to stride from this tempest. But in that instant the ghost did, shouting, ''Tis a wild night, too, in London.'

Val looked half-mad and brimful of joy. The wind that battered Will so hard he had to crouch had no effect on the priest. Val sauntered through it with every hair on head as smooth as if acolytes had just helped him don his vestments.

'London waits, Will.'

'So do ships to Holland.'

'London listens to you.'

'Why do you haunt me?'

'Your voice is louder than you think.'

'Then hear me, Ghost. My business is peace. Not fighting. I plea in my plays for peace. I plea for order. Your business is to break the peace, and you are so sure you are right, and so brave, that you will fight and die for it.'

'I would break any peace that sends martyrs to the gallows.'

Will asked, 'When does the slaughter stop?'

'Do you have an answer to that?' Val shot back.

The priest hunters were shouting, suddenly near.

'They're coming,' said Val.

'Good-bye, Val. Good-bye, my friend. We have had a long and interesting time together and will never agree.'

'What is your answer?'

'Observe it!'

Will Shakespeare jumped over the stones. Val's ghost spread its arms and moved in front of him, whether to stop him or embrace him Will did not know, but he opened his arms too, as wide as he could, and shambled into the ruin and searched among the tumbled walls. The vapors that were Val gathered around him. If not warmer than the wind, neither were they bitter.

'Do you believe,' Val droned in his ear, 'that saving a handful of souls from the priest hunters is peace?'

'For them it will be. But they are not my sole intent.'

'You are too mysterious,' said the ghost. The vapors turned cold. 'What is your intent?'

'My swiftest possible return to London.'

'You are more mysterious.'

'To return to London I must warn the worshipers to quiet their song before the priest hunters hear it. But first I have to find them. Somewhere in the ruin candlelight gleams from a cellar. Somewhere are lookouts.'

> *In had lacrimarum valle.*
> Mourning and weeping in this valley of tears.

Val asked, 'Do you recognize what you smell?'

A sudden whiff of smoldering tallow.

The wind whirled it from Will's nostrils but not before he knew. 'Candles!'

Burning nearby. In that same instant that he learned he had found the worshipers, powerful arms closed around him and dragged him to the ground. He had found a lookout in the person of a broad-shouldered shepherd who reeked of his flock.

'Priest hunters!' Will shouted in the man's ear. 'Silence your brethren!'

The shepherd clamped a calloused hand over Will's mouth.

Will bit down hard. 'Not me, you ninny! Quiet your people before the priest hunters hear them singing. I will try to lead them away.'

'God bless you,' whispered the shepherd.

Will ran from the ruin toward the sound of the hunters. Behind him he heard snatches of music.

'O clement, O loving, O sweet virgin—'

Was their song cut short? Or was it a trick of the wind? He ran harder to lead them astray.

'I mark your intent,' the ghost called from afar. 'You will cozen the priest hunters to convey you to London.'

'So I hope,' said Will. 'Promise, Val, we will be merry in Heaven.'

The ghost made no promise and spoke only to repeat, 'Your voice is louder than you think.'

Will pulled his table-book from his pocket. 'So I hope.'

TWENTY-ONE

'**S**top that man!'

The shouts sliced through the roar of the wind.

Will kept running. His scheme – cobbled in a flash and as self-serving as it was saintlike – was to lead them on a long chase into the storm until safely away from the Catholic mass. They would catch him eventually. There were too many to outrun, and the Kentish men would know where the ground lay, which he certainly did not.

But what he saw behind him when an extraordinary gust swept the rain aside froze the blood in his veins. The same gust whipped away their leader's bonnet, revealing an old man with a white beard. If by some monstrous trick of fate he was the priest hunter Topcliffe, there would be no duping such a veteran officer with the title sheet from Francis Bacon's pile of pages. Too late now to deal better cards for the game, and praying he had led them far enough, he slowed gradually to let them closer. He stopped suddenly in the blessed shelter of a stone cattle shed with a storm-shredded roof.

Boisterous youths bounded in after him and seized his arms, whooping victoriously as if they had captured a French army. Their leader staggered in, breathing hard. He was not, thank God, the fanatic Topcliffe, just another white-haired old man.

Will took him for an example of middling countryside gentry accustomed to lording it over his inferiors and bowing to his betters. His minions would be gamekeepers' sons who'd learned their craft tracking poachers. He had likely turned to priest hunting for official favor and the money.

'I arrest you for recusancy and most vile treason in Her Majesty's name.'

'*Her Majesty?*' Will shot back. 'Did you say, *Her Majesty?* Thank God. I thought you brutes were brigands.'

'Search him!'

A youth plucked his table-book from his hand and waved it triumphantly.

Show no fear, Will told himself, and ordered haughtily. 'Give that to your master. Immediately!'

'What is it?'

'You have taken my table-book. When you look inside you will find a folded sheet of paper. When you unfold it and read it – if you can read – your master will convey me directly to Francis Bacon.'

The priest hunter stared in disbelief. 'Francis Bacon, the Queen's Counsel Extraordinary?'

Thanking God that the bumpkin knew who Francis Bacon was, Will said, 'Or, you will be summoned to London to answer personally when Counsellor Bacon discovers that you have failed in your duty to him and the Queen.'

Will made a show of a glance of deep suspicion at the minions and beckoned the still dubious commander closer. 'I was separated from my men in the course of my duty. What are *you* doing here?'

'Hunting vile Catholics.'

'I saw a crowd scurrying by.'

'Catholics?'

'How would I know? I hid from them as I tried to hide from you, not knowing who to trust in this godforsaken land.'

'Where did you see them?'

'Somewhere out here. I just told you, I was lost.'

'When did you see them?'

'Not more than two hours past.'

The hunter's face fell. 'All gone by now . . .' Then, looking searchingly at Will, he said, 'I have seen you, somewhere . . . In London, perhaps? What is your name?'

'Ask Counsellor Bacon!'

'What are *you* doing on this heath in a tempest?'

'Serving Counsellor Bacon.'

The commander peered closely at the title sheet.

Will said, 'Sure you are a man who knows who is who at court. You understand why I charge you to keep this information to yourself. Release it only when Counsellor Bacon allows you to. First, however,' he added with a chilly smile, 'you will do him a service when you convey me to an inn where I may find a livery horse to London.'

TWENTY-TWO

'Good morning, Ned!'

The Southampton House buttery door groom tipped his halberd to his bonnet in friendly salute. 'Good morning, Master Shakespeare.'

Will swung down from his exhausted horse, a mud-drenched, sway-back with a motley saddle and mismatched stirrups. An ostler led the poor animal to the stable, and Will climbed to his room where he packed hurriedly, wondering to whom Ned reported his return. Would Southampton summon him? Or the countess? Or Frances Mowery, who was usually the first to know doings in the house? Would the moon-faced butler appear at his door with a welcoming tray of cheese and small beer? Or would armed gentlemen he had never seen before escort him to the cellar?

'Master Shakespeare, you promised my lady you would be her ally.'

Frances Mowery peered from the hallway, eyes boring into him like a stone-cutter's drill. He was cramming paper and quill, ink pot, blotting sand, and *The Sister Queens* into an old leather satchel his father had helped him make for his schoolbooks. His larger traveling-player bag, as lovingly cared for, sat by the door, already stuffed.

'I have always prayed to be her ladyship's ally.'

'Is that why you disappeared? And now why you're packing your belongings?'

'I have no choice. Please tell her ladyship that I will write to her and explain.'

'She must hear why from your lips.'

'But I have no time to tarry. If you can't bring me into her presence immediately, I'll return another day.'

'Follow me!'

Frances marched him to Countess Southampton's chambers and withdrew.

The countess greeted him with a thin smile. 'Well, Will. I was surprised when Frances announced that you returned, suddenly, after leaving, suddenly, with no word to anyone. Did your muse lead you astray?'

Will began his answer with Southampton's letter summoning him to meet at Greenwich Palace. Her smile faded. When he had said all that he thought wise to, she looked as fierce as he had ever seen her.

'Surely you don't think my son betrayed you?'

'I pray not, my lady,' Will said, leaving unvoiced his aside that her new husband was an Essex man.

'And yet . . . the note in his hand, the lines from your poem, the taunting "Let your Lord Southampton save you now" . . . You don't know what to believe.'

Will looked away. He sensed her seeking his eye, drawing him back to her. When they were locked gaze to gaze, he said, 'The thought shatters my heart.'

'You will speak with him. I will arrange it.'

'But Will,' Southampton protested. He was reclining on his daybed, his cat perched on his chest. On his side table was a glass of sherris wine and a cloth coin purse. 'I sent you no letter.'

'Forgive me, your lordship, but it was written in a hand that looked like yours.'

'How much like mine?'

'Semblable-wise as a mirror.'

'Forgery!' barked Southampton, with no smile for the word play.

'Exact, my lord. Also, it contained lines of *Venus and Adonis*, for which you have expressed admiration.'

'Which lines?'

> '"For know, my heart stands armed in mine ear
> and will not let a false note enter there."'

'Oh, yes. Very touching. But Will . . . I sent you no summons to Greenwich Palace. And I surely sent no wherry man to row you there. If we were summoned to the Palace, wouldn't I have taken you in my barge?' He shook his head and searched Will's face.

Will had no idea what to say. And Southampton only confused

him in a worse way when he raised a point of logic. 'Besides, Will, how would I take you to Greenwich Palace when I – like my Lord Essex – am *persona non grata* in every palace the Queen inhabits?'

'I didn't think of that, sir. Forgive me. Surely, I was fooled by the excellent forgery of your hand.'

'That should lift a weight from your heart.'

But Will could not push entirely from his mind the suspicion that his patron had betrayed him to the wherry men who'd tried to drown him. *Let your Lord Southampton save you now.* And with each fresh leery thought came more uncertainty. Nor was Southampton inviting him to debate the question. All he could think to do was try another word game.

'Surely, sir. Nonetheless, I feel it will help me write, with your permission, if I may move to a quiet place where I can quickly finish the play.'

The earl stared.

Will said, 'To do my work, I need to hide away in a . . . say we say, "poet hole?"'

'Poet hole! Excellent, Will. Sensible thought. You've "holed" before to finish off a foul copy. What did you call it? "Holed up?" "Holed away?" What words! No one but we knew what they meant – but that was all that mattered. Recall?'

'I do, my lord.'

'Yes. Well . . . do recall it was I who suggested that the sooner you turn that very excellent sister queens invention into an actual work, the sooner you'll lift all this confusion from your mind.'

'Yes, my lord.'

'Off you go, then – do you need anything?'

'No, my lord,' said Will, touched despite his turmoil. 'Thank you for asking.'

'Money?'

'No, my lord. Thank you.'

'Considering your recent adventures, I'd be surprised if you had much coin still in your purse.'

'That is true, my lord.'

'Here! Take this.' He tossed Will the purse from the table. It felt like it held a practical mix of copper and silver useful in town, and Will suspected it had been waiting there for him.

'Thank you, my lord. It will come in handy.'

'Handy? I've not heard that. You mean convenient? Handy. Handy. Is there anything else? Don't hold back. What do you need?'

'Actually . . .'

'Name it.'

'Beeswax candles.'

'Beeswax – ah! Poet candles! You'll be scribbling through the nights. Beeswax poet candles will be waiting for you at the buttery door, whenever you need.'

'Thank you, my lord.'

'Off you go, then. Off to your poet hole.'

Will bowed and backed toward the door. Southampton called after him, 'By the way, Will, how did you *not* drown?'

'I know how to swim, my lord. I was taught as a boy.'

'Do you mean the wherry men threw you in the river and you just swam away?'

'My first clear memory is of waking up on a ship whose mariners pulled me out of the water.'

'A ship? So you were below the bridge. Did the wherry men shoot the bridge?'

'God no! Or at least I don't remember – but such, surely, my lord, how could I forget?'

Ned, standing watch at the buttery door, said, 'There is someone waiting for you, Master Shakespeare.' He nodded at the open Judas hole. Will looked out and saw Anthony Bacon's dark coach outside the tradesmen's gate. Ned said, 'If you like, I could direct you out another way.'

Bacon's burly footman stood beside the coach, holding his hat in his hand.

'Thank you, Ned. But I'll be safe in plain sight.'

'Yes, sir. But once you go out the gate, I cannot leave my post to help you.'

'I understand, and I thank you again.' Anthony Bacon was making himself visible. He wanted to talk.

The footman stepped back two paces as Will walked to the coach. Will kept one eye on the man's boots, hoping their sudden shift would signal in time for him to retreat to the buttery. The coach driver's long whip could snare a leg or a throat at some distance.

Bacon pulled open the side curtain. His gloves were off, his fingers gnarled by his running gout. Who will speak first, Will wondered, and resolved, Not I. Bacon leaned close to the open window. The daylight fell on a face that looked miraculously benign – a moldable face that belonged, Will had failed to realize at their previous encounters, to a born player.

'It was not I who tried to drown you.'

'I did not think you did.'

'Why?'

'The play is not done. Who did try to drown me?'

'I do not know. But I was deeply relieved to discover you can still write my play. And, incidentally, I find it difficult to believe your drowning was attempted by Cecil.'

'Why would the Secretary of State drown me?'

'Who do you think killed Niles the Brewer?'

'I would like very much to know,' said Will. 'The man died holding my hand. Can you prove it was Cecil?'

'How? Cecil is no fool. Neither am I. Had either of us decided to drown you, you would by now be isinglass.'

'Isinglass?'

'Fish-glue. It's boiled from the wind-bladders of sturgeon. Sturgeon eat on the river bottom.'

Will had to smile in spite of himself. What a word! Friends to all, Ben Jonson had warned. Bacon was cunning as Caesar. Fast and loose with all sides. Played 'em like puppets.

'Why would Secretary Cecil kill Niles Roper?'

'To ensure that the brewer didn't expose that Cecil's father contrived the Babington forgery.'

'I was led to believe that was Walsingham's plot. He's long dead.'

'Who do you suppose Walsingham answered to? Lord Burghley. Cecil's father. Dead only two years.'

'Did the Queen know?'

'Burghley told Her Majesty what it was best for her to know. In his judgement.'

'But you had a part in their forgery. How else would you have known of it?' And known of Isobel's years with Mary Queen of Scots.

Bacon opened both hands wide, the image of guilelessness. 'I heard of it only after the Scots Queen lost her head. I was young and new to such business.'

Will did not expect any more on the subject of the forged postscript, much less the truth. He said, 'Assuming that you didn't order me drowned and Cecil didn't, who did?'

Bacon shook his head. 'I am thoroughly baffled. The latest news I hear suggests an impetuous invention clumsily executed by the first swine-drunk wherry men the inventor's minions stumbled upon.'

'They *were* drunk,' said Will.

'Which confirms that you were attacked impetuously. Perhaps Cecil, for reasons of extreme secrecy, felt obliged to reach beyond his worthy cutthroats and mistakenly chose clumsy ones. Would you consider me busy-bodied if I asked how you happened to survive?'

Will realized belatedly that the spy had cozened him into confirming that the drowning rumor was based on facts. Now, he was fishing for clues. 'Are you now saying that you are *not* certain it wasn't Cecil?'

'I am speculating,' said Bacon. 'Clearly, some party did try to drown you and, just as clearly, we have no notion of the culprit. How did you manage to escape drowning?'

'I knew how to swim.'

'Didn't they try to stop you? Bang your head with an oar? Or throw rocks at you?'

'The current whisked me away from them.'

'Ah. So they threw you from a boat?'

'My first clear memory is of coming to my senses on a ship. Some time after its mariners saved me. I say "some time" because they had dried my clothes.'

'But is it possible they threw you from the riverbank?'

'All I know is that I awakened on the ship that saved me.'

'Do you know any enemy who would attack you so rashly?'

'I have no enemies of the sort you imply. Yourself excepted.'

Bacon returned the warm smile of an old friend chatting about events since they had last met. 'I have been accused of many faults, not always falsely, but never of rashness. More to the point, Master Shakespeare, an enemy like me could prove to be a friend.'

'A happy thought,' said Will, 'suggesting circumstances which I am utterly unable to imagine.' The footman was shifting his weight. 'Why did you send those rapier and dagger men to frighten me in Niles the Brewer's house?'

'Did we not establish that Cecil sent them?'

'You claimed that Cecil had Niles the Brewer murdered. By a foreigner, according to Niles. Those sent to frighten me were two men, not foreigners. Why did you send them to frighten me?'

'Who came to your aid?'

'He left as soon as he had disarmed them.'

'Who was he?'

'I had the impression he was a Good Samaritan.'

Bacon shook his head with a warm smile.

'Why did you have me attacked?'

'Assuming that is true, it would be to frighten you into obedience.'

'But you already held my mother's life over my head.'

'I have a habit of maintaining multiple advantages. Now regarding the "checking" of our mothers, I am willing to concede that you achieved what chess players call "No check-mate, but a stale."'

'A stale-mate? If so, it is a woefully mismatched stale-mate. I've reminded you of the existence of your mother. You've threatened to murder mine.'

'I might be persuaded to mull that mismatch,' said Bacon.

'Until "Might mull" becomes "Erase that mismatch," your threat is undiminished.' Will turned around and walked briskly toward the buttery gate, spine tingling, ears cocked for running boots. Bacon called after him, 'If you wish to further discuss diminishment, leave a message at the French bookstall at Paul's.'

The driver spoke softly to the horses and the coach rolled away.

Will collected his bags and hurried to the city.

Bacon's guess that Robert Cecil had Niles Roper murdered rang true. But the spy had left out the truth regarding motive. The brewer himself had confessed to sleepless nights in the event his unasked-for knowledge of the Babington forgery made him too dangerous to leave alive. The conspirator Robert Cecil, who Will had encountered in the Thames mansion scullery – Countess Southampton's 'patient spider' – was the sort to plan for the worst.

If his life-long enemy the Earl of Essex won the throne and Roper was still alive to testify to the Babington forgery, the first decree of the newly royalized Essex would hang Cecil at Tyburn.

Will, too, had left truth out. When Bacon asked if he had impetuous enemies, who else was called to mind but the impetuous schemer who lost all reason to red-faced fury if threatened with defeat? Will guessed that Bacon could not imagine Essex acting on his own. As Will himself hated to conceive of Southampton as worse than a fool in the schemer's thrall.

TWENTY-THREE

'I need to build a fire, Mrs Broad, but Master Jonson is short of sea coal.'

'Short, indeed, Master Shakespeare. Master Jonson has not paid for coal since early last winter.'

Mrs Broad, a widow so old her husband had manned an oar in King Harry's barge, was the landlady who rented the writing garret above a lane off Threadneedle Street that Ben called Jonson's House of Correction for the Poor and Idle. Mrs Broad had understandably mixed feelings about her tenant. But she had taken kindly to Will from the first time she met him helping Ben up the steep stairs. As Will had expected, she had let him in without question when he appeared at her door with his bags.

'Would you have room in your coal hole for a chaldron?'

'A full chaldron will cost him at least five shillings, Master Shakespeare.'

'Let us surprise Ben with a full chaldron. You can count on me for it. And would you have enough down there for me to start a fire right this very minute?'

'The house is warm today.' She turned her back on the small window feathered with ice and snugged her shawl tighter.

'But I'm feeling a chill. I've been on horseback from Kent.'

'Good God! You poor man. I'll have the boy bring it up instantly.'

Will built a brisk fire and started reading *The Sister Queens*.

He read slowly to memorize parts he would re-fashion. No history would turn the groundlings against Essex, much less make sense of the complications. But a tragedy could show what the sisters had in common and therefore what they had to lose. If he could portray what each woman was losing to the conspirators, the groundlings might embrace what the sisters had in common, and what they had in common with the groundlings – and that would clearly not be Essex. As he finished with each sheet, he tipped a corner into the fire and let go when the flames neared his fingers.

Ben staggered in, reeking of strong ale, when Will had done the last scene. His face lighted with a gratifying smile. 'You're here! Where've you been?' He shouldered past Will to warm his hands at the fire. 'Half of London asks where you've been these weeks. The other half – playmakers and poets – pray you'll stay there. Hold! Where'd you get coal?'

'Bought you a chaldron.'

'You didn't have to do that.'

'The winter's coming on.'

'I thank you. Where have you been?'

'You would not believe me if I told you.'

'Rumor had you drowned. Though few listened.'

'Rumor as usual was half right. Why didn't they listen?'

'The city's wild with heavier news. "Reports" of succession. The more outlandish the rumor, the sharper the nutcrackers cock their ears: a post from Edinburgh has King James marching Scottish armies from the north! Spain's latest armada is delivering the Infanta Isabella from the Netherlands! Lord Essex's army set sail from Ireland!'

Will asked, 'What makes you think they're outlandish?'

'King James is more patient than violent. And the newlywed Infanta Isabella is by all accounts happily content to reign over her dowry – the Spanish Netherlands – given by her loving father King Philip.'

'What about Essex's army?'

'It is no longer Essex's army. And its soldiers, if my old comrades can be believed, find themselves well led by their new general, Lord Mountjoy.'

'Mountjoy is Essex's sister's lover.'

'In my experience,' said Ben, 'there are less fraught ways to entertain one's mistress than lead a rebellion against the Queen of England. Where've you been?'

'Ben, do you ever wonder whether Essex might be the conspirators' tool? Their stalking horse rather than their leader?'

'No. He wants the throne and he needs the throne.'

'Yes, but I mean a tool like an automatical tool.'

'A meat spit?' Ben asked.

'Meat spit?'

'You've seen the joint-turner at the Queen's Hart, haven't you? Moves the roast all by itself on clock wheels.'

'Yes! Exactly. It turns by itself but will never move from the fire.'

Ben Jonson raised his voice. 'Out with it, Will! *Where have you been?*'

Will reported events since he was summoned to Greenwich Palace. As he had with Southampton and Anthony Bacon, he implied that the wherry men had thrown him in the Thames, without specifying from a boat or the riverbank, and made no reference to shooting the bridge. Ben was transfixed and listened without his usual interruptions to talk about himself until Will reached the Kentish ruin.

'Hold! Hold! Hold! Are you telling me you cozened the priest hunters with Francis Bacon's title sheet?'

'It came to me on the wing.'

'As would a hawk ripping a pigeon. You took an awful chance.'

'It got me back to London.'

'How long do you suppose before that cozened priest hunter is boasting about his connection to the famous Francis Bacon and selling the intelligence?'

'I'm hoping I frightened him into keeping it to himself.'

'Hope that human nature has changed radically. What happens when the priest hunter reports to his superiors?'

'I believe I have worse miseries at the moment.'

'*You boiled-brains goosecap!* Topcliffe – Topcliffe himself – takes reports directly or through minions from every priest hunter he employs and every agent the government employs. He commands a "tight and yare ship," as your new mariner mates say. Topcliffe will hear of this within the week. If he hasn't already.'

'You told me Topcliffe lost his privy council commission.'

'That didn't stop him from locking me in Marshalsea. It just made it hard to keep me more than a few weeks. How do you feel about spending a few weeks in prison? Particularly if you have no reason to believe you will get out ever.'

'I would wonder every night who they'll send to kill me.'

'The question is, who can you trust not to try again to kill you?'

'I can't *trust* anyone. I cannot even think for sure who is "directing" the play plot. Who is the "patron" of the players "company." All I can do is side with who seems to have the best motives.'

Ben barked a harsh laugh. 'Even if any party has pure motives, I see no hope, my friend, but to finish writing your history of *The Sister Queens* as fast as you can and pray it inspires peaceful citizens more than fanatics.'

'I burned the history.'

'You did what?'

Will pointed at the fire. Ben jumped to his hearth. The coal in the middle still flickered hotly, but surrounding it were stacks of thin ash layered as only paper burned.

'Will! How could you burn your play? Why?'

'Anthony Bacon and Francis Bacon want a play to inspire rebellion. Essex wants only what Essex wants. The Bacons are Essex men. And sadly, so is the naive Southampton. Which means that *The Sister Queens* is not a history play because such confusion can only lead to tragedy. I'll write a tragedy.'

'In favor of whom?'

'To favor King James is to favor sense over nonsense, peace over chaos, a monarch who will at least try to blunt the Catholic–Protestant hatred.'

'I am equally dubious and relieved. Dubious about your King James guess – the Catholics are praying for him, hoping he'll re-convert. But I am relieved that you have made a decision at last. Luck be with you. Choose your champion and beg him for protection.'

'Cecil schemes to destroy Essex. Cecil's my champion.'

Ben tossed Will his cloak. 'Grab your bags and get your bonnet. I am walking you directly to Secretary Cecil's offices where you will demand a safe place to write. And by safe, I mean guarded by his best men. Day and night.'

TWENTY-FOUR

'No need to escort me to Cecil's.' Will started down Mrs Broad's stairs with his bags. 'If they come for me there will be too many for you to fight, and you will end up dead too.'

But Ben bounded down after him. 'I am guarding you on the assumption they will send no more than three, which in their minds should be enough to dispatch one hapless poet. Did I mention on the subject of your drowning, that uncharitable souls suggested I was responsible?'

'Why you?'

'So I could replace you in more of your parts. I was quite the memorable Sly at the Blackfriars. Not surprisingly, there are mumblings about the city that I'll next play Hamlet senior's ghost – provided the Chamberlain's Men ever fall upon a finished copy of the play.'

On Fleet Street carousing veterans spilled from the taverns.

'The veterans,' said Will, 'were the first thing I noticed when I got back to London. More than ever in the streets.'

'And growing bold.' Ben shoved two out of their way and dared another to draw.

'Knights, too.' Will pulled Ben into the shelter of a doorway as a pair cantered wildly up the narrow street on tall Flemish horses. Their rich saddle cloths were as gaily embellished as Kit Marlowe's murderers' new doublets. The ornate pendants fluttering from their harnesses and saddle-bows were enameled tawny orange.

'Essex knights,' said Ben. 'Fire-new from the mint. His lordship made knights by the multitude in Ireland, just like at Cadiz and Rouen. Cadiz Knights. Rouen Knights. And Irish Knights. Every knight honorably qualified – when dubbed loyal to his Lord Essex – his hell-raking *army* of new knights. Ruffianly swashbucklers who couldn't even tame the Irish.'

Will said, 'Those two ride like they met their first horse yesterday.'

'Not likely to clank in the tilts with old Apple Head and Struck Blind By The Infidel,' Ben agreed. 'Even if they could lift the armor. By the by, you still owe me two pounds.'

'Lost it in the Thames.'

'Lord Essex!' the veterans saluted with pint stoups and ale pots.

'Fucked the Irish and broached 'em on his sword!' the horsemen shouted back.

'Ben, what draws the veterans? You're not an Essex man. Why not?'

'I have in common with my brothers-in-arms strong memories of our natural nobility, our bravery, our dogged strength, and our selfless devotion to each other. I would die for them and they would die for me. What I *do not* have in common with many of my brothers-in-arms is their lack of much else to believe in. I am not talking about belief as in faith, or heroes, but the belief that I have many, many hopes, many dreams, many works to work on – a belief so strong that I never even think about until you ask a question like that. Most of my fellows will end up back in the stinking camps, back on the field of battle, back putting their lives in the hands of fools, because they have nowhere else to go, no dreams to hope for, whether poems, or plays, or a blacksmith trade, or a shop, or a farm to plow, or a school to teach in. But along comes an Essex who can somehow make them believe that they can hope, too, and serve a cause that offers hope of position – a place in the world. Even if their cause is vague, it's a cause they can be part of. Add the trumpet effect of numerous stoups and cups, and the whispers of rebellion are amplified to a clarion call. And if you want to put this soliloquy in your play, my friend, you are welcome to it. Though it would be nice if you place it in the mouth of a grizzled veteran named Jonson.'

Will asked, 'Could they tame the Palace Guard?'

Ben said, 'It will hinge on the people, if enough people join their march. If enough riff-raff band together into a rabble, the rabble will elect Essex and Essex will be king. Bacon is getting what he wanted, just as you reckoned the moment you heard it – a play to sway the nutcrackers. Which means, by the by, that someone other than Anthony Bacon threw you in the river. He has no motive to kill you before you finish his play.'

'So he just told me.' Will related his meeting with Bacon.

'Swears he didn't do it. Ben, the man has a face like soft wax. You'd hardly recognize him. He's a natural actor.'

'Doubtless he's a natural actor. He's a *spy*, you goosecap. But . . .' Ben raised a large-knuckled cautionary finger. 'Once your play is done, then Bacon *should* kill you just to be on the sure side of the hedge. Killing the poet offers the schemers the great advantage of exonerating themselves if the rebellion fails. How can the government interrogate a dead poet? What will they do? Rack your corpse? But if he didn't try to drown you, who did?'

'What would you say if I answered, "Essex."'

'What gave you that idea?'

'The attempt to drown me was clumsy. Bacon assured me that if he or Cecil had tried, I'd be dead.'

'I believe that. And I believe that Essex could be clumsy. But what does Essex get out of drowning you?'

'No play? No play to make him look unkingly?'

'Nonsense! Bacon – an Essex man if there ever was one – "commissioned" you to write the play.'

'I don't look for strict logic in Essex. Something ignited him, discomfiture, or confusion, or simply not getting what he wanted. Something made him furious. Had he stopped to think at the time, he would not have lashed out so clumsily. Now he's had time to think.'

Ben shot him a cunning look. 'Did Bacon hint it was Essex?'

'No! But he might suspect it and will try to reason with Essex.'

'So you are perfectly safe until Essex resumes his natural impetuosity. All the more reason to throw yourself at Cecil's mercy and beg protection.'

Hoofbeats pounded behind them.

'Look out there! More knights.'

Will and Ben pressed into a gateway.

The horseman who raced past spurring his tired mount was no carousing knight, but a light-weight post-rider with dispatch bags bulging from his saddle. Another overtook them on a similarly weary animal. Then a post-rider on a fresh horse galloped the other way.

At Charing Cross, where the road from Hampstead and Oxford joined the Strand, the post-rider traffic grew dense, and denser still as they walked between Whitehall Palace and the tall brick wall of St James Park.

Will said, 'I am not precisely sure where Cecil houses his offices. Though I believe they are before the Parliament.'

'Follow the horses,' said Ben.

They were streaming in and of a wide gate that opened on an enormous courtyard. Mud-spattered post-riders trotted lathered horses into it. Sweating ostlers led weary animals to the stables. House grooms relieved their riders of their bags, and freshly mounted messengers galloped away.

Will and Ben agreed that nowhere else in Queen Elizabeth's realm would so many messengers convey royal correspondence but to and from the offices of the Secretary of the State.

Ben threw an enormous paw over Will's shoulder. 'I will pray to Thomas More that you recall his advice while he waited in the Tower to be martyred – choose Lady Luck for your serving man.'

At the steps, armed guards blocked Will with ax heads. But when the door grooms heard his name, it was clear that Secretary Cecil had ordered that the playmaker be admitted the instant he appeared.

The only State offices Will had ever been in were the Revels' at St Johns in Clerkenwell, where the work of overseeing plays, companies, and theaters made them lively as beehives. But they were dull and dwarfish compared to Cecil's, which were huge, though not opulent, and as mightily industrious as Cecil himself.

In chamber after vast chamber, room after commodious room, he saw clerks and pen men by the hundreds, message boys, readers, amanuenses, translators, accountants, and examiners opening the post-riders' packets of royal correspondence, deciphering dispatches, and drafting replies. Will imagined he was inside a pump-like engine, a heart that beat a secret lifeblood through England's veins.

Cecil's own office had an enormous window for reading light, set high in the wall so he could not be seen from the courtyard below. He looked surprised when his gentleman led Will in. Surprised or not, the Secretary of State gestured for scriveners to gather up pen and paper and leave.

He greeted Will coldly and left him standing before his orderly desk.

'I instructed you to report who else approaches you. Clearly, some have. Who are they?'

Will listed his encounters. He said nothing about cozening the priest hunter in Kent – the blunder Ben had noted might well bring Topcliffe down on his head. The way out of that danger was to secure a safe-guarded poet hole. Which meant convincing Cecil that Will Shakespeare was still indispensable to his scheme.

He saved Niles Roper's murder for last and described it in much detail, minus any mention of the mysterious Master Greenleaf Fogliaverde.

'Very moving,' said Cecil. 'The brewer actually quoted your Falstaff?'

'His dying words – other than "Run. Run for your life."'

'Were these Falstaff's words . . . "I have led my ragamuffins where they are peppered?"'

Will was astonished. 'How,' he marveled, 'can you know that?'

Cecil smiled. 'They are words cherished by those who would cherish Falstaff despite their better judgement.'

Will did not smile back. The Secretary of State was an erudite man who could edit entire scenes of *Richard III* on the fly. But a man, too, who could starve an army to undermine a rival. *And throw me to the wolves quicker than Anthony Bacon, if it serves his needs.*

'Anthony Bacon told me that you killed Niles Roper to conceal your father's part in the Babington forgery.'

'That was Walsingham. My father had no part in it.'

'Bacon said Walsingham answered to your father, and I have no doubt that you, Sir Robert, were already employed to work beside him.'

'My father served the Queen. He heard nothing from spies that would have disturbed Her Majesty.'

'Did you order Niles' death?'

'No. And if you believe Anthony Bacon over me, you are not the insight-filled poet you project yourself to be.'

'I ask you again, sir—'

Cecil cut him off angrily. 'I have told you no, I did not kill Niles Roper.'

'I was attempting to ask if you have finally decided which heir you choose? King James or the Earl of Essex?'

Cecil repeated, 'I am still watching until one is clearly ahead. Then I will try to stop the other before civil war drives brothers, friends, and neighbors to kill, rape, plunder, and burn.'

Will asked, 'Why won't the Queen anoint her heir? Wouldn't that stop the struggle before it explodes in war?'

'A poet may speculate upon a monarch's motives better than I.'

'I can *guess* why she didn't marry to birth an heir – fear the child's father would usurp her, with Parliament's help; or behead her as her father did her mother. But now 'why' won't she anoint her heir? Is she simply afraid to admit aloud she'll eventually die?'

Cecil asked, noncommittally, 'What if the "anointed" grew impatient?'

'Can you think of any other mistake she has made in her reign comparable to refusing to decide on succession?'

'I could not begin to guess.'

'But you are privy to information that I am not.'

Cecil sighed, looked out his large window, signaled a minion in high-born garb not to interrupt, and said softly, for only Will to hear, 'I have begged Her Majesty to name her successor. She will not. And if you ever repeat that, I will deny it.'

'Because,' said Will, 'the man she anoints would demand she step aside, immediately, so a "proper" manly king may mount her throne?'

Cecil nodded with a small smile. 'What man could resist the opportunity?'

'But this limbo – this purgatory – is equally dangerous. Not only to Her Majesty, but to England. Is there no way to convince her to make up her mind?'

'Your *Sister Queens,* if it can convince enough people to thwart a rebellion.'

'And if the play cannot, you would accept Essex? After all you know?'

Cecil's smile dissolved to a bleak stare. 'Have you ever been sued, Master Shakespeare? Have you ever been in a court of law?'

'My father was involved in cases of law several times.'

'We English love our lawsuits. Do you know why?'

'No, sir,' said Will, reminded again of Coxswain Mapes' airy snare of words.

Cecil said, 'Would you agree that regardless of the outcome, neither your father nor his adversary raised a hand against the other, much less drew a sword?'

'They did neither.'

'We flood our courts to celebrate civil peace. The memory of battling our neighbor tooth and claw is bred in our bones. The memory of civil war boils in our hearts. Civil peace is a luxury – a golden gift from Queen Elizabeth, long may she live. And you, Master Shakespeare, have been given the opportunity to help our Queen bestow on England a legacy of forty more years of peace – I will not have to choose a tyrant if your history play serves prosperity.'

'It has a become a tragedy.'

'What do you mean?'

'I burned the history.'

'*What?*'

'It would not serve. The story is a tragedy. The play will be a tragedy.'

Cecil's face turned red. A vein shaped like a thunderbolt pulsed across his forehead and he stammered in rage, 'Did you – did you – did you retain your foul copies?'

'All ash,' said Will.

'You fool! You ignorant, untrained, disorderly upstart.'

'I heard similar insults from Anthony Bacon – fame-thirsting "new man" projecting myself above my bounds, impertinent, etcetera. He also told me, just yesterday, that he did not try to drown me in the river.'

'Did you believe him?'

'Not until he also claimed that *you* did not try to drown me, either.'

'Bacon and I find common ground. Briefly.'

'You told me not to underestimate the risk of presenting *The Sister Queens* while Her Majesty still lives. Could it be that the Queen ordered her agents to drown me in the Thames?'

Expecting a forceful denial, Will was surprised when Cecil, who had dominated their conversation despite Will's best efforts, slumped behind his desk, rubbed his misshapen shoulder, and replied distractedly, 'Her Majesty employs many servants.'

'Surely none you don't know.'

'The Queen was Queen before I was born. She has many servants I don't know.'

Will was certain Cecil was lying. But at least he had made it clear that his tragedy would favor King James. Which should keep the Queen's advisor on his side.

'Write your tragedy,' Cecil commanded. 'As fast as you can. I have learned that the Queen's decision not to renew Essex's sweet wine monopoly is absolutely final. Without that income, Essex is bankrupt. He is days from ruin. He is desperate. He will take desperate measures.'

Will said, 'The Earl of Essex, and Anthony Bacon, and at least one spy have appeared where I had rooms at Southampton House. If I am to write swiftly, I need a place to work uninterrupted in safety.'

'I will order Anthonie Kingston and Cyrus Carew, my most formidable armed gentlemen – my personal guard – to convey you to a place you choose and watch day and night. When Kingston and Carew sleep, they will be relieved by trusted lieutenants. Where do you choose to write?'

Will looked Cecil full in the face. 'The inn where you take your pleasure.'

'Pleasure? I am widowed, still mourning, and chaste as a bishop.'

Will stared.

Cecil asked, 'Where might this fantastical abode be?'

'The Bel Savage Inn. You nurse your power there and power is your pleasure.'

Cecil shook his head emphatically. 'Spare me your poetical insights, Master Shakespeare. Perhaps you are not aware that until very recently "Queen's Clerk" was the traditional title of my office. I much prefer that to the vainglorious "Secretary of State." I am the Queen's servant. I do not seek power.'

'I claim no poetical insights. But I am a player as well as a poet and I have a player's keen ear for the rattle of inconsistency.'

'What did you hear that sounded inconsistent in that inn?'

'"Postscript." Who taught an illiterate laundry maid words like "postscript?". Surely someone who prompted her to tell me this tale different than Anthony Bacon wanted me to hear.'

Cecil gave him the merest nod.

Will said, 'Since then, I've wondered whether the reason the Bel Savage innkeeper never appears in the comfortable room that Isobel the Moor occupies is because the innkeeper serves you. He's probably been banished to the garret, since you likely own the inn.'

Cecil looked amused. His voice was soft, his eyes still intense. 'Surely you don't suppose I would sell you colored merchandise.'

Will took his time forming his reply. Essex's Ireland army had been betrayed by courtiers. Cecil had to have been aware, if not part of the plot to undermine his rival by robbing soldiers of food, warm garb, and gunpowder. If Anthony Bacon was the man of winter Will had spied on first meeting, Sir Robert Cecil, cloaked in the milder habits of a dutiful clerk, had his own icy fangs.

'No,' he answered, 'I do not suppose you would offer me colored glass in the name of gemstone. But you did sell colored glass to Anthony Bacon.'

'You flatter me. No one sells colored glass to Anthony Bacon. His brother Francis, surely, by playing to his pride. Or his fear. But Anthony casts the colder eye, even on his own talents.'

'Was it not you yourself who installed Isobel at the Bel Savage?'

Cecil said, 'The girl doesn't know.'

'Neither does Anthony Bacon, which must have taken some doing.'

'It did. And I do not count upon the cozening to last forever. He is far too sharp.'

Will said, 'Isobel is key to the story of *The Sister Queens*. You believe – rightly so – that she is a true living link to Mary Queen of Scots and a font of stories I can adapt. All told, I can't think of any place in London I'll be safer or more productive than at the Bel Savage.'

'Only briefly,' Cecil warned. 'And only if you can write the play before Anthony Bacon catches on or Essex lets slip his dogs. This treason's bird has been long a-hatching. Until now their number has been not so many that can't be concealed, but too few to act. Now, the many will arise of a sudden.'

'Yes, I saw more veterans than ever in Fleet Street.'

'Do you understand, now, why I would have you spy in their camp?'

'I will serve your plots better as a playmaker than a spy.'

Cecil gave a quiet laugh. 'You're thoroughly capable of both.'

'But tell me this,' said Will. 'What did you mean by Francis Bacon's fear?' He had heard Ben Jonson speak that same word for Francis the night they slept in the stable.

'Francis has so much more to lose than most men. Splendid careers in science and law lie ahead for many years, as well as higher and higher service for the government – and one day the chance to serve a new king. Also, he fears for Anthony. Francis loves Anthony with all his heart and will do anything to protect him.'

'I don't think of Anthony Bacon as one who needs protection.'

'His fortunes are tied to Essex's. If Essex goes down, Anthony will sink with him. But I predict that if Essex is tried for treason, Queen's Counsel Extraordinary Francis Bacon will lead the prosecution whether in name or effect. And I further predict that brother Francis will escape scot-free.'

'But they've both been part of the play plot since it started.'

'I have watched Francis edge away from Essex recently.'

Will picked up his bags. He believed Cecil but was somewhat thunderstruck. And his small voice was asking, why is Cecil telling me this?

'Secretary Cecil, have you ever considered that the Earl of Essex is not the leader of the plot to put him on the throne, but the king-makers' tool?'

'Like a puppet?'

'Not a puppet. More a tool like an automatical instrument. Imagine a clock or a watch with larums set to chime the hour.'

'How do the king-makers control him?'

'They don't control him. They allow him to exercise his natural instincts that dazzle the people.'

Cecil smiled. 'They would be well-advised to keep his hands off the key that winds the tool . . . And who might those conspirators be?'

'The Bacons, who else?'

Secretary Cecil's opaque smile put Will in mind of a chess

player challenged by a not entirely unexpected move. In truth, the Secretary of State appeared to be relieved, and Will Shakespeare's small voice spoke up again to tell him that he ought to ponder why.

TWENTY-FIVE

'I 've never heard the Bel Savage so quiet,' said Ben Jonson, shooting busy eyes about Will Shakespeare's poet hole.

'Blessedly quiet,' said Will, 'up here, at least, since Cecil's guard moved into the stews.'

The shifting about to make room for the formidable Anthonie Kingston and Cyrus Carew and their cold-eyed lieutenants (and the banishing of the poor women who worked in the stews) had yielded a second room connected to Isobel's by an interior door, and furnished for Will with a stool, a flat writing desk, table glasses to spread his candlelight, and a narrow bed.

'Good to see you, Ben. What brings you?'

Ben looked uncharacteristically solemn and anxious. But he began with a jest about Isobel who had gone out when Kingston had announced Will had a visitor. 'Most Socratick,' he said with a broad nod for the beds in separate rooms. 'Or do I mean Platonick?'

'That's been laughing in my brain since you asked at the tilts. It's better this way.'

'I can only hope you have good reason for that reasoning.'

'She trusts me, and I trust her. No small matter, considering the times.'

'You trust me,' said Ben. 'I trust you.'

'Maybe because we don't share a bed?'

'I stand enlightened, Gentle Shakespeare.'

Will said, 'Setting your jest aside, Isobel is a much less intrusive presence than I had feared. She is completely swallowed up by learning to read and write. She possesses a steely discipline. I suspect she honed it when mastering the virginals. Now she practices writing by copying my foul pages. Her hand improves every day.'

'A peerless partner,' said Ben, 'in an idyllic retreat. How goes the play?'

'Like most tragedies.'

'Slowly?'

Will repeated, 'Like most tragedies.' Deep in the midst of it was no time to call down misfortune by proclaiming hopes aloud. He changed the subject. 'I think I've reckoned why Cecil killed Niles the Brewer. He's preparing for the worst. Which is to say that if Lord Essex becomes King Essex, he will put Cecil on trial for treason—'

'A hanging crime,' Ben interrupted, 'for which Cecil surely hopes to hang Essex first.'

'Cecil is eliminating loose ends by killing witnesses ahead of a trial.'

'Admirable deduction,' said Ben. 'You continue to rival Machiavelli.' His smile vanished. 'Will, I wish I had better news for you. I finally found the only recusant "smuckler" I would trust with your and your mother's lives. A peerless fellow – quick-witted, hard as steel, and honest.'

'I hear nothing that displeases.'

'But he regrets that fugitive smuckling is currently impossible – yet another unpleasant consequence of Lord Essex's ambitions. The government is absolutely beside itself over the unrest brewing. Sheriffs, soldiers, beadles, priest hunters, and watchmen strangle the ports and borders, which are also crowded with Bacon's spies. Even honest smucklers of French wines into the country, and grain and butter out, are starved of their living. Fugitives haven't a hope in God. I'm sorry, Will.'

'Thank you for trying,' Will said. To God, he delivered an aside of thanks for the temporary respite of Mother-Check.

Ben was anxious to leave and paved his escape with a laugh. 'I wish you continued joy in your sleeping arrangements – at least they won't distract you from your writing.'

'It's better this way,' Will repeated, and walked Ben out the door and down the hall past the armed gentlemen's open doors to the top of the stairs. Again, he said, 'Thank you for trying, Ben,' then watched his friend clump down the steps and returned to his writing table.

It *was* better this way.

Isobel returned immediately – alerted by her friends in the kitchen or the taproom that Ben had gone – and burst through the door with her usual joy to enter the room she loved. 'Would music distract you, Will?'

'Not at all.'

As she brushed by him, she stood on tiptoe to offer, as she would on occasion, a kiss – half in jest, half a test of his resolve. As usual, both laughed with the shared link of a private bond.

That their bond was sealed by profound trust became apparent on a night when Isobel barred the door, pulled the table that held her virginals from the wall, and turned back the carpet to expose the wooden floor.

'Do you see?'

'See what?'

'You're not supposed to see, ninny. I'm showing you a secret.' She pressed down hard on the wood. The end of a wide board pivoted up. She lifted it away, pressed another, and pulled it up too. Below, beneath the floor, yawned a dark hollow. He traced the top three rungs of a ladder.

'A priest hole,' Will marveled. 'In the middle of London.'

Isobel shook her head, proud as always when she stumped him. 'Not a priest hole. Not to hide. It's my starting hole.'

'To escape! Where's the way out?'

'Ladders down to the cellar. Steps to a deeper cellar. Hidden doors through more cellars. And up to a close in Seacoal Lane.'

Will shook his head, mazed. A long, long way underground. But whoever first had reason to vanish on short notice from the Bel Savage had known his business. Seacoal Lane led into Fleet Street. From Fleet you could run to Westminster, or up a hundred alleys, or down to the Thames. Across the river were the suburbs, upriver the countryside, downriver the Narrow Sea.

It smacked of Anthony Bacon. 'Who showed it to you?'

'No one. I found it.'

'How?'

'Whenever I'm put in a room, I look for a way out.'

The starting hole was precious to her, but he had to ask, 'Is it possible that the cripple knows of it?'

'I worried that he did. What good is a starting hole if the priest hunters make it their back door? But it doesn't seem new-built. I saw no green timber, no fresh mortar, no footprints in the mud. I even found moss on wet stones.'

'It seems a miracle the ladders still stand.'

'They're very strong. The wood feels like oak.'

'You speak of things a country girl knows – timber, mortar, stone.'

'I told you, Will. The gamekeeper's bastard was my bedmate.'

'Did you learn about starting holes from him? Or from Queen Mary?'

'Both. We used his when we sneaked out at night to poach rabbits. Queen Mary always prayed for one. We searched and searched but never found it.'

She replaced the floorboards and covered them with the rug. Will helped her slide the virginals table back in place. She laid warm fingers on the back of his hand. 'You asked about the ladders to find out if they're strong enough to hold you. You must promise me never to go down there. If anyone ever saw you leaving or coming back—'

'I would never let that happen.'

'You could make a mistake, and they would make it a back door, and we would be trapped. I showed it to you because I knew you would never betray me.'

'What's wrong?'

Will discovered Isobel in tears when he rose stiff-legged after hours writing at his table. 'What is it?'

'I ruined the sheet.' She pointed at her fair copy. Her tears had splashed and the ink had run.

Will said, 'It's only one sheet. Why such wet eyes? What's wrong?'

'Queen Mary lost her last hope.'

It took Will a moment to realize that Isobel was referring to events in the play, and then only when she said, 'I worried and worried and it never got better for her. She worried that the other queen would never let her out of her jail. And she was right to worry. The other queen never wanted to let her go. You took away her last hope.'

'I can't change what happened. I can only tell it true.'

That did not matter to Isobel. Just as it would not have, he had to admit, to the likes of his shipmates on *Eliza*. She glared up at him and brushed angrily at her tears. 'Why did you do that to her?'

'I can't change that she was executed.'

'I *know* that!' she screamed. *'I'm not a fool.'*

Will had not seen that raw anger since the first time they met when he exposed that she couldn't read. She had contained it ever since, much the way Cecil's Cyrus and Anthonie would not draw their rapiers until they intended a deadly pass. 'I know she was executed. But you didn't have to take away her hope.'

'I'm sorry. I—'

'Will! When a woman fears she will be killed . . . When a woman fears she'll be tortured before they kill her, she has to hold hope. If she doesn't then she might as well be dead already.'

Gently as he could, Will said, 'There comes a moment in a tragedy when a playmaker has to be true. Or it won't be a tragedy.'

'She deserves better.'

Isobel wept harder. Will put his arm around her shoulder. No wonder she hunted for starting holes. He kept his arm around her shoulder until she at last dried her tears. When she thanked him, he thought that he had never in his brief times with his children felt so useful.

Will had raced through well over half the play when, one morning after Isobel had gone out, he remembered reading that Mary Queen of Scots was fond of pearls and usually wore a gold crucifix. He recalled many pearls on the jeweled crucifix Isobel showed him. He went looking for it and found it under her mattress wrapped in a perfumed silk handkerchief. He touched it to his nose. He knew the scent. Just as he knew when he unfurled it that the silk was embroidered with a cross between four hawks from the Wriothesley coat of arms.

TWENTY-SIX

The fool's fool has been fooled. It had never occurred to him what Southampton meant when the handsome earl promised, 'I'll see to her safety myself, good poet.'

He could not look at her bed. When? The first time while he was drowning? Again while he jested with the mariners about Falstaff? The long days the ship was battling the storm? When he was lost on the heath? Or huddling for a week in a rank inn waiting for the tempest to blow itself out and the flooded roads to dry? He knew that he had no right to be jealous. He knew he had no right to loyalty from Isobel.

How stupidly he confronted her.

Isobel claimed it had fallen from Southampton's sleeve unnoticed, when he visited to assure her safety, and she kept it for its wonderful scent. Will was sure she lied. He lied back, claiming that he believed her. He felt made a fool of and betrayed to be cuckolded by the patron he thought was his friend. Not quite cuckolded, he kept reminding himself. She's my student, my friend, my fair fair-copyist, not my mistress. By my choice.

Father Val's ghost visited in a dream that night. *'Beware Southampton.'*

Will flew awake as if he had fallen from a running horse. He drove the dream from his mind with the observation that his jealousy had invoked it. Besides, it was high time for Val's honest ghost to be called 'home.' This visitor was the Devil in disguise. A smile should be tugging his face. But he knew if he looked in the glass he would see the churning anger of a fool who doted and doubted, who hated himself, and yet still loved.

He wrote days by the window and long evenings by candlelight, stopping only when so drained that he had nothing left in his mind to hold unanswerable questions at bay. Nights when the questions grew too sharp to sleep, he wandered London, safe on the dark streets with Cecil's guard at his heels.

What if Essex ordered Anthony Bacon to drown him? Not
Southampton. Or if Essex was the rebels' tool, then the master of
spies could commission a forger to write the Southampton note?
Who had supplied the convincing lines from *Venus and Adonis*?
But wouldn't Bacon's spies include a reader of poetry? Like the
flatterer at the Cross Keys who had ranted about his poetry and
knew it line by line. His brain circled spirals of hope and despair.
It made no sense for the conspirators to drown him before the
play was done. Why had Anthony Bacon speculated an 'impetuous'
attack? *To steer me toward Essex?* Had Southampton recruited
Isobel into the play plot? Or was he merely tempted by the thought
of an exotic Mooress? 'Nobles do what nobles do.' Why had Isobel
let him woo her? 'Goosecap!' he scoffed at himself. How could
any girl alone in the world resist a handsome, rich, young
nobleman?

He felt like his head was spinning off his neck on one of his
dark wanders, when he stumbled into a pair of Essex knights. They
were singing a new-writ drinking song that equaled the earl to the
brave lions in the Tower of London, and they threatened to draw
swords if Will didn't sing with them. They fell back, hastily, when
Cyrus and Anthonie closed gloves on their pommels with chilling
self-assurance.

Cyrus laughed. 'There are more Essex knights in London than
he killed rebels in Ireland.'

'Watch now. They attack another fool.'

Hungry to torment, the drunken knights whirled against a gallant
in a tall cap sprinkled with colored-glass.

'I know that fellow,' said Will. 'Anthonie, would you—'

'We've seen him following us, Master Shakespeare.'

'He's harmless.'

'We've seen him more than once,' said Cyrus. 'He is following
you.'

'He's smitten by the stage. Help the poor devil before they hurt
him.'

Will's gentlemen touched their rapiers again. The Essex knights
melted into the dark. Will stepped close to the shabby gallant.
'Did you lay lines of my *Venus and Adonis* in a note written
to me?'

The shabby gallant blinked, utterly mazed, and Will realized the man had no idea what in the name of the Devil Master William Shakespeare was talking about. 'Did you?' he asked again, to be sure.

'I am sorry, Master Shakespeare, I did not. Did you mean for me to? I could. I could do so for you. I admire your every line.'

'No. A misunderstanding. Go.'

'But as I told you at the Keys, there is something you should know, Master Shakespeare.'

Will felt suddenly too weary to speak 'There is always something I should know. Go. Get away while you can.'

The gallant's face hardened with resolve, and he appeared, suddenly, as if a veil had lifted, to be a man of more substance than Will had imagined. 'At the Keys,' the gallant said, 'you would not allow me to relate a tale that bears on your project. Now I implore you, sir. Time is running out. You must read this. Before it is too late.'

The gallant stepped close. Anthonie and Cyrus rushed to stop him, but the gallant was too quick. He pressed a thick letter packet into Will's hand.

Will asked, 'Is this the letter you spoke of at the Cross Keys?'

'That's long gone to Scotland,' the gallant whispered. 'This is now.' He whirled about, eluded Will's guards, and ran full tilt.

'Let him go,' said Will. 'Whatever he wants, he is harmless.'

'Unless he was correct, Master Shakespeare, that there's something you should know.'

'What do you suppose is in that letter?' asked Anthonie.

'Fancy,' said Will, stuffing it in a pocket. 'The fellow is a wizard of exaggeration.'

Beeswax flame revealed what Will had not seen in the dark lane. The letter was addressed to the Earl of Southampton, and the writer had taken extraordinary pains to secure his secrets. As deft-handed a seal-cracker as Arthur Gregory would find it near-impossible to sneak a look without alerting Southampton that its contents had been violated. The packet was doubled-locked with paper stitching under sealing wax.

Will turned it over and over in the candlelight, trying to hold it gently with shaking hands, imagining the difficulty of reversing the locking process to open it secretly. The writer had folded his paper six or eight times, sliced a long sliver off one fold with a sharp blade, pierced the folded letter, then stitched the sliver through the hole, smeared it with sealing wax melted in a flame, and pressed the wax with a seal to lock the stitch.

He jumped. Isobel slept lightly the nights he walked. Soft-footed as a cat, she had crept up and whispered in his ear, 'What is that?'

'A letter to your earl.'

'He's not my earl. If he was, I'd live in a house in the countryside and lock you in the garden so I wouldn't have to worry about you wandering dark streets. Did you write it to him?'

'No.'

'How did you get it?'

'It was given to me.' He turned it over to show her the seal.

'A secret letter. Secret secret.'

'What do you mean?'

'Stitched and waxed.'

'Isobel, how do you know that?'

'Queen Mary stitched and waxed her secret'st letters. Near the end, when her fingers were stiff, she let me help her.'

'How did she trust you? Her every letter was a danger.'

'I knew that. I thought she trusted me because I loved her, and I was only a child, and her fingers were stiff. Looking back, now, I know better.'

'What?'

'She was lonely as a dragon.'

Will locked *lonely as a dragon* in his memory castle. 'Can you unseal this with no one knowing it was opened?'

'It's not possible. At least by me.'

Will shoved his pen knife under the seal, tore the hardened wax from the paper, cut the stitch, and unfolded the letter into a single flat sheet. He read it in one heart-pounding glance and put it down.

Isobel read slowly, out loud. As expert a copyist as she was becoming, voicing words from a page was considerably harder than drawing their shapes.

'"My Dear Southampton,

This is only for your own eyes – except for Mr Anthony Bacon, who in all these things is to me as the hand with which I write this. After you've read it, it goes in the fire. You will send to the palace the cream you've skimmed from the army, your best foot, horse, shot, and musketeers."'

She stumbled over 'musketeers,' then forged on with fresh confidence.

"'If it be well handled, they would tame the palace guard, surprise the court, and much advance the business. When you see my carefree smile, doubt not my resolve, nor my gratitude toward you. Secrecy is—"'

Will snatched it off the table. 'Did you read who signed it?'
'No. You took it before—'
'You must not know. You cannot know. Ever.'
Isobel said, 'I would never tell.' She laid a hand on Will's shoulder. 'My friend, you are weeping.'

TWENTY-SEVEN

'**A** forgery?' Will asked the countess, with little hope. 'That does not appear likely.'

She laid the letter on her writing desk, smoothed the folds with the tips of her fingers, and gazed past Will. She, like Cecil, had not invited him to sit in a chair. It was mid-morning. Sleet rattled the windows. Will's guard, increasingly concerned by the mood of the city, had driven him to Southampton House in a small hackney coach.

Will remembered what Isobel had said about a woman without hope. 'But, my lady, they forged Mary Queen of Scots' postscript. Why not this too?'

'To what end?'

'To slander both earls and set me chasing wild geese.'

The countess sat still as ice. 'I have seen many of the Earl of Essex's letters. He wrote often to my second husband, Heneage. If this is not Essex's own hand, it is either written by a new-discovered, hitherto-unknown twin brother as like as Essex in every sinew and heartbeat, or the work of the best forger in England.'

'So it could be forged.'

'I know you don't want to believe it.'

'I do not, my lady.'

'The point is this, Will, it doesn't matter if it is a forgery.'

'It matters to me.'

'Surely. As it matters to me, the mother of a son whose life hangs in the balance. But beyond our mental suffering – your fear you've lost a friend to betrayal, and my terror that I will lose my son to the headsman – it does not matter if this is or isn't a forgery.'

'Why not, my lady?'

'In their enemies' hands, it will be both their death warrants.'

'Throw it in the fire!'

But the settled look on the Countess of Southampton's beautiful face told Will that the wise survivor had resolved not to burn the letter from Essex the instant he showed it to her.

'Burning,' she said, 'will do no good. First of all, there will likely be copies. Better to have one ourselves, than brand ourselves guilty by destroying the evidence.'

'Who knows we have it?'

'Don't be silly, Will. Your gallant in the tall cap knows. Whoever gave it to him knows. Etcetera.'

Master Greenleaf's word for go-betweens.

'Besides – don't you see, Will – if Essex prevails and manages to anoint himself King, this letter to my son will be not a death warrant, but . . .' She turned on him a frank and open gaze as if to take his measure. Or consider it anew.

'But what, my lady? A badge of honor?'

'I could not put it better myself. Other than to amend your badge of "honor" to a badge of "royal service." Dukedoms are handed out for less.'

The countess spoke this with no hint of irony, no cynical smile, no minutely cocked brow, but as a statement of unassailable truth, and in this moment, Will understood why the nobility did not know fear. They were too eagle-eyed to overlook the main chance and too cold-blooded to hesitate.

'Will you show Essex's letter to your son?'

'I see no good coming of that. Let you and I pretend it is a forgery that fell accidentally into your hands. It is safe with me.'

'Doubtless, to be sure, my lady. But I must ask that if there are copies and if one somehow were to land in his hands, should you not forearm his lordship with the sight of this one?'

Her ladyship acknowledged with a brisk nod that Will's point was to protect her son. 'When I learn that he's received a copy I will show him this to show they are forgeries. And that he should steer clear of any plot that involves skimming cream from the army to attack the palace.'

She lowered her voice until even loyal Frances lurking at the door could not overhear. 'Lord Essex is the last noble still alive in England who can singlehandedly lead a rebellion to usurp the crown.'

Will was astonished. 'You maze me, my lady. Sure you don't profess that Essex is destined for domestical greatness?'

'Essex is void of greatness. A harsh simple nothing who is utterly empty. But people are drawn to emptiness. Perhaps they wish to be charmed by a void that mirrors their own. Depending upon how many of that ilk Essex attracts and how "well handled"' – she reached to trace the words of the letter – 'how swiftly he sends "the cream" skimmed from the army, best foot, horse, shot, and musketeers to the palace. If he "tames" the guard to "surprise the court," then this usurping Essex would in a twinkling "protect" the Queen in the Tower and mount her empty throne. But whether he succeeds or fails, the shambles he provokes will be a bloody war. You see, Will, your *Sister Queens* is needed more than ever.'

'It is not entirely my *Sister Queens*.'

'Then do what you have to, to make it so,' snapped the countess, and Will wondered, did he have to burn another?

'Why do you say that Essex is the last noble still alive who can lead a rebellion? Surely there are others, particularly with succession in doubt?'

Countess Southampton said, 'I could name as many as a hundred nobles, knights, and gentlemen who might *follow* Essex – if convinced of success. But not one of their number could lead the rest. Only Essex can lead a rebellion. Why?'

She cupped a hand and opened graceful fingers to mark each reason.

'Few nobles are so desperately bankrupt as Essex.

'Fewer are so stupid as Essex, so incapable of imagining failure.

'And none but Essex are so loved by the multitude who don't know, or care, that he is empty. Empty of treasure. Empty of brains. Empty of heart, soul, and imagination. A mere nothing. A cipher, or that new word I have heard spoken recently, a "zero."'

She touched a finger to her thumb to form an empty O. 'But he is formidable because he is a hero with nothing to lose whose time is running out.'

'But may I ask, my lady? Is it possible that one so empty as Essex is not the rebels' leader, but their tool? A sort of "automatical" tool or instrument, like a clock set to raise alarms.'

'An instrument that the rebels wind to run? Which rebels?'

'Those Essex considers in his ignorance to be his minions.'

The countess nodded. 'Anthony Bacon. His brother. Their friends at court.' Will knew her son's name was on the tip of her tongue. She shook her head and added, bleakly, 'Yes that is possible. Very likely. If true – which the more I think about it, the more I believe it is – the would-be kingmakers will turn against each other and make the shambles even bloodier. Because when all is said and done, they are conspirators, not leaders.'

She turned her face to the wall.

Will stood in silence, thinking, waiting for her to dismiss him. Against such a self-contained, self-blind adversary it was useless to grapple with Essex minions like Anthony Bacon and the countess's hapless son. Only face to face could Essex be persuaded to see what his followers and manipulators could not – that he was surely not destined for domestical greatness. That even if he won at first, he would fail, and it would be too late to convince his followers to give up a quest that would be no less bloody for its foolishness. How could he be persuaded that his cause was hopeless?

The answer struck Will with dazzling simplicity: wind his 'clockwork' to turn Essex against the king-makers. Reveal how they had made him their tool.

Will had to somehow confront Essex himself. To the earl's face. But to survive such an encounter he would have to confront him in the company of a personage whose presence would protect him.

'May I ask, Lady Southampton, do you know Sir Walter Raleigh?'

She kept staring at the wall. 'Not well. I know Raleigh's cousin Gorges better.'

'Sir Ferdinando Gorges?'

'Why do you ask?'

'Isn't Sir Ferdinando Gorges an Essex man?'

'I would not put it so strongly.'

'Forgive me, my lady, but is he not what they call an Essex knight?' Ben had rattled off a list of them the morning they saw Essex knights gallivanting on horses better trained than they were. Ferdinando Gorges had topped the list. Although Ben had made pains to say, Gorges was a worthy soldier.

The countess looked at him. Will saw that her patience was running out. Her eyes narrowed. Color flushed her cheeks. Her reply was acerbic.

'After Essex knighted Gorges for gallant service at the siege of Rouen, the Queen herself appointed him commander at Plymouth. Will, what are all these questions?'

'My I ask, my lady—'
'Enough!'
'Forgive me, Countess Southampton, but—'
She cut him off angrily. 'Next you'll remind me that my new husband is an Essex knight, too?'
'No!'
'And worry that I'll betray you?'
'You would never—'
'How can you be sure?'
Will Shakespeare turned away without asking her leave and fled the first harsh words that ever passed between them.
She called sharply, 'Where are you going?'
'To write,' he lied.
'Come back here!'
He had to confront Essex face to face, poet eye to noble eye, before he skimmed cream from the army to attack the palace.
'Will!'
Disobeying her – disrespecting the rank between them, ignoring their gulf of stations and, worst, dishonoring their many years' bond – surely meant she would never allow him inside her house again. But if he did not challenge Essex, who could? And if she could not help him get to Essex, he would have to on his own.
Halfway to the Bel Savage, he shouted, 'Hold! Take me back. Back to Southampton House!'
His guard protested. Will jumped out of the hackney and started running back to beg forgiveness for ignoring how even the strongest woman would suffer when she feared for her son's life. The hackney clattered up behind him and they persuaded him into it, promising, 'We will drive you, Master Shakespeare.'
At the buttery door, he sent a message to Frances Mowery and waited until the page returned and piped her reply in his little boy's voice: 'Her ladyship is closeted in her chambers.'

'Promise that you will never show anyone.'
Will said, 'I promise.'
Isobel pleaded, 'Not even by accident. Swear!'
'I swear that I will never lead anyone to your starting hole. I will be doubly vigilant never to let anyone see me come out. And I will be especially careful never to let anyone follow me back.'

They were crouched on the floor, having slid the virginals aside and turned back the carpet, and were peering down the ladder into the dark. Isobel said, 'I am so afraid they will come for me.'

He wished that he had not let her fair copy portions of the tragedy. She used to be so fearless – singing her hymns, brandishing her gifts from Mary. Now she feared the priest hunters every minute. She could not separate herself from the tale and was terrified that Queen Mary's fate would be her fate. No explaining could persuade her that it was only a story. For Isobel, the tragedy of *The Sister Queens* was as real as the air she breathed, and Mary Queen of Scot's lost hope – 'You made her lose her hope!' – was as true as the execution of the Queen she loved.

'Are you sure you have to go without Cyrus and Anthonie?'

'Yes.'

'Why? It's dangerous.'

'It would be more dangerous for me to pretend that my armed protectors are not Cecil's men.'

They carried poet candles down the ladders in the narrow shaft between her room and the Bel Savage cellar. They heard the patrons carousing, first through the walls, then overhead. From the Bel Savage cellar, she led him deeper down a hidden stair into a silent maze of connected cellars girdled by wet stone walls. As old John Stow never tired of marveling, London had been settled for so many hundreds of years – these older parts from Roman times, more than a thousand – that the city was riddled underground with forgotten cellars, tombs, treasure stores, dungeons, and tunnels.

They reached at last a partially filled coal hole. The inclined chute, Isobel told him, led to a walled close with a wood gate at the end that would open onto Seacoal Lane.

'Listen very carefully before you open it,' she warned. 'Make sure no one is in the lane.'

'I will listen,' he promised.

'Can you remember how you will find your way back?' she asked.

'I remember what I rehearse. So before I go out to your close, we will return to the ladder where we began for another run.'

They repeated the route, twice.

When Will was ready to leave the coal hole, she showed him a tinder box she had hidden in the wall to re-light candles.

'I promise, again,' he said, 'that I will not be followed, accidentally or otherwise.' He climbed the chute. He paused at the gate, listening closely for footsteps until he was sure he was alone in the dark. Then he slipped out the gate and onto Seacoal Lane. Sticking to shadows, he hurried down Seacoal to Fleet. The winter night had fallen. Dots of flame flickered. A link boy ran to him with his cone of pitch-soaked rushes burning brightly.

'To the wherries,' said Will. With strong memories of his last time in a boat, he would greatly prefer to walk. But he could not risk being recognized crossing London Bridge.

The boy lighted the way down to the Thames and demanded a half-penny – double the usual price. Will gave him a full penny from Southampton's purse for good luck. Wherry boats splashed to the landing, oarsmen shouting 'Westward Ho!' or 'Eastward Ho.'

'West!' said Will.

He stepped aboard a fast one-man sculler. The wherry man reeked of spirits and Will had a sudden, unexpected, and very hopeful thought. *Let your Lord Southampton save you now*, the swine-drunk wherry men had taunted him, because they'd been paid by Essex minions to cast the blame on Southampton.

The sculler rowed him to a dark patch of Bankside. From there, it was a short walk to the tavern that supplied the noonday dinners for the players at the Globe.

TWENTY-EIGHT

'**F**etch me a gray beard,' Will told Marc Handler. 'But not a long hermit beard. I wish to disappear, not stand out.'

'Cony skin or fox fur, master?'

'Use your judgement.'

Like the best of the boy actors, his apprentice was skilled at disguises. Marc not only played women, but could also pass, costumed and bearded, as a grown man to fill a part for a missing male actor. Will had surprised him in the arms of a new admirer – the tavern-keep's wife. She was, happily, not a woman to be made pregnant by folly. The boy was still catching his breath.

'I need a wig to cover my brow and a bonnet with a broad brim to shadow my eyes. Also, a dark cloak. Rich enough to make a cutthroat worry I've got a rapier under it.'

'May I suggest, master?'

'Surely.'

'Your eyes are not soon forgotten. Perhaps some kohl to black your lashes. Darken the fire?'

'Make it so.'

Marc scampered off and Will thought, I've spent more time and spoken more words with this orphan than my own Hamnet. How sad to regret; what joy to feel blessed.

Three hours later Will Shakespeare turned off Fleet Street into a narrow close, passed a rank midden and a ranker jakes, and knocked on the scullery door of a Thames-side mansion. A groom stepped out with a light and inquired firmly but politely, which spoke well for his costume, 'Have you business here, sir?'

'I would resume a conversation with Coxswain Mapes. Will I find him in the scullery?'

'Very likely, sir.' The groom's smile said that the mariner's interest in the kitchen maid was known to the house. 'I'll walk you to the door.'

Unlike Marc Handler, Mapes did not have to be pried loose

from his young lady, at least at this moment. The scar-faced coxswain and the plump maid were hunched over cups of tea in the back of the big kitchen, gazing into each other's eyes. Mapes rose to his full height to confront a stranger. 'May I help you, squire?'

'A private matter.'

Will let his cloak fall open to show he had no sword and hanger. Mapes looked him over, slowly. Finally, he said, 'This gentleman and I would have a cup of wine. Could you bring it, please?'

When she had brought the wine and left them alone, Mapes said, 'It seems that talk of your drowning is but a rumor. And yet you go disguised. Did the river make a near run of it?'

'I'd not have had it any nearer.'

'Sit down, Master Shakespeare, you had me well fooled. And only face to face. I'd not notice across a room or in the street.'

'I'm relieved to hear that, Jim. I'm caught up in doings I don't fully understand. I have some questions for you and hope you can answer them.'

'As I can, and my duty allows.'

'Where does Sir Walter Raleigh stand with the Earl of Essex?'

'At a cable length.'

'Why so distant?' There'd been no cable length distance when Essex's troop arrived at Southampton House. They were not riding by side – Essex led alone – but Raleigh was in the thick of the earl's entourage.

'Captain Raleigh knows that the government is watching for the possibility of an Essex conspiracy.'

It sounded like Raleigh could be spying for the government. 'Conspiring to do what?'

'You would know more about that than I, sir.'

Will shrugged his shoulders. 'With succession in doubt, what could it be but to usurp the throne?'

Mapes said, 'Again, sir, you would know more about that than I.'

'I wish that were so.'

Mapes lowered his voice to say, 'You should also know that the government suspects your patron is part of it.'

'Does your captain believe that of my Lord Southampton?'

'Sir Walter does not know what to believe. But he wonders will the government manufacture a conspiracy if they can't find one.'

Which could describe neatly – but from a twisted angle – Will Shakespeare's theory that Cecil had planted *The Sister Queens* in the Bacons' minds. Would the government inspire Essex supporters to rebel and give courage to Essex himself, or even put the scheme in Essex's mind in order to arrest, prosecute, and behead him?

'You say "government," Jim, but isn't Secretary of State Cecil part and parcel of the government – if not the entire amount of it?'

'You are asking a simple mariner to guess about matters above his ken.'

Will laughed. 'If you are a simple mariner, I am a poet of dumb shows. Do you serve Secretary Cecil?'

'I serve Sir Walter Raleigh. Sir Robert and Sir Walter are friends of many years.'

'That night at Paul's, how did you happen to appear at such a sudden?'

'It was not at such a sudden. Sir Robert was keen to take your measure. I had my orders to stand my watch upon you. Sir Robert liked what I saw.'

'What did Cecil like?'

'He liked how you went right to it. Any otherwise, you'd never have met him.'

Mapes' concise answers indicated to Will that the tall mariner was not hiding in his usual sea of words. He was confirming that the events of that night were staged, just as Will had told Ben in the stable of this very house. But truth was missing. Will said, 'You saved my neck. You led me and carried Ben Jonson directly here. At no point could you have sent Cecil a message. Yet Cecil arrived soon after.'

'Sir Robert's spies who were watching *me* watch *you* reported the news from Paul's.'

Staged, as Will had guessed. 'So it was no accident that you were the new stage-keeper at the Globe?'

'Surely not. When Sir Walter heard a whisper of Anthony Bacon's "play plot" to force you to write a play favoring Essex, Sir Walter told Sir Robert.'

'*Hold!* What whisper? Such a plot demands strict secrecy. How did Sir Walter hear a whisper that a master of spies did not? Or is he also an intelligencer?'

Mapes shook his head emphatically. 'Sir Walter Raleigh does not possess the double face required of beagles. No, he overheard by accident – in a jakes at court. When he told Sir Robert, Sir Robert claimed he already knew of it.'

'Claimed?'

'I know only that Sir Robert asked my captain for a trusty mariner. Sir Walter gave me leave.'

Will gave Mapes a smile. 'So Sir Robert weaves webs like a spider?'

Mapes returned a lion's grin. 'Quicker. Taller. Wider. Deeper.'

'Do you recall I was looking for a seal-cracker?'

'Surely.'

'The seal-cracker told me that back in the time of the Babington conspiracy, a spy named Gifford recruited Sir Walter Raleigh's followers to assassinate the Queen.'

The mariner rose to his feet, shoulders broadening, eyes and mouth narrowing, a man primed to give his life to defend Sir Walter Raleigh or take another's. 'What would you have of my captain, Master Shakespeare?'

Will returned a hard stare of his own. 'I would have you make it possible for me to talk in secret with Sir Walter.'

'Why?'

'That he would present me to his cousin Ferdinando Gorges.'

Mapes looked surprised. 'You want to be presented?' Drained of suspicion, he uncoiled and sat back down, transformed from a big-boned, dangerous man to an amiable fellow. 'Why not ask Cecil?'

'If it came from Cecil, Gorges would be of no use. Besides, I must speak with your captain first.'

Now Coxswain Mapes embarked on a sea of words. 'Master Shakespeare, I am a simple mariner, not one to tell you your business, and I love my master Raleigh. I know little of what your business is. But if you seek my captain's support in your projects, whatever they may be, you should be aware that when time moves on, the tide turns.'

'What is that supposed to mean?'

'It saddens me to tell you that Sir Walter is not the man at court he used to be.'

'He is a Member of Parliament.'

'No Member draws the admiration paid a successful sea captain.'

'He's been made Governor of Jersey.'

'The island of Jersey, Master Shakespeare, is a long sail from London. But I will do what I can for you.'

'Without Secretary Cecil's knowledge, please.'

Mapes clearly did not like that. He said, 'But Cecil is your champion.'

'Surely Cecil is my champion. You yourself "presented" me to Cecil in this very kitchen.'

'There you are, then, sir. Cecil's your champion.'

'But not in this tilt.'

Mapes asked, 'Why not in this tilt?'

'Because I don't know whether Cecil is Sir Ferdinando's champion.'

'Cecil is friends of both Sir Walter Raleigh and Sir Ferdinando Gorges.'

Will asked, 'Who did Cecil ask to install a new stage-keeper at the Globe to stand watch upon me? Raleigh or Gorges?'

'My Captain Raleigh.'

Will stood up and slung his cloak over his shoulders. 'There you have it, Jim.'

Mapes ducked his head. 'I will do what I can for you, Master Shakespeare.'

Will was not sure he believed him, but there was nothing more to say. He pulled his bonnet brim over his eyes and found another link boy on Fleet Street to lead him near, but not too near, Seacoal Lane.

TWENTY-NINE

'Pray tell me,' shouted Ben Jonson, bursting through Isobel's door, 'that you are not burning another play!' He hurled himself at her hearth. Will moved quickly to stop him. Ben tossed him across the room as a bear would throw a dog and grabbed the water pitcher. Only a quarter full, it scattered wet ash but did not quench the flames.

'Why? Why? Why?'

Will picked himself up off Isobel's bed. 'It's the best play I've yet written. But it's too disruptive, too provocative. Cecil's smooth succession from an aging Elizabeth to a vigorous young James far more legitimate than Essex depends on making James's mother as heroic as Elizabeth. But if Mary Queen of Scots is as heroic, Elizabeth's heroism is tainted when she beheads her, which will inflame Mary's followers for centuries.'

Ben scoffed. 'It's just a play.'

'Three thousand people do not listen rapt in contemplation to "just a play," and rush back to the city to shout in the ears of ten thousand, gripping their hearers' wrists to tell the news they heard in "just a play." If I have learned anything these arsy-versy days since Val died at Tyburn, it's that a well-told story spoken by well-graced players is as real to the audience as their breath in their chests. Besides, you haven't read it. Believe me, it touches the heart, and it would mean slaughter. Fortunately, no one will hear it.'

Ben stared mournfully at the ashes. 'God's wounds, Will. What a waste.'

'I've started another. It won't be as good, but it will serve peace.'

'Tragedy? History?'

'You decide. I'll speak you my Prologue.'

Ben listened intently. A smile softened his scarred face. 'I mark your intent.'

'Would you hear the end lines?'

'You've written the last act before your first?'

'Just the last scene. Sometimes I like to know where I'm going.'

'Yes please, Master Playmaker, your final lines.'

Will spoke them. Ben laughed aloud.

'And here is my last stage direction.' Will hesitated for an instant, as if to be sure he remembered precisely, then spoke it.

'Wonderful,' Ben roared, and slapped his thigh. 'Wonderful . . . But –' He sobered abruptly. 'Your hopes rest in a Queen not always noted for her gentle-hearted nature.'

'The Queen likes a good laugh and Cecil wants me to destroy Essex.'

'The only soul in England who can destroy Essex,' Ben answered, somberly, 'is Queen Elizabeth Tudor.'

Will barely heard him. 'Cecil can . . . with my help.'

'Consider this very grim possibility – what will the Queen make of Sir Robert Cecil and Master William Shakespeare destroying her Earl of Essex?'

Will flashed forth a smile he did not entirely feel. 'I would hope she expresses gratitude for securing her throne and saving England from civil war by elevating Cecil to an earldom and dubbing me a knight – a true Queen's knight.'

Ben did not smile.

'Rub that sad scowl from your face, Ben! I'm praying for a Queen who loves a jest.'

'Ask yourself will she love your unauthorized destruction of a former favorite for whom she still harbors a fondness.'

'No monarch remains fond of a usurper. No monarch loves a rebel.'

'She is no ordinary monarch and never a woman to provoke. She is her father's daughter, only fiercer than old King Harry at his worst. She has reigned forty years following her own star. If your and Sir Robert's "star" does not please her, you will find yourselves not ennobled, but diminished. Painfully. Or have you forgotten how she "thanked" John Stubbs when he tried to "secure her throne" from France and "save England" from the Catholics?'

Will answered soberly, 'I have not forgotten Stubbs. Who could?'

The Puritan fanatic John Stubbs wrote a pamphlet protesting mightily against Queen Elizabeth's courtship by brother of the King of France, the Catholic Francis Duke of Alençon and Anjou. Stubbs unwisely compared the wooing, which Her Majesty had encouraged with warm hopes, to 'an uneven yoking of the clean ox to the unclean ass', and declared her too old to bear children. Convicted of seditious writing, Stubbs had the hand that penned the pamphlet hacked from his wrist with a cleaver.

Will said, 'She is all the things you say, but still a woman who likes to laugh.'

Ben said, 'Holinshed did not record whether she laughed that day. All we know for sure is that Stubbs did not.'

Will went out of Isobel's starting hole disguised, again, and walked to the Cross Keys in search of Stefano Fogliaverde. The rapier man was not at the Keys. Will looked in the Boar's Head and the Queen's Hart, and finally saw the Italian at the Mermaid on Bread Street, peering in its arched front window as if about to enter. Will stepped into the dim glow of the light that flickered beside the door and asked, 'A word, sir?'

Fogliaverde took in Will's bearded countenance, brimmed bonnet, and cloak in a glance. '"What news on the Rialto?"' he asked with a hint of a smile. '"Who is he comes here?"'

Will shook his head, chagrined and dismayed. 'Burbage told me you liked his Shylock.'

'I liked your play. And I believe your disguise would fool most. May I suggest you go in first. I will follow shortly, bump against you, spilling your wine, apologize by standing you a cup, and we will converse as strangers becoming hail-fellows well-met.'

Will said, 'Master Greenleaf, you put me in remembrance of being told to wait in the street and leave the swordplay to you.'

'Our best actions fit the moment.'

Will went into the crowded taproom.

Despite Fogliaverde's protestation on their first meeting that he had no talent for the stage, he played his part as if he believed it. Progressing from bump to apology to a call for cups, they found stools at a small table. Fogliaverde said, 'I did not believe the rumors, but to remain on the secure side of the bush, I prayed you remembered how to swim.'

'I thank you for your prayers. Now, may I ask you? You spoke of go-betweens and thieves as if such men inhabit your natural sphere.'

'They orbit on occasion.'

Will asked, 'If I had to suddenly leave England for France or Italy with a recusant fleeing priest hunters, could you direct me to someone who could arrange passage?'

Fogliaverde said, 'Yes, I have known many such. Some still alive.'

'Thank you, Stefano. You've taken some weight off my mind.'

'If you have such a need, it will be my pleasure to try. But I must warn conditions in this moment are not the best. The government and its officers are up in arms.'

'Yes, I've been told that.'

'It doesn't mean one cannot prevail, but it would not be easy. Now, I am sorry to report that I have made no progress discovering who set those rapier and dagger men on you.'

'I'm not as concerned as I was. I've come to believe they confessed to you truly that they were ordered to frighten me, not kill me.' Will touched his wine to his lips, touched again, and drank deeply.

'Do you know if Sir Walter Raleigh is with Essex?' he asked Stefano.

'All I know is Raleigh is a man of sudden enthusiasms. He could be for or against with equal passion.'

'How about Ferdinando Gorges?'

'Gorges is a man who knows everyone. Though his chief interest seems to lie in the New World. The section called Maine.'

'Do you know Anthony Bacon?'

'I know his reputation. Wise in the ways of Europe. He's served the Earl of Essex since Walsingham died. He is another who knows everyone. But whereas Sir Ferdinando Gorges knows everyone good, relatively speaking, Anthony Bacon knows everyone one should *not* know if one has an honest heart and a relatively unblemished soul.'

'Stefano? Are you going to explain your interest in me?'

'Not until the day I am able. Please let me hasten to explain that my interest is benign, as it has always been, in your continued long life as a fine maker of plays. I had no idea of what had swept you up. May I offer advice?'

'Surely.'

'Trust those armed gentlemen protecting you. Don't go about London without them.'

'But what if their master turns on me?'

'Cecil?'

'You know so much about me.'

'A simple guess, Master Shakespeare, based on the knowledge in my circles that Secretary Cecil employs only the best armed guards, who also happen to be as short of stature as he.'

'Very good guess.' Will smiled back.

'I will also venture this, my dear Master Shakespeare. If, God forbid, Sir Robert Cecil does turn on you, whether you are in company with those armed gentlemen or not, will make no difference to your outcome.'

'I hesitate to ask you another kindness, but—'

'Ask!'

'There is a fellow I think of as "the shabby gallant" by his costume – once-gorgeous garb worn poor. He approached me first at the Keys. He insinuated he knew about the play they want me to write. More recently he pressed a letter packet in my hand. A letter from Essex to Southampton – almost surely a forgery, but maybe not – in which he directs Southampton to "surprise the court."'

'Describe him for me.'

'He is tall, he is thin, he is obsequious, then suddenly not.'

'His age?'

'Less than thirty. And he wears a young man's colored-glass gems in a tall cap. You know, he could be someone's messenger, passing secret letters.'

'Perhaps he got your Essex letter from Essex himself. I will beagle about and see what I hear,' said Fogliaverde.

Will rose from his stool and shook the Italian's hand – the picture of one new friend saying good-night to another. 'I must ask you not to follow me now.'

'I am obliged to protect you.'

'To whom are you obliged?'

'Myself.'

'But I am obliged too. I have promised that I would not reveal our starting hole. I cannot let you see me go into it.'

Fogliaverde's face hardened. 'I had hoped by now you would trust me.'

'My friend, I do trust you. But I gave my promise to someone who trusts me, too.'

The Italian bowed his head. 'Then I will vow my word that I will not follow you as you leave. May I at least walk you out the door?'

'Certainly.'

Outside on Bread Street, beside the flickering door light, Fogliaverde said, 'You leave me disappointed that I cannot help you.'

'But you can.'

'Name it.'

'I must gain an audience with the Earl of Essex. I have no one who can present me, other than Southampton, and I cannot have him involved. I am trying to gain a presentation through Sir Walter Raleigh and Ferdinando Gorges, but I doubt it will happen. Would you be acquainted with any high-born personage – perhaps a student of the rapier with whom you have grown friendly – who you could ask to present me to the Earl of Essex?'

'Can you tell me what it is you want to say to the earl?'

Will heard his quiet voice counsel, Time is flying. This man, whoever he is, seems truly your friend and a man of honor. Ben Jonson had repeated the common slur that Italians were not to be trusted for serving all princes at once, but from their first encounter, Will had seen 'Greenleaf' as a man he admired. 'Yes, I can,' he answered. 'I am inclined to believe – and certainly hope – that the letter from Essex to Southampton is a forgery. I must see how Essex reacts when I ask him about it.'

'To what purpose?'

'To decide whether or not the rebellion he is using me to incite is mere talk or treason.' Will was surprised when Fogliaverde smiled. But it was not a smile of amusement, rather of delight in being trusted.

'I thank you for confiding in me. Know that nothing you have said to me will be heard further than this doorstep. What will you do if it is not mere talk?'

'If treason, I will attempt to separate him from his conspirators.'

'How?'

'Plant in him seeds of discord.'

'But how?'

'Provoke him into a fury. Make him lose all reason. Bare him open like a fresh-plowed field.'

'Provoke. Yes. But how?'

Will was reminded of arguing with a Jesuit who raised the questions that demanded clarity. 'By thwarting him,' he said. 'I have learned not so much how Essex thinks, but how he feels. He is crippled by self-love, blind to the prospect of failure, until he sees it in the face, and enraged by defeat.'

'Disappointment could have the same effect,' said Fogliaverde. 'I have noticed that nobles hold in common a sort of hierarchical assumption that they are never wrong. That can lead to disappointment. Which nobles find as noisome as defeat. But in either instance, you run the risk of *murderous* fury.'

'I will bear that in mind. Meantime, while hoping to find my way inside Essex House, I have to redouble my efforts to finish a play that will *not* incite a rebellion.'

'May I suggest a simpler method to place yourself inside Essex House immediately?'

'How?'

'To enter Essex House, Master William Shakespeare need only knock on the front door.'

Will envisioned beating his bare fist on a monumental slab of oak studded with iron bolt-heads. Next he envisioned Sir John Falstaff sucking his bloody knuckles. But the vision was less comic than frightful.

'I doubt a peer of the realm allows commoners in his front door.'

'From what I have heard, the Earl of Essex is the sort of hero who would fancy himself portrayed by a popular playmaker.'

Will shook his head.

Fogliaverde said, 'You are not unknown in London, young poet. You are a prince of the theater.'

Will thought it unlikely that a noble plotting to usurp a monarch would be dazzled by any prince, much less one of the theater. And the risks of going alone into Essex House were enormous.

'Nor have you never conversed with a noble. Your patron for one. His mother the countess for another.'

Will fell silent. Fogliaverde waited. Finally, he asked casually – though clearly to put him at ease – 'Is the countess as beautiful as people say?'

'Her carriage and countenance mirror her wit, her courage, and her soul.'

'Every moment in her presence,' the older man said, drily, 'must be a pleasure.'

'A joy,' said Will, mourning those moments ended.

'So all you must do is keep Lady Southampton in your mind while you speak with Lord Essex. Your voice is louder than you think.'

Will was startled. 'I was told that recently.'

'Told what?'

'That my voice is louder than I think.'

'By the countess?'

'No.'

Fogliaverde took his arm firmly. 'May I ask by whom?'

'A ghost.'

The Italian neither laughed nor recoiled but tightened his grasp. 'Whose?'

'An executed priest's.'

Will felt the strong hand slip from his arm.

Fogliaverde stepped back, suddenly unsteady, and whispered, 'None other.'

Will guessed that were the door light brighter his face would look pale. 'Are you not well, Stefano?'

'I should have been at Tyburn.'

'You knew Val?'

'Long, long ago.'

'How?'

'Good-night young poet. I cannot meet your face in this moment.'

'But why? Tell me how you knew him?'

'I should have been with Father Val. But I didn't have the courage.'

The Italian glided toward the dark.

'Courage?' Will called after him. 'Then please understand that *I* don't have the courage to knock on that door. Not without a personage like Raleigh or Gorges whose presence would protect me – allow me to get out safely.'

Fogliaverde stopped and returned to Will's side. 'A prince can't wait for safety. A prince must decide. A prince must act.'

'If I were a prince, I might forget that Dr Lopez – Queen Elizabeth's own physician-in-chief – was dragged through that door, and that when Essex was done interrogating him, the government hanged him.'

'A prince can always summon up a reason not to act. But a prince who *won't* act is caught betwixt and between.'

THIRTY

'If upon opening Essex's front door,' Ben Jonson warned with no hint of a jest, 'they snatch you inside like a fat goose strutting outside the kitchen, neither your armed gentlemen nor I can save you before they slam the door shut.'

But Coxswain Mapes had reported no progress with Sir Walter Raleigh, and Will was on his own and out of time. Trailed at a short distance by a puzzled Anthonie Kingston and Cyrus Carew, and further back by Ben, he trudged beyond London Wall and through the rain pelting Fleet Street toward the Strand, rehearsing the line he would speak when he knocked. 'Tell the Earl of Essex that Master William Shakespeare is here to discuss *The Sister Queens.*'

'Is here to discuss' was hideously awkward on the tongue. 'Has come to' would be some improvement. But with nerves growing infirm, this was no time to new-write. At the door, he'd end up mumbling, 'has come here.'

Essex House sprawled adjacent to the Middle Temple, so enormous that it blocked any view of the distant Thames, which its gardens bordered. It appeared recently built, and even more recently fortified with iron shutters on the lower windows. 'We would need a cannon to get you out of there,' Ben had added. 'As we neglected to bring one, you would be wise to reconsider.'

The front door of oak wood Will had imagined had been armored in steel. The hammer dents looked fresh. He pulled from his purse a half-brick he had pried from Isobel's hearth. Brick struck steel like a funeral bell trolling a dirge-mass. If it *was* Essex who tried to kill him, he was making it easier for him this time.

He heard, inside, bars being lifted from their barricade brackets. The door swung inward. The weight of the armor made the hinges groan. Immense house grooms gripping halberds peered down at him.

'Tell the Earl of Essex that Master William Shakespeare is here to discuss *The Sister Queens.*'

The hinges groaned. The door thundered shut.

Will waited in the rain, unable to predict what would happen next.

Quite suddenly the door opened again. The halberd men stood aside. A rapier and dagger man dressed in noble livery gestured for Will to follow. Wondering if he would ever see the sky again, he was led into a vast mansion that felt like a soldiers' camp. Room after room was crowded with gentlemen in arms or rugged mercenaries. These were not the boisterous gallants awaiting dinner at Southampton House. They were solemn troops girding for battle. Hearing a preacher drone, Will glanced into a large chapel. The Reverend Charles Mills, the priest he had heard sermonizing, 'Death to Papists that taketh away the life of the soul!' at the open-air Paul's pulpit, was now beseeching God to 'Bless the mighty Earl of Essex and all who endeavor with him.' Fifty armed men prayed at his feet.

Being new-built, the rooms were larger than Southampton's, all but the Great Hall. The grooms closed its doors behind him. Will found himself alone in a banqueting chamber of a size more suited to a city house yet would still seat one hundred. It had elaborate inlaid wood floors instead of stone, decorated plaster walls, and a painted ceiling, only half-finished, that depicted angels and cherubs flocking toward an empty space. The absence of scaffolds and the scent of oil suggested that the painters had stopped work abruptly when their employer lost his sweet wine monopoly and ran out of money.

A door on the far side flew open.

'Broached on my sword!'

Robert Devereux, 2nd Earl of Essex, swept in with an exuberant bellow. He halved the distance between them in long, elegant strides and greeted Will with a dazzling smile. 'My soldiers love your words, Master Shakespeare. As they love my deeds. I am told that you are writing a new play. What is it called? *Sister?*'

Will doffed his bonnet and bowed. *Truly the first you've heard of it?*

'It is called *The Sister Queens,* Lord Essex.'

'Something like that. What's it about?'

'Monarchs old and new, my lord. And their minions who betray them.'

'When will we hear it?'

'Within the week, I pray, though my muse has been quarrelsome of late, fickle, and perverse.'

The nobleman surprised Will with an infectious laugh, an engaging rustle that seduced the ear. *Does he even remember trying to drown me in a fit of lashing out?* 'You make it sound as if poets grapple with life itself.'

'Well, yes, my lord. I suppose we have no choice. But the muse tells me that there are important matters I still must learn before I finish writing.'

'Matters? What matters? How do you mean that?'

'As you said, your lordship, poets, like everyone, must grapple with life. Only far less consequentially surely, than men who embrace great affairs. For the affairs of kingdoms turn on deeds, not mere words.'

'Surely,' said Essex, 'men who are remembered will be those who led not followed. And when all is said and done, what's done will be remembered more than what was said.'

Unsure what that meant, Will said, 'Exactly, your lordship. Your thoughts are the sort my muse insists I be informed of before I finish the play. May I ask—'

'Hold!' A change of mood was flashing on the rim of high dudgeon, and Will could only guess, what next?

'Yes, my lord?'

'What is this talk that keeps coming to our ears that you drowned while shooting London Bridge at the tide turn?'

'I am not aware, my lord, of having drowned.'

Will waited for the Earl of Essex to smile. Instead, a flush gathered in his face. 'Well?'

'I am not aware of shooting the bridge, my lord. I *did* almost drown. True, I remember little of what happened before I came to my senses on a ship whose mariners had pulled me from the river. But I certainly do not remember shooting the bridge and I would think I would if I had. I do recall a wherry to Greenwich Palace.'

'Who were you seeing at Greenwich Palace?'

'I thought I had been summoned by my Lord Southampton. Now I know the summons letter was a forgery.'

'Forgery? Clearly, you are confused. Go on, ask your questions.'

'Thank you, my lord. Were I writing a play about a new English monarch, what do you suppose would be the first deed he would perform?'

Essex answered promptly. 'He will lay his subjects' hearts at rest that there will be peace and prosperity in our island. And mastery overseas.'

'How would such a monarch achieve— Excuse me, lordship, by your leave may I write down your thoughts that I may ponder them later, more deeply than in the moment?' Will tugged a table-book out of his doublet, opened it, scratched gesso with pin. 'I dare not rely on memory in the excitement of the moment, your lordship . . . You were informing me how the new monarch would achieve peace and prosperity.'

'As the people say, "The new broom sweeps clean."' An inviting smile coaxed Will to smile with him and Will saw a difference between Essex and Southampton. Their elegant bearing was similar. So was their assumption of command. But where Southampton dealt in studied irony, affecting careless indifference, Essex was plainspoken. Southampton spoke for effect. Essex spoke forth-rightly. Southampton's fellow officers and brother nobility enjoyed his company. So would Essex's. But his foot-soldiers might cherish him, too.

'New broom,' said Will, writing quickly. He poised his pen and looked up expectantly.

Essex said, 'I would start by sweeping the court.'

'The court, my lord?'

'The court is a sinkhole of corruption.'

Will widened his eyes. 'The Queen's court?'

Essex gestured sternly at Will's table-book. 'Mark well, I love my Queen. It is her corrupt counsellors I abhor. Their depravity. Their ceaseless conspiracies. I heard such in one of your plays. The words you put in the mouth of Queen Margaret – which of the plays?'

'*Henry VI Part 3.*'

'Do you remember Margaret's plight?' asked Essex.

Am I to recite? wondered Will. But Essex did it for him:

> '"Our people and our peers are both misled,
> Our treasures seized, our soldiers put to flight,
> And, as thou seest, ourselves in heavy plight."'

Will nodded in spite of himself. Essex's recitation was letter-perfect. Unlike chief-clerk-and-master-spy Cecil cropping twenty-seven lines to six, Essex the soldier let every word live. Now he revisited them, embellishing dramatically.

'*Misled?* Then as now!' He began pacing his hall. A lion? thought Will. No. This man was no animal caged in the Tower, but the long-legged stallion, born beneath an open sky. Or, asked his quiet voice, an ambitious actor who pranced the stage like a stallion to command attention?

'Her Majesty misled. Her nobles misled. Her common subjects misled. All misled by corrupt counsellors – I mean Secretary Robert Cecil.

'I lament and I grieve how they proclaim that none in the world but the infanta of Spain has a right to the crown of England. From *Spain*, Master Shakespeare! Could any Englishman alive stomach the torturers of the Catholic Inquisition reigning from Whitehall Palace? Could any deny a proven law of nature – our beloved Queen being the one exception, never to be repeated – *that women are not fit to rule*?'

'Women are not fit to rule,' Will repeated, and wrote diligently.

'*Treasures seized?* My sweet wine monopoly – my treasure granted me by the Queen for my loyal service – snatched back when Cecil tricked her, turned her against me. Against me, Her Majesty's most loyal warrior.'

No wonder he remembers the words, thought Will. Three lines only and he nurses them daily. Something tells me he never heard the play, but was read these lines by Southampton.

Essex paced faster. '*Our soldiers put to flight?* Cecil starved our soldiers in Ireland, drove them naked into battle. Cecil saw to that business. Cecil and his courtiers conspired to turn Parliament against my army. *Heavy plight?* Good Christ! Brave English soldiers deserve so much better.'

He stopped, suddenly, and addressed Will in a whisper as commanding as any Dick Burbage projected from the stage. 'England cries for better. But Cecil's conspirators hold a grip on the Queen so tight that even when she was young – which, let me be honest, she no longer is – but even if she were still young, even then she could not break free. Thank God that when conspirators flourish ugly deeds, it is the ordained duty of the Queen's nobles to defend her. She needs our protection. Without me, she will die as Cecil's puppet.'

He flushed scarlet.

Will saw a chance to establish whether the letter to Southampton was forged or authentic. 'I have heard it rumored in the street that you would instruct your supporters to "surprise" the court.'

But Essex recovered his poise in an instant and with it an acerbity that would do Countess Southampton proud. 'I do not inhabit "the street," I have not heard this rumor.'

'But your lordship, all say that you are rightfully proud of possessing the "common touch."'

Essex threw back his head and proclaimed, 'My common touch does not embrace common gossip.'

Will loosed a hearty burst of laughter. 'Well said, my lord.'

Essex was watching him intently, and Will warned himself that despite the countess's judgement, Essex was not entirely stupid.

'What else do you hear in the street, Master Shakespeare?'

'The news is outlandish. A report goes that your army is sailing from Ireland.'

'If such were happening,' Essex replied smoothly, 'I would be the last to know. It is Mountjoy's army now, not mine.'

'Is it possible, my lord, that Lord Mountjoy might bring it home to you?'

Essex's demeanor changed. He grew somber and deliberate, like a war-seasoned general of the army informing a green lieutenant. 'A winter crossing of the Irish Sea is never to be undertaken lightly in ships laden with troops. Even if it were achieved without suffering undue losses, the army would still face a long, cold, hungry march to London, since the ports of Plymouth and Southampton would not let them land if Cecil's government forbade it. Nor would Dover, Portsmouth, and certainly not the port of London. Perhaps a secret landing could be achieved at Poole or Newhaven, if it be well-handled.'

Will had the eeriest sense that Essex had just admitted that he was trying to find a port to convey ashore his Irish army. The phrase 'if it be well-handled' was chillingly familiar.

'Forgive me, my lord, I have heard of a letter in your hand,

surely a forgery, that you wrote to my lord the Earl of Southampton
instructing him to amass a force of soldiers to surprise the court.'

Essex shrugged like a man growing bored and continued pacing,
wall to wall in long, fluid strides. 'That sounds like the same gossip
you just rumored. I asked had you heard any different.'

'They say that King James is leading an army from the north.'

'The Scotch King lost his nerve. If he ever had it.'

Will called on all his stage-magic to hide his astonishment. Had
the Earl of Essex confessed that he had expected Scotland's intervention? It did not seem possible that he would admit to a stranger's
face that he had conspired in secret with the King of Scotland.
'Your lordship, do you imply—'

Up snapped the earl's powerful hand to parry Will's thrust.
'Never imply. Tell "the street" that the Scotch King waits for evil
counsellors like Cecil to *invite* him to England.'

Will glanced up from scribbling in his table-book. Essex was
about to turn around and walk away unless his attention was riveted
by something new. 'May I ask, my lord, did you hear that in the
time of the Babington conspiracy, a spy named Gifford recruited
Sir Walter Raleigh's followers to assassinate the Queen?'

Another shrug. 'Raleigh ran with atheists. I would believe
anything of his followers.'

'Would Sir Walter himself have known of the plot?'

'Assassinating the Queen is not his way. By all accounts, Raleigh
was in love with her. At least before he married Bess. Besides,
one does not assassinate his queen just because she jilts you.'
Essex flashed a smile that could light a coal hole on a dead night.
'Am I not living proof of that?'

The intimate jest caught Will far off guard, and he could only
smile back while he scrambled for another approach to the letter.

But Essex destroyed that hope with an unmistakable end to their
conversation. 'One last matter. To inform your informers in the
street. If I ever were to "surprise the court," I would do it solely
to plant men there to prevent hindrance by my enemies who would
stop my passage to the Queen. All I wish is to prostrate myself
at her feet and submit to Her Majesty's mercy. As is my duty to
my Queen.'

Typical of the common actor who played for himself instead
of the audience, Essex had thundered onto the stage, delivered less

than promised, and now was staying a deadly moment too long. His voice took on a funereal tone. 'As is my noble duty to my beloved Queen, my dear friend, whom I have loved and worshiped and obeyed all my life since I was a boy.'

And here, thought Will, comes the bluster.

Essex marched straight at him and glared down at his face. 'Have I answered your question, Master Playmaker?'

'You have indeed, my lord. Thank you.'

'Have I satisfied your muse?'

'I am certain, my lord, that she lays prostrate at my quill.'

Essex did not smile. 'What does she sing to you?'

Will was startled to hear his own voice speak words that until now had dodged him like a tardy debtor. They were true for *The Sister Queens* and even truer for *Hamlet*. 'The muse sings of purposes mistook that fall on their inventors' heads. She tells me that what's truly broken cannot be repaired by any of the court. The election will light on a new broom.'

'When will you be done with it?'

The brave prince, Will thought, *has just been handed his last chance to provoke Essex to explode in a murderous red-faced fury.* He said, 'The first attempts did not go to my liking. The hero who would serve his nation as the new monarch seemed old-fashioned and too trusting of his minions. It was impossible to believe that such a ridiculous figure could be king.'

'Why do you call him ridiculous?' The earl's fine features glowed pink.

'The supposed hero who strove to become king failed to act when a minion proclaimed, "Every honest man ought forsake his friend rather than forsake his queen."'

Essex looked puzzled. 'What did the hero do to his minion?'

'Nothing! The supposed hero who claimed that he would replace the old monarch to serve the realm did absolutely *nothing* when he heard the scurrilous insult, "Every honest man will forsake his friend rather than forsake his queen."'

'I have heard that phrase before,' Essex said sharply, his flush deepening.

Will pretended not to hear him and raised his own voice indignantly. 'When betrayed, a true hero condemns his minion's disloyalty, then tosses the traitor on a pike. The supposed hero, the empty hero, failed to act. So I burned the sheets and set forth, immediately, on a true play about a true hero.'

'Who did you take those words from?' Essex asked.

'My lord, surely not "take" in the sense of stealing, forgive me my lord, but—'

The earl cut him off. 'Who did you take them from?' he demanded. '"Every honest man will forsake his friend rather than forsake his queen." I know them well!'

'I may have read them some—'

'I know them well!' Essex shouted in sudden red-faced fury. 'It goes in total, "Every honest man will forsake his queen rather than forsake God, and forsake his friend rather than forsake his queen." Answer me!' he yelled at Will. 'Who did you take those words from?'

Will hung his head in abject embarrassment. 'Actually, I may have heard them spoken at a lecture, sir.'

'*By whom?*'

'Queen's Counsel Francis Bacon, I believe, sir. If so, I would pray that Counsellor Bacon would take it as an admiring tribute were it to be heard in the play – which it won't. I burned the sheets.'

Breathing hard, Essex stood stiff and silent but for the heavy air storming in and out of his lungs. Then, gradually, his fury seemed to abate, to Will's great relief. The seeds were laid. But he still had to get out of the house alive.

'When will you be done?'

'Much sooner than I had hoped, my lord. Now that I know how these things came about. You may hear *The Sister Queens* at the Globe next Saturday.'

'Saturday?'

'All this I can truly deliver Saturday, but especially a new broom. Saturday at the Globe. Saturday for all who dare be inspired by a new broom.'

Essex's mood shifted like a flash of lightning. 'Burbage!' he exclaimed happily. 'Burbage will play the new king.'

'Burbage for certain,' Will lied.

'Burbage is manly.'

'Burbage worships that quality in you, my lord. In truth, he cherishes you as his model. Manly.'

'Off you go then!' Essex turned on his heel and strode away.

'Saturday for all who dare,' Will repeated, and hurried to a door pulled open by a groom waiting behind it. Head swimming, he followed more grooms through more doors and, finally, out the armored outside door. The rain had stopped and he found himself in the street, surprised to be blinking in sunlight.

THIRTY-ONE

'Did you provoke him?' Ben Jonson asked as he hurried across the Strand to join Will.

'I surely tried, but he slides everywhere at once, quick as quicksilver.'

'Will he come to the show?'

'I don't know. But I do know, now, the difference between Hamlet and Essex. Essex is ridiculous. So ridiculous that I still wonder whether he's the rebels' leader or their tool. Whereas Hamlet is hopeless. But Hamlet at least knows that he can't be king. Essex has no idea.'

'You brave Essex House to serve *The Sister Queens*. You come out spouting Hamlet.'

'I am spouting succession. Hamlet knows in his heart that he is not the prince who would be king. The damage his uncle inflicted by murdering his father outstrips Hamlet's capacity to repair it. Only a leader outside the madness can save Denmark. Thank God I left a Norwegian invader standing by.'

'What about *The Sister Queens*?'

'Exactly the same: what's irrevocably broken can't be repaired, whether a murdered monarch or an ancient monarch who's anointed no heir. With no orderly succession, only an outsider can build anew. Hamlet's anoints the Norwegian invader with his dying wish. Secretary Cecil invites his Scottish king.'

'What of King Essex?'

'King Essex would set England afire and sink her every ship at sea. Nonetheless, good news!' Will threw his arm around Ben's mighty shoulder. 'Thanks to Essex, it's a play, at last. It's got it all. It might even have a role for you – if Burbage doesn't want it – a part equal to your talents, a ridiculous, self-loving, greedy knight named Sir Chester Checks. Chet-Checks. Has a certain echo to it, doesn't it? But Essex House is packed with fighting men. I have to write like a demon to finish immediately.'

'While writing a whole new character?'

'Not entirely new. Chet-Checks has been lurking in my mind for a month.'

Ben nodded across the Strand where Anthonie and Cyrus were waiting. 'Those two are sure to report your visit.'

'I'm reporting first.'

'I've been to Essex House.'

'What for?' asked Robert Cecil.

'To speak with Essex.'

The vein Will had seen only once before began pulsing on Cecil's brow. Will reminded him, 'You did ask me to spy on all I encounter.'

'What did you learn?'

'Most I'm sure you already know or suspect. For one, King James is not coming to London until you invite him.'

Cecil nodded.

'Second, Essex does not believe that he can land the army from Ireland. Nor does Mountjoy, unless Mountjoy can somehow make a secret landing at Poole or Newhaven. Both of which, I imagine, you are watching.'

'Did he mention any other ports?'

'No, Sir Robert.'

'Continue.'

'He claims that he has no intention of "surprising" the court.'

'Do you believe him?'

'He has concocted a story that if he surprised the court he would only do it to get access to the Queen so he could tell her how much he loves her.'

'Who does he intend to tell this story to?'

'Himself.'

'Arrogance!'

'He suffers from a disabling trait – what I've heard called a hierarchal assumption of always being right.'

Cecil asked, 'Did your "visit" lend new insight to your notion of Essex the automatical tool of Anthony Bacon's conspirators?'

'You suggested that the conspirators keep the winding key out of Essex hands. In truth, he could not see the key if it were sticking out of his chest because he can't imagine the possibility. But Essex admitted, without realizing it, that it was he who ordered me drowned.'

'But Bacon told you Essex didn't. Not that his word means anything.'

'Bacon told me *he* didn't. By now he might suspect his dazzling automatical instrument. But I *know* Essex did because Essex is the only one who knows that the wherry men were paid to kill me by shooting the bridge at the height of the outgoing tide.'

Cecil raised an appreciative brow. 'You did not tell me that. You told no one? But he knew it?'

'He did, sir.'

'Why didn't he kill you today? He had you in his house.'

'Today his house is full of soldiers who are listening to priests sermonize that God will make him king. He can't imagine a lowly playmaker stopping him from surprising the court.'

'All the more reason for you to race back to the Bel Savage and finish my play.'

'*The Sister Queens* is not your play, sir.'

Will strode to Cecil's desk and stared down at him. Cecil glanced toward his door groom as if to summon help.

'I thought for quite some time it might be yours, but it never was.'

'Francis Bacon invented it.'

'Francis Bacon invented *nothing*. Neither the play, nor the plot to inspire rebellion. But you somehow wedged it into Francis Bacon's brain.'

'Now you say it's my play. Make up your mind.'

'It is not your play. Nor is the plot to inspire rebellion your idea, either.'

'You are full of yourself today, Master Shakespeare. Unusually so.'

'It has been an unusually full day.'

Will thought it interesting that Cecil did not ask him whose ideas the play and plot were. He still put Will in mind of a chess player relieved to be challenged by a move he had expected. Will had listened to his small voice that told him he ought to ponder why. And he had, at last, a loose possibility swirling in his mind. But for it, he could not conceive the motive.

'Your automatical theory makes him no less the threat.'

'Which is why,' said Will, 'I will finish my play tomorrow.'

THIRTY-TWO

[Exeunt SIR JOHN FALSTAFF pursued by –

Will scraped the bottom of his ink pot to complete his final stage direction. Pen to paper one last time. Then tuck this sheet into his playbook bag. Seven more words would end his third and last *The Sister Queens*.

He and Isobel already had a supper table set for a Done-At-Last-Thank-God-Almighty-Done-At-Last festival of poached oysters, a capon fricasy, and the best bottle of sack wine the inn had to offer, which menu the Bel Savage cook had proudly proclaimed 'Falstaffian.' He lifted his pen, glanced at what he had written, and thought for an instant he had lost his brains. Falstaff? He had meant to write 'Sir John Quiver-Spear,' the name he had settled on to free himself of Falstaff, and here was Falstaff jumping off the page at him.

To be Quiver-Spear or to be Falstaff? A line from Ben's *Cynthia's Revels* answered for him: 'Only I can take it for no good omen, to find mine honor so dejected.'

Sir John, I am not a man to turn my back on omens good or bad. Farewell, Quiver-Spear. Falstaff you would be. Falstaff you are. He reached for a fresh sheet to record the pact. His mind's eye filled with a strange and frightful vision. A long-legged stallion bunched its hooves and skidded to a sudden stop. Strange it was, and frightful, too, but he recognized it instantly.

The Earl of Essex had paced his banquet hall, sleek as a race horse. But now Will saw the menace he had failed to see in the instant *after* Essex blurted that the Scotch King had lost his nerve. He stopped pacing.

The long-legged stallion had smelled danger on the wind.

Will closed his eyes to recall the sequence of events. Essex confessed casually (impetuously?), that he had expected Scotland's intervention. He had admitted to secret discourse with the King of Scotland. Through intermediaries or letters by post-riders, the nobleman had attempted to suborn King James to march his armies on London. Conspiracy, to usurp the Queen. Death, the penalty.

Essex had smoothed it over by shifting the blame – the Scotch King was going to wait for evil counsellors like Cecil to *invite* him to England – and he was soon gliding about the floor again. But upon confessing seditious conspiracy, even the least empathetic earl in the realm could envision Will Shakespeare stretched on the Tower of London rack by a government interrogator like Topcliffe. *And tell us, too, what treason did you hear spoken in Essex House?*

Days too late, Will knew that he had underestimated Essex. Worse, he had let his own 'boiled-brains' drift to *Hamlet* in that crucial instant. So distracted, he had let himself be gulled into overlooking the deeper implications of the earl's foolish blunder. Full of himself? Cecil had mocked Will. To the brim! But why had Essex let him escape from the house with that confession in his ears? Because there was no escape. The Earl of Essex had Anthony Bacon to chastise upstart poets.

'What is that?' asked Isobel, ear cocked to the hall.

Will had heard it too. Thinking, *my God, what have I done?*, he opened the door just as the upstairs of the Bel Savage exploded in shouts and crashes. The battle in the long, dark, narrow hall looked like a staged vision from the past – older than jousts in ancient armor. Men encased in stiff cowhide jerkins stormed from the stairs, wielding short cudgels and old-fashioned bucklers. Anthonie and Cyrus and their lieutenants sprang from their doorways, only to be pushed back into their rooms before they could draw their rapiers. Cudgels and heavy round shields were weapons made to command the cramped space.

Anthony Bacon's burly footman and the veterans who had waylaid Will at Tyburn led the attack. Behind them surged the mercenaries he'd seen attending Bacon at the Southampton kitchens. Last up the stairs was white-haired Sir Richard Topcliffe, whose hunter-eye pierced the mad clamber in the hall and landed straight on Will.

'Surrender yourself, playmaker!' Topcliffe shouted. 'You can't escape.'

The footman broke from the tangle of fighting men and charged the length of the hall with murder in his eyes. Will slammed the door shut. Isobel slid a wooden bar in its bracket. Fists and clubs

pounded the door. Will lifted the other bar in place, thanking God
for Anthonie and Cyrus's barricade. But where was their man who
guarded the stair? Turned traitor by Bacon?

Isobel was frantic. 'I saw the priest hunter.' She threw herself
to the bed, reached under the mattress, and grabbed her pearl-
encrusted crucifix, still wrapped in Southampton's handkerchief.
'They'll torture me.'

The pounding bounced the door in its frame. It wouldn't hold
long. Will jumped to move the virginals from the starting hole.
Before he could touch it, the entire table fell over with a crash.
They had discovered the starting hole and were attacking from
below. He threw an arm around Isobel and backed away, trapped
between the door and the tunnel that had been their last hope.

THIRTY-THREE

The rug and floorboards flew. A steely shadow levered off the ladder into the room.

Will crushed Isobel to his chest and clamped a hand over her mouth. 'Be still. He's our friend.'

Stefano Fogliaverde swooped to his feet, drawing rapier and dagger in liquid motion, and gestured for Will and Isobel to jump down the ladder. 'Take your play. They can't kill you without it.'

Will grabbed the bag with his playbook. Isobel was already halfway down the ladder.

'How we can conceal the starting hole?'

'We can't. We'll take the ladders to slow them.'

The door split apart.

'Go!' said Fogliaverde.

As Will stepped into the hole, Bacon's footman shoved his hands through the smashed wood and knocked the bars out of their brackets. He hurtled into the room, unsheathing a dagger. The needle tip of Stefano Fogliaverde's rapier skidded off his leather jerkin. A second lightning thrust skewered the footman's eye, and he collapsed in front of the door. Another attacker charged in. The Italian cut him down and snapped over his shoulder, 'Go!,' then faced a third, who was aiming a flintlock pistol. He triggered it at Fogliaverde even as the Italian ran him through the neck.

There was a moment's delay for the flint spark to explode the gunpowder. Fogliaverde staggered backward, knees buckling. Will reached up to catch his legs and guided him down the ladder. He was shaking head to toe and Will had the awful feeling that the man was disappearing in his arms.

'You are hurt, my friend. Give me your rapier.'

'It is yours when it falls from my hand. Pull the ladder . . . Good! Now follow my candles. Isobel, can you lead us? Will, blow them out as we pass.'

Fogliaverde covered their retreat, backing across the Bel Savage cellar, down the lower ladders, through the deeper basements, and along the wet stone tunnel walls. In the dark gaps between the candles, Will could hear him gasping for breath. A clatter echoed behind them. Whether a pursuer fallen in the dark, or a dropped weapon, the sounds kept coming.

'Help me, Will,' Fogliaverde gasped.

Will felt along the wet stones, thinking to help him walk. Fogliaverde said, 'Lift this.'

It was a massive wood beam. Together they heaved one end up and propped it precariously on a wall stud the Italian had placed earlier for the purpose. 'Dead-fall,' he whispered. 'Quick, now!'

They caught up with Isobel who was waiting by a candle and forged on, with Fogliaverde fighting to stay on his feet. A scream behind them announced that the dead-fall had claimed a pursuer. Frightened shouts sounded as if the rest were following more cautiously. At last, they were through the tunnels and up the coal hole chute that led to the close.

They listened at the wooden door that opened on Seacoal Lane. 'There will be a hackney coach,' Fogliaverde whispered.

'Where do we go?'

'The driver is well-paid and honorable. He will take you wherever you feel safe to go.'

'What about you?'

'You will be safer without me.'

'I will not leave you like this.'

'I will be perfectly fine,' said the Italian. He flashed white teeth in a reassuring smile and fell at Will and Isobel's feet.

The dark lane off Threadneedle Street that led to Ben Jonson's House of Correction for the Poor and Idle was too narrow for the hackney coach. Will and Isobel propped the half-conscious Fogliaverde between them and struggled to Mrs Broad's door. Will knocked, hoping she was not the sort of landlady – of which there were many – who would not allow a Moor on her property.

'It's Will Shakespeare, Mrs Broad,' he whispered, when she called through a peep-hole, 'Who is that there?' She stepped out with a tallow light. 'Is Ben here?' Will asked.

Mrs Broad's quick eye fell on Fogliaverde sagging like a

drunkard and fixed onto Isobel. 'A Moor?' She stared for a long moment, then broke into a smile. 'Come inside, dear. Come in. You know, my late husband Clement was a Moor. Manned an oar on the Royal Barge. Old King Harry took a fancy to him. Made him bowman. Said the hearts of half his court were blacker than Clement's cheeks. What is your name, dear?'

'Isobel.'

'I am Mrs Broad. Come in the house, Isobel.' She got them inside, barred the door, and took a second look at Fogliaverde. 'This man's not drunk. He's hurt.'

Will asked, 'Can we stay in Ben's room? Just for the night. We'll be gone in the morning.'

'You'll never get him up the stairs in this condition.' She led them into a large room with a bed. 'No one's living here at the moment. Put him on the bed. Master Shakespeare, run up to Master Jonson's. Yes, yes, he's there, scribbling. Master Jonson should find you the right sort of doctor.'

Ben's right sort of doctor was a surgeon, a former comrade returned from the Irish war. When he was done pulling a pistol ball and splintered bone from Fogliaverde's shoulder, he said with field-of-battle bluntness, 'I've seen smaller holes in men tossed on a pike. And they were corpses.'

'But he is strong,' said Will. 'A certain force of nature works in him.'

'Certain he will need it,' said the surgeon.

Isobel sat beside him and held his hand. When he whispered something to her, she fetched his rapier and placed it beside him, guiding his fingers around the hilt.

Will asked Mrs Broad to hire the best woman she knew to nurse and feed him. 'Can Isobel stay with you?'

'I have already asked her. She said she's going away. Somewhere. She's terribly afraid, Master Shakespeare.'

A reminder to Will that their escape was a temporary respite. Isobel had served the purpose of spreading the stories about Mary Queen of Scots and was now a problematical witness to conspiracy – as Will would be too, the instant his play was heard. An hour earlier, finishing the play, he had felt such hope that the unasked-for trial was nearly over. Now the dying Italian clutched his rapier, and Isobel pressed her beloved crucifix to her chest.

'I need it close to my heart.'

She prayed aloud over the cross, and Will began to sense that she was trying to collect her spirit. Suddenly she opened her eyes and said to him, 'Queen Mary didn't give it to me. I stole it from her.'

'You're no thief. That would never have been your way, even when you were a child.'

'I stole it so that Queen Mary couldn't kill herself.'

'What do you mean?'

'It's the only starting hole she ever found. Good-bye, my friend.'

'Stop her!' cried Fogliaverde.

With a practiced twist of the cross, she peeled the diamond crust from the long base arm. It had been a sheath to conceal a gleaming dagger. And Will Shakespeare realized as he lunged and fell short, that she had always known she was Anthony Bacon's tool and so had planned her escape from torture. She gripped the cross bar in both hands to pull the blade into her heart. Will heard Fogliaverde gasp in pain. His rapier flickered its needle tip against the back of Isobel's hand.

'Do not!'

Her eyes glinted at the Italian. 'I'll do it another way.'

'You can,' gasped Fogliaverde, struggling to breathe. 'Or you might twice think so that Will won't blame himself for predicamenting you.'

She looked at Will. He said, 'I blundered with Essex. Because I did, Essex sent the priest hunters.'

'Why didn't he send the cripple?'

Fogliaverde whispered, 'So the priest hunters would be blamed if something went wrong for them. Not the cripple.'

Isobel's eyes traced his rapier from its point in the blood on the back of her hand up the steel to Fogliaverde. '*You* were what went wrong. I thank you.'

The Italian bowed his head slightly. 'Your servant, Signorina Isobel. Please do not kill yourself.'

'What will happen to me?'

'I regret with all my heart that I am unable to keep any promise to you, no matter how much I wish to make it,' said the Italian.

'I can,' Will said in a desperate rush of words. 'I will do everything I can to make Secretary of State Robert Cecil protect you. Remember, now that the play is done, you are ready to begin reading the Bible, which has many less different words than the play. In it, you will read the divine prohibition against self-slaughter. You will read that you are the temple of God, and that the Spirit of God dwells within you. And you will read, "Be not foolish. Why would you die before your time?" God does not want you to kill yourself, Isobel. Just as you did not want Queen Mary to kill herself.'

Isobel looked at the crucifix-dagger still touching her chest and asked with a small smile, 'Do you suppose Secretary of State Cecil will let me keep Queen Mary's crucifix, which must certainly be the most horrible piece of Mariolatry in England?'

'I will persuade him,' said Will, 'to make an exception – but I have a better idea. You asked what will happen to you. If we reach a point where you feel safe and don't need Mary's crucifix to kill yourself, would you trade it with Cecil?'

'For what? What does he have that I would want? – Hold! He's the Queen's Secretary of State. Can he make me Ambassador to Rome?'

Fogliaverde convulsed. What started as an unexpected laugh escalated to brutal coughing. Isobel dropped her crucifix and nestled to his side, wiping blood from his mouth with the linen Will handed her. 'Oh, you poor sweet creature. I am so sorry, Master Fogliaverde.'

When he could speak, the Italian said, 'I could use a jest. Thank you, young Isobel.'

'Close your eyes. You will sleep. I promise I won't kill myself. I will stay beside you.'

Fogliaverde closed his eyes and in seconds was still. 'This poor man,' Isobel whispered to Will. She stroked his brow. After a while she whispered, 'What would I want Cecil to trade me?'

'Would you settle for the Bel Savage Inn?'

'What do you mean?'

'Cecil owns it. If we get out of this, if the Queen is safe, then Cecil is safe and if Cecil is safe, we are safe.'

Isobel said, 'There are many ifs.'

'I fear so,' said Will. 'But I am hopeful.'

'You would make me an innkeeper?'

'Would you like that?'

Her smile put Will in mind of Niles Roper beaming at his prized

Queen's Hart. 'A place in the world? Very, very much. How can you do it?'

'Cecil is wealthy. He has the power to reward loyal servants. If I handle it well, I can convince him that it's the least he could do to thank you for *The Sister Queens*.'

'So many ifs . . .'

'They will depend,' said Will, 'upon the success of our play.'

'Arrest Bacon!' Will Shakespeare shouted at Sir Robert Cecil. 'Arrest Topcliffe!'

The Secretary of State was hurrying to his office so early the watch was still out. His guard, reinforced to a dozen spread about the Strand, had let Will near having recognized him before he started shouting at the top of his lungs. Now two strong men seized his arms and a third had a sword in his fist.

'What are you shouting about?' Cecil demanded.

'They attacked the Bel Savage.'

'I am aware of that. My Anthonie and Cyrus are with the surgeons, still.'

'I have a friend mortally wounded and the Moor threatening to kill herself.'

'How did you escape?'

'By a miracle.'

'Where is the play?'

'Arrest Bacon. Arrest Topcliffe. Or you and the play can go to hell.'

'I cannot arrest Bacon and Topcliffe.'

'Detain them to protect me and mine or your play can go to hell.'

'I can and will detain Topcliffe to mollify you. But I cannot detain Anthony Bacon.'

'Why?'

'No one saw Bacon at the Bel Savage.'

'I saw his footman. And his minions who seized me at Tyburn.'

'They were led by Sir Richard Topcliffe. Do you expect me to arrest Anthony Bacon for not being there?'

'He would have been there if he was capable of running up the stairs.'

'You're wide of the mark, Master Shakespeare,' Cecil said softly. 'Bacon paid Topcliffe to take the blame for the attack. We cannot charge him.'

'But you are the Queen's first servant. You can do anything you want to.'

'My powers are to protect the Queen.'

'You didn't murder Niles the Brewer to protect the Queen. Don't tell me Bacon lied. I didn't need Bacon to tell me you killed Niles. You had to kill the witness who could testify that your father advised the Queen to behead Queen Mary wrongfully, falsely, illegally – while you were in your father's employ.'

'You are shouting sedition in a public street. Stop or I'll lay you into the Tower.'

Will lowered his voice, sure he had Cecil's attention. 'You killed Niles the Brewer to protect yourself. If Essex wins, he will put you on trial and hang you. I understand. I will even try to forgive you Roper, who deserved better.'

'Who are you to forgive me? The brewer conspired for the Scots Queen. He was an opportunist who saw his chance and took his reward – the best tavern in London.'

Will looked Cecil in his eye. 'He was an English war veteran. A simple English patriot making his new living as a brewer until conspirators snared him.'

Cecil turned his face, his mouth working, his jaw loose.

'Look at me, Sir Robert! You cannot ignore me. I have served you well. I may even have touched a better part of you that you never knew existed.'

'You will make a mistake appealing to what you misconstrue as my better side.'

'It's my only chance,' said Will. If this patient spider had a weak strand in his web it was his belief in alliance, which was also his strength. The man sought partners. 'We totter on the cusp of your play plot, Sir Robert. We verge on our chance to stop Essex before blood flows.'

Cecil turned his face back to Will and gestured for his guards to let go of his arms. 'I will detain Topcliffe until after your play settles this one way or another. I will not detain Anthony Bacon, but I will put him on strict notice that if he comes anywhere near you I will charge him.'

'And any of his people.'

'And his people. Where is the play?'

'In the arms of the book-holder. We start rehearsal this morning.'

THIRTY-FOUR

'I have never seen so many properties called for on one stage,' said the Chamberlain's Men's prop-man. 'A jig or a bawdy should plenty satisfy the nutcrackers.'

'*Props?*' Will Shakespeare scorned. 'When I apprenticed for the Queen's progress show at Castle Elvetham, the Earl of Hertford dug a *lake* to sail a full-rigged *ship* to entertain Her Majesty. All we're asking for the Globe is a low wall and some horses. And your usual crowns and coronets.'

The prop-man's protest was the third interruption of Will's inaugural rehearsal address to *The Sister Queens* company, though the rising sun had yet to clear the gallery roof. First Edmund the book-holder and then stage-keeper Mapes had galloped breathlessly onto the stage to report that they still could not find Clown Kempe.

The company was shivering in the open air under a February sky brewing snow. Wintry gusts plucked paper sides-rolls clutched in frozen fingers. If only there was time, he would write to his father for a packet of inexpensive gloves in sizes to fit men and boys. But there was no time and the city so wild that Will had to wonder whether the rebellion would start before the play he wrote to stop it. Ben reported rumors that the Lord Mayor and the Lord Sheriff had promised to provide Essex with a thousand men. Mercenaries were said to be streaming into the city in the dark of night with armor and weapons. Mounted knights were galloping across London Bridge. And inside Essex House, fortified with strong defense and ammunition, Will himself had heard fighters pray while preachers sermonized that God demanded the earl be made king.

Little of this penetrated the Globe. As during any rehearsal, a city on fire would not be noticed until flaming embers showered the stage. Will saw faces that looked expectant and mostly hopeful. Winter shows were rare in the outdoor theaters. The hired men were glad to be paid for unanticipated work. The shareholders were grateful for a chance to replenish the coffers.

'Our play,' Will told them, 'presents rival kingdoms, Isla and Islay, divided by a Hadrian's Wall-like tilting barrier and reigned over by warring Sister Queens. Virgin Queen Elspeth who rules Isla and thrice-widowed Queen Isobel who rules Islay have been arguing since their father divided his kingdom between them. They agree only once: joust for victory instead of bloody war. In the words of Widow Queen Isobel: "If being unseated fails to cool the blood, then drop thy lance and draw thy sword." If the jousts fail, their subjects will die and their nations fall. Which fate, we players will not allow in a comedy. In rehearsal, until we find proper mounts, you'll have to imagine Queen Elspeth and Queen Isobel are on horseback.'

'We'll ride horses?' asked Marc Handler, who was playing Virgin Queen Elspeth of Isla.

'Huzza!' roared Dick Burbage's son, Robbie, the apprentice who was playing the thrice-married, childless Queen Isobel of Islay. *'Horses!'* Will and the book-holder exchanged a glance as alarmed as it was private. Young Robbie's shout suddenly sounded manly for a boy playing a queen.

'This stage won't fit two ponies,' said the prop-man. 'Never mind carry horse weight.'

'We are rehearsing a play due to show Saturday. Please tend to your lances and armor and crowns and coronets. I'll deal with the horses. Now shall we be—'

Dick Burbage ran on stage from the tiring-house. 'Will! There's a fellow here selling barrels.'

'They're for the carpenter, already paid for.'

'And two wheelwrights delivering eight wheels.'

'Pay them.'

Instead of his usual complaint that a property borrowed was superior to any prop purchased, Burbage said, 'The strangest thing just happened at the Revels.'

Will said, 'I am attempting to rehearse, among others, your son who claims whenever he forgets a line that his father is to blame for teaching him the part in a manner difficult to remember.'

Burbage asked, 'Remember that thoroughly unpleasant clerk at the Revels? Doffed his bonnet most graciously and informed me that the Chamberlain's Men are directed to ask for anything we need.'

Cecil's orders. Firm on Will's side, for the moment, with the guard at the Bel Savage tripled, trusted swordsmen at Mrs Broad's, and a whole squadron guarding rehearsals.

'The clerk even called me "sir."'

'Could be a knighthood in this for you, Dick.'

Burbage beamed. 'The first player ever knighted? Who better . . .? He also told me that the Revels' official listing for *The Sister Queens* is *Richard II*. Do you know anything about that?'

'No,' Will lied. By bribing the Revels to post his weak-king history *Richard II* as Saturday's state-licensed play, Secretary Cecil gave himself several ways out if *The Sister Queens* scheme went wide of the mark. He might cozen Essex supporters into paying the Chamberlain to perform the weak-king history *Richard II* and charge them after with sedition. Or, less likely, Will hoped, the Crown might charge the Chamberlain's Men with sedition. In return for not questioning Cecil's self-serving scheme, Will had bargained the secretary's sworn promise to deed the Bel Savage to Isobel the Moor in the event of success. *(You try my patience, Master Shakespeare. But not your needs, Mr Secretary.)*

'We begin with the Queens' double-fool – a Falstaffian character named Sir John Falstaff – who will also serve as our Chorus and present a Prologue similar to our Prologue for *Henry V*, though lighter of tone. Since Master Kempe has yet to appear to rehearse Sir John Falstaff this morning, I will speak the Prologue for you now:

> "Two warring Queens, between them a wall,
> With one secret tunnel unknown to them all . . ."'

He searched their faces as he recited. But, as always, God alone knew whether the players liked the play. Some might claim to. Others would raise odd questions. Harry Condell spouted one such at the end of the Prologue.

'Did I hear you speak the phrase, "Essex knight," Will?'

'"Chet-Checked knight." Let us begin – Act One, Scene One: Rude Mechanicals Prepare the Tiltyard.'

An apprentice bolted from the tiring-house and whispered in Dick Burbage's ear. Burbage turned to the company. 'The news is bad indeed.' He inhaled as portentously as a man about to step

into his grave and announced, 'Master Kempe just informed his
fellow morning sluppers at the Mermaid that he will be dancing
backward to Scotland.'

'*When?*' God's wounds! Kempe's monkey face and gravel
tongue could make deep-chest laughs out of plague sores and
mirthful howls for a feeble jest that would fall from any other
player's lips like a lame beggar.

'His show is leaving this afternoon, leaving us short one Sir
John Falstaff.' Burbage opened his arms to address the company
in his mightiest voice. 'Fear not. Master Kempe as Falstaff is small
loss. No one who heard him in *Merry Wives* would pay to hear
his next Falstaff.'

Easy for you to say, Will thought, knowing what Burbage would
say next.

'Fortunately, Will, if anyone knows the part it's you. Sure you're
busy directing the players where to stand. But I'll carry the weight
in our Chet-Checks scenes, and I will ease your burden by shifting
any number of the Falstaff lines my way – those better suited to
me. I will prepare you a list.'

'I thought that went well,' said Coxswain Mapes, who was still
new to the stage. 'You must be pleased.'

'It felt like an unmitigated disaster,' answered Will Shakespeare.
He had stopped the rehearsal when the dusky sky made it impossible to read the sides.

'The book-holder said the very same thing to me. But he did
not look anxious. Neither do you, sir.'

'The book-holder is a wise old hand. It'll come together.
Although I could cheerfully burn Clown Kempe at the stake. No,
what worries me, Jim, is the cold. If it gets any colder. Or if it
snows, God forbid, how will we get spectators to cross London
Bridge? You're a mariner. What does your "weather eye" tell you?'

Playmaker and stage-keeper jumped off stage and hurried
across the pit to where they could see more of the darkening sky
above the loom of the galleries. Mapes examined it from several
directions. The tall flag turret atop the theater was barely visible,
the giant flag itself a wisp.

'Mares' tails. Changes are coming. Pray for the best, plan
for the worst.'

'In other words, sail against the wind?'

'Be *prepared* to sail against the wind.'

Something about the flag turret looked different, and Will asked, 'Is that the white flag up so soon?'

'No one told me not to fly it and I was feeling optimistic that you would still play the comedy.'

'Why wouldn't we play the comedy?'

'The Revels sent me a red flag. Told me to keep it handy in case we show a history. White for comedy, red for history.'

At this point, clearly, the Revels and Cecil were one. Again, the cautious Secretary of State was planning for all events.

'Shall I strike the flag, Master Shakespeare?'

'No, the more people see it, the more will cross the bridge for a comedy.'

'You could have the seamstress run up a second flag that names the day.'

'Like a broadside advertisement? Why not? Make it so, Jim.' They crossed the pit, gathering speed the last few paces, and vaulted easily the five feet to the stage. Mapes said, 'If you like, I could put some of my mates in boats. Row along the bridge flying white comedy flags with Saturday on them.'

A cold gust raked the stage.

'Could they fly flags in shapes?'

'What do you mean, sir? Shapes?'

'Could they fashion silhouettes of knights jousting?'

'Don't see why not. Step a little mast and rig it out of sailcloth.'

'Make it so.'

Will was just about to hurry with his guard to Mrs Broad's, nursing a forlorn hope that Stefano Fogliaverde might survive his grievous wound, when a toymaker's apprentices arrived lugging large boxes. Will hurried them to the carpenter's workshop.

'Are those what I hope they are?' asked the carpenter, who was fixing small wheels to a large barrel.

They pulled two hobby horse heads from the boxes. The horse heads were double standard measure, painted white, and large enough to be recognized from the upper regions of the galleries and across the groundlings pit.

The prop-man crowded into the carpenter's workshop. He

nodded approvingly at the barrels, wheels, and horse heads. 'They won't eat much. Nor drop the results on the stage.'

The tire-man said, 'Master Shakespeare, the bladders have arrived.'

'Which?'

'Cow, pig, and sturgeon.'

Early on the third morning of rehearsal – only two days before the show – Marc Handler found Will on the stage where he was leading young Burbage through Queen Isobel's lines. He had a strange, baffled look on his face when he said, 'Master, someone has come to see you.'

The armed gentlemen ordered to let no outsiders into the theater had made an exception for a trim middle-aged woman in sturdy country clothes, who possessed work-roughed hands, a gentle's erect posture, and a deep blue gaze that riveted all she faced. Theater apprentices were flocked around her, as if enchanted by a magical visitation from another world, and Will heard one boy whisper, 'Master Shakespeare has her eyes.'

'And her carriage,' said another.

'Mother?'

Will was shocked to see her in London and feared the worst. On his last visit home, his father had seemed much older than his years and he had wondered whether his next visit would be to bury him. He asked with dread in his heart, 'Where is Father? Is he not well?'

'Father is at home,' said Mary Arden Shakespeare. 'Take me to Stefano Fogliaverde.'

THIRTY-FIVE

Will Shakespeare hurried across London Bridge with his mother, mystified silent, terrified that he had to get her out of London before the showing of the play lifted the constraints on Anthony Bacon, and thanking God for Topcliffe's temporary jailing in the Clink. She set a rapid pace and stared straight ahead, taking no notice of the bustling crowds that parted for her, nor the arresting vision of St Paul's towering over the city, nor the boats flying white flags, theater flags of Hercules carrying the Globe on his shoulders, and canvas silhouettes of jousting knights. A dangerous tide was racing, but Coxswain Mapes' mariners – sun-blackened Walter Raleigh deep-sea men – rowed blithely close for all to see SATURDAY.

'Mother?' Will asked when they turned off Gracious Street into Threadneedle. 'How does it happen that you know Stefano Fogliaverde?'

'He was Father Val's armed gentleman.'

Isobel was at Mrs Broad's, and when Will's mother rushed into the room where Fogliaverde lay, she stopped Will with a whispered, 'Hold.' Mazed, he watched from the door as his middle-aged mother and the dying Italian rapier and dagger man wept in each other's arms.

'Give them time,' Isobel whispered.

'What is this?'

'They love each other.'

'I see that. But . . . how . . . what?'

'Go back to the theater. Come here later.'

Will hurried back to the Globe, pondering questions that had troubled him for years. What caused his father's long decline from a vigorous man of means? How had an ever-rising 'new man,' an illiterate farmer's son who married a gentle, an ambitious craftsman who mastered merchant arts and reveled in political wiles, how had he withdrawn from public life to end his years an ordinary glover?

Had this betrayal started the fatal engine of descent that wrenched him from his frame of hopeful expectation?

He forced himself to close his mind to betrayal in order to give his company the rehearsal they deserved, and surely needed. Not to mention a sympathetic ear for cares and troubles. The book-holder, cradling *The Sister Queens* book in his arms, greeted him with a compliment. 'Your jousting silhouettes are having the effect you hoped for, Master Shakespeare. The whole world sees *The Sister Queens* tilt, even before the play is shown.'

'Thank you, Edmund – but why your long face?'

'My wife is an honest woman who would never dream of crossing to the Southwark suburb, even for a play for which book I am holding. Thanks to your silhouettes catching her eye, she is venturing over from London to attend the show with her mother and her aunt.'

'Wonderful!'

'Wonderful? My Southwark friend, who hears every play we do in the Globe, will not think it wonderful when I ask her not to attend.'

An observation both soothing and manly was expected, but the best Will could muster was, 'Well, they're not likely to meet in the multitude we're praying for.'

'God is a jester, Master Shakespeare. He will seat them side by side.'

Will tutored the players and stage-keepers through dusk, applauded the tire-man's costumes, encouraged the prop-man to find longer lances that weighed less, and raced back to Mrs Broad's. His mother invited him to come into the room where she had the Italian propped half-sitting against pillows. If any man could look happy dying, Stefan Fogliaverde was that man. He was pale, his voice weak.

'Will,' he said, 'I could never tell you this without her. But now, I die happy as your mother says I must tell you . . .' His eyes drifted to the ceiling and around the room as he collected his emotion. 'We met before you were born, when the Jesuits hired me to smuggle Father Val into England and protect him. We loved, as your old friend Marlowe said so wisely, never deliberating, but at first sight. We knew we sinned. We sinned regardless. But whatever we might regret, we cannot ever regret you.'

Will's breath caught in his lungs. 'Stefano? What are you saying?'

'I am saying I have the honor of being your father.'

His father's wound, doubled. Betrayed and reminded of it daily by a bastard in his house. 'My father, John Shakespeare,' he said to Stefano Fogliaverde, 'is a good man.'

'Were he not,' said Fogliaverde, 'none of this would matter, would it? Instead, it matters great worlds of matter because John Shakespeare is a good man.'

Will turned to his mother.

She looked him straight in the eye, with a gaze as sure as the Countess of Southampton's. 'You have no need to judge, Will. I face a sterner judgement when I die. Until then, a scorpion stings in my heart for my husband's broken heart.'

'Did he forgive you?'

She seemed glad he had asked. 'His anger was ferocious. He raged with the cruelest words you could imagine. It was as if he blamed, detested, and cursed the vices of every woman who ever lived. For my betrayal, all vices became mine: lying, flattering, deceiving, lust, and rank thoughts, mine. All faults that may be named in Hell. He said things I had never heard from his lips before – or since. For, yes, he did forgive me, but at terrible cost to his spirit . . . Stefano and I have talked of this these last hours. Few can believe in our own death until the last hours. But for your father . . . it was as if I made your father believe his own death. God and Satan will never prick me deeper than when I watched him wither.'

'Did Father forgive me?'

Anger blazed in his mother's eyes. 'Did he ever *once* give you cause to make you think otherwise?'

'Never.'

She took Will's hand for the first time. 'Busy young men don't much notice their children, but for you he reminded himself daily to take notice with small kindnesses. It was as if by assuring you he didn't hate you, he loved you more. Do you understand that?'

'I carry my book satchel that we made together. And my traveling player bag.'

'I thank you for that,' Mary Arden Shakespeare whispered. She sat on the edge of the bed, shaking her head.

Will took out his goatskin table-book and showed his mother the dent in the cover board. 'And Stefano knows I pocket my table-book over my heart. Do you not, Stefano?'

'We would not be having this discourse if you didn't,' whispered Fogliaverde.

Will's mother's eyes shifted to Fogliaverde and filled with tears. 'Tell Will the rest.'

'It is not as important.'

'It is who you are,' she urged firmly.

'It is *part* of who I am.' Fogliaverde tried to smile. 'Will, the Italian rapier and dagger man you see sinking on this bed was never only as he appeared. To begin at the beginning, I am not Italian. I am Portuguese. Nor am I truly Portuguese, though I was raised here in London by kindly Portuguese refugees.'

That would explain the absence of an accent, thought Will. 'But if not Portuguese, who?'

'I am a Jew.'

'A Jew? But we have no Jews in England. Haven't for hundreds of years, except perhaps a few merchants of the Netherlands. I have never met a Jew.'

'To the best of your knowledge . . . In truth, we worshiped in our homes, alone, out of the community, invisible. Like Catholics!'

'I suppose I should be proud you liked my *Merchant*.'

'You did your best within the constraints.'

That stung, and Will admitted, 'I lacked the courage to say it all.'

'To speak to all from the stage you have to have the courage to be circumspect. If not circumspect, if too loud a judge, only fragments of the crowd will hear you. Fragments are for poets.'

'Did Father Valente know you were a Jew?'

'Not from my lips. But I suppose he did. Val was too wise to be fooled.'

'I'm surprised he never raised the question.'

Fogliaverde said, 'Father Val was my knight. I was his lance. He was too good a soldier, too valiant, and too loyal to his god to dull his weapon with questions better left unasked.'

'How did you happen to be Val's guard?'

'My father – my Portuguese stepfather – I never knew my father – wanted me to learn a trade that would let me live more free than a Jew hiding in England. He sent me to friends in Rome where I learned the sword. My masters sent me to guard Father Val. He made me his acolyte, until I resisted.'

'I did, too,' said Will.

'Do you know why?'

'I used to think it was because I didn't have the courage to be Catholic in England. I've come to realize that I resisted the obedience the Roman Church demands. I was already subject to the Queen and happy for it.' Will glanced at his mother, who was listening closely, and held her eye. 'I did not want a Pope. I did not want to be Catholic. Just as now, I don't want to be a Jew.'

'How do you mean?'

'I am an Englishman.'

Stefano Fogliaverde's eyes warmed with a small smile.

'Surely you are an Englishman. *You* of all Englishmen are as English as the roast beef of England. England is where you were formed. John Shakespeare and your mother reared you English, made you English, gave you England. As I was formed in Italy. My masters gave me Italy, made me think Italian and feel Italian. I returned to England with Father Val a "new leaf" – far more Italian than Jew or Portuguese or acolyte of the Roman Church.'

'Yet you stayed with Val, unlike me.'

Fogliaverde said, 'I stayed on to guard him – not for his faith, but his bravery.' He gave another weak smile. 'As I said, I am Italian.'

'And returned to England, still hiding,' Mary Arden Shakespeare interrupted with an ironic and proud smile. 'Disguised as a Catholic spy.'

'Who failed in the end,' Fogliaverde said bleakly. He started to cough, contained it, and whispered, 'I envied you his ghost, Will. But you earned it by being there when they killed him.'

The coughing grew harsh and wracked his face with pain. Will's mother moved to his side. When she had settled him, she beckoned Will closer. 'He wants to say good-bye to you.'

Will took his hand. He was trembling, his fingers soft.

'I am sorry, Stefano, that I never received your fencing lessons.'

'Life intrudes,' said Fogliaverde. 'For which I am sorry, too.

Come closer, please.' Will knelt beside the bed. Fogliaverde whispered in his ear, 'Not for your mother to hear but be warned: I found your shabby gallant. He was a spy who carried messages to Scotland for Essex. He gave you that letter because Bacon tried to kill him to silence him. He took umbrage. As you noticed, there is more resolve in the man than is apparent at first. He claims he has joined with Raleigh and Gorges.'

'Do you trust him?'

'With your life, young poet. It was he who warned me that Bacon's crew was headed to the Bel Savage.'

'Did he do it for revenge?'

'Not solely. I believe he truly loves your writing. But he further claimed he had information for you about Sir Walter Raleigh.'

Events, thought Will, had likely overtaken that information, whatever it was. Still, best to be on the safe side of the hedge and ask Coxswain Mapes to look into it.

'Fortunately,' said Fogliaverde, 'I had already bent my word to you. When next I saw you disguised in the street, I did follow to your starting hole.'

Will had sneaked out to press Coxswain Mapes, again, hoping in vain for an introduction to Raleigh. He had been vigilant, listening intently, clinging to shadows. Extra-vigilant to never let a link-boy's light fall on his face when entering or leaving Seacoal Lane. But somewhere in those shadows, he had failed to see the night-wandering Stefano.

'Thus I knew how to spirit you away from them, but I was moments late.'

'Stefano, did you serve Cecil?'

'I served myself to find my son. And you made these few days in London my happiest since the day you were born.' His voice drifted. His eyes closed.

Will rose and let his mother steer him toward the door.

'Remember Stefano.'

'Remember?' he asked his mother. 'You ask me to remember?'

'He – and we – are you.'

Protest hammered Will's heart. He wanted to shout *No!* I am my father, John Shakespeare. He knew it was wrong to shout it, cruel to double their pain at this terrible end to their love. But he wanted to shout, I am not the two of you . . . I am my own. Was that true? he wondered as he struggled to smother a voice that raged against betrayal, against what they had done to his father, against Southampton with Isobel, against Southampton's letter, against Southampton conspiring with Essex – and he felt that shout bursting from his breast like a flaming *Vulcano*.

I am my own.

THIRTY-SIX

'Remember?' Will Shakespeare demanded. 'You ask me to remember?'

Hold, whispered his quiet voice. *Hold! Hold! Hold! Remember. Go to your castle.*

His memory castle had rooms, vaults, coffers, chests, and strong boxes. He stormed through it, flinging open doors, lifting traps, sliding lids.

'*Lonely as a dragon.*'

'*A blow no less cruel for its poverty.*'

'*She was a brave lady, Master Shakespeare. More queen in death than ever she was in life. Forgave the headsman.*'

Deeper in, he found Father Val's *Ego te absolvo.* Tethered hands lifted the sign of the cross to forgive the hangman's apprentice for bringing the knife. And Val's final gift when his eyes glinted at Will. 'You too, my friend.' His mother spoke in a voice so clear that his castle vanished.

'You were born when I needed you.'

'How do you mean?'

'Your sister Joan died. Your sister Margaret died. Twice then after I miscarried of child. Your father and I had been married six years and we still had no children when Stefano came with Father Val . . . Stefano is surely right that we loved at first sight. But had I not been so empty, I may have been strong enough to resist. *May,* to speak true, for I do not know. All I know is that even though I loved your father – and I love him still, you must know – I loved Stefano, too. And I was not strong enough. What we felt, what we knew, was stronger.'

'How did you know Stefano fathered me?'

'I did not know for sure until you opened your eyes. Then I knew.'

'But everyone says I have your eyes.'

'I saw you had *our* eyes.'

'How did Father learn?'

'Oh, my dear. We were so careful not to hurt him. Besides, Stefano and Val were very rarely with us, always steps ahead of the priest hunters. It happened one day when you were four years old. It was almost as if your father allowed himself to see what he must have seen all along. Your father is a sharp-eyed man. You get your sharp eye from him.'

'And my inner eye from you?'

'For what it's worth.'

Will saw himself swimming – saw under the bridge the shadow of Stefano guarding them, saw his mother laughing in sunlight. His father watched them from the bridge. Stefano's shadow filled his mother's eyes and when they blended as one, John Shakespeare turned around and shambled away like Thomas Kyd.

Taint not thy mind against thy mother!

Will heard the ghost of Hamlet's murdered father demand a second promise from his son. Not only to take revenge, but a heartful promise of tenderness, and Will knew that he had discovered, at last, the manful plea by a king who was stronger than his son begging his son, *Leave her to heaven.*

'Remember?' he asked. 'How could I not remember? Two true men for fathers? My good mother who loves them both? Not one would I wipe from my table-book.'

'Tell Stefano!'

Will went back into the room. The Italian sensed his rush to the bed and opened his eyes. Will knelt and kissed his brow. 'I know now what you meant when you said you prayed that I *remembered* how to swim.'

'A tongue slip. I did not mean to give it away. And I was glad you didn't notice.'

'I noticed. I did not understand. I could not imagine.'

'Your mother had to make the decision with me.'

Will saw the light stray from Stefano's eyes, and he said, 'Mother should be with you now. Good-bye, Father. God speed.'

'May I ask, young poet, what will you tell John Shakespeare?'

'I will tell him the truth: Stefano Fogliaverde saved John Shakespeare's son's life. Twice. And you each in your way showed your son how to make his way.'

THIRTY-SEVEN

'Hell's mouths are open,' Will Shakespeare shouted in the dark to warn Ben Jonson. 'Mind you don't fall in.'

'Hell's mouths' were trapdoors in the stage floor that covered steep stairs down to the cellar that the players nicknamed Hell. For *The Sister Queens* they allowed the double-fool Falstaff and the Earl of Chet-Checks to descend from Queen Isobel's side of Hadrian's Wall and emerge in Queen Elspeth's realm. The cellar extended back under the tiring-house where stairs up to the tiring-house itself presented a third way on and off stage. Properties were stored in it, and the company's playbooks were locked in the book-holder's vault.

The traps should not be open, but when their last rehearsal ended in dying daylight – placing *The Sister Queens* in the hands of the gods – the freezing company had fled so fast into the tiring-house that no one had remembered to close them. Will was feeling his way in the dark to do the job himself when Ben stepped out of the tiring-house.

Will said, 'Well timed. I was about to send you news.'

Ben said, 'I wish I were bearing better news.'

'Stefano?'

'I'm sorry, my friend. 'Scaped the world with his sword in his hand and a smile for your mother.'

'Where is she?'

'Headed home on horseback.'

'Alone?'

'Safe with brother veterans conveying a costly Spanish breeding mare to Tewkesbury. God help highway robbers that try to steal the animal, much less trouble your mother. She prays you will understand she needed the long ride alone with her thoughts.'

'Thank you, Ben. Thank you for looking out for her. And would you thank Mrs Broad for taking us all in – wasn't that wonderful that her husband was a Moor.'

Ben laughed at him. 'Mrs Broad's husband was no more Moor

than you are. She told me it was the first thing to jump in her head when she saw how frightened Isobel was.'

'I'll be. Well, thank her and tell her I will bear all the expenses and the burial.'

'I already took care of the burial. Stefano told me he was a Jew. They like to bury in a day. What's my news?'

'You will play Chet-Checks after all. The book-keeper has fresh sides revised in rehearsal for you to study. But say nothing until I've spoken with Burbage.'

'He holds double shares. You can't just take away his part.'

'I am shifting him to young Robbie's part.'

'Why in the name of all holy would Master Richard Burbage – a tragedian of great name, he'll inform us often – agree to play a queen?'

'Robbie's voice is cracking.'

'God's blood!'

'Your son may yelp like a broken bell,' Will told Dick Burbage, 'and still play the part of Queen Isobel. Or he may bark like a fox. Robbie may even squeak like a mouse and play Isobel. But I will not have him on stage barking, squeaking, and yelping all three in the same line. And surely not if he rumbles like a kettle drum, which I've heard him do twice between yelps.'

The nightmare of every London theater that employed boy apprentices to play women's roles had struck with a vengeance. Young Robbie Burbage's voice had cracked – fragmenting into unpredictable spurts of noise as horrible as Will had ever heard. The clamor of falsetto pitches and bass booms would quiet, even- tually, into a manly baritone as solid as his father's. But not by tomorrow afternoon.

'Who will replace him?'

'Fortunately, we have an actor who knows every line – because he tutored his apprentice to play them.'

Dick Burbage said, 'What are you saying?'

'Shave your beard and pluck those eyebrows.'

'I can't play a woman. I haven't played a woman in twenty years . . . fifteen.'

'Beneath all that hair you have fairly fine features with a quality observers might view as a sort of beauty. And don't tell me you've grown too stout. Your character is thrice married, thrice widowed, the *older* sister, grown slab-sided, as you have. The tire-man will labor through the night – letting out seams and affixing panels until you fit smartly into your Queen Isobel costume.'

'But my voice—'

'Your voice has a musical character that would do an older woman proud. It is consistent and compelling and the many who love you have never, ever heard a single yelp, bark, or squeak. Off you go!'

'Who will play Chet-Checks?'

'Since we heard Robbie's first rumble, the book-holder has been tutoring Ben Jonson.'

'*God's blood!*'

'The company will pay your barber. Off. You. Go!'

'I will never play a woman with that man on the stage!' Burbage declaimed and stormed into the tiring-house.

Will closed the traps. The tavern would have sent hot pies and mulled wine to the tiring-house by now, but he stayed on the stage, alone in the dark, weary, deeply worried, and very unhappy. He had no idea at this moment what play they would do tomorrow. He had already burned two full *Sister Queens* playbooks and had completed a third. Was that fall back to be knocked back by a gutted *Richard II*? He wandered, looked for stars, saw none in clouds that threatened snow.

His sudden, unexpected richness in fathers had not lasted long. But even if he had not learned of it, he would still be saddened by the death of Stefano Fogliaverde. He had enjoyed their every encounter. Having your life saved from rapier and dagger men will do that, he thought with a very small smile. As would being rescued from murderous priest hunters. But he had truly enjoyed every conversation. The man courted me, Will thought. Every marvelously mangled phrase, every unusual notion, and every reflection in his stranger's eye had left its mark.

'You have to have the courage to be circumspect,' would stir debate in his bosom for a very long while, and 'To the best of your knowledge,' in answer to, 'I have never met a Jew,' would spark a smile for the rest of his life.

He wooed me. Successfully. He wanted his son to love his father.

'*Will! Will Shakespeare!*' Dick bustled out of the tiring-house with a flaming link light held high. 'There you are, Will!' He had wrapped himself in a huge piece of black cloth, and he was still neither plucked nor shaven.

'What is that around your shoulders?'

'The black flag of tragedy. We will show a tragedy tomorrow. I will play King Richard II. If Ben Jonson wants, he can play my queen.'

Will thought, *I have broken my cardinal rule with Burbage and now am paying for it: never antagonize Narcissus.*

'I am a tragedian of great—'

'Dick, if you won't play Queen Isobel of Islay, then the last and final show the Chamberlain's Men will ever play will be *our* tragedy.'

'*Richard II* is the play for these tumultuous times – a far greater show to persuade the nutcrackers to defend the Queen.'

'*Richard II* is more likely to dispatch the groundlings to court with burning torches.'

'Some nobles,' said Burbage, 'just offered us forty-shillings extra to play it.'

'Those nobles would buy themselves gallery, and us gallery seats in the Tower. It's too late, Dick. We are set on course to show *The Sister Queens*.'

'We all know the *Richard* book. Played it for years. If you'll prune a few more lines and cobble me just one rousing speech of a dozen or thirty lines, I'll handle the business. The Queen's throne is safe.'

'The Queen hates the play. She won't blame the Revels. She'll blame the players. And so will the groundlings. They love a comedy.' Will pointed at the night sky where the white flag flew from the turret. 'The groundlings trust us to deliver.'

Burbage roared, 'I trust the Revels and the Revels say we are performing *Richard II.*'

A trapdoor banged open beside them and the Cyclops-huge figure of Coxswain Mapes loomed halfway up from Hell. 'Is all yare, masters? I thought I heard mayhem – Master Shakespeare, I must speak with you on an urgent matter.'

Will said, 'Wait here, Dick, I will come right back.'

Will followed Mapes down the stairs and pulled the trap shut.

Mapes said, 'I found the shabby gallant fellow you wanted. Name of Lyle Leet. You were right. He's serving my Captain Raleigh.'

Bless Stefano, Will thought. 'Where is he?'

'I put him down here. When I came back, Hell was empty. He's afraid to be seen. But he left this.'

Mapes shined his link light on a leaf cut from a table-book. On it, the shabby gallant had scratched. 'DAWN. BRIDGE. UPSTREAM.'

'What did he tell you?'

'Sir Walter's been at Essex House these past days. Heard everything they're plotting and he's come to think that not only is the rebels' intent wrong, it's doubly dangerous because they've started fighting among themselves.'

Excellent, thought Will. Wily Cecil had wisely hinted that Francis Bacon might renounce Essex to protect his brother. The seeds of discord had sunk roots. 'Over what are they fighting?'

'Betraying Essex. Betraying the cause. Cowardice.'

'What will Raleigh do about it?'

'He's left the house to warn the court that Essex will attack.'

'Good!'

'Let us hope. But your shabby Leet says that Ferdinando Gorges was commanded by Essex to kill Raleigh. Unfortunately, Raleigh has agreed to meet with Gorges before he warns the court.'

'Why? Why would he do that?'

Coxswain Mapes shook his head sadly. 'My valiant Captain Raleigh broached the Irish, defeated the Spaniard Armada, sailed the seven seas, and founded colonies in the New World. But he remains a bull-headed innocent with a habit of falling in with the wrong sort. And he is certain his cousin Gorges would never harm him.'

'Where will they meet?'

Mapes held up the table-book leaf. 'On the river, a fine place to harm bull-headed innocents.'

'Do you trust this Lyle Leet?' Will asked.

'I believe he loves Raleigh, and he does truly seem to love your poems.'

Stefano had trusted Leet, too. 'Perhaps he's not all bad. Please wake me before dawn.'

'Shall I get one of the boats?'

'Get them all – but first help me try to persuade Burbage to listen to sense.'

They climbed to the stage where Burbage was blowing on his fingers to warm them. He slung the black flag off his shoulders and thrust it at Mapes. 'At first light, fly this up the flagpole. It is the black flag that signals the message to all London that means we're playing a tragedy tomorrow, not a comedy.'

Mapes shot a stealthy glance at Will, who raised one eyebrow a hair's-breadth.

'What play, squire, may I ask?'

'*The History of Richard II.*'

'But that's a history, squire. Not a tragedy.'

'I believe I know the difference, having played it a hundred times.'

'Surely, squire. I may be new to the theater, but I do know that the flag that signals history is a red flag.'

'Then raise a red flag, for the Devil's sake.'

'But we have no red flag, sir.'

'We surely do. And if we somehow lost them all, I was personally informed that the Revels sent a new red one the other day.'

'Overboard,' said Mapes. 'From our boats.'

'Boats? Oh, with those silly sails.'

'Silhouettes,' Will interrupted. 'Floating broadsides. The advertising seems to have had an effect. If reports from the taverns can be believed, we'll have many spectators crossing the bridge tomorrow. More nutcrackers than usual, even in this cold. As for the new red flag, Dick, one of the mariners who Coxswain Mapes paid in cakes and ale to man the boats had, shall we say, a few too many.' Will glanced at Mapes.

Mapes said, 'Fell in the river, the lad did. God's grace, we pulled him out before he drowned. But the Revels' red flag went over in the process – small price, wouldn't you say, squire, to save a man's life?'

Will said, 'Coxswain Mapes, you should sleep. Tomorrow will be a long day.'

When they were alone, Will asked Burbage, 'Would you be remembered as he who laid a-bed when so great an honor would be won? Or will you be remembered from this day to the ending

of the world, as the happy brother who played for we few actors
in our band?'

'You are shameless,' said Burbage. 'And if you must quote your
own play, at least get the lines right. The Crispin Day speech goes,
"We few, we happy few, we band of brothers." I'll tell you what,
Will. My final offer: you play Queen Isobel. I'll do Falstaff.'

'*NO!*'

Burbage jumped back, quick as a frightened cat. 'Well,' he said.
'Well . . . Touched to the quick, as they say.'

Will had stepped back too, as astounded by his fury as Burbage
looked to be. He repeated softly, 'No. I will play Falstaff.'

'It appears he's important to you.'

'Shockingly so, I must admit. Sorry if I shouted at you.'

'Why so suddenly important? You never minded Kempe playing
him.'

'I love Falstaff. He says what he wants to. He can't imagine
being circumspect.'

Dick Burbage loosed a sigh as dramatic as a house fire and
shambled off. 'You win, old friend. I'll find the barber.'

'The other thing about Falstaff?' Will called after him. 'For
most roles the playmaker has to hunt words to put in their mouths.
With Falstaff I run alongside him, scratching what he says in my
table-book.'

The tiring-house was crammed with snoring apprentices and stank
of the mulled wine that had put the boys to sleep before they could
return to their lodgings. Will took the black flag Burbage had left
there and climbed back down the ladder to Hell, which was blessedly quiet and smelled of nothing more noxious than the river. He
made a bed of the flag, wrapped himself in his heavy cloak, and
fell asleep while tugging his bonnet to his ears and wondering
whether dreams or ghosts would visit after such a day.

He dreamed of his mother camped alone in a wood with a horse.
A sun beam lighted her face and she awakened with a smile, as
young and beautiful as he had ever remembered her. She saddled
the horse with the quick and sure hands he had always envied –
she had learned to ride as a child. He had not, until much later,
and horses knew it. She mounted as assuredly and cantered from
the wood to the front door of their house, where all their family

waited inside – Will's sisters, living and dead, cheerful Hamnet, his father still robust, and Stefano Fogliaverde still standing his watch. Val was in the house, too, but not a ghost. Suddenly they all sat at a table set for dinner. Will looked for himself, looked everywhere, but he was not there. Two chairs remained empty. Would they wait or pick up their spoons? Val bent his head to lead them saying grace, and Coxswain Mapes said, 'Good Morning, Master Shakespeare.'

The wind was picking up and blowing fog off the river. As the oarsmen of the Globe's leading boat pulled, Will, seated in front beside Coxswain Mapes, saw two wherry boats near the bridge, midstream, each with two oarsmen and a single passenger. A third larger boat stood off at some distance with eight men. Four were at the oars, four were seated.

'The shots?' he asked Mapes.

'Yes. And my Sir Walter is too thick headed to hide from them. While we have no muskets. That is my captain in the starboard boat – your right, Master Shakespeare – and his cousin to port.'

Mapes grunted a command and the oars pulled harder. Raleigh's and Ferdinando Gorges' boats were converging. Gorges stood up and removed his cloak.

'What is he doing?' asked Will.

'Showing he's not armed,' said Mapes. 'It looks to me like Gorges had second thoughts about murdering his cousin for Essex. He's bringing his boat alongside his cousin's so the musketeers won't shoot. Brave man. Must know in his heart they'll probably shoot anyway – *Pull harder, lads! Put your backs in it.*'

Raleigh's and Gorges' boats touched while the Globe boats were still a hundred paces off. Gorges went to shift into Raleigh's boat, but Raleigh was quicker and swung into Gorges' boat, moving lithely for a man of nearly fifty.

Mapes said, 'I should not have let you come with us, Master Shakespeare.'

'What would you do if I were not in this boat?'

'Ram the shot.'

'Instead of rowing unarmed against four musket men,' said Will, 'may I suggest we circle our boats around your captain and his cousin and screen them with our jousters silhouettes.'

Mapes grinned. 'The shots can't shoot what they can't see.' He signaled his convoy to follow closely. 'And they're not too likely to shoot at four Globe Theatre *Sister Queens* boats flying white comedy flags in plain sight of London Bridge. I should have thought of that myself.'

'You're a mariner, Jim. You sail straight at the enemy. Playmakers have to sail circles to see what we can see.'

'A good morning's work, Master Shakespeare, all before the tide turns.'

Except if Sir Walter Raleigh's own tide had turned, as Mapes had warned, and he was not the man at court he used to be. The same held for Ferdinando Gorges, an Essex knight shifted from court to the distant isle of Jersey. How long would it take men of diminished influence to convince someone at court that the threat was real; how long for that courtier to convince others? Even then, would they face the fight? As Ben Jonson had warned, repeatedly, and the spy master Anthony Bacon knew the instant he heard the play plot, it would be up to the people. The crowd would choose, or not, to swarm with Essex.

THIRTY-EIGHT

Will cinched 'fat-guts, great-belly' Sir John Falstaff padding around his waist, smeared rouge on his drunkard's nose and cheeks, and folded cloth helmets, one red, one blue, into his bulging doublet. Then he clapped on his head the white helmet he would wear to deliver the Prologue in the role of Chorus, inspected the effect in the tiring-house glass, and climbed to the top of the flag turret to count the audience pouring into the Globe.

Predictions from the taverns looked to be true. If anything, they had underestimated the crowd. Multitudes had crossed the Thames. And still they came – walking on London Bridge and rowed in wherry boats and private barges – bundled against the cold, glancing at the sky, which loomed heavy with snow, and anxiously back at London as if at any minute they would see the rumor-plagued city on fire.

Back down in the tiring-house, he told Ben Jonson that he imagined the great orb of the theater swelling like one of the bladders they had inflated for the final act.

'And does the Globe shrink when the people go home?' asked Ben.

'Always,' said Will.

The tire-man had Ben decked up in heroic Earl of Chet-Checks magnificence, glittering head to toe in a gaudy shade of gold, with a peacock feather in his bonnet. The prop-man had found Ben a sword long enough to trip on.

Dick Burbage was peering out a curtain to the stage and rubbing his hands gleefully. 'Pennies are falling like rain. God bless our clever boats. What did we name them? Advertising?'

He was arrayed in queenly splendor, wearing a crown on his head and a voluminous red gown on his back. His beard was shorn and his eyebrows concealed – by merciful compromise – under the same hog-bone paste that whitened his face like a beautiful woman's pale skin.

'Three thousand in the pit alone. Thick as bones in a churchyard and growling for a bawdy.'

'They'll have to settle for a jig,' said Will, 'if the Queen attends.'

Each of those three thousand had dropped a penny at the door into boxes held by eagle-eyed collectors. Others had paid another penny to ascend the stairs to the first gallery. A third penny took them higher, a fourth higher yet, with cushions to sit on. Five pennies secured a seat in the Lords' Room, behind the stage, where they could see little of the actors, but were more likely to hear every word, or so they believed.

The theater doors swung shut. The collectors carried their boxes to the box office and Will felt the company forming up behind him. He nodded to a stage-keeper. Trumpeters in the musicians' gallery above the stage blew a long, loud fanfare. Will turned around to tell the company, 'Trust the groundlings!' Then he stepped onto a loop of rope dangling from the flies. Coxswain Mapes swayed him up and out of the tiring-house and over the stage and lowered Sir John Falstaff to the boards like an unlikely visitor from Heaven.

The first spectators he saw in the pit were a crew of mariners who had somehow survived the sinking of *Eliza*. A wonderful omen, he thought, until he remembered they were his harshest critics and not shy to speak their mind. A stupendous voice that could only belong to the master of the good ship *Eliza* thundered, *'Falstaff?'*

'Aye!' cheered some groundlings.

'Nay!' groaned others who'd likely heard last summer's *Merry Wives*.

The galleries remained decorously hushed

Will stepped from his foot loop as the stage-keeper whisked it away, doffed his white helmet, bowed toward the more welcoming voices, and lifted his own.

> 'Your Chorus, Gentles, that
> Our Prologue you may hear
> of Beauteous Princes and a noble they should fear—'

Ben Jonson/Chet-Checks strutted over the stage. He tripped, credibly, over his sword, then stood still as a tree. 'Bow!' Will muttered through clenched teeth. Ben bowed. Groundlings applauded and Will continued:

> 'Sister Queens at war, between them a wall,
> With a secret tunnel unknown to all
> Except their double-dealing twice-paid fool
> And a Chet-Checked Earl with morals small,
> who woos the Queens to their both realms rule . . .'

Prologu-ing on, Will searched the audience for the Queen. He saw Secretary Cecil instead, ludicrously disguised as an old woman with a hunched shoulder who happened to be guarded by Anthonie Kingston and Cyrus Carew wearing beaver pilches and bandages on their faces. No sight of Her Majesty.

He saw the Countess of Southampton some distance from Cecil and the vision of her lifted his heart. She wore a black half mask, but anyone who had feasted on the sight of her smile would recognize her instantly. Even if she hid her face behind a full *vizard* Will would recognize her carriage. He looked for Southampton, hoping against hope that he was safely above the fray escorting his mother to the theater. But she was accompanied only by Frances Mowery disguised as a country squire in town for the day gripping a sword cane suspiciously.

Isobel and Mrs Broad had treated themselves to the three-penny gallery. Banished to a lower gallery, under Cecil's watchful eye, was Anthony Bacon with the fixed features of a man gripped by defeat. Nearby sat a grim-faced Sir Richard Topcliffe, who looked hollowed, a husk of himself, like a tree rotting from within, a doubly satisfying sight as the heavy-set Grinner of the Clink hulked beside him with Topcliffe's arm firmly in his powerful paw.

Will spoke his last line of the chorus, removed his white Prologue bonnet, and exited down the Isla trapdoor. He crossed through Hell, under the wall, and emerged on the Islay side of the stage where he donned his blue hat and thrust his fat-guts belly in a Falstaffian bow. Mariner appreciation stoked a round of clapping that rippled across the pit and rattled the gallery.

Falstaff exited into the tiring-house as flocks of jousting grooms, squires, and rude mechanicals bounded out of it, and Act I, Scene 1 sprang to life on either side of the low wall that divided the tilt yard. Players preparing armor, helmets, shields, lances, and saddling barrel horses argued which queen had Elspeth and Isobel's father loved most. Words evoked threats, threats provoked raised fists, raised fists flew, and flying fists made a punching and kicking brawl. Down in the pit, groundlings with fond memories of warring Montagues and Capulets bellowed, 'Romeo and Juliet.'

Peacemakers intervened. How appalled the beloved old king would be to hear his subjects battle. How dangerous their battle was to their nations' safety. How long before foreigners from Spain, France, and Rome invaded their weakened realms? Knights in black armor lurked behind columns. A mustachioed king and an ermine-robed Pope peered from a balcony.

A peacemaker was pushed, pushed back, and the brawl resumed.

Marc Handler, attired in Queen Elspeth's blue gown, and Richard Burbage Isobel in red, entered their separated courts and commanded peace. Spying each other across the wall, they exchanged greetings, words, insults, and entered into shrieking battle over which daughter their father had loved more.

The galleries cheered when Marc seized possession of the younger queen's role, conveying both a girl's petulance and a wise woman's concern that the sisters were on a dangerous course. A dazzled Will wondered how Dick Burbage would handle such business, which he had to admit he had not written.

Burbage showed who Burbage was. Choosing Queen Elizabeth for his lode star, he extracted from a word here, and a thin hint there, an older woman proud of her own beauty, yet envious of her sister's youth, and terrified that her time on earth was passing. From the pit to the highest gallery, the audience was silently intent until Dick's last word detonated applause. They sounded, Will thought, grateful to be moved to fear that both women might well lose what both deserved to keep.

Falstaff told Queen Isobel that her name meant 'God is my oath' in the olden language and she rewarded him with a purse of gold coins. Will changed hats and jumped into the secret tunnel to tell Elspeth that her name meant 'God is my oath' in the olden language. Elspeth rewarded Falstaff with a purse of gold coins. Falstaff bowed for the laughs and reached for an ale pot that a generous spectator – Robbie Burbage, appareled in a butcher's apprentice cap and apron – offered up. Will drained the water in a long gulp, tossed the pot back to him, and re-introduced Chet-Checks as Ben Jonson strutted on from the tiring-house.

> 'Hail Noble Chet-Checks:
> Late to battle
> And early to feast,
> The happy warrior's a hungry beast!'

Eliza's mariners roared:

> 'To the latter end of a fray
> and the beginning of a feast
> Fits a dull fighter and a keen guest,'

the original *Henry IV* lines Will had pilfered. The pit exploded with shouts and claps and Ben muttered, 'Are those Essex men?'

'My old shipmates.'

'With your shipmates, who need pirates?'

The snorts and snickers ringing about the theater died suddenly. Puzzled whispers were succeeded by the deadest silence Will Shakespeare had ever heard from a stage. Outside the wooden walls he heard a distant murmur. The sound grew louder in seconds, a rumble, a roar, a violent bellow, swelling suddenly as deep as thunder. Veterans in the pit looked at each other in open-mouthed bewilderment. The great rolling clamor could only be massed cavalry – one-hundred horse at least – charging the Globe at full gallop.

Will looked up at the galleries. Anthony Bacon wore a smile.

Theater box-men opened a door at the back of the pit, peered out, and fell back.

'*Essex!*'

THIRTY-NINE

'The earl!'
'The Earl of Essex!'
'*Essex, Essex. Essex!*'

He wore a uniform of silver-colored cloth that gleamed like armor, field-of-battle cavalry boots, and a glistening saber. Head high, helmet sparkling with diamonds, he marched across the pit, parting the startled groundlings as a plow furrowed a soft field. Some cheered. Some, Will noticed, look less enchanted.

'Broached on his sword!' a veteran shouted, provoking an ale wife to fling a full pot in his face. His sputters sparked laughter, then a fight, a flurry of fists and boots soon smothered by *Eliza*'s mariners and the bellows of their master, 'Play the show! Play the show!'

Halfway across the pit Essex stopped to greet a middle-aged fellow dressed in the threadbare garb of a veteran who had known better days. The victor of Cadiz and Rouen embraced the brave foot-soldier for all to see.

'Who is that knave?' Ben muttered to Will. 'I know him, but not from warring.'

'Moser – shilling-a-day player in veteran's attire.'

Essex strode toward the gallery stairs, carpeting his way with warm gestures and a gracious smile. He tossed a coin to the dumbfounded box-man at the foot of the steps, and pounded loudly up two flights, boots ringing on the treads. A minion planted for his entrance vacated a seat in the front row. Essex stood tall and still until every eye in the theater had fixed on his uniform.

Will watched the three- and four-penny galleries. He sensed fear and fascination in equal measure. Some gentles had left their seats as if to retreat before fighting erupted. Several aristocrats were escorted out by their armed gentlemen. Others watched, feigning placidity and awaiting developments, afraid to commit to the noble's rebellion, but loath to offend him in the event he prevailed.

Essex took his seat and gestured for the play to continue.

Will stage-whispered new directions to the company: 'Sweet Wine; then shift straight to the jousts.'

Traitorous Islay and Isla courtiers, played by the mustachioed actors seen earlier as the foreign king and the Pope, gave Chet-Checks sacks of gold. Chet-Checks stuffed them in his pockets, raced off stage, and returned with empty pockets and wheeling a huge cask labeled SWEET WINE.

The galleries laughed. The pit howled. Will could not tell at the distance between them whether Essex flushed. He glanced behind at the split in the curtain where Coxswain Mapes stood watch from the tiring-house.

'Bladders,' he mouthed and Mapes raised a thumb.

Queen Isobel and Queen Elspeth jumped on their barrels-on-wheels horses. Their squires armed them with lances. Thunder under the stage mimicked hooves as the queens jousted for their monarchies' honor. Gentles in the galleries and groundlings in the pit clapped hands and stamped their feet.

'They're applauding the props!' Ben Jonson groaned to Will.

'I applaud all applause.'

The queens invaded each other's realms by vaulting the wall. When neither queen could find her enemy, Falstaff and Chet-Checks helped them search. Suddenly Falstaff and Chet-Checks were wearing the queens' crowns.

'Traitors!' roared a choral singer with a huge bass voice who Will had stationed in the pit for two shillings. 'Treason!' bellowed another, deeper yet. Then a bedazzling boy soprano: 'Se . . . di . . . tion!'

Worth every shilling.

Loyal rude mechanicals grabbed Chet-Checks and Falstaff's crowns and clapped them back on the queens' heads. Isobel and Elspeth were simultaneously welcomed to their new realms by their new subjects.

The Earl of Essex disrupted the scene by storming down the gallery stairs in an exit as showy as his entrance.

'Bladders!' Will called to the company. 'All bladders on stage.'

Queen Isobel presented Chet-Checks with a long, orange sheep bladder. Chet-Checks waved it triumphantly over his head. It collapsed when the air rushed out of it, accompanied by the breaking wind noise of apprentice boys blowing hard through closed lips.

Queen Elspeth rushed up with a bigger orange cow bladder, which deflated the instant Chet-Checks held it up. The apprentices blew harder as every character in the play handed Chet-Checks a bladder which deflated when he touched it.

Red-faced with rage, the Earl of Essex struggled across the pit, trapped by the packed crowd who were laughing at the drooping-bladders bawdy show. Falstaff waved good-bye. He looked to the gallery and saw the countess curl a finger to her thumb to form an empty O. Who was she signaling? Me, Will realized. She is signaling me that Essex is empty.

The queens saw Falstaff and Chet-Checks sneaking away. They seized their lances and leapt on their wheeled barrel horses and chased the False Fool and the False Knight chorusing,

> 'Sister battling Sister we Queened our realms
> Now always we will steer with doubled helms.
> Like oaks and elms that side by side agree
> Hand in hand we sail in company.'

Ben Jonson, running circles with Will Shakespeare, asked, 'Are those the worst four lines ever penned?'

Will quoted Stefano Fogliaverde: 'They fit the moment.'

> 'And if foolish nobles conspire to oust us
> Be they warned, they first must joust us.'

The queens caught Noble Chet-Checks and gave him the smallest orange bladders of all – tiny sturgeon wind-bladders narrow as their lances – that drooped in Chet-Checks' hands.

Sir John Falstaff waved good-bye to the Earl of Essex as he broke free of the crowd and ran from the Globe – a retreat to the drum beat of his cavalry galloping back to London.

Waving empty bladders, the Chamberlain's Men took mighty bows to stoke the laughter sweeping the Globe like a tempest wind. It swelled from the pit, pounded the stage, and flooded the galleries, echoed by the spectators pouring from the Globe and racing to London Bridge.

'They are laughing like hyenas,' said Ben Jonson.

'At the Earl of Essex,' said Will Shakespeare, praying that they were laughing loud enough to be heard all over the city.

There was snow on the wind and fear in the streets, and night had begun to gather, but Will Shakespeare stayed on the stage, thanking his company until the last men and boys hurried home. Finally, he left the theater too, thinking to brave the city, catch up with Ben celebrating at the Mermaid if it wasn't in flames, and help him to his writing room while he could still walk. And there, perhaps, hear what Isobel and Mrs Broad thought of the play.

A dark four-horse coach with no coat of arms stood at the theater door. Four men, grim as war, swept from behind it. Two blocked his path. Two seized his arms and marched him between them. It felt as familiar as it was frightening. He knew what to do, all he could do, which was watch for a chance to escape. But now he saw horsemen gathered in the shadow of the Globe.

FORTY

t was dark inside the coach. A glimmer of the daylight seeping from the sky shone on the figure of an old woman who looked exactly like Secretary Robert Cecil in his lame disguise. Why this charade? Will wondered.

The figure spoke and Will realized with a mix of astonishment and terror that the disguise was ingenious. The Cecil hunched shoulder, the Cecil guard in the gallery, the hat shading the face, and the ruff to the chin conspired to conceal Elizabeth Tudor, Queen of England, who had had herself spirited into the Globe to hear *The Sister Queens.*

'We are never a tyrant for tyranny,' she told Will in a voice that slurred a little and was hard to understand. 'Were we a tyrant, we might well resent being portrayed, warts and pimples, in *your play.*

'We might resent Master Burbage, who never fails to astound. But we cannot charge him for that revolting bawdy at the end of the show. Is there anything you would say, Master Shakespeare?'

'Had I but known you attended, Your Majesty, I'd not have played a bawdy.'

'Had you not played that bawdy, you'd have lost your spectators.'

Her face was barely visible in the dark, but some of her teeth were likely missing, which caused her slur and lisp. She banged her stick on the coach floor. A helmeted officer appeared instantly in the door's window.

'To Essex House,' said the Queen.

'Essex House, Your Majesty.'

Horses clattered and the coach rolled smoothly, cushioned by springs, as did cars built in Europe.

The Queen said, 'After the end of your play, the Earl of Essex returned to the city on horseback to arouse his followers. His entreaties to march on my court were heard by a crowd at Paul's led by people arriving from the Globe, and rejected. When his troop galloped to the mayor, trailed closely by that crowd, he was rejected again, as he was, next, by the high sheriff. He retreated to Essex House. And that is where the fool is now.'

A thousand torches lighted Essex House brighter than the dinner hour on a sunny day. A wheeled cannon had been somehow hoisted to a Middle Temple tower next door and pointed down at the armored windows on the first floor of the earl's mansion. Will could see smoke rising from the gunner's tapers, and the gunner poised to light fire to the touch hole. The helmeted officer appeared the instant the coach stopped.

'Report,' said the Queen.

'The earl has been instructed to surrender himself.'

'Who is in there with him?'

'The Earl of Southampton.'

The Queen glanced at Will. 'Convey my command to surrender themselves in two minutes.'

'Two minutes, Your Majesty. Thank you, Your Majesty.'

'Off you go.'

The officer ran, the Queen banged her cane, and ordered the next face at the window, 'Bring a small light.'

A shielded candle was produced in seconds and placed between her and Will Shakespeare. Her face was furrowed, her teeth yellow and as sparse as Will had guessed. There was weariness in her eyes, but they landed sharply on Will's face and stayed there.

'You played your part well in this scheme, Master Shakespeare. We would reward you. What do you want?'

'Spare Southampton.'

'That is all?'

'That is everything. I have known and tutored him since he was a lad.'

'We have known him since he was a boy, as we did Essex. We hoped they would grow better. We were wrong about Essex to believe he would serve England rather than destroy it. And we assure you, Master Shakespeare, that Essex will lose his head for his crimes. Why are we not wrong about Southampton?'

'There is something within Southampton as yet to be unwrapped.'

'How long are we to wait for this . . . unveiling?'

'Your Majesty, even if you had to wait five long years for him to flourish, he would still be a man young enough to serve England for a full generation. And serve her well.'

'What is this "something within" that you see?'

They were interrupted by shouting.

'Hold,' said the Queen.

Will saw the gunner lean closer to the cannon. When his officer raised his sword to give the signal to fire, the gunner extended his taper toward the touch hole. Commencing his downward sweep, the officer suddenly froze. The gunner jerked his taper back, and Will saw the armored front door that he had banged on with Isobel's brick swing slowly inside the darkened house. The Earl of Essex strode out boldly, then paused as if awaiting an ovation. When greeted by nothing but a curt shout, he took another step and raised his head to stare at the cannon on the Temple tower. Southampton came out behind him, blinking in the light.

Soldiers surrounded them. In seconds the earls were led away with their hands shackled to chains around their waists.

The Queen banged her cane. Footmen closed curtains over the windows, and the coach broke into motion.

'We repeat. What is this "something within" that you see?'

'His mother.'

The Queen sat back on her cushions. 'We are relieved, but not surprised, that you did not credit his father, who was as big a fool as Essex, only not so ambitious . . . Tell us what do you make of this scheme to write a play to inspire rebellion?'

Will's head was reeling. What of Southampton?

'Master Playmaker! What do you make of this scheme to write a play to inspire rebellion?'

Will formed his answer from fragments. 'The scheme was a test, Your Majesty.'

'A test? A test? Of whom?'

'A final test.'

'Of *whom*?'

'The earl was given every chance. And he betrayed.'

'Do you know who invented the scheme?'

'I thought for some time that the inventor was Sir Robert Cecil, which would have meant he somehow cozened Francis Bacon into taking credit for the play.'

'Do you believe that Francis Bacon was, shall we say, "cozen-able?"'

Will almost laughed. It was a word Ben Jonson would enjoy, too.

'To be clear,' said the Queen, 'Cecil could cozen almost anyone. No monarch was ever better served since our father by Cromwell. He has no desire to be a prince, only to serve a prince. So, since you changed your mind that it was Cecil, to whom do you credit the scheme?'

'Strangely, Your Majesty, after I told Secretary Cecil that I had changed my mind about the inventor, he did not ask me who I thought was the real inventor.'

'Why do you suppose that was?'

'I don't think he wanted to hear it from me.'

'Did you wish to tell him?'

'No, Your Majesty.'

'Could you have told him if he asked?'

'I could have named someone I suspected was the inventor.'

'Suspected implies not sure.'

'Motive was the puzzle, Your Majesty. I simply could not understand the inventor's motive.'

'You do now?'

'Beyond doubt, Your Majesty.'

'What was the inventor's motive?'

'The motive was love.'

The Queen stiffened. She stared hard at Will and he could never in this life divine what the monarch would do or speak next. She held that pose, then, suddenly, slumped on her bench and passed a hand wrinkled as wet parchment over her long, thin features. She slurred so when she spoke that Will was forced to say, 'Forgive me, Your Majesty, I could not hear what you said.'

She straightened up and answered loudly, 'We said that you know too much for your years, Master Shakespeare.'

'Thank you, Your Majesty.'

She fell into a deep silence. Finally she asked, as a child might ask a wise old man, 'Was it only for love?'

'And hope.'

'The hope that he would not betray?'

'The hope that this one time he would be different. At last. Somehow.'

'But Lord Essex failed even that test?'

'He was given every chance. And he still betrayed.'

She spoke loudly again, and slowly, to enunciate every word. 'And the inventor of the scheme, Master Playmaker? What of the inventor?'

Will Shakespeare took a very deep breath. 'The inventor took full, direct command in a time of peril and trusted no minions, even the most trustworthy, to keep their clear eye and wits about them. And now that the inventor has put the peril to rest, *she* will guarantee – as she always has, from Accession Day to this very day – that peace makes smiling plenty and fair prosperous days, Your Majesty.'

Again a silence, deeper than before, and longer. At last, the Queen spoke.

'We learned years ago that when the wrong element seizes control, order is doomed. Do you know where we learned that?'

'I do not, Your Majesty.'

'Your *Richard III*. A simple play. A very simple play. But true. Cecil suggested we hear it . . . As often happens, he was right. But – Master Playmaker – the wrong element are sometimes the *only* element who can serve smiling plenty and fair prosperous days. It remains the prerogative of the sovereign, and her duty, to employ the wrong element to oust the wrong element when it is necessary. That demands the clearest eye of all, the honest eye that shows the sovereign when she strays from what she knows in her heart. We have spoken to Anthony Bacon. We will speak to Sir Richard Topcliffe. Neither is likely to outlive us; Topcliffe is old; and Bacon, a walking shambles. Regardless, we will ensure that they will never trouble you and yours.'

'Thank you, Your Majesty. May I beg that the girl Isobel the Moor, who served well your invention, be embraced by your graciously extended protection?'

'We will make it so . . .'

'Thank you, Your Majesty. Thank you . . . May I, Your Majesty, ask pray what of Southampton?'

This drew from her a long silence.

'You ask us to consider the man Southampton might be in the future. We are not surprised. We've read your sonnets. We suspect we know where lies your heart . . . We wonder whether your eyes are clear or blind . . .'

'Clear, Your Majesty. Clear as is the summer's sun. Not blinded by all Your Majesty might imagine.'

'You were his tutor. What did you teach him?'

'I tried, Your Majesty, to teach him to project himself into the minds of others so that he might understand their needs and wants.'

The Queen's face lighted, offering Will a glimpse of the lively wit that had sustained her through years of grappling with opposition. 'You were expecting a lot of the nobility.'

'His mother inferred that was what she hoped for her son.'

Queen Elizabeth lowered her head in a small nod as if to admit that in the end hope was all that mattered. 'Your patron will be released after a suitable length of penance in the Tower of London.'

Will bowed his head and swallowed hard, nearly overcome. 'Thank you, Your Majesty. Thank you. Thank you.'

Her carriage tilted forward as it rolled down a slope. Will could smell the water and hear the horses' shoes sliding on stone. Ostlers shouted and he sensed strong men seizing harness to help the animals stop.

The Queen said, 'We ask you to accompany an old friend safely home. Will you do us that favor?'

'As you bid, Your Majesty.'

'Good-night then, Master Playmaker.'

'Good-night, Your Majesty.'

Will backed down the carriage steps, bowing deeply. The Royal Barge was waiting at a landing ablaze in torchlight and bonfires. He saw what he had not seen from the coach – a strong detachment of outriders clad not for a public procession, but armed for war with swords, lances, pistols, and muskets. The horsemen's faces, however, showed more clearly than any proclamation that the battle was over and won square.

The Queen called down, 'As we said, young poet, we have read your sonnets.'

'Yes, Your Majesty?'

'You did say love.'

FORTY-ONE

Lights burned the long length of the Royal Barge. Snow twirled in the wind. Mary Wriothesley, Countess of Southampton, sat beneath a canopy high above the oarsmen, wrapped to her eyes in sable fur. The barge master stood at his tiller twenty feet behind her. Armed gentlemen made way for Will, who ascended to the canopy as lines were loosed at some silent command, men dipped their oars, and the barge pulled from the landing.

Will bowed. 'By your leave, your ladyship, Her Majesty asked that I see you safely home.'

She appeared puzzled to see him and dreadfully anxious. But she still possessed her deliberate gaze. 'Safely? What is Her Majesty thinking? She already has me encircled by four musket-boats and attended by sufficient armed gentlemen to fight a battle – or deliver me to the Tower, if she chooses.'

'I believe the Queen's purpose is for me to inform you that my Lord Southampton is safe in the Tower of London where he will remain for what Her Majesty named a "suitable length of penance."'

The countess lowered the sable from her face. 'Thank God! Thank God! . . . Thank you for telling me . . . Will, are you sure?'

'Absolutely sure, your ladyship. He will be freed.'

There was a second seat in the small covered space, inches from hers, and she gave it a brisk pat. 'Come. Come sit here, tell me everything.'

Will began with his surprise that it was the Queen and not Cecil in the coach.

The countess said, 'She's always loved her disguises. As I was seated close by in the theater, I knew it had to be her, but she never once looked my way. I don't believe she had made her mind up yet.'

'Perhaps, but she obviously feels affection for his lordship. And for you, certainly.'

'She's known him since he was born and me since I was a maid. What did you tell her?'

Will related every word of their conversation.

'I thank you,' said the countess.

'I would guess, my lady, that the Queen hoped all along that your son was not cut of the same cloth as Essex.'

'God bless her. And you, Will.' She fell silent for a few moments, then changed the subject so abruptly that it could only be to tear free of many long days and nights of uncertainty. 'I am told,' she said, 'that you've completed a new *Hamlet*.'

'Almost, my lady.'

'Are you pleased?'

'It will be the best I've had London hear . . . May I ask, your ladyship, what you thought of *The Sister Queens*?'

'Well, it was as thoroughly amusing as a farce. If light of weight and measure. Which was right as events have been anything but light.'

She lowered her voice, though it was unlikely that the nearest oarsmen could hear over the wind.

'I have in my possession your earlier *Sister Queens*.'

'That cannot be.'

'The tragedy you burned.'

'But how?'

'The Moor girl made a copy. She passed it to my son.'

'Did my lord read it?'

'Oh, yes. He gave it to me for safekeeping.'

Will's heart soared with the unexpected and absolute proof that there was indeed something true in Southampton. He had not used *The Sister Queens* to advance Essex's stately schemes.

'It should not be heard in our time, my lady.'

'It is the truest piece you've ever written.'

Will Shakespeare said, 'That is why I burned it. *The Tragedy of the Sister Queens* must wait until these hatreds are dead and forgotten.'

'I promise you it will wait until all of us are gone from memory. It is hidden, sealed in lead, safe from meddling by court conspirators. Safe from rot, flood, fire, and nibbling mice. Safe, too,' she added with a smile, 'from new-writing poets.'

The Royal Barge turned toward a bonfire that marked the river landing for her carriage to Southampton House.

'Will, you saved my son's life. I would reward you.'

'To be embraced again in your friendship is reward enough.'

'That you are. Never doubt. What will you say if I say to you, one night? But only one night.'

'I long to accept such a reward, but I cannot. It would be far more precious than anything I have done or could do.'

She watched the lights grow brighter as the barge neared, then turned to him and looked him full in the face. 'If not your reward, could you accept that I would celebrate?'

'Celebrate?'

'I have much to celebrate. My son lives and peace will reign and my poet believes that he is writing his best play yet.'

My poet filled his heart.

'Will you celebrate with me, Will?'

'Surely. On such stuff are dreams made.'

'But I mean it when I say, one night. I am married – but for this one night. There will be no return, no repeat. Only one. What do you say?'

Will Shakespeare spoke truth from the bottom of his heart. 'I say that I am grateful beyond words.'

The bonfire on the landing lighted a playful smile that danced from her lips to her eyes. 'Grateful that I would celebrate *only* one night? Would you be less grateful for two?'

Will was careful not to touch her glove, nor let any oarsman see his smile. 'No, my lady. I mean that I am grateful for winter.'

'Winter? Winter is icicles and empty pots.' A bitter gust blasted down the river and rattled the canopy. A snowflake lodged in the silvery fur caressing her cheek. 'What do you mean, Will?'

'I am grateful that winter nights are long nights. Mary.'